RUTH PRAWER JHABVALA'S FICTION

Existential Modes and Stylistic Patterns

RUTH PRAWER JHABVALA'S FICTION

Existential Modes and Stylistic Patterns

By

A.A. Khan

Ashish Sharma

ADHYAYAN

ADHYAYAN PUBLISHERS & DISTRIBUTORS

NEW DELHI (INDIA)

Published by
ADHYAYAN PUBLISHERS & DISTRIBUTORS
4378/4B, 105, J.M.D House, Murari Lal Street
Ansari Road, Darya Ganj, New Delhi-110 002
Ph: 011- 23263018, 011-23277156, FAX: 011-23280028
E-mail: adhyayanpublishers@yanoo.com

Ruth Prawer Jhabvala's Fiction: Existential Modes and Stylistic Patterns

First Edition 2011

ISBN 978-81-8435-264-1

Printed in India

Published by Harish Chandra Yadav for Adhyayan Publishers & Distributors, Laser Typesetting at A.V. Rao Laser Typesettings, New Delhi and Printed at Tarun Offset Printers, Delhi.

The present book is

Dedicated

to

Hon'ble K. Subramaniam I.F.S.

for his Life Time Contribution

to

Higher Education and Literary Studies

Preface

Indo-Anglian literature would be incomplete if it fails to take note of the writings of Ruth Pawer Jhabvala. Born and educated in Europe but married to an Indian and settled in the country of her adoption, she brings to contemplation of the life around her certain advantages and limitations. These qualities distinguish her writings from those of the foreigners passing through India and the writers native to the soil. Thoroughly familiar with the life and manners of her adopted country, she is able to have a close peep into the typical traits of Indians, particularly urban, upper and middle classes as they keep on balancing between tradition and modernity. It is said that Ruth Prawer Jhabvala has not been able to receive the kind of attention she really deserves. Most of her novels deal with sentiments and manners of both men and women belonging to the middle class family. It has been seen that Indian writers in English generally make a virtue of mysticism and sentimentalism. In this connection, Raja Rao's journey into the Vendantic philosophy and Narayan's concern for the ritual to get rich can be cited as examples.

Mrs. Jhabvala's novels do not indicate these traits. She deals with social problems and Indian predicament in her own typical way. It is for this reason that we find all her novels endowed with local colour shade. In her novels a clear line can be drawn between tradition and modernism, between the east and the west and the confusion that follows as a result of these clashes. Her vision is not limited to one or two persons alone. She deals with corporate life of many families, and her novels are free from accidents, coincidences and sudden shifts of fortune. On the contrary, they are expressive of the dull routine of daily life, resulting in being repetitive and boring It is for this reason that she has been able to describe the domestic and social life of Indians as no other writer writing in English has ever done. In this respect, she is undoubtedly unbeatable.

Her first novels ***To Whom She Will*** (1955) revolves round the theme of arranged *versus* love marriage and gives rise to family tension when Amrita and Hari think themselves to be in love but face resistance from their elders. Their two families succeed in arranging Hari's marriage to Sushila Anand.

Amrita, much to her own as well as that of her family's satisfaction, is not left to marry Krishna Sen Gupta, whom she actually loves. The novel is a light hearted comedy presenting various view points on the issue of marriage.

The Nature of Passion (1956) is the story of a successful patriarchal businessman's love for money and his family who uses his money as a powerful weapon to further his business empire, to generate corruption in bureaucratic circles, and also to ensure a luxurious future for his children. The novel remains an interesting social document.

Her third novel Esmond in India (1980) is the story of Esmond Still Wood's marriage with Gulab, an Indian beauty, and deals with the theme of cultural confrontation. Esmond poses to be an expert on Indian culture and earns his living by serving as a tourist guide and by teaching Indian culture to young society ladies,. Shakuntala, the pampered daughter of the industrialist Har Dayal and Madhuri falls for Esmond's charm. The secondary thematic stand is the issue of Shakutala's marriage. Her ambitious and snobbish mother rejects an idealist Narayan in favour of Prof. Bhatnagar's England based son. The novel is an objective portrayal of the urban upper class life.

The Householder (1960) lightheartedly deals with Prem's dilemma of maturing into a householder. His new status brings Prem face to face with the problem of adjustment between the pulls of mother and wife. He is also gripped by the economic constraints of running a household. In ***Get Ready for Battle*** (1962) the main thematic concern is the vast economic disparity between the worlds inhabited by the poor and the rich. Sarla Devi, a determined idealist falls apart from her capitalist husband on ideological grounds. On behalf of the poor slum dwellers of a refugee colony she wages a war against her husband's materialistic concerns and the government apathy. In this novel Jhabvala treats the theme of social and political apathy, and exploitation with bitterness.

A Backward Place (1965) revolves round the three western girls' experiences in India. Judy's marital life to Bal, a dreamy Indian, presents a reverse view of Esmond-Gulab marriage in ***Esmond in India.*** Judy submits to her husband's wishes and makes her life successful. The novel also refers to the theme of exploitation at a peripheral level.

In ***A New Dominion*** (1973), Jhabvala continues to dwell upon the theme of cultural confrontation through the experiences of another set of three girls and an American tourist in India. The novel serves as a sardonic comment upon the emergence of a new dominion consisting of dubious swamis, lusty women and self-seekers in contemporary India. For the first time Jhabvala uses the narrative technique of a travelogue to present a comprehensive picture of Indian society.

Heat and Dust (1975) too centres round the theme of Westerners' experiences in India. Using the flashback technique of narration Jhabvala presents two stories—one of Olivia and the other of the narrator. Olivia, the wife of Douglas, a district officer at Satipur, falls for the charms of an Indian Nawab and leaves her husband to stay back in India as the Nawab's mistress. Curiosity about the story of Olivia who happens to be the grandmother of the narrator brings her to India after a gap of nearly half a century. Olivia's history repeats itself in experiences of the narrator. She too falls for the mystery and charms of India, gets pregnant, and like Olivia resolves to stay back in India. Jhabvala remains sneering rather than objective in her treatment of India in this novel.

Her novels are like windows through which the reader can see the changing image of Indian society as Jhabvala saw it. Jhabvala wrote all her novels like a detached observer. Initially she wrote as an observer writing about things which enchanted her and later on about things she knew too well and found them to be beyond her tolerance, and naturally she became bitter and critical. Jhabvala observes the life around her in a detached and dispassionate manner. She is often compared with Jane Austen for a realistic delineation of the familial and social scene in urban middle class life. Some of her novels are ironic illustrations of inter-cultural dichotomy. She is a novelist who seems to be better known abroad than in India. In the present study authors I have tried to examine the novels which she wrote in India during her stay of almost two decades and have endeavoured to trace her thematic patters of these novels.

—Dr. (Smt.) Qamar Talat

Contents

1

Introduction

Throughout the past three decades during which Indo-English Literature has received the attention of scholars and critics, emphasis has been given to its special nature and its nearly unique situation. The term 'Indo-English' or "Indo-Anglian"[1] suggests only a part of the difficulty in trying to place the literature produced by Indians in English within clear national, regional or linguistic boundaries. This situation has drawn from scholars and critics a variety of descriptions and labels.[2] The critical issues regarding Indo-English writing are many, but most of them are centred on these writers' choice of English for creative expression. It would be improper to treat these writers as English merely because they write in English—after all what Americans and Australians write is no more called English literature either. On the other hand, it is argued that if these writers are Indians their natural medium for expression should be the Indian languages. The only other literature that perhaps faces the same basic questions about its existence is that produced by West African writers who have preferred English to their native tribal dialects. And yet, too many, the Indian writer's choice of English seems less logical than the African's because of the highly developed State of Indian regional languages and literatures when juxtaposed with the largely oral unwritten literary traditions of the African dialects.

It is perhaps possible to divide the various approaches to Indo-English literature into the following distinct categories— *(a)* as a part of English literature; *(b)* as a part of Commonwealth or 'third-world' literature; *(c)* as a part of Indian literature *(d)* as a representative Indian literature that synthesizes responses and traditions in ways that no single Indian regional literature perhaps can. The habit of treating Indo-English literature as an extension of English literature has died a natural death. It has been recognized that the more recent Indo-English writing, unlike the work of Toru Dutt, Manmohan Ghose, does not respond well to such a treatment. The rejection of this approach has been okayed even by librarians, who, as we know are never in a great hurry in such matters. Today, Indo-english literature is also being studied as a part of Commonwealth literature. While this approach has some bases insofar as it encourages comparative studies, its thematic implications are quite limited and confused.[3]

Most available criticism on Indo-English literature having any value looks upon it as a part of Indian literature. Recent studies have made its Indianness the main issue of critical focus and they have used Indianness or a lack of it as their primary criterion for judgement. This approach is quite in line with the Indo-English writer's own sense of his being a part of the Indian literary scene. At the same time, most of them would take exception to defining Indianness in a special way to exclude them. They see nothing an Indian in their use of English for creative expressions. The Indo-English writers must keep in view the needs of the time while writing a novel or composing a poem. According to some, there is no necessary or binding relationship between Indianness and the use of English for creative expression— As K.D.Katrak says

"A poet is not the product of an ethnic stud."[4]

Indo-English literature like any other growth area, has created its own vested interests which have sometimes tried to project it as the most significant Indian literature on the ground that this is the only one which is not limited to a particular Indian state or region and is widely accessible to audiences in India and abroad. This argument is advanced to assert the representativeness of Indo-English literature, highlighting its capacity to pull together the various levels of linguistic and cultural tradition in the country. In this connection, one notices with sorrow the tendency in the West to concentrate on Indo-English literature to the complete neglect of literatures in regional languages. The underlying assumption has been that in all Indo-English writing, there is a gap between the cultural experience that is expressed and the languages chosen to express it. The writer may exploit this gap to his advantage in his work to heighten the clash of cultures (the East -West encounter in the work of Raja Rao, Mulk Raj Anand, Arun Joshi, Anita Desai or Ruth Prawer Jhabvala). We may counter this assumption by underscoring the immense possibilities inherent in the availability to English to Indians for use at a variety of levels. Despite the fears often expressed in certain circles, the banishment of English from the Indian soil seems, to be a remote possibility. But even if we were to imagine a situation where English would leave the Indian shores we will never be able to root out the far- reaching psychological and linguistic impact it has on Indian life since 1835, when Macaulay sought to establish the "imperishable empire" of ideas through a massive introduction of English in Indian education. India has demonstrated that even if she is sometimes reluctant to admit it, that provincialism has no place in matters of literary and cultural expression.

The years between 1980 and 1990 have been very prolific ones, for Indian English fiction. More novels and collections of short stories have been published in this decade than ever before in the history of Indian English writing. In this decade, not only have new writers appeared, but older writers like R.K.Narayan and Mulk Raj Anand have also produced significant new work. In his "Overview" of the Indian English novel of the 80s G.N.Devy, has considered the questions of marginality and social consciousness of Indian English writing. In this essay Devy has assigned to Indian English literature the status of "Pocket literature", as it exists in the pockets and lacks a regional base. He has argued that this literature is a peripheral literature, as it does not concern itself with the vast majority of Indians. In sharp contrast to this view, some critics focus on the socio-political commitment of Indian writers. Another interesting aspect of Indian English fiction of 80s is that of the expatriate writers. A substantial number of novels published in the 80s were written by women. In this early year of Indian English writing, its philosophical content was much stressed. This was supposed to portray the essential Indianness of Indian English fiction.

This has over the years been exposed as a colonial stereotype of the "philosophical Indian". The Indian English writers of the 80s are not especially inclined to be philosophers. However, Raja Rao has published a major new novel and this novel is much dependent on Indian philosophy. Recent Indian English fiction displays a sense of social consciousness, is concerned with Indian socio-political realities and is authentically Indian. It is no more a literature which is aimed deliberately at a western audience. The rising middle class, in India has assured it of an indigenous readership.

It is now a literature of self-definition and assimilation into the Indian ethos. The analysis provided here cannot however be taken as definitive. Twenty years back one rarely spoke of Indian English fiction. Ten years back, the writers like R.K.Narayan, Raja Rao, Mulk Raj Anand, Manohar Malgonkar and Kamala Markandaya were inducted in the university courses of English. In comparison the quantity and variety, fiction published during the last ten years are very impressive. Writers like Nayantara Saghal, Anita Desai and Ruth Prawer Jhabvala have made it possible to speak of women's Indian English fiction. One of the major international movements of the last decade was the Feminist literature movement. The English speaking Indian women found the new ideology of subversion is very attractive. That they did so feel was in itself a desirable event. But since most of them have little interest in activism at the grassroot levels in Indian society, they found it liberating to imitate American and French Feminism and produce fiction giving their ego-graphs. The motivation of the fiction of the 80s creates some aberrations in the perception of these bodies of literature.

The interactions between two cultures, European and Indian is Ruth Prawer Jhabvala's forte. It forms the substance and also shapes the process by which her personal experience in India is transformed into the art of fiction. In a revealing autobiographical essay "Living in India" Jhabvala writes:

> "I have lived in India for most of my adult life. My husband is Indian and so are my children. I am not, and less so, very year."[5]

Jhabvala in this essay has expressed her varied relations to India and its people. She declare that India reacts strongly on foreigner and they either love it or hate it or do both. She has herself passed through this cycle and her fiction is a part of this cyclical growth. Jhabvala's world signifies space—the space that is India, the India moulded by her experience and fictional art. Her endeavour should be designated as time-art, since her narrative mode is conceived in terms of history or a sequence of time. Her mode of narration follows the traditional time span, the individual's and family's cyclic development or decline. Jhabvala writes about India and her culture and presents it in a graphic way. Her fiction is a part of what she has experienced and seen and it is for this reason that we feel drawn towards her world in spite of the fact that most of the things that she talks about in her fiction do not win our approval. That Ruth Prawer Jhabvala is an interesting writer is beyond any doubt and dispute.

Jhabvala writes about one part of India which she knows by first hand experience. She happens to write about day-to-day problems of living; avoiding more obvious sensational, melodramatic or heroic subjects and avoids political controversy. The background and history of Jhabvala is sufficiently distinctive to invite comment at the outset. Jhabvala is Indian neither by blood nor by birth. She is of polish Jewish educated in England where she took a degree at London University and she came to India (Delhi) after the world war second as the wife of a Parsi architect. Yet the subject of her novels and her collections of short stories since 1955 has been exclusively India and like R.K. Narayan she writes about one part of it— Delhi. But unlike Narayan she encounters the Indian scene as something alien and new, and there is considerable evidence in her novels of the (outsider) approach to India. Jhabvala keeps herself to one locality and writes about professional people and expatriates like herself or about the rich business elite who would regard themselves as above others in social status. By declaring the setting of her novel to be Delhi Jhabvala manifests her desire to remain within the confines of naturalistic fiction. Jhabvala returns repeatedly to the same subjects, the joint family houses, arranged marriages, romantic love affairs, children and parents, divorce and keeping mistress among the ideal rich. Her first novel ***To Whom She Will*** (1955) shows a girl in love with a boy whose parents arrange a marriage with some one else more suitable to their class and way of life. This is also one of the plots of ***The Nature of Passion*** (1956). Expatriate bohemian artists appear in ***Esmond in India*** (1958) and in ***A Backward Place*** (1965). Jhabvala's main occupation in her fiction is her exclusion of fantasy poetry and exaggerated comedy. Jhabvala seems to be cool, detached and often sardonic. Love and Marriage in Indian family life are Jhabvala's favourite subject. Indian family life in particular exerts considerable fascination on her and she comes back again and again to the subject. Jhabvala treats young fascinating love with elements of irony and in her first novel ***To Whom She Will*** her foolish young people, Amrita and Hari, fall in love and then out of love with equal ease and the system of arranged marriage does not appear to be so tyrannous after all, especially when Amrita falls in love in the end with some one approved by her own mother. Similarly, the young female rebel in ***The Nature of Passion*** Lala's favourite daughter Nimmi who goes out and dates with a man of her choice and even has her hair cut short - all to the scandal of her orthodox family — falls out of love with one boy friend and into love with another who also happens to be the husband arranged for her. Romantic love is ephemeral and comic. Arranged marriages work out just as well or just as badly as ones that depend on falling in love. It amuses Jhabvala to manipulate her plots to suggest this. An apparent love marriage like that of Esmond and Gulab in ***Esmond in India*** (for no other explanation is offered of this strange marriage except love) can be completely disastrous.

Jhabvala is pessimistic about the marriages of her characters whether arranged or not. The marriage of Sarla Devi and Gulzari Lal in ***Get Ready for Battle*** (1962) has come to grief on their incompatible temperaments, and Gulzari Lal has a mistress, a lovely passionate woman of a great strength of character whose intrigues provide a major thread of the action. In her study of the joint family of the Punjabi business tycoon Lalaji in ***The Nature of Passion,*** Jhabvala makes fun of the maliciousness of the women, and show the stuffy atmosphere of the women's quarter driving the son. OM to seek escape in the arms of prostitutes. It is interesting that some of Jhabvala's more villainous characters are amorous and adulterous, Esmond and Gulzari Lal, for example. Sarla Devi's materialistic son has an eye for the ladies like her brother Brij Mohan who keeps a prostitute as his mistress and quarrels with her violently and noisily. In only two of her novels does Jhabvala show a marriage turning out successfully Prem and Indu achieve a kind of harmony by the end of ***The Householder*** (1960), and the marriage of Judy and Bal is saved after being imperilled in ***A Backward Place*** by the example of heroic acceptance of life shown by an old Indian woman aunt Bhuaji. Jhabvala chooses classes of the Indian community where adultery and divorce are not unknown, the rich upper middle class of Delhi and the circle of artists, bohemian and expatriates. Etta, one of the central characters of ***A Backward Place*** has had a failed marriage and has been the mistress of several men since the break-up. Kusum is the mistress of Sarla Devi's estranged husband. Jhabvala presents in ***Get Ready for Battle*** the life of a fast–living group of young people who drink, dance and have affairs in Delhi. Even innocent girls like Shakuntala in ***Esmond in Indian,*** fall easy victims to phony sexual charms. Love is a destructive force sharply in opposition to the peace and security of marriage. As in the life and literature of medieval Europe, love and marriage do not mix.

Ruth Prawer Jhabvala's consuming interest in the nature of the Indian joint family reflects perhaps her European origin. In Europe the families are nowadays often a small unit, it is not common for three generations to live together as they often were 30 years ago. Jhabvala with her own personal history of exile and expatriation comes with great curiosity to such an immensely secure and complex institution and yet within which such tensions and rebellions, can occur. Her most elaborate exploration of the undivided Hindu family is *The Nature of Passion,* her ironical novel of the "Rajasa" temperament which centres round the great Lalaji's attempts to keep his family together and save himself from the disgrace and ruin of being prosecuted by the government for corrupt business practices within the family. The tensions are feverish, young people in revolt worship at the shrine of) emancipated love and art, and Lalaji has only the dour Om (his eldest son) on his side and prepared to follow in his foot steps. Most alienated from him is another son, Chandra, the 'England - returned' civil servant. He, with his social-climbing wife doesn't live in the joint family, they keep apart and are reluctant to allow their children to be petted by Lalaji. Yet the key to Lalaji's very survival as a business man lies with his son; and it is one of the best ironies of the book that when he does act in his civil service capacity to protect his father, he does it out of self-interest and with no real filial loyalty at all. Self-interest is seen generating unity within Lalaji's family when the rebellious son Viddi is back by the judicious use of money and influence.

Ruth Prawer Jhabvala consistently bases the conflicts that arise between Indians and Westerners in her novels upon the complexities of culture, history and psychology, avoiding the simpler, more obvious issue of colour. Her Indian characters, as seen by Western eyes, range from the sexually titillating to the grotesque. By using descriptive terms that are non-associative in terms of colour, she keeps her subject clear of the superficial, and the boring. Once they have crossed the initial barrier set up by what is unfamiliar or foreign, her characters respond to one another as individuals. Those who are unable to do so reveal their immaturity or the falseness of their claims to liberalism or spirituality. Prem ***(The Householder)*** Gopi ***(A New Dominion),*** Nalini ***(A Course of English Studies),*** Clarissa *(A Backward Place),* and the Swami ***(In an Experience of India)*** are characters on both sides of the cultural 'fence' who, when angry, uncertain or excited, comically reveal cultural prejudices that betray their immaturity. The prejudices that distorted human relationships in India's colonial past are reflected in E.M Forster's ***A Passage to India*** and lesser novels that emerged from that past are dwarfed, in Ruth Prawer Jhabvala's picture of the new India, by a theme which is equally impressive and more moving in its tragic implications in our world and our times. There begins to emerge as early as in her second novel, ***The Nature of Passion,*** an impression of India as a mysterious presence half- medieval, half-modern, intensely spiritual, immensely old and scarred by an inescapable poverty, that looks ironically down upon the unheroic antics of the present breed of" gazetted Government officers" business tycoons and shallow socialites who multiply in her new society.

Ruth Prawer Jhabvala's scale shifts from the comic incongruities of Indian life to focus more and more searchingly on those who pretend that such knowledge is easily acquired or inherited by birth. Her portraits of 'experts' on India include a number of Indian characters such as Har Dayal ***(Esmond in India)*** and Pt. Ram Bahadur ***(To Whom she Will)*** who present a picture of India to their youthful relations and Western friends that is severely limited by the narrowness of their own views and experience. Gopi ***(A New Dominion)*** is possibly Jabvala's most satiric study of an ignorant Indian who sets himself up as an authority on India's cultural traditions, deeming himself better qualified by his Indianness to penetrate to essential truths than any western seekers after knowledge however intelligent they may be. These sketches acquire a deeper ironic shading when they begin to include westerns who seek to interpret India to the Indians, characters such as Prof. Hoch ***(To Whom She Will),*** Esmond ***(Esmond in India)*** and the western experts on Yoga whom Prem encounters with wondering perplexity at a party in ***The Householder.***

In 1960, Ruth Prawer Jhabvala paid a brief visit to Britain and found, on her return to India, that her attitude to India had undergone a change. Some of the sources of her discontent are to be found in her fourth novel ***Get Ready for Battle*** (1962) the only one among the eight she has published to centre almost exclusively upon India's extreme poverty, and upon the exploitation of the poor and helpless by the corrupt, the wealthy and the hypocritical. Ruth Jhabvala had taken up the subject of corruption in business and political life before, in ***The Nature of Passion,*** but in that novel the dishonesty of an Indian tycoon had appeared forthright, even endearing, in comparison with the pretentious social climbing of his selfish children. There are no such moderating factors in ***(Get Ready for Battle)*** in which, as H.M. William's has noted, the moral values put forward propose a straight forward conflict between the' Babbittry' represented by big business and the spiritual values embodied in the novels, 'Yogi' figure, the high principled Sarala Devi:

> "The tragedy of Modern India as depicted in Jhabvala's novels is the total failure of communication between the Babbit and the Yogi".[6]

Ruth Jhabvala disillusionment with India that she had begun by loving so passionately found additional expression between 1960 and 1975 in three collections of short-stories. In one of these short stories Ruth Jhabvala westerner in India, of a cycle of intense emotional variations to which she sees all sensitive Westerners who spend any appreciable time in India as being inevitably bound:

> "There is a cycle that Europeans — by Europeans I mean all Westerner, including Americans — tend to pass through. It goes like this: First stage, tremendous enthusiasm — everything Indian is marvellous; second stage, everything Indian not so marvellous; third stage everything Indian abominable. For some people it ends there, for others the cycle renews itself and goes on. I have been through it so many times that now I think of myself as strapped to a wheel that goes round and round and sometimes I am up and sometimes I am down. When I meet other Europeans, I can usually tell after a few moments conversation at what stage of the cycle they happen to be".[7]

These feelings are mirrored in the yearning for Europe that overtakes her Western characters in the three novels published during this period: ***A Backward Place*** (1965), ***A New Dominion*** (1972) and ***Heat and Dust (1975).*** Ruth Prawer Jhabvala applies her theory to the characterisations of Westerners in India that are a feature of ***A Backward Place.*** Etta, Judy and Clarissa are poised at different points on a turning wheel of emotional experience, and their respective fates result as much from their being Westerners in India as from individual temperament or social and cultural background. For her novel ***A New Dominion,*** she selects a time – span identical with the period of time. It takes her two Western characters Raymond and Lee, to experience the intense effects of a full turn of the wheel of torture and disillusionment. Raymond plans, as Esmond did before him, to leave India; for Lee. In ***Heat and Dust*** the experiences of an English woman in the India of 1923 are recreated and analysed, after a pause of fifty years, by another of extraordinary courage for whom the cycle 'renews itself' and is poised to make another revolution. Just when India appeared to have failed the novelist as a source of spiritual and emotional sustenance, a new challenge directed her energies to another 'battle', this time to an artistic kind. She was invited to write the screenplays for a series of film directed by James Ivory in association with Ismail Merchant, beginning with a cinematic version of her own novel ***The Householder.*** The recurrence of similar characters and subjects in the film scripts and fictions she worked on alternately during this period indicates the nature and intensity of Ruth Jhabvala' s preoccupations as a woman and as an artist in these crucial years.

The characters of Ruth Jhabvala's early novels are, in a sense, near -contemporaries. Some of them, like the Saxena's of ***To Whom She Will*** and Gulab's parents in ***Esmond in India*** have lived in Delhi for many years, others-like the Bengali intellectuals Krishna and Sudhir, and the provincial school teacher, Prem— are comparative newcomers. Some like Santi in ***A Backward Place,*** have never gone out of Delhi, some like Guppy in the same novel are continually on the march while others like Etta, appear to be trapped there for life. A network of fictional relationships is built up so convincingly in the early novels that the reader can with a very slight stretch of imagination, extend that network from one novel to another. The Mathur family with whom Nimmi is on friendly terms in ***The Nature of Passion*** could quite easily be related by marriage to Amrita's aunt Tarala Mathur in ***To Whom She Will*** and include a young relative for whom Indira selects a wedding present in Esmond in India. Mrs. Bhatnagar, the social service queen of ***Get Ready for Battle*** could well be Shakuntala's future mother-in-law in ***Esmond in India.*** Ruth Prawer Jhabvala is quite at home while writing about India to draw characters and situations that were parts of the solid, observable world she knew at first hand.

Everything in the world is subject to change and keeping this in view Ruth Prawer Jhabvala's Delhi reflects social and cultural developments over a period of twenty-four years that need not affect an invented community such as Narayan's Malgudi or Jane Austen's; ***Mansfield Park,*** which can remain essentially the same whatever changes may take place in the metropolis. Indian society, which in the past was as rigidly stratified as any feudal Europe, has undergone radical social changes in the last half century. Delhi, as the Indian capital, is necessarily in the forefront of such change. Immediately after British left India, when traditional Indian courtesies were beginning to be revived and respected, the dividing line in society could be drawn on the point of manners and behaviours; in keeping with the thinking of other youthful liberals of her time. Amrita in ***To Whom She Will*** turns away from the vaunted 'breeding and fortune' of her westernized family to have identification with simple, true and unassuming people. The decline in the status of English and the rise of a powerful business class are two agents of social change in India that Ruth Jabvala presents in ***The Nature of Passion.*** Although Nimmi may admire 'England-returned' Pheroz's sophistication, and Kanta may think of educating her children beyond all point of contact with their grand-father's world, it is with Lalaji that real power lies. In Ruth Jhabvala's novels such discoveries are constantly made.

Her early satiric studies of middle and upper class Indian society prompted the comparison of her work by readers and critics to Jane Austen's novels. Some of the reviewers even went to the extent of calling her an Indian Jane Austen. "If you have never read novel by her, start now. She is as astringent as Jane Austen"[8] is a typical comment. Most comparisons of Ruth Prawer Jhabvala's work with those of other authors have indeed concerned themselves chiefly with similarities between the societies described; post-independence India on the one hand, and Regency England or pre- revolutionary Russia on the other. Her own thoughts on likenesses that might go very much deeper are tentatively offered in connection with Jane Austen– "A Sort of ironic detachment and yet, she was never ceased to study the art of fiction with a special interest in European writer of the late 18th and early 19th centuries"[9] In fact, even her earliest novels resemble Jane Austen; not only in their settings and racial backgrounds, but in theme. Acid satirical portraits of Indian snobs, social worker and literary giants are presented with amusing errors made by youthful, misguided but ultimately maturing or contented lovers that bring to mind ***Pride and Prejudice*** **and** ***Emma***. The similarity goes beyond even these external through language of these early works, a habit of ironic undercutting within a sentence frequently brings Jane Austen to mind, as in the following description of an Indian part in ***Get Ready for Battle***.

> "These being modern times, many people had brought their wives who sat in a semi-circle at one end of the room and sipped pine-apple Juice."

Haydn Moore Williams, in one of the serious studies of Ruth Prawer Jhabvala's fictions, refers to Jane Austen as her 'Literary ancestor', underlining the dependence of both authors on an 'acute' observation of contemporary life[10] for their material, the predominance of satire and irony in their work, and the self-imposed limitations, in regard to setting and social class that both display. The impact of Jane Austen, Fanny Burney and other English writers of the 18th century on Ruth Prawer Jhabvala's fiction is most clearly visible in ***To Whom She Will*** and ***The Nature of Passion,*** the two novels she wrote when she was still a newcomer to India and her approach to it inevitably guided by her literary studies in Britain. ***To Whom She Will*** brings to mind ***Pride and Prejudice*** both in directing a good deal of satire and marriage in middle class society and in being a novel about growing up. The superior wisdom of the young lovers' elders is shown to be quite often motivated, and although the activities of these elder are directed towards, the ending of their 'unsuitable' love affair, it is really brought to an end by the gradual emergence of hitherto unrecognized attitudes and feelings in the lovers themselves. Having been influenced by their own emotional and physical maturing, the young people grow out of sentimentality into sense, out of romantic dreams into real life. Conflicts occur between sense and sensibility on the one hand and between literature and sentimental trash on the other. In fact, romantic sentimentality is generally a warning signal in Ruth Jhabvala's novel as it is in Jane Austen's. It is to be met with again and again in such flawed characters as Viddi in ***The Nature of Passion,*** Asha and Gopi in ***A New Dominion,*** and Major Minnies in ***Heat and Dust,*** all of whom display taste for poetry with too much moonlight, too many roses and nightingales.

Ruth Jhabvala's development of the characters of Krishna and Amrita, and of their relationship with each other has much in common with Jane Austen's treatment of her more sensitive heroes and heroines. Krishna, whom Amrita makes her confidant and go-between in her love affair with Hari, spends, a good part of the novel in the anguished frame of mind to which Edward's engagement to Lucy and Edmund Bertram's admiration of Mary Crawford reduce Elinor Dashwood and Fanny in ***Sense and Sensibility*** and ***Mansfield Park*** respectively. Both Krishna and Amrita are accused of being heartless by her mother, Radha- None of you young people has any feelings I (page 161). Yet their silence marks more genuine feeling than is possessed by any of the other characters in the story, and their sensibility if far greater than the shallow sentimental emotion of such advocates of 'feeling' as Radha and Hari contrasts, that recall those between Catherine and Isabella in ***Northanager Abbey,*** Elizabeth Bennet and her mother in ***Pride and Prejudice*** and Elinor and Lucy in ***Sense and Sensibility.*** A delicacy emerging as a concern for others and for moral principle even at the cost of personal pain or loss, is common to Amrita and Krishna, making the gradual development of relations, something to wonder at and to value.

Similarly, ***To Whom She Will*** introduces the three Saxena sisters, Amrita's mother and aunts, as Indian avatars of indolent, selfish and kindly lady, Bertram(Mira), restless Mrs. Norries (Tarla) and dull and slow Mrs.Price (Radha) in ***Mansfield Park.*** Tarala's Delhi mansion, inhabited by people of wealth and who achieve little communication with one another puts us in mind of Bertram's residence. Radha's arrival at the Sahni household, undertaken in order to put an end to Amrita's romance with Hari, resembles Lady Catherine calls on Elizabeth Bennet in ***Pride and Prejudice.*** Amrita, fragile in appearance yet morally firm, has a good deal in common with heroines of Jane Austen as Fanny Price and Anne Elliot. Such resemblances like the imposition of comic dramatic structure on the events of real life, strike the reader of ***To Whom She Will*** as imported element. In writing her first novel, Ruth Jhabvala appears to have been experimenting with style and techniques, fitting what she found in India in the 1950s into moulds that were familiar to her.

To whom She Will is "an uneasy blending of two world" not only of the conservative and modern in a changing society but of material and methods drawn from the west and the orient. The blending of different elements is 'uneasy' because, despite all the youthful author's efforts, there appears to be something missing. This uneasiness is best seen in Ruth Prawer Jhabvala's contrasting pictures of the Saxena and Mathur households on the one hand and the Sahni and Anand households on the other. The drawing room comedy chiefly verbal, of the former does not only represent another kind of Indian life from that represented by the vigorous slapstick that obtains among the Sahnis and Anands, but is presented in a different literary mode. That mode is imported, and it does not succeed in blending with what is 'indigenous' in the novel.

In describing the Punjabi family life Ruth Jhabvala brings out their vigour, resourcefulness, energy and health, drawing her material from her observations of the large Punjabi family of her husband Hindu partner[12]. The delight in detail and in every aspect of a rich subject that emerges in her descriptions of Indian family life in both ***To Whom She Will*** and **The *Nature of Passion*** is part of the 'rapture' with which, at the age of twenty-four, she first encountered India:

> "Perhaps, I loved it then because of my being Jewish. The Indian family life, the humour was closer to the Jewish world I knew than the Anglo-Saxon world"[13]

It is significant that when drawing the conservative Saxenas, Ruth Jhabvala turned for her models to the' Anglo-Saxon world' of 18th century fiction and satiric comedy that had been the subject of her academic study. When confronted with the rich material yielded by her observation of Punjabi family life she turned instinctively to the Jewish spring of her own nature. Recent critics do not throw much light on 18th century literary influence on Ruth Jhabvala's writing. One reason for this seems to be that by moving so clearly beyond satire in her most recent fiction, she has ceased to present marriage debates that immediately recall ***Pride and Prejudice*** or character portraits such as those of Kanta and Viddi in ***The Nature of Passion*** that bring Jane Austen's Fanny Dashwood or Fanny Burney's young Mr. Branghton of Evelina to mind. Another reason might be that her fiction though comic in content, is no longer light — hearted, and appears to concern itself more with self analysis of the psychological condition of various characters than with social criticism. The influence of the 18th century in Ruth Prawer Jhabvala's fiction goes much deeper. Far from being dead or outmoded, it may be traced throughout her writing, and should be recognised for what it is — a source from which she constantly draws strength in matters relating to both style and sensibility.

It can be said with certainty that Ruth Jhabvala is most "Augustan" in the propriety and skill which she selects material from 18th century and other sources and utilises them for own artistic purpose. She imitates in fact, in the 18th century manner recreating her model in terms and images of modern India in her earliest novels: concentrating on the human and essential truth to life of her selected originals. She places them in carefully observed Indian settings, and filters their speech through an artistically modified form of spoken Indian English idiom.

In her later works, the literary sources of her inspiration become much less easy to identify in any specific way. Her characters of worth in both ***A New Dominion*** and ***Heat and Dust*** for example, observe standards of decency in their personal relationships with others that originate in such Augustan virtue as elegance of mind and delicacy of behaviour.

Ruth Jhabvala first made her mark as a satirist with a sharp eye for hypocrisy and inconsistency. Her novels make consistent use of a character whose habit of mind-critical of flaws in society and in himself and carefully controlled behaviour indicate a person of sensitivity. This character (Krishna Sen Gupta in ***To Whom She Will,*** Shudhir Banerjee in ***A Backward Place.*** Ramnath In ***Esmond in India,*** Raymond in ***A New Dominion*** are example) becomes in a sense the author's representative in the novels, fictional world, establishing through his thoughts actions and the words a standard by which the behaviour of the other characters may be judged. Ruth Jhabvala's targets are not specified nor exclusively Indian faults but human weaknesses that have been diagnosed and subjected to satiric scrutiny by writers as far apart in time and locality as Chaucer, Alexander Pope, Vlotaire, Jhonathan Swift, Shakespeare, Chekhov and V.S. Naipaul, and the unknown authors of the ***Jataka Tales*** and ***The Book of Job.*** They are in fact, the classic targets of the satirist. Selfishness, vanity and egotism that interpret the world incorrectly because the place, the self and its centre, affectation and insensitivity, hypocrisy that manipulates others for selfish or immoral purpose. Although Ruth Jhabvala' s narrative tone remains cool and polite," her temperament remains more or less feminine and sentimental. The pretensions of western experts an Indian culture who fit India to their theories are occasionally exposed by a satiric persona, but are most consistently satirized by being viewed against Ruth Jhabvala's evocation in her novels, of the infinite mystery and variety of India. Her experience of India and knowledge of its culture have been limited by the very short time that she has been able to observe them fully. These limitations do not inhibit her in the least from believing that India has no surprises for her. Ruth Jhabvala exposes people's lack of sense and judgement and superficiality of their contact with land.

Ruth Jhabvala reveals her stature as a satirist in her choice of a worthy target. Despite her occasional use of traditional satiric techniques, the readers of Ruth Jhabvala find themselves led far more frequently towards sympathetic understanding of morally confused character than they find themselves pitched into easy laughter.

> "Perhaps I do tend to see the ridiculous aspects first, both in situations and in characters. But I don't think I just sit and laugh at them. On the contrary I am beginning to feel that what ludicrous on the surface may be tragic underneath that is especially surface may be tragic underneath that is especially true in India. Afterward you see that it is not comic at all but quite the opposite. Then one stops laughing at which point perhaps one's writing opens up."[14]

The coop detachment of her tone in A Background place as she takes the Hochstadts apart for her reader's instruction and pleasure and the flexibility of a narrative style that can appear to take on the colour of character's voice and habit of thought are features of Ruth Jhabvala's writing that developed more and more with each published novel. Ruth Jhabvala's movement from the comparative simplicity of satire towards the complexity of an ironic mode can be seen from a literary point of view a maturing process and from a personal one as a means of survival. The use of irony becomes for her a means of self-discipline. The Nawab of Khatam in ***Heat and Dust,*** who would be glad like his heroic ancestor, to visit a ferocious punishment on those who insult and persecute him, develops a studied courtesy with which he masks his contempt and hatred for the Britishers. He does not, however, try to develop an understanding of their difficulties or sympathy for their point of view. The times come when his nature can support the tension of this situation longer, and personality that once possessed the potential for true leadership develops into a nonentity. It is from frustration and tension comparable to that of Nawab, possibly, that Ruth Jhabvala has developed her ironic style.

> "I know I am the wrong type of person to live in India. To stay and endure, one should have a mission and a cause to be patient cheerful, unselfish, strong. I am a central European with an English education and a deplorable tendency to constant self analysis. I am irritable and have weak nerves."[15]

Ruth Jhabvala' s mature novels, far from being the cynical attacks upon India that some critics have taken them to be, seem to be most properly viewed as artistic expressions of the process of understanding life and of coming to terms with it. As in real life there are no answers provided in either ***A New Dominion*** or ***Heat and Dust.*** Her early novels are neatly balanced with greater grace and ease. In ***A New Dominion,*** what is unfamiliar to a western reader is skilfully interwoven with the thought and experiences of Raymond, a newcomer to India, whose habit of writing detailed letters to his mother about every moment of his day, is part of his character. By these means Ruth Jhabvala tries to direct her reader's eye through what seems to secret depth. As Raymond and Lee travel from Delhi to Banaras and from secret depth. As Raymond and Lee travel from Delhi to Banaras and from Banaras to Maupur Ruth Jhabvala's descriptions of landscapes and interiors take on symbolic colour that turn these characters into seekers after truth. Raymond's travel in and out of India brings out the hidden mystery of India. The vividness of the images that she presents indicates the intensity of her Indian agony. It is through her novels that Ruth Jhabvala presents the intricate nature of India. Equally interesting is the manner in which Ruth Jhabvala handles situations in which communication between characters has become impossible or nonexistent. Music, like dialogue is often used effectively in Ruth Jhabvala's fiction. A close study of her novels clearly shows that Jhabvala seems to be more concerned with internal development of her character's personality and this is something which gives her a chance to analyse her character minutely.

Jhabvala seems to believe in the inner development of her character. A close examination of her novels would bring out the fact that she is greatly concerned with that mystery and nature which takes one into the depth of character. Ruth Jhabvala looks at her character with a dramatised eye and moves from simplicity to complexity. The impulses to personal and artistic expression that have united in shaping Ruth Jhabvala work to a strong continuous development towards increased understanding and skill reverberate through her words clearly and effectively. She has written not only for entertainment but also for artistic gratification. What counts more than anything else is the inner satisfaction that one strives for. Despite the fact that Ruth Jhabvala's technical skill as a writer has helped her to devise ways and means to make her fiction more acceptable and effective, there is still something that we see is missing. Ruth Jhabvala is not one who claims perfection and also who claims to be near perfection. At most she can be near perfectibility and this is something that she tries to achieve in her fiction.

After 1975, Ruth Jhabvala published comparatively little fiction. Her four novels — ***in Search of Love and Beauty*** (1983) and ***Three Continents*** (1987), ***Poet and Dancer*** (1993); ***Shards of Memory*** (1995) and several short stories make up the entire body of her fictional output today. The decline has been qualitative as well. Ruth Jhabvala herself admitted to Paul Grimes: "Obviously I have lost my subjects, all my work seems to end up being about parasites and perverts".[16] Two distinct features; mark the writing of this period. One is a hangover from the novelist's old theme of India feeding on the vulnerable alien. The other centres on the break down of the natural order that is fast becoming a feature of the west. These two feature exist, sometimes independently and some times together in her fiction of these periods. An effort to combine their backgrounds - European, Indian and American.[17]

A very special 'fate' return soon after Ruth Jhabvala's departure from India, keeps the stories of an English women's self-imposed exile in India following a recoil from the west. Like her predecessors Nancy Tennyson had come out to India in the wake of what she believed was a spiritual call but what was in reality a passionate infatuation with a spiritual charlatan. Her fate is taken beyond theirs in the fact that thirty years after Dr. Mohanty's death Nancy, the only survivor of the vast number of disciples who had believed in synthesis unlimited, is still in India guarding the decay centre in Cooch Nahin.[18] The extent of Nancy personal synthesis with India, however, is far from encouraging to Westerners.

In a ***Summer by the Sea*** the two themes are even more properly blended. Ruth Jhabvala' s comment on the degeneration that had permitted American life, is presented in the depiction of perverse sexual and emotional relationship that are taken for granted by the younger generation. The life of a group of young men in a isolated cottage resembles that of secluded women in an eastern harem. Strifes and jealousies, rejections and favouritism had once centre around the blond and beautiful boy. The husband of the narrator Susie and Hamid, a handsome Indian comes into their lives and becomes the cynosure of all eyes. As a result of the life he leads, boy's natural instincts have been eroded to a point at which he believes Hamid, who is a pervert, to be a descendant of a line of famous saints who have handed their sainthood down from generation to generation. Susi's irrational love for Boy has drained her of all resistance and rendered her insensitive to humiliation. In the final scene, Hamid makes it clear that he is indifferent as to who makes up a couple with him — Boy or Bee. The tussle between the son-in-law and mother-in-law ends with both realising that to keep Hamid each must endure the presence of the other.

Parasites published a few months before a ***Summer by the Sea*** exposes the rapaciousness and the predatory tendency let loose by the breakdown of tradition in American society. In this story Ruth Jhabvala brings together a group of people who, out of their varying needs in the strange world in which they live feed on one another. Paul and Annette make a living out of rich, mentally undeveloped Stella who in her turn depends upon Annette for her personal fulfilment.

In the entire body of Ruth Jhabvala's fiction 'Expiation' is the only work in which an exploration of the criminal consciousness seems to be the novelist's sole purpose, Although the story is told by a man who is sympathetic to the two boys, they are never the less, depicted in animal terms. The aspect of Indian spiritualism is once again brought out in Ruth Jhabvala's novel ***In Search of Love Beauty.***[19] Set in an around New York during the 1980s the story follows the lives and aspirations of a family of German Jewish immigrants— Louise and Bruno their daughter Marietta and their grand children Mark and Natasha. Although their lives - are closely involved with those of other Jewish expatriates in the old clannish way a sense of displacement haunts them, leading each in a special way to engage in a quest for meaningful experience of life.

Published two years early ***Poet and Dancer***[20] is set in Manhattan's community and focuses on the passionate intimacy that develops between two cousins. This intimacy, with its lesbian under currents proves fatal for Angel who has taken upon herself the mission of protecting the mentally imbalanced, self-destructive Lara. "And this truly is what a perfect lover must always do. Angel had underlined in a medieval text, utterly and entirely despoiling himself of himself for the sake of the thing he loves, and that not only for a time but everlastingly: This is the exercise of love, which no one can know except he who feels it"[21] With such a view of love, it is no wonder that Angel's attachment to Lara, stronger than reason pushes her into taking her own life.

A central concern in all Ruth Jhabvala's writing after 1975 is the helplessness of western youth in the face of a stronger personality. Why does Angel allow Lara to manipulate her the way she does? Why do Harriet and Rupert not assert–even after they grasp the truth of their situations? What is it in their culture that drains youth of all resistance? Ruth Jhabvala does not answer these questions, but in a revealing passage in ***Three Continents,*** she presents the death of western civilization.

> "It was a long underground rite anonymous and a ghost like as though I had just died and did not know where it was bound for and neither did the other people who got in and out as the doors slid open at the stations, there was an unending stream of them, all smelling damp as if in their grave clothes"[23] (page 166).

Twelve years before writing this passage Ruth Jhabvala had undertaken a real journey from India to America in order to escape the alienation that Indian had brought for her and in the hope of being assimilated in the mainstream of western life. Now she confesses in Harviet's voice, that she does not know where the stream is taking her and neither do her fellow Westerners. Judging from her fiction and recorded statement[22] of last twenty-two years she has found loneliness, neurosis and lack of direction where she had hoped to find her roots. Incapable of accepting alienation as a way of life Ruth Jhabvala is perhaps like a fickle woman. She declared that she was getting ready to change the country once again in the hope of acquiring a life pattern that promises stability and meaning. The impulse to move out of America, Ruth Jhabvala believes, will come from within. "One just has to go on-learning, being." She declare in her 'Testament,' "throughout however many twenty years stretches is however in many different countries or places actual physical ones or countries of the mind – to which one may be called."[24]

REFERENCES

1. Despite many attempts by V.K. Gokak, Sujit Mukherji and other, the literature written directly in English continues to be known variously as "Indo-Anglian literature", "Indo-English Literature and *Indian Writing in English*

2. It is to suggest the sense of harmony between the language used and the culture expresses that Indo- English writing has been described humorsufy as "Mathew Arnold in a Sari" or Shakuntala in Skirts."
3. For a further comment on the viability of common literature as an area of study the article "The commonness of Common" Wealth Literature Indian *The Chronicle* Vol. IIIrd no. 3 "New Delhi 1st February 1978, p. 67.
4. Modern Indian Poetry in English *An Anthology and a Credo* (Calcutta-writers worksshop -1969), p. 291.
5. Ruth Prawer Jhabvala- *Living in India* (London Magazine September 1970) p. 41.
6. H.M. Williams (The Yogi and the Babbit Themes and Character of the New India in the novels of Ruth Prawer Jhabvala) Twentieth Century Literature, July 1969, p. 89.
7. Jhabvala-"My self in India" *An Experience of India* John Murrary, London 1966, p. 7
8. An Early review, quoted by R. Agarwal "Outsider with unusual Inside" *Times of India,* 25 March 1973.
9. R.P. Jhabvala *Myself in India,* p. 10.
10. H.M. Williams, "English Writing in Free India" *Twentieth Cenguty Literature,* January 1970, p.10.
11. Glasgow Herald review of *To Whom She Will*
12. A Rutherford and K.H. Petersen, *World Literature Written in English,* p. 375.
13. *New York Times,* Article of 1973
14. R. Agarwal- Ruth Jhabvala's fiction *Critical Review,* p. 34
15. R.P. Jhabvala *Myself in India* p. 81.
16. An Interview with Paul Yime, *The New York Times,* 15th May 1976, p. 14.
17. Another Dimension of Living New Week, 31 October 1977, p. 52.
18. Ruth Prawer Jhabvala— A very special fate New York, 29th March 1976, p. 27.
19. The Literal meaning of Cooch Nahin in Hindustan is "Nothing"

20. R.P. Jhabvala-In *Search of Love and Beauty* (1983 London Penguine Books).
21. R.P. Jhabvala— *Poet and Dancer* (1993) Landon, Penguine Books 1994.
22. *Ibid.*, p. 7.
23. Another Dimension of Living an Interview with R.P. Jhabvala.
24. R.P. Jhabvala's "Testament," *The Hindustan Times,* weekly 27th July, 1980.

2

Panoramas of Fictional World

No survey of the contemporary Indian literary scene would be complete if it failed to take note of the writings of Ruth Prawer Jhabvala. Here is a unique situation among those writings in India. Born and educated in Europe but married to an Indian and settled in India, she brings to the contemplation of the life around here certain advantages and limitations, which distinguish her writings from those of the foreigners passing through India and the writers native to the soil. Thoroughly familiar with the life and manners of her adopted country, she has been at the same time, gifted with the western sensibility which endows her with an uncommon insight into the typical traits of Indians, particularly the urban, upper and middle classes as they keep on undulating between tradition and modernity.

In spite of being a good writer in many respects, Ruth Jhabvala has been one of the neglected writer writing in and about India. Mrs. Jhabvala has published as many as eight novels and three collections of short stories in India. In his well written article on Mrs. Jhabvala, Mr. R.L. Agarwal enumerates several reasons for the neglect of the gifted writer. Some scholar— critics think that she cannot be regarded as an Indian writer as she is not one by birth. Others think that she is doing her bit of finger— wagging, as Mrs. E.V. Savi and Flora Annie Steel did in the past, that will be lost in the limbo of time as they are today. Still others believe that her novels are 'social novels' written in the most matter– of– fact manner and that she does not deal with such popular subjects as 'Spiritual Quest' or 'Nature of Reality'

She writes about the social problems and evils in the presentday India. Jhabvala's novels are full of local colour and clamour, dealing with the young who are inert, romantic and foolish, and the old who are cool, calculating and rigid. She describes the head-on collision between the traditional and the modernism, the East and the West and the confusion that follows in the wake of these collisions. Mrs. Jhabvala's world is upper class North India. The world she portrays is peopled by sophisticated and Anglicised, where husbands make love to their wives in broad day light. It is a world crowded with people who make a virtue of decay, depravity and coarseness: people who are indolent, sensuous and violently emotional; people who have not intellectual curiosity, and in the absence of this they lead a sort of life emptied of any quality in it. Mrs. Jhabvala does not write about one or two persons. She writes about the corporate life of two or three families. Her novels are singularly devoid of accidents, coincidences and sudden shifts of fortune. On the contrary they are full of the drab routine of daily life, so much so that they appear to be repetitive. But Mrs. Jhabvala is not afraid of being repetitive. It is for this reason that she has been able to describe the domestic and social life of Indians as no other writing in English has ever done.

Obviously, the novelist has observed her Indians at very close quarters. She depicts the uneasy and comic manner in which East and West are shown meeting, but only superficially. She describes, as no other writer writing in English has been able to describe, how funny, incongruous and tragic such a meeting could be. She is quick, sharp and intelligent to perceive that under western influence only surface changes have taken place in the Indian society. Its core remains unaffected and unchanged. At the same time the blind imitation of the West is bound to have dangerous repercussions. In her novels she employs the qualities of Jane Austen, of exposing the smug self-consequence and pompous triviality, the sentimentalism and cheap romance characteristic of the middle class.

The dialogues catch the vernacular flavour to some extent and reproduce its idiosyncrasies of speech through the peculiar mode of Indian English and more often through a literal translation of the vernacularism. The spicy flavour of her novels owes much to her rich, ironic descriptions. She does it sometimes with perfect comic reticence and sometimes offering her own remarks while describing a scene. She also deliberately uses expressions which give the characteristic Indian touch to her dialogues.

The technique of the novel only helps to throw the task of adding irony, of making fine moral discrimination on reader; it runs the risks of monotony undue repetitiveness, a narrative structure of a string of similar episodes. In Mrs. Jhabvala's world, suggests Meenakshi Puri[1] romance is confined to the four walls and the garden where there is one. What kind of romance can there be in a Delhi by-lane with litter lying dumped everywhere — the gutter flowing down with children squatting along? One should imagine a quick brutal attack and that is all. Well, not according to Mrs. Jhabvala; in her world the litter is not even mentioned, nor the gutter. No flies, no mosquitoes, no picturesque and florid abuses with accent on incest. And in this world after dismissing all this, husband and wife can make love on the terrace in pouring rain. This exactly happens in ***The Householder.*** How can any couple dare this in the city — unless they are hippies — we fail to understand. But still strange things happen in Mrs. Jhabvala's world. A young couple elopes. The third class compartment where they find themselves is presented through some coincidence. And, the entire third class compartment witnesses how an aristocratic lady chops onions, after prayers before the picture of her Guru to help her servant. Later, she strokes her son-in-law's hand to console him because her daughter is about to divorce him. But in spite of all these slipshod and glaring inaccuracies, she has portrayed her world and its people so fascinatingly that we cannot help liking them at once.

About her keen insight and sensitive observation John Reed wrote, "No western writers, not even E.M. Forster, is better equipped to deal with the mysteries of the Indian psych than this sensitive observer"[2] In "The Testament of a Novelist", Mrs. Jhabvala strongly protests against some critic's charge that she loathes India. She explained that it is neither love nor loathing, but the articulation of the "truth about her feeling for India and Indians."[3] But she confesses the charge in her perspective. In the earlier work her attitude is marked with compassion and love. At that time she loved everyone — even beggar, the poverty didn't bother her. It was life as one must read about it in the Bible "Whole, I thought pure I thought."[4] But in the process of becoming herself she became a European again. Whatever, she wrote about India was seen from a European point of view "I become a European sensibility again. I was no longer emerged in sensuous delight but had to struggle against in India. The tide of poverty, disease and squalor rising all around the heat the? frayed nerves, the strange alien after inexplicable often maddening Indian character"[5] Significantly this alienation and change in the novelist's perspective is accountable to the Cuckoo or Chameleon qualities that appear to be the part of her heritage.

Mrs. Jhabvala is hard on Indians as well as on Europeans if she is critical of the Indian tendency to sloppiness and self- indulgence, she is equally unsparing in her criticism of the pretentiousness of Europeans living in India. The theme of pseudo-modernism and false display of the women's craze for their emancipation finds mention in some of her novels. The Indian society has been in a considerable light position, losing its ancient heritage and stability, but is not ready for a change. Modernity has had only a superficial impact on the Indian elite class, who are still undecided about their social and personal norms. It goes without saying that Mrs. Jhabvala has observed Indians very closely and accordingly depicts the uneasy and comic manner in which east and west are so meeting, but only superficially. She describes, as no other writer writing in English has been able to describe, how funny incongruous and tragic such a meeting could be. She is quick, sharp and intelligent to notice that under the Western influence only surface changes have taken place in the Indian society. Its core remains unaffected and at the same time the blind imitation of the west is bound to have an adverse effect. In her novels she employs the technique of Jane Austen of exposing the empty self consequence and pompous triviality, the sentimentalism and cheap romance, characteristics of the middle class.

Jhabvala represents India with all its plus and minus points. Her feeling of India, its miseries and its excitement is in fact nothing more than skipping over the surface of Indian life with all too clever observations of its external characteristics. Sometimes we find strange things happening in her fiction not only because India is strange but because Jhabvala has "made the country stranger in her imagination over-heated by hatred."[6] All this can be accounted for her own secret non-acceptance of the country of her adoption. She confesses this rather bluntly in her autobiography "However, I must admit that I am no longer interested in India. What I am interested now is myself in India."[7] It can be said with a fair amount of certainty that Ruth Prawer Jhabvala belongs to that school which believes in presenting things as they are without caring whether this is liked by others or not. One can level the charge that her novels neglect the fate of the individual in a particular human situation, and that these do not deal with a personal and private predicament. But it must be remembered that dealing with a social milieu such novels are more concerned with presenting the entire picture of society rather than with individual's personal history. The characters in these novels tend to be, therefore, types rather than individuals as is found throughout the 19th century's sociopolitical novels of England. The Indo-English novelist like any good creative writer writes with a social consciousness born of the phenomena enacted around him. He is essentially a realist who moves around the society and experiences the social tensions of the struggling classes. It is this that arouses his deep creative impulse and ultimately makes him a writer.

Critics may argue that since Jhabvala is mainly concerned with the contemporary or topical event in life, her work ceases to have a universal appeal. By now Mrs. Jhabvala has produced a considerable body of fiction from the point of view of both, quantity and quality. Mrs. Jhabvala has drawn material from various aspects of life, chiefly the upper middle class people of India. There is enough material in the society to buy communal frenzy, social disparities and corruption in bureaucracy for the thematic treatment by the novelist to stir the imagination of the countrymen to a new awakening. And this can best be done through the medium of novel. Mrs. Jhabvala like Shelley, well realised that so long as the imagination of the people is not stirred, the seeds of reform will keep lying on the road to be trodden upon by the unweary traveller.

Modern and liberal in outlook, Mrs. Jhabvala believes in new humanism and a new morality according to which woman is not to be taken as a sex object and glamour girl, fed on fake dreams of perpetual youth, lulled into passive role that requires no individual identities, but as man's equal and honoured partner. In Mrs. Jhabvala, one can easily discern a happy blend of two sensitivities — the sensitivity of an artist and sensitivity of a humanist. As a humanist, she is for unfettered freedom and urges us to realise that "Human Personality is a precious, hard one achievement worthy of nurture, irrespective of sex."[8] She regrets that in this modern age when monumental problems have been resolved by science and research, the human relationship still seems largely unresearched.

She, therefore, pleads for the new marital morality based on mutual trust, consideration generosity and absence of pretence, selfishness and self-centredness. Not that Jhabvala's women characters alone have been portrayed as victims of conjugal unhappiness or hankering after extramarital freedom. Her men are no better either, Jhabvala seems to suggest that the sound basis of happy married life is mutual understanding, because much that goes wrong between men and women lies in what they withhold from each other. She lashes out vehemently and sarcastically that if chastity is so important and so well preserving it would be easier to safeguard it by keeping men in seclusion, not women. She wants the generation to come out of the shackles of bondage to the air of freedom as freshness to break off the rules, the regulations, the laws that make people fearful of each other.

The concept of individual freedom continuous to be the central concern of the novelist and that is why her heroines so deeply and loyally rooted in Indian culture are portrayed to be struggling for freedom and trying to assert their individuality in their own right. A trenchant defender of human values, Mrs. Jhabvala in all her novels pleads for enduring, frank and friendly communication, a compassionate approach in order to untangle the personal and social problems, more particularly the problem of man-woman relationships. Mrs. Jhabvala has eminently succeeded in impressing this idea

On the reader's mind.

The estrangement between men and women in her novels have been treated with a brutal frankness and in realistic terms. One can, if one wishes, dub and damn these characters using any epithet for them, say, degenerate, corrupt, frustrated, aimless, unrestrained, insane, nihilist and infidel. But few can refute the dispassionate honesty of the novelist in treating the discord and relationship, fictionality. She carefully avoids to be sentimental, nor does she evade facing the situations and destinies. She has also been careful enough not to pronounce her value, judgement - especially of incompatible or ill-matched couple, which were earlier considered taboo for the Indian writers, particularly when the writer happens to be a woman.

What distinguishes Mrs. Jhabvala from other writers is her occupation with the individual and his inner world of sensibility. She chooses the social background for comedies, tragic comedies, farces. Of all the women Indian-English novelists Mrs. Jhabvala is perhaps the only writer who presents her character and situation comically. Her fiction seems to assuage both the traditions of American and English novels. And as a result of this her fiction takes its form and tone from polarity, dislocation of normal life, recklessness of behaviour, morbidity of temperament – these together with the profound poetry of disorder radical form of alienation, mal adjustments and contradictions – seem to have been preserved as the best of both great traditions. Mrs. Jhabvala sees more deeply, darkly and privately and her emphasis is on an appropriation of reality with the high purpose of bringing disorder. This aspect of Jhabvala's fiction undoubtedly adds a new dimension to the Indian English novel. It is therefore imperative that the modern English novel should seek new techniques to articulate these newly experienced inner and outer realities. Mrs. Jhabvala spotlights the extremely complex nature of life. Real life has an infinite variety. It may take as many forms as there are individuals. Her notion of reality of life seems to have been greatly influenced by Varginia Woolf's, who maintains that "Life is not a series of gig lamps symmetrically arranged, life is a luminous hallow a semi transparent envelop surrounding from the beginning of consciousness to the end."[9]

It would be wrong to link Jhabvala with other creative Indian writers writing in English such as Mulk Raj Anand, Raja Rao or R.K. Narayan, nor with women novelists such as Kamala Markandaya or Nayantara Sahgal. She stands a part from them and the merits as well as demerits of her literary situation are particular to her. Her advantage is in her being a European living in India, the disadvantage, too lies in her not being a genuine, grassrooted Indian. It is for this reason that she can afford to be detached, ironic and satirical. She can judge and evaluate the human affairs in an Indian family from a point of view which is both objective and unsentimental. John Reed, while evaluating ***An Experience of India*** finds Jhabvala better equipped than even E.M.Forster. "To deal with mysteries of India psyche."[10] She is, unlike E.M.Forster, not really concerned with the mysteries or muddles that India or Indian's presents to a creative western writer. Her worldliness and down- to-earth approach to life indirectly helps her in avoiding the defects of sentimentality or superficial involvement with varieties of Indian religious or mystical beliefs.

Jhabvala's merit as a creative writer lies in her being fully aware to her limitations. She writes about possibly only social segment of urban India that she knows at first hand. The general belief that she writes about only the sophisticated upper class is unjustified because her writing as in ***A Backward Place,*** portray the lower middle class with sympathy and understanding. She also touches upon the rising commercial class which is by no means really sophisticated. In reality this constitutes the new rich class which has risen from the brink of want and bare necessities and which is hungry for culture, refinement and a respectable social status. Thus, enlarging the scope of her social and cultural background in her fictions, Jhabvala shows her awareness of the variety and complexity of the post-Independence Indian society. Her urban India is not urbane, in fact, it may even be described as a 'backward place'. Her basic literary aim is to portray the human picture of the society caught into the conflict of a change from tradition to modernity.

Jhabvala's art of fiction follows the path of the comic and develops the form of a social comedy of manners. George Meredith says that comedy presents men and women in society, that the setting of comedy is primarily urban, and that the comic writer projects a social and cultural outlook with a ideal, and this norm often gives rise to a sense of proportion a value. All writers of comedy present a point of view in which this norm is implicit, and for eccentricity, abnormality one must have a moral yardstick in view. These incongruities of human behaviour clearly show departures from this norm. Jhabvala has no equal in presenting incongruities of human character and situations. These incongruities have social and cultural implications and hence they become the source of the comic. In ***The Nature of Passion*** Nimmi speaks of her college and the lecture on Keats' poetry and Om makes fun of the whole business of girls going to college –

> "This college, said Om talking more loudly, it is only a waste of time and of good money and will perhaps even give her wrong ideas. How much money was spent on her education and what has it led to now? Usha laughed. She had failed many times to pass her inter and reference to this always moved her to good – humoured laughter" (Page 17).

The idea of sending girls to college in Lalaji's family creates the conflict between the old and the young, orthodox and reform, tradition and modernity. But this difference in values is presented in a very comic and sarcastic manner. The incongruities in human behaviour are shown in the character and behaviour of Lalaji sitting in his office and receiving persons who call upon him for help. Please command me~ he said, and they went through the preliminary formula of disinterested affection. The visitor declared that his sole purpose in coming was to regale his eyes on Lalaji. Laliji said that it was too long a time since he had the pleasure of seeing his visitor. The visitor solicitously enquired after Lalaji's health and after the health of his family, they continued in this strain for some five minutes both very cordial and both of them thinking of something else." (page 50).

This small incident of social give–and–take has beautifully presented Jhabvala's keen observation of Indian specially Punjabi, modes of behaviour. However, the novelist displays her ironic mode in clarifying the difference between the sweet surface graces of the two Punjabis and their real submerged motives. The lndianness of Indian writers in English or European writers on India has often been raised in relevant critical forums. Sometimes this question itself has been considered superficial and insubstantial because creative literature deals for more with the universal in human passion and reason than what may doubtfully come into the category specified as 'Indian'. However, the Indianness of Jhabvala's fiction raises some important points since she is not really an Indian, at least by birth. Her Polish parentage German upbringing, British schooling and finally life in India after marriage and her living in New York only heighten the complex nature of this problem. After taking into account all these facts of her life, some may ask as to how far Indian is Ruth Prawer Jhabvala? This question is different in tone and quality from the other as for example, how far Indian is Kamala Markandaya or Nayantara Sahgal?

The Indianness of Indian creative writing in English will have to be judged by the awareness of the author of certain specified and special characteristics of societies and cultural patterns in India. For example, Indian society has always been an 'in group' society than its counterpart in the west. Although the joint family system is getting shattered under various economic and social pressures, Indian society even in urban areas still preserves this 'in group' feeling, mental outlook and the get togetherness of families ties. The west has not yet affected the spirit of Indian society and the heart of the emotionally generous individual. Jhabvala presents her deep awareness of this aspect of Indian society. In fact, many of her novels are basically concerned with portraying either the fulfilment or the frustration of individuals in the undivided Hindu joint family system. Lalaji in ***The Nature of Passion*** almost like a benevolent and generous head of the family keeping in mind the welfare and happiness of his children. ***The Nature of Passion*** is almost like a family chronicle and in this sense essentially Indian. It is also Indian in the way in which it brings out the clashes between two families or two individuals in the family in the context of the present day changes in metro cities of India. The tensions in Indian societies today such as those between the old and the young, the upholders of orthodox traditions and the rebels against that tradition underline the social world of Jhabvala's fictions. These situations are individual in the deepest sense as well as being representative of social change and almost universal in their appeal and content. The experience of such individual caught up in the whirlpool of social change is essentially Indian as much as it is universal in a larger sense.

Jhabvala is much preoccupied with portraying the plight of individuals In their relationship to the family, to the social group, in ways which demonstrate her Indianness. Lalaji's second son, Chandra Prakash, a government official who is married to Kanta, is in part isolated from the family and in part still united with it. He is very conscious of his career as the head of the department and his wife is deeply aware of their western culture. He considers himself intellectualized and therefore different from his father and his brothers who know only the art of making money. He and his wife, both, however need the money and the financial help from the joint family, which specially Lalaji provides. The dislike of the commercial class is thus combined with a peculiar sense of dependence on the class and this is a good example of the present day dilemma in which people live with a lot of contradictions. It is these aspects of the Indian society which find, expression in Jhabvala's fiction.

There is another aspect of this Indian familial setting which Jhabvala presents with considerable power and acute sense of inward understanding. The experience of European women married to Indians or of Indian women married to Europeans who are faced with this unusual situation of the Hindu joint families is finally projected in her fiction. Gulab's marriage to Esmond has not changed her life-style. She looks forward to the spicy food that her mother or the cook prepares for her and Esmond simply averse to the strong smells of spices. European women such as Peggy in ***The Aliens*** are in for cultural shocks when her sister-in-law enters her room and opens all the drawers without caring even to ask her. This is indicative of not merely a minor question of social manners, but one which projects the difference between the individualistic European families and the socially close - knit Indian families. Jhabvala shows her deep awareness of this difference in these characters and situations they are in. In this context she is both European and Indian thereby underscoring her distinctive position among creative writers in English on India. In ***The Aliens*** Jhabvala presents the pains and predicaments of Peggy, an English girl married to Dev, and made to live in a joint family of Punjabi Hindu businessman. She feels rather isolated in the family because she is averse to the coarseness of her mother-in-law. Peggy with her English background is against the insensitivity and coarseness of men and women of a society wholly guided by the profit -motive. However, she does nothing to make her feelings known to her parents in England as she has become accustomed to their stoical way of life. She feels isolated, and yet she manages to "live and let live" in her Indian husband's family. Peggy does not approve¢- of Indian manners and ways of behaviour and Jhabvala brings out this negative aspects of Indian modes of behaviour quite sharply.

The interaction between two cultures, European and Indian, is Jhabvala's favourite theme. In fact, it is her forte since it is in this area that her personal experience in India finds expression in art. In a revealing autobiographical essay 'Living in India', Jhabvala writes-

> "I have lived in India for most of my adult life. My husband is Indian and so are my children. I am not less so every year"[11]

Jhabvala in this personal article has spoken of her varied reactions to this country and its people. She knows that India reacts strongly on foreigners and they either love it or loathe or do both. She has herself passed through this stage in India where everything appears to be marvellous and remarkable. This kind of attitude makes the writer to write more about this aspect of Indian life and this, in turn, finds mention in art. Jhabvala's creative self seems to be the sole occupant of her especial, individually designed room, 'a room of one's own' from where she can view the outside world. It is of great help to her in maintaining an attitude of ironic detachment since it is a room of very distinctive, and also different from the world outside. Yet there is a change within the room itself as, for instance, when the air conditioner works, it is cool and comfortable. It creates the right atmosphere for Jhabvala sense of the comic. But sometimes the electric power goes out of order and the room cooler stops functioning and the atmosphere becomes oppressive. This outer weather affects the inner weather of Jhabvala' s sensitivity. It is then that her attitude to India and the world of her fiction undergoes a drastic change and she grows critical, ironic, even bitter. Empathy gives place to antipathy because the room is no longer her own, it is invaded by the outside atmosphere. It loses itself in a larger India and the creator of fiction feels identified with her created world. She gives expression to it in the following lines -

> "India swallows me up and now it seems to me that I am no longer in my room but in the white-hot city streets under a white-hot sky" (page 42).

The heat in India is oppressive and murderous, yet Jhabvala figures out many figures in it which take possession of her imagination and creative self. A smiling leper being driven in a cart by another leper and the image of the lord Shiva being worshipped by people presents aspect of India which are both human and divine. She very well realizes that religion and religious devotion are potent forces in India. Even old and semi-starved widows can be seen dancing in the countryside. The Indian sky which is huge, expansive and clear appears to be dominating the destiny of man. Jhabvala is all praise for Indian devotional songs of the Bhakti cult on the themes which draw parallels between man's love of God and man's love for woman.

Jhabvala is sincere in exposing false labels, and is very keen on bringing out the hollowness and emptiness of Indian middle class life. She is also tempted to be 'defiant and European', but in the end she appears to be ready to become one with the Indian soil:

> "Of course, this can't go on indefinitely and in the end I'm bound to lose, if only at the point where my ashes are immersed in the Ganges to accompaniment of

> Vedic hymns, and then who will say that I have not truly merged with India"? page 51.

Jhabvala's later reaction to Europe, the place of her birth and upbringing is not one of nostalgia but restlessness—a restlessness which often impels to return to India, the country of her voluntary residence

> "I do sometimes go back to Europe. But after a time I get bored there and want to come back here. I also find it hard now to come back here. I also find it hard now to stand the European Climate. I have got used to intense heat and seem to need it" (page 51).

This transparent sincerity of Jhabvala in revealing her responses to the phenomenon that is India brings out the process of her creative faculty. She may perhaps be called a European writer on India, yet her creative work provides enough evidence of her Indianness, the aesthetic design of her art, shaped by her experience of life in India. It is the European's "Passage to India" but very different from that of Kipling or E.M. Forster. Jhabvala in the early years of her experience of this country seems to try to establish a little Europe of her own in India, but with the passage of time the plant has developed into a tree, with a native growth, which is sustained and nourished by the Indian earth. The question what is 'Un-Indian' in the image of India as projected in Jhabvala' s world of fiction is similar to raising another question about the autonomy of her art.

The growth of Ruth Prawer Jhavbala as an artist in fiction shows the working of a process of isolation– alienation in a mild form, and its transformation into art. But in Jhabvala's world the context and meaning of alienation is basically social. Her fiction depicts the breakdown of a traditional social order thereby highlighting the isolation between one individual and another in marital relations, in family life and in society at large. Those having leanings, towards Marxism may describe it as a satirical comment on a decadent, capitalist, commercial society. From such societies only springs inevitable fountain called alienation.

The breakdown of a world-view, divinely ordained and supported by tradition, is the primary source of this alienation. Its social context presents man against the power of money and position. Alienation results from man's reduction to the status of a mere thing, as he is isolated from the earth and his fellow men. Once reduced to the level of a thng, he falls a victim of the power and lure of money.

Ruth Prawer Jhabvala' s personal experience of displacement and exile has had a profound effect on the fiction that she has produced. Her earlier novels, which are all set in India, generally reinforce the values of home, family and community. Plot move comfortably towards closure, and the view of the world presented is secure and conservative. While characters may initially be straining to loosen themselves from the strictures of tradition, they are artfully manoeurved into positions of acceptance. They are always brought back home. As Jhabvala's years of residence in India stretched on, there is a noticeable shift in her work. The outsides! living in a foreign country- Jhabvala' s own position becomes the main focus. While the early novels seek to resolve internal conflicts within families and communities, the later works remain more fragmented. Typically, ending are decidedly more ambiguous. The reader is never quite sure if the English character Lee in ***A New Dominion*** and Judy in ***A Backward Place,*** who decide to stay in India permanently, are in fact happy and secure in their adopted homes.

Home is invoked most immediately by the image of the house. In Indian Jhabvala's novels, the manner in which her characters are housed.Where they live, how they live, and how they feel about their homes – is integral to the construction of the fiction. The salient fact about Ruth Prawer Jhabvala is that she is a writer in permanent exile.[12] Although Jhabvala is an exile, she does not follow the typical pattern. She does not re-create her original home in her fiction; on the contrary, she avoids it. Her silence is intriguing. It suggests that home and the memories associated with home, are simply too painful to face. When considered in the light of early fiction she produced, it seems that Jhabvala dealt with her feeling about home by writing herself into her adopted place. She made a new home both physically and imaginatively in India.

The sensitive readers rightly understand the alienation in her novels, but unable to explain it in concrete terms. The world of Jhabvala's fiction is guided by this mild soft sense of alienation. And it is because of this she responds to it rather obliquely. As a European writer in India, she is placed in a position which is naturally subjected to the pressures of alienation. As a representative of western culture and tradition, she inherits a life - view which does not seem 'native' to the sons of the soil. She consciously as well as unconsciously brings to the fore the Indian ethos combined with the western rational and scientific attitudes which inevitably become the criteria for judging Indian's, their moral behaviour and their emotional responses to environment. This situation is a source of her strength as well as her weakness as artist. She is at her best projecting conflicts of individuals and domestic friction, which are social or familial manifestations of alienation. Alienation is not restricted to foreign wives in their relationship with native husband or vice-versa, but is a dominant feature of here created cosmos in which even Indian wives and husband are up against barrier created by their selves. The implications of alienation in Jhabvala's fictions go far beyond the boundaries of domestic life. They extend to a world in which man is reduced to the level of an object, man is subjected to manipulation by his fellow men in pursuit of wealth and material gains. Man becomes a part of the commercial world where money making and acquIring positions is the main occupation of our present day civilization.

Jhabvala's great achievement as an artist lies in the fact that she gives an artistic expression to the mild alienation in her projection of man and society in India. Man and society in India are involved not merely to change from tradition to modernity but are also in a process of cultural and mental fragmentation. Man is not what he used to be in the past. Today, he seems to have lost his moorings and does not know what to do and what not to do in a given situation. He finds himself in a peculiar dilemma where he is unable to find himself, thus allowing himself to be victimized by the temptation and lure of money. Jhabvala portrays all this with a remarkable sense of awareness of sensitivity. Jhabvala also shows here remarkable capacity to combine her portrayal of material reality with the portrayal of aspects of India's spiritual reality. In her fiction, we find that man has lost touch with reality and is engaged in looking for his lost identity. Whereas other Indian writers in English are also isolated to some extent from their native soil, they have an advantage of getting back to their grassroots. It is not possible for Jhabvala to achieve this objective. This Journey is not for her a return to the earth, but her sincere attempt to have the feel of the soil itself. The search for the Sadhus and the pursuit of the spirit in her novels can be interpreted in terms of her journey to the Indian earth. Jhabvala is busy in searching for the hidden beauty and truth of the objects. She is confronted with and this is something she appears to be working for. The transformation of isolation into art is the most sign.

The major themes in Jhabvala's fictions are 'East-West encounter' and 'marital dissonance' which are mutually inter linked in their negative context. In the positive context they may be described as fruitful and happy relationship between East and West resulting in marital harmony and joy. Jhabvala brings out both these aspects, but the elements of encounter and dissonance play a very vital role in her world of fiction. In her two novels ***Esmond in India*** and ***A Backward place*** these two themes are treated in a very remarkable way. In ***Esmond in India*** we find Gulab having a European as a life partner and their marriage cannot be termed as a marriage of true minds. They represent the two opposite views of the east and west. This difference in their cultural patterns and values is skilfully brought out by Jhabvala. Towards the end of the novel we find their married happiness breaking down and resulting in failure.

Gulab and Esmond move away from each other due to temperamental and cultural gap that exists between the two. Whereas in ***A Backward Place*** Judy, who is married to Bal, a handsome youth dreaming of career in films, makes an apparent success of her marriage. Gulab and Esmond ruin their marital union through errors of misunderstanding and loss of perspective. Jhabvala beautifully brings out the problems and conflicts facing people belonging to the eastern and western parts of the world. They do not come to terms with one another because no sincere effort is made to narrow down the gap separating the east from the west. There is a desire for friendship and relationship and sometimes it appears to be coming from the heart but even then it does not have an element of solidity and firmness because though it comes from the heart, it does not include the heart. The theme of marital conflict in Jhabvala's fiction has a much larger scope than is evident in East-West confrontation or coexistence. Indian husbands and their Indian wives too appear to be falling apart in a purely Indian familial and social situation. This has its roots in the clash of personalities, temperaments and also values. Jhabvala appears to be suggesting to us that getting married does not mean enjoying the bliss of heaven and this is clearly brought out in novel after novel by Ruth Prawer Jhabvala. In ***Get Ready for Battle*** Gulzari Lal and his wife Sarla differ basically in their attitude to life. Both of them are opposed to each other as Gulzari Lal is governed purely by materialism whereas Sarla, his wife, is guided by idealism. Their conflict is a conflict between materialism and idealism and this is the core of Jhabvala's theme of the novel.

The clash of personalities is dramatically presented in ***The Householder*** between Prem and Indu, who are married only to discover that their ways of life are more contradictory than complementary. He tries to assert his position as the dominant husband. The conflict between a growing sense of individualism and the orthodox tradition of a man-ridden Indian society is suggestive of the post-second world war phase of Indian society. In ***To Whom She Will*** Prema and Suri also displays dislike of marital harmony. Marriage, according to Jhabvala, is only an adjustment, rather than a real involvement in human relationships and love. Mrs. Kaul in ***A Backward Place*** becomes a society lady immersed in social work and cultural activities simply because her husband, Mr. Kaul is too busy traversing the road to self glory and advancement of social status. She is "a bird in a golden cage" who seems to be a willing victim of self deception. The satirist in Jhabvala artistically brings out Shaw's estimate of the British institution of marriage as a convenient solution of Britain's acute housing problem of allotting one room for two people. Jhabvala makes fun of this aspect of the Indian society today which is caught in the whirlpool of a major conflict between the old and the new.

The new society woman in urban India is a phenomenon in itself, but what is of significance to note in Jhabvala's portrayal is her deeper awareness of woman's condition. In her search for the outer life there is a hidden sense of frustration, a sense of failure of the inner life. Mrs. Kaul in ***A Backward Place*** or Sarla in ***Get Ready for Battle*** clearly bring out the Indian society lady's personal perplexities. The theme of East-West encounter in Jhabvala's fiction has social, cultural and spiritual aspect. In the social context Indians and Europeans meet, fall in love, get married and face either mutual dissonance or familial fractions. In the cultural context they face the problems of adjustment of diverse backgrounds. Jhabvala is, of course, very much concerned with the problems of European men and women trying to get adjusted to Indian society and its customs. In the spiritual context she portrays Europeans who are fascinated by Gurus, the torch bearers of India's ancient spiritual heritage. The spiritual element in these Gurus may be fake or genuine, yet the charm they have for Europeans is beyond any doubt. The relationship between Indians and Europeans is thus varied. It has at least three prominently portrayed dimensions in Jhabvala's fictional world.

Jhabvala as an artist in the realism of fiction thus presents three kinds of reality– the social reality, the cultural reality and the spiritual reality. She is basically a novelist of domestic life, its joys and sorrows, its harmony and conflict, its fulfillment and frustration. Since she is concerned with a materialistic civilization in its domestic setting, she tries to present the material reality which is significant in the metaphysics of her art. However, this metaphysics in her world of fiction has also a spiritual dimension partly revealed in the charm that Europeans have for the Gurus, the inheritors of India's spiritual glory. In this way Jhabvala's guest for the material reality is supplemented by, and harmonized with, her search for a spiritual reality. This dual quest ultimately leads to the basic unity of her art in which the real and the ideal, the material and the spiritual are blended into a unified vision of her art.

Art is both a mode of expression as well as of communication. Jhabvala is very clear about her own position among creative writers of English in India. As a writer, she is very deeply conscious of western readers and this awareness has greatly affected her craft of fiction. As a practitioner of the art of fiction, the choice of idiom the mode of the European's vision of India appear to be the central problems of Jhabvala. Her basic position is that she is a European writer, and second, she writes primarily for western public. Her strength as well as her weakness as an artist in the realm of fiction has to be judged in the light of this specific point of view.

In her novels Jhabvala acts as an omniscient narrator. ln this method she presents a story with a perspective or several perspectives without, of course, personally getting involved in any of them. She is present at the side of her characters, in the author's corner of her scenes, she watches them and comments on their actions mode of feeling and thought processes. She is at the centre, but the centre is outside the varied and overall circles of her creations. She thus seems to be an outsider for a while, yet she plunges into small circles, enter the consciousness of her characters and then describes what she has observed and assessed so meticulously.

As a European writer, Jhabvala's persistent emphasis upon painting or describing minute details of apparently unimportant scenes or events is an important element of her art. The western intelligence thrives on comprehensiveness and throughness in the subject under review. As an artist Jhabvala inherits this western intellectual discipline and projects it on her fictional canvas. She is also aware that she is writing for western audiences who are not familiar with Indian culture or modes, and therefore her comprehensiveness receives additional impact. Her area of observation is very wide and she presents all that she observes in an effective way. Sometimes this tendency towards reproducing an actual scene is carried to an excessive degree with the result that an Indian reader is almost bored, but the western reader, who is unfamiliar with the scene feels thrilled. For example, Suraj in ***A Star and Two Girls*** visits an actress friend. She and her mother fuss over him and there is a good deal of teasing and the actress sits with her hand in her lap with her eyelids lowered except when she throws a look of fire at him. The whole scene establishes the fact that Jhabvala is adept in presenting even minor scenes and events graphically and effectively. The following passage can be cited as an example –

> "Then some photographer came to taker her publicity picture, and although Swaraj wanted her to send them away, she wouldn't, but posed for them in various attitudes in her drawing room. Now she looked reflective by a vase of flowers and holding one flower in hand, now she struck her finger through the bars of her parrot's cage and tenderly puckered her mouth at him, now she was gay and threw back her head and laughed wit spontaneous laughter into the cameras."[13]

This meticulous attention to every small movement of characters their actions, their gestures is an interesting aspect of her craft of fiction. For example, Lee in ***A New***

Dominion at one stage is divided between two compelling figures and voices, who claim her soul and the Swamiji. About Raymond, Lee Writes-

> "I knew he had been watching me all the time. Not in curiosity but in concern. And that was the way he looked at me too. Soon after the Swamiji cast her eyes on Lee and she was almost mesmerized by him - Yes, of course, his eyes were on me" (page 154).

This description of the setting and the scene of action is part of Jhabvala' s visual perspective. There are so many soul scene on situation, which she describes so comprehensively and convincingly. Her pictorial imagination covers almost every small movement of nature and man. This visual side in Jhabvala's created world is only a preview of a wider and deeper moral perspective. Her technique reminds one of that of Robert Browning in his famous dramatic monologues. Browning too projects a visual perspective in his poems like Fra Lippo Lippi or Andrea Del Sarto and it functions as an objective correlative to the moral perspective. Similarly, in Jhabvala's fiction descriptions of men and things create a wide visual canvas. They are so concrete that one can almost feel them, touch them and smell them. But they also concretize the abstractions of a moral perspective. They give substance to the feelings and points of view of the characters in her novels. Minuteness and exactness of detail in Jhabvala's fictions contribute to the making of a disposition or attitude. It is in fact a complete visual organization of the world. Since she writes basically for the western readers who was not quite acquainted with the Indian landscape, the modes of Indian behaviour or patterns of Indian culture, she feels obliged to create a large, comprehensive visual canvas aimed at objectifying these complex patterns. This visual organization constitutes part of her world view as an artist.

Jhabvala's world signifies space – the space that is India, the India moulded by her experience and fictional art. The way in which she presents India or Indian characters can be termed as important since the entire canvas covering India is projected. Jhabvala's mode of narration follows the traditional time – span, the individual's or family's cyclic development or decline. The time - dimension in her fictional art is so dominant that her art does not show any substantial spatial development and far remote from the concept of space–time polarity as reflected in the novels of Virginia Woolf.

Whereas Jhabvala' s fiction is essentially a time – art, her modes of narration of description are direct and comprehensive. As an ever present narrator, Jhabvala is well aware of the utility and the effect of what the direct telling can perform. Either the main character in her fiction speaks or the all- knowledgeable novelist describes, or comments in the third person. However, she sometimes overplays the role of the omniscient narrator, and in consequence takes the entire range of the knowledge of her characters for her private province. Whenever such things happens she seems rather boring to the reader. And her language too appears to be pedestrian.

The conventional 19th century method of the novelist was to separate his character descriptions from setting descriptions or nature descriptions from the body and movement of his novel, and treat them as separate components. The reader is treated to a long, romantic, decorative description of sun rise or sunset without any real link with the characters or their consciousness. Modern novelists make description an organic art implying that it is an essential part of the plot, action, characterization or symbol. Jhabvala's art of fiction displays this organic quality, the deft interweaving of description of scenes, the modes of narration and the methods of characterization. In her novels, she has given excessive emphasis upon food. However, this makes an unpleasant deviation from the modes of her organic art and the description having nothing to do either to the characters delineation or to the elaboration of plot or theme. They appear to have loose connection with characters or situations without much significance. However, the love of individuals.

Gulab, the Indian wife of an English man, Esmond in ***Esmond in India*** is very fond of dishes and this is characteristic of Jhabvala's mode of organic art, emphasizing food habits.

Jhabvala's use of irony must be distinguished from her employment of sarcasm or satire Irony, according to H.W. Fowler, is a kind of utterance, which projects a double audience comprising one party that hears as well as realizes the deeper significance of the expression. Jhabvala in her ironic mode succeeds in splitting her audience between those who perceive and those who don't. Her language thus becomes exclusive or private to set a character, and the knowledge escapes others. She, however, expects the reader to perceive the hidden meaning that lies beneath the surface statement, the gulf that lies between the aberrance of a situation and the reality that underlies it. Jhabvala uses different forms of irony such as verbal irony or rhetorical irony, but her fiction does not produce many examples of dramatic or tragic irony. Her fiction is ironic partly because it recognises the complexities and incongruities of her aesthetic experience.

Jhabvala's style is the 'subject' and this 'subject' is India in relation to a western creative writer's sensibility. This Indian landscape, natural as well as human, comes within the range of her descriptive and narrative ability and she projects upon it her visionary power greatly circumscribed by her naturalistic and ironic traits– although technique is in a certain sense discovery or vision, after a point technique and talent appear to be going their own ways in different directions. Modern fiction in English is peculiarly conscious of its techniques and tools. The modern novelist does all he can to explore and interpret the complexity of the modern spirit and in this context almost all Indo-Anglian writers, with the exception of Raja Rao, appear to have met with failure. In a realist like Ruth Prawer Jhabvala we find a very sensitive creative writer. However, she is mostly preoccupied with the environment only, with India as its central points.

Jhabvala usually presents the traditional undivided Hindu family and only by implication she criticises it. Sociologically it is a vital element in Indian society and at the same time, it protects many of its member from the effects of poverty, unemployment and loneliness. It generates both misery and relief from misery. The undivided family is the embodiment of traditional middle-class India, the old ruling but protecting the young. Outside the family Jhabvala's novels present political corruption and the poverty in India, usually the poverty of those who have come down in the world. Jhabvala is interested in the fact that traditionally Hinduism has recognised the validity of the life of the house holder husband, father, and breadwinner, as long as this life is limited to a phase of a man's life, giving way to the spiritual as he grows older and older with the passage of time.

But above all sympathy and not anger dominates Jhabvala's treatment. She stands apart from the subject she creates characters and events as a whole, as part of the consistent pattern. She has drawn, and her concern is to show how art can arrange and rearrange the shifting events of Indian life. She is against preaching and hardly exaggerates. On the contrary, her genius is for the miniature and the minor. Jhabvala's method is to lead her characters into complicated situations, which generate the solution of the problems. Her plots are usually slow to be developed. There are few major incidents. Sometimes, the action is minor even trivial.

Jhabvala is the most sophisticated novelist of the Indian scene. Her treatment of the Hindu undivided family and of the tension between old and new, young and old, western and eastern, all within modern Indian life, is certainly highly sophisticated. She takes a balanced view of life and never favours completely the young rebels or the old conservatives. The young are confused while the old self-deceived and disillusioned. Out of such cliches, however, Jhabvala creates a new and fresh patterns. In India the conflict between old and new, between old and young, is complicated by the question of national identity. As a rule Jhabvala seems to bring about the changes between social comedy and tragic comedy from novel to novel. The blackness of ***Esmond in India,*** for example, was followed by the sunniness of ***The Householder.*** Jhabvala's ability to write with great skill about the darker side of life, about abnormal psychology and social and spiritual problems is shown vividly in some of her novels. Jhabvala is a sincere novelist and this sincerity can be seen in all her novels. Jhabvala's love - hate relationship with India is dramatically captured in her novel ***Heat and Dust,*** which brought her universal recognition which won the Booker Prize in 1975 and was filmed in 1982. The story is told on two planes - the story of Olivia and the story of the narrator. The narrator tells Olivia's story after visiting Satipur fifty years later. The two separate stories of Anne and Olivia give Jhabvala a chance to portray a double view of Indian society. She observes–

> "My last novel written in India– about India– ***Heat and Dust,*** has come from within a double pretence. On the one hand, as far as the Indian character and their society and thoughts and values were concerned, I pretended to be them, on the other hand, when I wrote about the Anglo-Indian character and their tradition I pretended to be them. So I exited from India on a double lie – one it took me 24 years to manufacture."[14]

Jhabvala says that even the poverty in India did not bother her during these early years as is apparent from this picturesque description of a street scene in ***To Whom She Will*** as Hari walks down it.

> "The houses oozed brown wounds and bulged out of doors and windows with children and washing and jutting ends of furniture. Banana - peels, tomato-skins and rotting bits of vegetable lay squashed in the dust, sniffed by skinny pariah - dogs." (page 13)

It was after ***Heat and Dust*** when Jhabvala could no longer come to terms with India, that she decided against staying in India. However, even twenty - five years after living in India Jhabvala could not keep herself away from her Indian experience and continued to write abroad. However, Jhabvala tries to overcome this problem through her western character and through her narrative techniques using not only evocative syntax but also regional colour. In her development as a writer she has learnt from her favourite novelists and also from her experiences as a screenplay writer and absorbed themes and techniques from these into her fiction. To be in the world of Jhabvala is to be in a world of reality and every event and incident that she describes is something we are familiar with. It is for this reason that we feel at home in the world of Jhabvala and this is one of the important characteristics of Jhabvala as a writer.

REFERENCES

1. Meenakshi Puri– Trends in Indian fiction publish in thought (Weekly June 16th 1973 issue.
2. John Reed Christian Science Monitor, p. 75.
3. R.P. Jhabvala *The Hindustan Time* (Sunday Magazine) July 27 1980, p. 1.
4. *Ibid.*
5. *Ibid.*
6. Nissim Ezekil "Distorting Mirror (review)". *The Times of India* (Sunday Magnu June 4 1976) p. 8.
7. Jhabvala— *An Experience of India* 1972, p. 41
8. M.L. Malhotra— *The Bridge of Literature* (Ajmer Sunanda Publication 1971), p. 224.
9. Varginia Woolf *The Common reader* The Hograth Press, London, 1953, p. 177.
10. The Christian Science Monitor Quoted by Shyam M Asnani in Jhabvala's novels, A Thematic study, the Journal of India Writing in English Vol. I No.2 Janurary 1974, p. 47.

11. Ruth Jhabvala in her autobiographical easy "Living in India" Published in the London Magazine in September 1970.
12. The Term "exite used because Jhabvala, like James Joyce, feals that the return home is impossible, p. 35.
13. Jhabvala, "An Experience of India" p. 60.
14. *Hindustan Times,* Magazine 27th July 1980.

3

Experimenting with the Indian Middle Class

Women's writing continues to occupy a place of importance for reasons more than one. It projects the responses of more than half of humanity and reflects, a consciousness constructed by gender. It remains a fact that it is possible to identify some issues that are of immense importance and constant debate ever when it is no longer possible to call one self an unqualified feminist. The stereo typed visions of women have undergone a great change and female characters are now presented as strong and active beings rather than passive side kicks. In England, almost all women novelists have stabilized themselves as great forces to be reckoned with. They no longer suffer from financial dependence and they also have a place of their own. Early novels by women writers in India established the fact that they have their own voice carrying weight with the readers. It is only after the Second World War that women novelists of quality have begun enriching Indian English fiction.Of these Ruth Prawer Jhabvala occupies an important place.

Female quest for identity has been a pet theme for many women novelists. Ruth Prawer Jhabvala is one writer who makes an effort to understand the inner dimensions of the female characters. It goes without saying that the fictional world of Ruth Prawer Jhabvala is thematically wide as her concern is social, economic, cultural and sometimes historical. Poverty, hunger, fear, despair and corruption are her recurrent themes. Ruth Jhabvala presents a realistic picture of the impact of industrialization on the people of India. The east-west encounter also gets treatment in her fiction. A study of her fiction reveals that it is a world of multicolour threads woven together and as such it has thematic complexity. During the last three decades a large number of Indian women novelists writing in English have attracted a great deal of attraction and favourable comment. Ruth Prawer Jhabvala is one of the most significant fiction writers among them. The existential absurdity and lack of communication bring mental crisis to her central characters who are seen in the quest of their individual identity. Her chief concern is human relationship and existential predicament of an individual which she projects through incompatible couple, very sensitive wives and ill matched husbands. Jhabvala is a mute observer perceiving everything minutely and delicately. Whenever she creates a typical situation she gives it a perfect treatment in every detail.

Though Ruth Prawer Jhabvala is basically a social-political novelist dealing with families in transaction in post-colonial Indian set up with female character at the central focus, yet she has started enlarging her thematic pattern leading towards spirituality. In Jhabvala's fiction we come across socia-familial intrigues in post independent India where neo-colonial consciousness specially amongst the ladies, unmarried and married both, results in disharmony due to existentialist dilemma of attempting to compromise between the traditional set up which has not completely disappeared and the so-called new awakening, a sort of women – liberation which has not yet completely set in.

> "The relationship of woman to their parents and husband and to other women are totally devalued today. I have never come across a woman who does not suffer from the problem of not being able to resolve in harmony, in the present system, her relationship with her parents and with other woman. Psycho-analysis has totally censored the positive value of these relationships."[1]

Gender discrimination is one of the prominent themes in Indian women writing in English and in other Indian languages. Ruth Jhabvala seems to suggest that women should be judged as subject and not as object. Women is not a mere tradition — tossed toy in the hands of conservative society. She is not a spineless, wooden creature subjected to male authority — like tragic heroes of William Shakespeare, Her female characters learn by suffering. It is suffering which purifies the 'dross of desire' in the characters. Moreover, her outlook is not vague, partial and monotonous but is always suffused with rich moral imagination.

In analysing Ruth Prawer Jhabvala's fiction certain factors have to be kept in mind. Her focus is on the limited world of Delhi. Her work reveals the trauma, insecurity and agony that lie beneath the structure of such women's, lives. Her writings appear to be a definite attempt to drive home the fact that the trials and tribulations faced by these women are no less if not greater than the pangs of the comparatively economically weaker women. One of the prime concerns of Ruth Prawer Jhabvala's women is marriage. Marriage is not totally ruled out in the life of the modern and liberated women. As Simone de Beauvoir mention in her *Second Sex* "Marriage is destiny traditionally offered by society. History proves that marriage is essential to the well being of human society and that celibacy brings ruin upon states."[2]

According to Indian tradition marriage is a point of maturing and the beginning of a new way of life. Our Sastras and Epics glorify marriage as a holy union. Once the women do not find happiness in marriage they feel frustrated and out of tune with life. Allied to the issue of marriage is the issue of social status in Jhabvala's fictions. Jhabvala focuses her attention on social domestic problem that the members belonging to the middle class face in day-to-day life.

It goes without saying that domestic happiness depends upon the favourable situation and environment one finds one self in. In India, almost every person belonging to this state has to struggle hard for survival. It is interesting to note that Jhabvala has given expression to these aspects in a very subtle way. Crushed by the traditions and customs of society, the members of this class pass through various stages of hatred and anger and these, in turn, blur their vision. Hatred creates more problems than it solves. Love alone conquers because it heals and redeems. Ruth Prawer Jhabvala focuses on this aspect of life and brings out its inherent contradictions. What makes any writer with a social conscience angry is the fact that poetic sensibilities, fine arts, religion and culture are 'luxuries' that well - fed plutocrats only can afford. For the middle class man day-to-day existence is struggle for survival. It is in a very remarkable way that Jhabvala brings out the fact and also the inherent and basic concern of the middle class people.

Jhabvala's first novel, ***To Whom She Will*** reflects the spirit that is in tune with that of the people belonging to the middle class. While its individual theme is projected through the personal conflict of Amrita and Hari, the social theme is stated through the complications with parents, as the responsible agents of social institutions, induct into the marriage. The reconciliation that makes the final marriage possible comes about when Amrita, who, in the beginning loves Hari, gets reconciled to the notion of marriage with Krishna Sen Gupta. Amrita under the influence of her mother and grandfather moves away from her attachment to and love for Hari. The manner in which Hari makes love brings out the middle class mentality. The social setup presented by Jhabvala is quite often shown as emerging from the human predicament. The freer the society, the greater the variety of the individuality. Amrita and Hari both represent the female and the male agents of this free society. The young men and women in the novel are caught up in the wave of social change from a tradition-bound society to an open society free from social customs and conventions. We can term this as a change from tradition to modernity. Hari is so uncertain of himself, and although he is conscious of Amrita's feelings for him, his response to her has been far from encouraging. His failure to come to terms which in reality is a failure which people of this class generally experience.

The conversation between Krishna and Hari at the Bombay Coffee House, the haunt of disillusionment about Amrita and Hari's real intention expose the cavalier quality of the youngman's responses. Krishna comes to restaurant as Amrita's agent and representative, and wants to know Hari's real intentions. It is from Krishna that Hari learnt, that Amrita is shortly leaving for England. That he does not look his character and personality, but of the entire narrative and thematic structure of the novel himself. Hari keeps avoiding the questions put to him partly because he is not sure of himself and partly because he has almost followed his parents proposal for an arranged marriage with Sushila Anand, a pretty singer. Sushila is introduced to us a prettier girl than Amrita, she 'has a melodious Voice, she is very intelligent, and moreover she is a girl from the same community. If we look at the Hari - Amrita relationship, we find that it has its own inherent complications and contradictions.

Amrita's character and personality is viewed by other characters in the novel from various angels. She declares her passionate love for Hari who, in turn, admires her as a Goddess in human form. He looks upon her as a modern Belinda who perspires and gives ample evidence of being human, a real woman. Pt. Ram Bahadur, Amrita's grandfather though not opposed to her marrying outside the community, is against her marrying Hari on grounds which are primary social and cultural. He sincerely feels that Hari is unsuitable for Amrita as he is a misfit in mind and soul and also in acquired culture and refinement. Had Hari belonged to the sophisticated and. intellectual class Pt. Ram Bahadur would have had no difficulty in giving his approval. However, Pt. Ram Bahadur's behaviour and conduct is guided by worldly wisdom and down to earth experience and it is for this reason that whatever he says carries weight.

However, tradition and custom continued to have its impact on the members and this impact is something we see operative in the middle class families. For example, the concept of arranging a family-meet to enable the prospective bridegroom to see the prospective bride is a fairly new social development in Indian families. This is an important step in the direction of arranged marriages. Hari goes to the house of the Anand and is almost captivated by Sushila Anand. Anand's grandmother is totally opposed to the idea of showing the girl to the boy and this is a suggestive of conservative and conventional approach to the problem of marriage as a social institution in India. Hari finally marries Sushila and Amrita falls into the arms of Krishna Sengupta, who is her paying guest and quite typically the messenger of her love for Hari. Though he sincerely tries to narrow down the gap between Hari and Amrita, but finally fills in the gap himself.

Jhabvala portrays these situations with a genuine spirit of gaiety. The scene of 'booking the boy' is not without its light-hearted flourishes and ceremonial playfulness. Mr. Anand makes every attempt to prove that he is equal to the situation in which he finds himself. This booking' event leads to the usual sentimentalism of elderly women, their sobs of self pity, a curious combination of joy and grief. The novel ultimately ends on a note of reconciliation achieved through marriage. The wedding of Hari and Sushila is celebrated with great pomp and show while the union of Amrita and Krishna is portrayed in a low key. The title, having its roots in the ***Pànchatantra*** story, is suggestive of the situation in the novel and the conflict in the original are brought in close association with the central triangle of marriages. The wisdom of thc ancicnt oagoo of India, is dramatised through the character of Hari and Amrita, Sushila and Krishna. Amrita makes a bold, though fertile or fruitless attempt to marry for love but doesn't succeed. Sushila Anand and Hari married at a tender age and there is no question of their marrying for love. Hari marries Shushila not for love, but for social respectability and for preserving the values of the community and family life. Marriage is thus presented as a compromise in the social sense, a sort of social adjustment where two individuals try to adjust to a social norm. The two marriages that takefil place in the novel bring out the spirit of a social compromise. Jhabvala projects woman as a more powerful agent of revolt than man. Hari is introduced as passive and stupid, but quite ironically persons like him becomes the object of love of the Amrita's world. In this novel, we come across situations and episodes which presents a conflict between tradition and modernity and what ultimately happens is the compromising attitude between the two families or two communities. Jhabvala seems to suggest that it is through adjustment and compromise attitude that one can get success in life and this is what Jhabvala aims at in this novel.

In her second novel, ***The Nature of Passions***[3] which is the story of a successful businessman called Lalaji, Jhabvala projects the acceptance of selfishness and crudity under the pretext of fate. The title of novel is a little intriguing and is foundto be pretentious. However, we come across lines in the novel which remind us of the philosophy of life and human behaviour. Dr. Radha Krishna says:

> "The three modes are present in all human beings, though in different degrees. No one is free from them and in each soul one or the other predominates. Men are said to be *satvika*, rajas or tamasa according to the mode which prevails..... While the activities of a sativika temperament are free, calm and selfless,. the rajas nature wishes to be always active and cannot sit still and its activities are tainted by selfish desries."[4]

The novel throws light on the *rajsa* nature, Lalaji' s is a *rajsa* nature and hence he is always restless and his actions are guided by selfish desire. When he learns that he has to give away his daughter Nimmi in marriage to a boy he does not like in order to secure a twenty-five lakh contract, he gives his approval. He knows that money is the ruling God of life. He accepts the fact because he also believes that money is so ordained and it has to be so. Jhabvala comments on this theme of acceptance in the introduction, "Myie lf in India" in ***An Experience of India*** She says:

> "Another approach to India's basic conditions is to accept them. This seems to be the approach favoured by most Indians. Perhaps it has something to do with their belief in reincarnation. If things are not to your liking in this life, there is always the chance that in your next life, everything will be different. It appears to be a consoling thought for both rich and poor... However, this path of acceptance is not open to you if you don't have a belief in reincarnation ingrained within you."[5]

Lala Narayan Das Verma is the head of a large family of three sons and three daughters including in-laws. He is a successful contractor who, by manipulating his financial faculties, has risen from rags to riches. In keeping with his rising social status, he has bought for himself a modern house having all the facilities and amenities. Though he has seven well equipped bathrooms, he still prefers to wash by the garden-tap and clean his teeth with a twig from the Margose tree. He is mainly pre-occupied with two things—making money and looking after his family. Luckily for him, these two things go hand in hand. He picks up the morning newspaper to see advertisements and matrimonial columns. But business and family are also, constant sources of worry. Therefore, Lalaji is very much worried about its income tax arrears and a bribe case that is likely to come-up against him any time. He is also worried over the future of Viddi and Nimmi, who have adopted the modern ways of visiting clubs and talking about art and independence just to show that they are well acquainted with the latest trend of the society. His attachment to his family is deep rooted. As soon as Lalaji receives the news of the birth of a granddaughter he feels very happy as he considers it to be a good omen. The other members of his house are not as happy as Lalaji. Lalaji is free from the petty jealousies of his womenfolk. He is a down-to-earth man and knows how to reckon with the situations in a realistic manner. He does his business by indulging in corrupt practices and he sees nothing wrong in this. He is of view that bribe and corruption are foreign words. According to him giving presents and gifts to government officers is a sign of courtesy and respectability. Therefore, he is against people going to 'foreign countries'. He had sent his son Chandra Prakash to England and lost him because Chandra was against bribery and preferred to be a government employee rather than a successful businessman. This, however, has not come in the way of his sending of disapproval from the other members of his house. In his day-to-day life Lalaji meets applicants and promises to help them in every possible ways. As a shrewed businessman he does everything possible to make use of all opportunities for the advancement of his business. In the meantime he comes, to know about the twenty-five Lakh contract from the Happy Hindustan Company he is keen on getting it. One of the directors of the company wishes to marry off his son and he tells Lalaji that he would help him to get the contract if he agreed to give away Nimmi in marriage to his son. Here for the first time Lalaji's two interests clash and this disturbs him very much. He finds himself in a dilemma and doesn't know what to do in this given situation. Jhabvala brings out this state of mind very effectively.

> "She is too young, he told himself, though he knew she was not. It is necessary for her to finish her education, though he knew it was not. The match is not suitable, though it would have been hard to think of one more so. She who is worthy of a king, he would tell himself, to be married only to the so of a director of a trading company."[6]

His clerk who is well conversant with Sanskrit, draws his attention to the wisdom of the Gita: "Man attains perfection being engaged to his own duty. He who does the duty born of his own nature incurs no sin."[7] Lalaji remembers his early humble life and how he was happy but realizes that all that was gone and convinces himself that to be true to his own nature he has to earn more and more and get reconciled to the idea of marrying his daughter off to the son of a director in order to secure the contract.

Chandra, Lalaji's second son, is well qualified and wishes to lead an independent life. But he is also guided by the same considerations in the end. A letter about the tax-bribery and corruption case which has been worrying his father, it happens, is in a file which, as a Government servant, he has been handling.

Chandra and his wife Kanta are against the letter being removed from the file as they do not wish to help Lalaji. Both of them are against corruption but both know the importance of money which they need badly to decorate their houses and wear good clothes and throw parties to please their superiors, without generous help from Lalaji they will not able to do much. Lalaji finally manages to convince Chandra to take out the paper by talking about the prestige of the family that is at stake and the money everyone needs to live with decency. Chandra takes the hint and quietly removes the paper. Chandra's case is an overwhelming example of the force of the value by which Lalaji lives and the role of the joint family. Towards the end of the novel we find Lalaji coming out of the web of worries and anxieties. The boy he had chosen for Nimmi turns out to be the boy Nimmi had taken a liking to. In this way, the twenty-five lakh contract is sure to be awarded to him. Viddi soon realizes the power of money and is back in the fold and does all he can to climb the ladder of success in life.

In portrayal of Lalaji Jhabvala succeeds in giving a full portrait of a typical Indian businessman. The ***Gita*** of course, does not teach corruption. But Lalaji resolves the moment of crisis in his life by a convenient reading of the ***Gita*** and pacified his conscience. He is in full agreement with his clerk who says that if one has a desire for making money, he should do all he can to fulfil his desire and there is no sin in doing so. His own logic that daughters are meant to be given away and money is to be preserved also means much the same. So Lalaji realizes that his is a *rajasa* nature and money is the guiding principle of his life. Similarly almost all the characters of the novel have more or less, identical philosophy of life. Viddi and Nimmi are superficial modern and Phuphiji is an orthodox woman, and between them they present two sides of India. The former operates in hotel and club and the later in Indian homes. Thus the novel brings out the typical middle class mentality, thereby projecting the values that people of this class generally stand for.

In ***Esmond in India,*** we get introduced to Esmond, an Englishman who instead of returning home, stays on to guide tourists around the ruins of the ancient country. Later on he falls in love with Gulab and marries her. He is very particular about his ways of life and believes in keeping his house clean and beautiful. He expects Gulab to take to western ways of life which she is opposed to. He wants her to be his companion and treats her as an asset in his career as an expert on Indian culture. But Gulab is opposed to the idea and refuses to be in the company of foreigners with whom she feels uncomfortable. Ravi, their son, becomes a matter of dispute between the two. Esmond wants him to be trained in British ways of life, expects him to developed a taste for boiled English food and to sleep in a separate bed. Gulab, true to her tradition is in favour of giving him spicy and oily Indian dishes and pet him all the time. These things irritate Esmond and he becomes rough and inconsiderate. He starts insulting Gulab but Gulab bears this insult or contempt with meekness and this, ultimately tells on his nerves. Though Gulab allows herself to be insulted by Esmond, her mother Uma does not. Fed up with the ill treatment of Esmond, she keeps asking Gulab to leave her husband for good, but Gulab, true to type, looks upon Esmond as her lord who is at liberty to treat her as he liked. Gulab and Esmond do not understand each other as they are not on the same wave length. In due course of time, their marriage becomes a cold affair. Bored and irritated Esmond leaves for Agra and get involved in an affair with Shakuntala, a silly college girl. When Esmond goes out to meet her again in a market place, his servant finds Gulab alone and advances towards her. This irritates the usually docile Gulab. She becomes furious and takes the servant to task for the liberty he has taken with her. She now thinks that it is time for her to leave her husband. She feels that he has failed in his duty to protect her.

She can bear any kind of ill-treatment from her husband, but she would be the last person to allow anyone to spoil her chastity. She expects Esmond at least to protect her chastity and in his failure to do anything in this regards that she decides to leave him. Esmond meets Shakuntala in a busy market and finds her in a joyous mood. When he looks into her eyes, they appear to be reminding him of Gulab's eyes as they had been when they first met and made love to each other. This is suggestive of the fact that Shakuntala will be another Gulab in due course of time.

Jhabvala at one level, deals with the clash and conflict between two cultures. She also seems to suggest that life is made up of trivialities and much depends on them in our day-to-day life. At another level, she shows the basic difference between the English and the Indian characters that keep them apart. What Jhabvala seems to emphasize is that the English are rational and the Indians emotional. The other theme which Jhabvala takes up is the theme of social change. In the novel this theme is dealt with at length. Ramnath belongs to a rich family and could have settled down to a comfortable life. But he thought more about the freedom of the country than about his own comfort and even went to jail. He even compelled his wife to part with her jewellery and lead a simple life. He inculcated the same spirit in his son Narayan. Narayan is a doctor and chooses to work in remote villages without even basic comforts. Ramnath's friend Har Dayal too had been to Cambridge, but he had returned home to make money and climb the ladder of success. His son Amrit like his father has the same attitude towards life and takes up a profitable job with an English firm. Consequently, Ramnath remains poor and helpless, whereas Har Dayal becomes rich and move about in circle of respectable men and women.

Jhabvala's understanding of Indian women is greater than her understanding of men. Of all the Indian novelists writing in English, she alone has been able to project their excessive possessiveness and dominating nature their greed and soft-headedness. Uma, after the death of her husband lives only to look after her daughter. There is hardly any moment in her life when her mind is without the thought of Gulab. She does not allow Gulab to live peacefully with Esmond, she does not even lead her brother Ramnath to live in peace, because she is in favour of Gulab leaving her husband and coming back to her. Laxmi is all the time thinking about his son Narayan and blames her husband for wasting all the family property. Madhuri keeps asking her husband about her son Raj, who is at Cambridge. These women are like tigresses guarding their children, and they are all endowed with possessive temperaments.

Shakuntala is brought up in an upper middle-class family. Her father sends her to college. Shakuntala does not mind having affairs herself to the middle aged Esmond. In a tone full of pathos she says, "Let me be your slave, please allow me. I want to humble myself before you.[8] Shakuntala's infatuation with Esmond, who is married to her cousin, is something disgusting and leaves a bad taste in the mouth. Gulab's readiness to play the role of a meek wife is presented without any redeeming qualities. Esmond, an Englishman, is shown to be a pathetic figure in Independent India. He earns his living by giving lectures on Indian culture which he hates. But he is clever enough not to show his hatred. His fondness for India was similar to his fondness for Gulab. But staying in India and with Gulab under the same roof makes him realize that beneath the beautiful side of life there is something which causes repulsion and hatred. As Gulab proves to be a submissive woman, India the land of Taj Mahal, turns out to be a place of unredeemed poverty:

> "There was no romance about life in India, Esmond knew: only for the tourists, he bitterly thought, who clapped their hands in delight over what was, he knew, only shabbiness and poverty repeated to a point where the spirit yawned at the boredom and fatuity of it all."[9]

Esmond then turns to Betty because she can talk his own language and share his attitudes. During their Agra trip Shakuntala loses her heart to him. He is against getting involved with her, but is forced by Shakuntala to do so. His stay in India, his uncertain financial position, his marriage to an Indian woman, the treatment he metes out to her and his affair with Shakuntala persuit him to an insensitive, irritable and irritating character. Of all the characters created by Jhabvala Esmond is perhaps the most intelligent. He has a remarkable capacity for seeing through the glittering facade of the land of the Taj. He has also a great capacity for seeing the poverty and shabbiness of India. He is a sensitive but is unable to give expression to his thought and ideas about India in clear and specific terms. ***Esmond in India*** reminds us of Nirad Chowdhari's statements in ***The Continent of Circe*** that there is something in Indian climate which dwarfs human spirit.

In this novel, we find Jhabvala in a less tolerant and less forgiving mood than she was in her earlier novels. This change in her outlook has been noticed by reviewers too.) This may be due to the fact that she is no longer completely detached from the scenes she writes about. In the earlier novels she appeared to be an observer but in this novel she seems to have been confronted by her own experience of India. It is for this reason that the novel is replete with intensity and passion. The novel presents a scene of the present cultural and social situation in India. Jhabvala has a limited purview but her limitation appears to be her strength. ***Esmond in India*** is concerned with the problem of appearance and reality. Esmond falls a victim to appearance. The Taj and Gulab's eyes, deep sad eyes, which he took to be full of all the wisdom of the East. When he finds himself in a world of reality, the poverty and squalor that surround the Taj and the mere wooden and expression less eyes of Gulab - it is too late. Gulab in Esmond in India accepts without any complaint the code of conduct prescribed for Indian wives by the holy books of the Hindus. The code, however is a part of her personality:

> "Gulab was never, in anything, undecided-probably because she did not form decisions about anything but followed whatever her instinct dictated. And just as before her instinct had told her that she must leave him. She was quite sure about it. So sure that she did not have to sit and reflect but could at once start getting her things out, ready to pack them."[10]

The theme of East-West encounter has been one of the most favourite themes of Indo-Anglian as well as Anglo-Indian writers. It means coming to terms between two cultures. In The ***Twice Born Fiction*** Meenakshi Mukherjee examines how this theme is handled by individual writers and concludes that "the Indo-Anglian novelist more often than not is trying to reconcile within himself two conflicting systems of value."[11] It was E.M.Forster who took up the theme of East-West encounter more seriously than any of his predecessors. In ***A Passage to India*** he makes an attempt to understand the spirit and the meaning of India. He also tries to examine whether it is possible for the Britisher to be friendly with Indians. On examination, he finds that so long as the Britishers and the Indians do not get ride of their prejudice and preconceived ideas, any attempt to bridge the gap between the two races is sure to result in failure. In this novel he lays emphasis on the need to connect. This connection is possible only when the desire for friendship comes from the depth of the heart. But this alone will not be enough. Unless it includes the heart, any attempt to form friendship will be futile.This is the conclusion he arrives at the close of the novel. In ***Esmond in India*** Jhabvala takes up the theme of East-west encounter where For ster left it off. But while taking up this theme, she adopts an altogether different approaches to it. While Forster raises it to a religious and mystical level, Jhabvala brings it down to the mundane. Forster used symbol and rhythm to communicate his feeling while Jhabvala uses a down-to-earth approach to it. Forster's characters are round in the sense that they grow. Where as Jhabvala's characters remain static. "The main effect in ***A Passage to India*** is of order in the Universe, but order that can merely glimpsed, never seized for sure."[12] The effect of ***Esmond in India*** is restricted to cultural differences that can tell on one's nerves and how they can give rise to unhappiness and misery.

Jhabvala's ***The Householder*** is unique in many respects. It is the only novel throwing light on lower-middle class people. It is also unique in the sense that the overall atmosphere is one of humour and sympathy rather than of irony, though the latter is not totally absent. The householder unfolds the story of an ordinary young man's slow attainment of a status of the householder, the second stage of life I.e. the *grahasta* ashram in the traditional social structure according to the Hindu tradition. Its strength lies in its faithful exemplification of the process in matter of authentic character and situation.

Prem, the protagonist of the novel, is a young teacher in Mr. Khanna's private college. He is simply a second class B.A., who teaches Hindi and is married to Indu, a very ordinary girl selected by his parents. He suffers from diffidence but at the same time intelligent enough to deal with the situation in a realistic manner. He is well aware of the precarious financial position he is in. He sticks to this job, in spite of being paid poorly because he knows that he cannot get a better job because of his poor qualifications. His position becomes even more precarious when he learns that his wife is in the family way. In view of this, he decides to better his condition by either getting raise in his salary or reduction in rent. He knows very well that his present qualifications will not allow him to make any honourable bargain with the management. He also knows that any assertive tone on his part in this regard is sure to meet with disapproval. He also knows that he cannot maintain discipline in his class. So when he meets principal he feels terribly diffident and does not know how to stake his claim. Since he is unable to get over his diffident in the Principal's chamber he decides to call upon him at his residence. He is soon overwhelmed by the authority of the Principal and intolerant behaviour of his wife and comes back home without making his feeling known to the Principal regarding his salary. It is here that Jhabvala is at her best to bring out the comedy of the situation:

> "Prem stood hesitating outside the sitting-room door, but he made himself brave and entered. Mr. Khanna was sitting eating his breakfast, Prem was shy, he hovered by the door and kept his eyes lowered. Mr. Khanna was in a jovial mood. You see me enjoying my breakfast, he explained. Prem looked up and nodded. He saw that Mr. Khanna was having an English breakfast of eggs and toast. He could not speak, he was so overwhelmed with shyness. Not only because of what he had come to say, but also because the Principal's sitting room always made him feel shy"[13]

The dialogue is a good example of Jhabvala's comic Juxtaposition. When Prem reaches home he finds his wife conversing with Mr. Seigal, his land-lord. When Mr. Seigal sees Prem he asks as to why he keeps his wife locked up all the time. Prem is about to defend himself when he realizes that it is only a joke.

At this point Prem is so preoccupied with his own problem that he hardly understands the simple fact that his wife is a human being having her own desires and aspirations. He has seen Seigal's meeting people inviting them entertaining them and spending money lavishly. This sort of life-style is out of question for him. He approaches Seigal with desire to request them to reduce his rent but comes back without uttering a single word about it. This situation is as comic as Prem's meeting Mr. Khanna. This shows how the lower-middle class people like Prem suffer from lack of confidence and feel disturbed when they see some people enjoying the pleasure and comfort of life. Prem wants to be friendly with Raj who is at the moment a Government servants in Delhi. It is with the sole desire of discussing his problem with him that he was embarked upon the idea of being friendly with him. But when they actually meet there is hardly any communication between the two in the real sense.

In his immaturity Prem does not take notice of the inevitability of change in human relations. For example, he believes that relationship which he had with Raj, his college mate, would continue unabated for ever. Prem does not feel sure of himself even at home. He lives his wife as all married man do and expects her to help in his problem, but the kind of cooperation he expects in not forthcoming to him. Prem's problems multiply with the arrival of two letters. The first comes from his mother announcing to visit Delhi and the other comes from Indu's father asking her to be ready to be taken home by her uncle who will be visiting Delhi shortly. Prem tells Indu that it is not possible for her to go home since his mother is arriving but Indu insists on going. This conflict is something common between wife and husband in the middle class families. This conflict poses a threat in Prem because he thinks that a husband must be obeyed by his wife in all circumstances. In this respect, he has his father as his model, who was Principal of a college and commanded unquestioning obedience both at home and at college. When his mother arrives, she shows her concern for Prem as all mothers belonging to this class are generally found to be doing. She has brought with her all the dishes Prem is fond of, and she expects him to eat them in her presence. Late in the evening she wants him to sit near her and talk to her. The more the mother starts caring for him, the more Indu starts fretting and fuming. One-day when Prem returns home after a very tedious day at the college, he finds Indu gone without even caring to inform him about that. Prem feels greatly hurt. The increasing indiscipline in his class, his anxiety about his financial problems and about his wife render him in a very helpless condition.

It is at this juncture that Sohan Lal, one of his colleagues in the college, and older man with a family living far away takes him to a Swami. Prem does not mind going to Swami as it enables him to get away from his worries and problems. But the Swami has not much to offer Prem. It was while waiting for Raj that he comes across a German youth called Hans. Hans is in India because of a dream in which he saw a palm tree and a temple. Under the palm tree sat a sadhu in whose eyes there was pity and kindness. It was this that drew Prem to the sadhu. Hans is under the impression that all Indian men have spiritual faces and all women beautiful. He mistakes Prem's emptiness for a meditative and reflective mind and wants to be inmates with him. In his desperate attempts to establish connections, Prem allows Hans misunderstanding to continue and even visits him in his room. It is here that he meets Kitty, Hans's landlady, who also has a liking for meditation and spiritual exercises.

Till this point in the story we find Prem as incapable of relating with people, first with his own wife and then with the others with whom he comes into contact. The turning point occurs when Indu, his wife returns after her visit to her parents. By now Prem's mother has left, and this gives the husband and wife a chance to know each other and accordingly developed their changed relationship. Jhabvala creates a number of incidents which mark Prem's graduation to the status of a householder. The novel is remarkable not only for its remarkable portrayals of the slow and painful process of Prem's growth to maturity, but also for its handling of relationships in the Indian context. Though the novel is about lower middle class people, money plays a very vital place by its absence. The world of Amrita, Lalaji and Shakuntala is the world of the rich. In the novel Jhabvala shows how Prem's domestic life is jaded for want of it at every stage, it is money that preoccupies him. He is unable to ask for a raise in his salary because he is overpowered by Mr. Khanna's opulence.

In ***Get Ready for Battle***[14] Jhabvala goes a step further and shows the process of disintegration. In her earlier novel Jhabvala throws light on the solidarity of joint family system erodeds an individual member's freedom and initiative, it also stands by him and gives him a sense of security and belonging. In the novel, we get introduced to a worse set of characters. In the novel, Gulzari Lal is introduced to us as a businessman. He is in the habit of throwing big parties just to impress petty government officials. Having been deserted by his wife, he lives a very colourless and drab life. He has mistress called Kusum an army officer's widow. Kusum spends most of her time with Gulzari Lal and rules his household. Vishnu, Gulzaria Lal's son gets used to her presence in the house. Gulzaria Lal does not find it wrong to having mistress in the house. Kusum wants Gulzari Lal to divorce his wife in order to be his legal wife. Gulzarilal is against divorcing his wife, because such a skip would bring disgrace to him and spoil his business prospect. He believes in eating his cake and having it too. He is not guided by any moral values. Brij Mohan Gulzari Lal's brother-in-law is an immoral aristocrat who spends most of his time in the company of prostitutes. We can take him to be a larger edition of Gulzaria Lal.

In addition to these two characters there is Sarla Devi, who feels for the poor and is always eager to improve their lot by organising them and representing their case to the government. But she loses her battle with her unscrupulous husband. In spite of this, she does not lose heart and continues to care for the poor and the downtrodden. Sarla Devi also loses the battle on the house front. Her son Vishnu and her daughter-in-law Mala side with her husband, and Kusum finally succeeds in convincing Gulzari Lal of the need to divorce Sarla Devi.

Sarla Devi however, is not an idealised character. Her philosophy of treating pleasure and pain, profit and loss, victory and defeat alike makes her a little too unworldly. It is because of this that she is unable to make her presence felt in society. She has sympathy for Kusum, though she does everything possible to make her leak the dust. She sympathises with Tara the prostitute, though Tara does not need her sympathy. She is eager to help the poor of Bundi Busti, but she does not know how to do it. Ramchandra, the leader of Bundi Busti ditches Sarla Devi but she refuses even to say a harsh word about him. Though her brother Brij Mohan lives a sinful life, she remains blind to it and does not comment on it. She even develops a liking for Kusum; who is eager to replace her as Gulzarilal's wife. In a way Sarla Devi fails to take any moral stand at any step of her life as she lacks moral realism. Her moral vision has its roots in her belief in the philosophy of ***the Gita.*** She accepts the role of crusader because she feels that she cannot opt out.

> "All her life she had wanted to be free and alone, like this, thinking nothing and being nothing, only a disembodied state of acceptance and all her life she had been tugged back by her compassion into a world where nothing could be accepted and everything has to be fought against."[15]

In Sarla Devi's character we find two contradictory elements in her personality. It is perhaps because of these contradictory elements that she does not prove herself to be a good wife and a good crusader. If Sarla Devi is unworldly in her dealings with others, Kusum, her counterpart is a little too shrewd and practical. She has Gulzari Lal under her spell and even plays tricks on him. Her love for Vishnu and Mala is only for show and not genuine. When she finds that everything is according to her plan, she persuades Gulzari Lal to send Vishnu and Mala away, so that she may have complete control over the house. Even as Sarla Devi and Kusum present a study in contrast, so do Gulzari Lal and his son Vishnu. Gulzari Lal is known for his ruthlessness and selfishness, while Vishnu is weak and unsure of himself. He wants to be on his own but has no idea about how to proceed. He is not happy with his mother and wife Mala, in this fluctuating mood he becomes a victim of social dropout

Jhabvala makes her characters move in a world of their own. We find them in a state of changelessness. Even at the end of the novel they remain what they are at the start. They don't grow nor do they show any sign of growth in their attitudes to others. In an article called "The Yogi and the Babbitt" Williams Moore recognised this truth about Jhabvala's characters and says

> "The tragedy of modern India as depicted in Jhavbala's novels is the total failure of communication between the Babbitt and the Yogi."[16]

This observation is full of wisdom, the title of the novel has its origin in the ***Gita.*** In this novel Jhabvala presents the Yogi and the Babbitt in their extremely perverted forms. Gulzari Lal is insensitive and blind to the moral values of life. He attaches much importance to money and thinks money is essential for enjoying the pleasures of life. He does not mind in seeking pleasure even at the cost of his children. He decides to send Vishnu away so that he can carryon his improper and questionable relationships with his mistress Kusum. Gulzari Lal is an extreme example of the degenerate businessman. Sarla Devi represents the other extreme example of a social reformer. Her mistaken vision of life and her blindness to social reality bring out her inability to function in any capacity. It is through these characters that Jhabvala develops the theme of her novel just to show how money and religion, the two great agents of cultural renaissance, can create problems for the people of the society and even degrade them to the maximum. We find money and religion playing a sinister role in the novel.

In *A Backward Place*[17], Jhabvala introduces an altogether new theme for her fiction namely, the problems of adjustment generally confront Westerners living in India. Many of Jhabvala's characters are in Indian to "find themselves". It is the gurus, the temples, the chanting of hymns and talk about spiritual matters that draw a lot of Westerners. There are also quite a few who are in India because of a chance marriage. In most cases such marriages break-up sooner or later but by the time this comes about it is too late for them to return to their own countries.

Finally there are Westerners who pay a visit to this country just to understand her. They get so involved in the country with the passage of time that their return to their own countries becomes difficult. In her introduction to ***An Experience of India,*** Jhabvala comments on Westerners passing in India and observes:

> "First stage, tremendous enthusiasm-everything Indian abominable. For some people it ends there, for others the cycle renews itself and goes on."[18]

Westerners who are In India for a short while usually pass through the first stage and before reaching the second stage, they are back home. The problem of living in a country which is completely different from their own becomes really serious for those who for one reason or another cannot get back to their own countries. Those who have strong personalities display great patience and courage to present their identities.

Here in the novel the Western characters meet Indian characters, the types we have met before in her earlier novels. Bal is an incarnation of Viddi. Unlike his brother, Mukund who is content to lead an ordinary life, he wants to be an artist and thinks that he could become one by paying frequent visit to cafes and restaurants. He dreams of becoming a film actor by hanging around Kishanchand, a famous film actor from Bombay. Bal also represents another basic quality so common to modern Indian youth that is the dilly dallying. Once, Bal hits upon the idea to start a theatre group, but when Judy entertains the same idea and when it starts taking shape Bal loses interest in the project. He is quick to take insult but is negligent towards his duties as a husband and as a father. Prithvi his son, falls sick and wants him to be with him. But Bal gets dressed in a finely starched Muslim *kurta* and *pyjama*, which had come back from the laundry only that morning and black slippers with little coloured flowers embroidered on them. Prithvi wants ice but Bal does not seem to be interested in looking after his needs. What is true of Bal is also true of Sudhir and

Jayakar. Sudhir has an M.A. degree. He had a teaching job at an evening college in Calcutta but soon started disliking it and, through a politician, he gets another job at Cultural Dais. He does not take interest in this job too. Jayaker talks of revolutionary changes in society and goes on talking about it but actually does nothing.

A Backward Place is, like Jhabvala's previous novels, a portrait of society which bubbles with Western and lower-middle class people. All these characters have fixed aims and characteristic and there is no interaction even when they come in contact with one another.

They remain unchanged. This unchangeability of characters is a feature of the novel of character and it effectively brings out the clear - cut diversity

At the end of the novel we find Sudhir boarding the train for Calcutta and Bal is seen moving towards Bombay. From the way Sudhir and Bal are introduced in the novel we can quite guess that these journeys are endless and futile, not only for them but for all those who belongs to such categories especially middle class family.

In ***A New Dominion***[19], Jhabvala depicts characters who live in a world in which everything is accepted and nothing is questioned. This is particularly true of the European characters in the novel. Jhabvala uses an altogether new setting for a New Dominion. In this novel Jhabvala moves away from the centre of social activities to the centre of spiritual activities. Gopi doesn't take any interest in his study. He meets Raymond and spends most of the time with him. Through Raymond he gets introduced to other westerners in like Lee, Margaret and Evie. It is through Lee that he meets, Asha, the sister of Rao Sahib - Prince who lost his princedom in Independent India. There is the Swamiji playing a very important role in the novel. He represents the strong fasicnation that the East exerts on Westerners fed up with their own society. He represents Indian spirituality, though of wrong type. The way in which he talks is incoherent and puzzling and this contributes to the charm of his personality. The Swamiji is a fraud and his spirituality is only a mask. He is one of the thousands of Swamis in India who take the religion because they have no other job to which they can cling. Like many Swamis this Swami also exploits his disciples to the maximum. The characters in this novel are once again a strange group of European an Indian types. Jhabvala introduces many scenes and episodes focusing their activities. Reviewing the novel V.S. Prichett says.

> "Forster's and Jhabvala's characters are matched. Raymond, the sensitive spinsterly English aesthete and inquirer, is another Fielding plus unconscious homosexuality, his Indian friend, the ingenuous and ludicrous student Gopi, is in some ways a budding ill-educated, up-to-date version of Dr. Aziz."[20]

Though Jhabvala matches her characters with Forster's, she charts out a different course of activity for them with the sole purpose of emphasizing the change in the Indian situation. In Forster's India, it was a pertinent question to ask whether the English and the Indians could be friends. In modern India this question has no validity.

In ***Heat and Dust***[21] Jhabvala describes how India overwhelms two English women who are sensitive and receptive to it. Unlike Lee, Evie and Margaret they are not on a spiritual quest in India. Olivia is in India because her husband Douglas, is a District Collector at Satipur. The other English woman, her granddaughter, becomes interested in her and comes out to India to reconstruct her life. Both these women are different from Westerners depicted earlier in Jhabvala's novels. Olivia is happily married and lives a very comfortable life with her husband. It is only when she meets the Nawab of Khatm, a small princely state, that she finds herself drawn towards him. She is carried away by his wealth, his authority, his hospitality and above all by his carrying affection for her. At the first meeting itself Olivia realizes that "here at last was one person in India to be interested in her the way she was used to."[22]

Olivia is against mixing with the English community at Satipur and keeps herself aloof all day. It is from now onwards that we find a change both in her outlook and attitude towards many things including her husband and India. She finds that the Britishers at Satipur do not have a good opinion about the Nawab and thus avoid making him the subject of discussion in her presence. They however make comment on his marriage and on his connection with dacoits, which displeases and shocks Olivia. Her regard for the Nawab is part of her attitude to the Natives which is radically different from that of the others in her community. This regard is due to her innate goodness and her ignorance of the people and customs of India. She develops a very critical attitude to her community and to her husband in particular. Olivia looks upon the Nawab as friend. She has no idea, owing to her innocence, that the Nawab IS connected with dacoits. Even when she comes to know about the Nawab's dealings with dacoits, it makes no difference to her relationship with him. It is her interest in him as a human being which brings her closer to him, but in the end she is totally captivated by him and her surrender to him is complete. The Nawab's attitude to Olivia is quite different, he finds Olivia attractive and sympathetic to him and makes deliberate attempts to win over her heart. By the time the young woman arrives in India, the palace in which the Nawab lived has become a deserted place. All its splendour and glory have vanished; She rents a small room from Inder Lal who also acts as her guide to the places around Satipur. Ultimately we find her going to the Himalayas in search of spiritual comfort.

Heat and Dust shuttles between the past and the present. Though the two heroines are separated by half a century, they are similar in their sensitiveness and receptiveness to India and both of them go through identical experiences. According to Trilling, "The Novel is a perpetual quest for reality, the field of its research being always manners as the indication of the direction of man's soul."[23]

The quest for reality through the study of manners has always been Jhabvala's preoccupation. What is true of the Nawab is also true of Inder Lal and the other characters. We know Inder Lal through his preoccupation with his office work, his relationship with his mother and wife. Jhabvala's characters move in a crowded country where the pressure of its climate and complicated tradition of manners are great. In the novel Jhabvala manners are great. In the novel Jhabvala shows that the two English heroines of the novels lack moral vision. They fall victims to illusions generated by their liberalism and their sensitivity. They are carried away by their generosity.

The novel is Jhabvala's last novel about India. novel published in *The Times of India*[24] Nissim Ezekiel talks about Jhabvala's static characters. He appears to have forgotten the fact that in a novel of character the characters are bound to be static and larger than life. George Orwell in his essay" Charles Dickens"[25] points out what critics thought were Dickens' defects. Dickens has acquired a permanent place in English Literature and this is true of Dickens as it is of Jhabvala. Jhabvala deals with India at the social, cultural and intellectual levels. She is more concerned with the social realities than with abstract philosophies. Jhabvala is closer to R. K. Narayan as both of them look at the world ironically and with detachment. They differ from each other in their approach and vision. R.K. Narayan observes petty villainies and follies with amusement. In the writings of Jhabvala religion is kept out of her fictions. She is not concerned with ideological interpretations. Her only concern is with the presentation of a graphic picture of the society around her. She presents two different points of view and hence one can find her describing the collision between the tradition and the modern, the East and the West and the confusion that follows in the wake of these collisions. In each of her novels she presents the life of two or three families and they are devoid of accidents and coincidences. It is for this reason that she has been able to describe the domestic and social life of

Indians as no other writers writing in English have ever done. She deals with the strong hold of tradition and traditional wisdom and how in modern India tradition and modernity go hand-in-hand. In most of her novels Jhabvala deals with marriage, money, the Indian wife, the Indian house holders and the Indian social reformers. Even the titles of her novels are indicative of this approach. She presents Indians in terms of Indian codes of conduct for businessmen, wives, householders and social reformers. Indian society, for its progress in science and technology, is traditional to the core. It is still at work and exercises great enfluence on the minds of the Indian peoples.

Jhabvala is at her best when she deals with the whims and temperaments of the middle class people of India. She does her job in such a way that the readers feel automatically drawn towards her. What appeals to us more than anything else is Jhabvala' s concern for reality. Her characters act and react as anyone would do in a given situation. The way in which she presents her characters at once impresses us and it is due to its impact that we feel more at ease in the world of Jhabvala.

Her area of exploration is the social world and material of her analysis is manners. To Jhabvala, reality is whatever is external and hard, though it could be unpleasant. She writes the novels of character which are concerned with expressing the modes of existence rather than the images of experience. Since her fiction has social problems as her theme, thrills and violence find no place in the world of Jhabvala. She writes mainly about the middle class because this is the class with which she is most conversant. There are critics who opine that Jhabvala deals with things in a superficial way but in fact her novels bring out Indian wisdom and philosophy. Though she writes about the middle class society, she shows an admirable awareness of Indian problem by and large. She is aware of Indian poverty and of the indifference, callousness and moral bankruptcy that afflict the middle class. She succeeds in presenting the wavering and drifting lives of Indian youth, the bickering and possessive Indian mother and the rising callous and unscrupulous middle class in post - Independence India. Jhabvala writes about antiheroes who are conditioned by their religious, social and economic traditions and oppressed by scorching heat. Small wonder if they lead false and empty lives. It is not Indians alone who are presented in this manner but also the English and the Americans who get attracted to the charm of the East. She takes a group of men and women and describes them as they move from day to day. Jhabvala has an eye for the ridiculous but she is also aware of the fact, that what is ludicrous on the surface is tragic underneath. Jhabvala's characters are given just enough definite traits to carryon.

Jhabvala's fictional strategy in creating her fictional world is to take a central character and build around him or her a set of incidents which are so arranged as to reinforce the validity of the kind of world she creates. Jhabvala's first concern is to know and then impart all she knows in terms that would make her readers see and hear and feel a lively sense of actuality. In her first five novels Jhabvala presents the Indian codes of conduct. In order to do so she plays up certain character-traits and introduces extreme situations. The situations are so arranged as to highlight the character-traits. This strategy suits Jhabvala's purpose because she is not interested in individuals or their psychology. She is interested in social life. But while their characters are busy reaffirming their various points of views Jhabvala is busy showing how the overall reality of India affects them. Jhabvala's distinctive achievement as a novelist lies in the fact that, while Indian writers writing about Indian mores tend to deviate from British tradition of the novel and develops a more indigenous form especially suited to Indian life in terms that would be acceptable to the Western readers. She sees India in a western perspective. Radha and Uma, the two anxious mothers in ***To Whom She Will*** and ***Esmond in India,*** for example, are presented ironically rather than sentimentally as they would be by Indian writers. What is sentimental for Indian writers is comic to her. The material that would get a melodramatic treatment from Indian writers gets ironical treatment from her. She never allows her Western sensibility to be overpowered by the Indian scene.

Writers like Kipling and Forster were highly fascinated by Indian mysticism but not so Jhabvala. So her fictional presentation of Indian life with a Western perspective is unique. A theme running through her novels about Indians in post Independence India is the frustration of people who fought for Independence. It is fully treated in her first three novels. Few writers writing about India have dealt with it more poignantly. Running parallel to this theme is the theme of moral bankruptcy among the newly rich. For over a quarter of a century Jhabvala's novels and stories have been the Westerner's window on India. her tecnical skill, her remarkable insight, her cool and cotrolled brilliance and her sustained work have created for her a place in the hearts of the writrs of the world. It is with a rare insight into the establishment of a cultural identity of the people she writes about In an article on Dickens George Orwell says" Tolstoy's characters are strugling to make their soul where as Dicken's people are presented far more often and far more vividly than Tolstoy's but always in a single unchangeabe attitude like pictures or pieces of furniture."[26] Perhas unchangeability is the cause of th epopularity of Dickens's characters. And what is true of Dickens's characters is also true of Jhabvala's.

REFERENCES

1. Irigaray Luce: *Women's Exile Ideology and Consciousness*-1977, p. 75.
2. Simone de Beauvoir *The Second Sex* Penguine, p. 45.
3. R.P. Jhabvala, *The Nature of Passion* London: George Allen and Unwin, 1956.
4. *Ibid*, p. 5.
5. R.P. Jhabvala, *An Experience ofIndia* (London John Murry, 1971, pp. 9-10.

6. R.P. Jhabvala The Nature of Passion, p. 164.
7. *Ibid.,* p. 240.
8. R.P.Jhabvala, *Esmond In India* (London Greoge Allen and union, 1958), p. 184.
9. *Ibid.,* p. 252.
10. *Ibid.,* p. 249.
11. Meenakshi Mukherjee, *Twice Born Fiction* (New Delhi: Heinemann, 1971), p. 136.
12. E.K. Brown, ***Forster,*** P. 159
13. R.P.Jhabvala, *The Householder* (London' John Murray, 1960)
14. R.P .Jhabvala *Get Ready for Battle* (London John Murray, 1962)
15. *Ibid.,* p. 169.
16. H.W. Moore, "The Yogi and The Babbitt": Themes and Characters of New India in the Novels of R.P.Jhabvala *Twentith Century Literature* 15th July 1969, pp. 89-90.
17. R.P Jhabvala,A *Backward Place* (New Delhi Orient Paperbacks, 1965).
18. R.P.Jhabvala, *An Experience of India* (Londan John Murry, 1971), p. 7.
19. R.P.Jhabvala, *A New Dominion* (London John Murray, 1972).
20. V.A. Pritchett *Snares and Delusion* review of *A New Domion.* The New Yorker, Jun. 16 1973,P.106
21. R.P.Jhabvala, *Heat and Dust* (London: John Murray, 1975)
22. *Ibid.,* p. 17.
23. Lionel Trilling, *The Liberal Imagination* (London: Penguin Books 1970), p. 214.
24. Nissim Ezekiel A Distorting Mirror review of Heat and Dust, *The Times of India,* January 4, 1976, p. 10.
25. George Orwell, "Charles Dickens" *The Dickens Critics,* Ed. George Ford and Lane (New York: Cornell University Press, 1961), p. 166.
26. *Ibid.,* p. 166.

4

Thematological Concerns

A writer will have his own vision which may be peculiar and unique. His perspective changes according to his experience and understanding of the world in which he or she lives. It may be national ethos or the various patterns of life adopted by a people in response to the demands of a particular environment natural, social or political, which influence the writer and his perception. A writer is apt to be more sensitive to the disturbing day-to-day happenings and changes around him and tends to react and respond intensely. He creates a world of his own depending upon the view from which he observes the world. It is because of this that fiction today has become the most popular literary medium of expression. Indian fiction writing though began in the 20th century, the significant era began with writers like Mulk Raj Anand, R.K. Narayan and Raja Rao. In the early thirties of 20th century we noticed two types of novelists writing in English — the Indo-Anglian and the Anglo-Indian. The works that they lay before the novelists during pre-independenc time, was to focus on foreign oppression and atrocities and nation's struggle for freedom and in post-independence time was to explore and affirm the Indian identity at various levels. Today domestic problems and social concerns have found expression in most of the novels, written by the writers and in this connection, Ruth Prawer Jhabvala's contribution to the enrichment of fiction has assumed special significance.

Though Ruth Prawer Jhabvala has been established as an Anglo-Indian novelist by the modern critics, she can in no way be compared with any of the Indo-Anglion novelists, as the basic difference in their writings lies in the fact that these writers are basically Indians, writing in English to get a worldwide recognition. But as far as Anglo-Indian writers are concerned they are themselves alien, for they don't know well about the country in which they live. As a result what they write have a note of detachment which makes their works entirely different from those of Indo-Anglian writers. Though the mode of writing is different but they were writing about the same country same people and problems they were faced with, before and after its independence.

Jhabvala's plea that she should be considered an European who happened to write about India is confirmed by the fact that her two novels of the period, ***In Search of Love and Beauty*** (Morre 1983) and the ***The Three Continent*** (1987) shift their attention away from India. Jhabvala deals with many problems relating to India and specially to the people living in city like Delhi. Ruth Prawer Jhabvala focuses her attention on many aspects of Indian life and hence there are many themes and issues that come across in her novels.

As is clear from an account of her literary career, the major and minor concerns that interweave in Ruth Prawer Jhabvala's novels arise from personal experiences. It is, no doubt, tempting to speculate on the extent to which her fiction reflects her personal life. When we go through her novels, we come across many aspects of life in her novels, we find her characters discovering their own identity. It is in this context that a critical study of her novels is a must in order to acquaint ourselves with the various themes and aspects of life with which we get acquainted in the course of our reading those novels.

> "***To Whom She Will*** was a novel about India, written by an English lady. Well written too, Amrita could see that, all the proper elements of style and sensibility, but Amrita could not understand why the lady had given Indian names to her characters"[1]

The Plot of ***To Whom She Will*** appears to bring out the wisdom of that institution dear to oriental conservatism, the marriage arranged by family elders between young people who lack the experience are denied the opportunity to choose partners for themselves. Amrita finds her western style of living uncongenial, and thinks herself in love with Hari Sahni, a poor young Punjabi who works at the New Delhi radio station where she is a part-time announcer. Their families do not agree that the marriage between the two should be materialised Amrita's grandfather is opposed to it, her mother and her aunts entertain the idea of looking for a more acceptable partner for her. Hari's family is also engaged in negotiating a marriage settlement for him with Anand, a family of their own community. Worn down at last by family pressure, Amrita and Hari settle for marriage with partner from socially suitable backgrounds. To ***Whom She Will*** is a story about young Amrita whose feeling for Hari is guided by an idealized concept of the 'Indianness'. Hayden Moore Williams has pointed out that Ruth Jhabvala, like her literary ancestor, Jane Austen likes to develop plots in which romantic love is less than adequate[2]. It is not accident that an early review described ***To Whom She Will*** in terms that are applicable to ***Pride and Prejudice.*** ***"To Whom She Will*** might be described as a social comedy .... The tale of family matchmaking is told with a delightfully gentle irony"[3] like Jane Austen's novel this book also entertains us greatly. Although Ruth Jhabvala derives much comedy from the romantic excess of her sentimental lovers, and ends the novel by resolving the conflict between youth and aged in a manner satisfactory to all concerned, the picture she draws of the Indian family as a 'loving and protective cocoon' is, to say ate least, ambiguous. Amrita's mother does not appreciate her brave attempts to earn her own living. Pt. Saxena plans to send Amrita to England in order to show his own importance and justifies the compulsion of the situation. Lovers find happiness in their several ways in the teeth of family insensitivity to their deepest feelings.

The reader is aware of the fact that Amrita's decision to marry Krishna will cause no re-thinking, no restatement of established values in Saxena's household. Amrita's feelings have taken her grandfather, mother and aunts by surprise. Within this ambiguous but generally compassionate picture of youth and aged in conflict, Ruth Prawer Jhabvala finds plenty of opportunity to satirse the whole scene. Ram Bahadur Saxena values what he calls his family's "breeding and fortune" and though he considers himself a man of liberal views his treatment of his social inferiors marks him out as a self-deceiving snob. The changes in Indian society after independence have isolated the old man. All that he values has either disappeared or reduced to very confined limits. As he grows older, he finds himself more and more unfit to cope with the society he lives in. Though his house presents a picture of opulence, it betrays a moral and cultural emptiness. It is quite natural that the idealistic Amrita should turn away from this empty respectability to worship "Indianness". But it is a sign of her immaturity that her quest for 'Indianness' leads her to Hari's elder sister Prema, in whom she discovers the familiar combination of wealth and ostentation, together with a new kind of emptiness. Their newly acquired money gives Prema and her husband Suri superior status in their own community. It is this attitude that makes them to challenge the arrogance of the Saxena's comic incongruities enrich Prem's tea-party for Amrita, their humour sparingly comes out partly from a contrast intention between the two characters and partly from a conflict in expectation. Prema tries to impress Amrita with her luxurious style of living, Amrita for her part hopes to find in Hari's sister the 'supreme simplicity' with which she would like to identify herself. While Prema talks of her recent Simla holiday, her fondness for Delhi's most expensive pastries her imported car, her husband's choice for new and fashionable things occupy most of her conversation. She tries to make a show of her wealth and position just to impress Amrita and the other members of the family so as to be thought of highly by them. It is the wish to be thought of well that impels Prema to talk about her position and status and it is this attitude which has been signalled out for satiric treatment by Ruth Prawer Jhabvala.

In this novels Mrs. Jhabvala makes fun of the young Indian generation who while thinking themselves to be modern and weternised try to do a thing which the traditional Hindu society is opposed to, that is falling in love with a boy or a girl outside one's own caste, community and social status. What is ironical is that tradition scores victory over modernization and Jhabvala has succeeded in describing these two types in the modern Indian Society. The entire episode of Hari's and Amrita's love has been presented in a humorous manner by Jhabvala. In fact, many times she seems to be ridiculing the whole thing. Amrita asserts her love in a dramatic manner for Hari in the studio. It is through this relationship that Jhabvala has been able to develop the main theme of novel arranged V /s love marriage. Hari has been presented as a weak character as compared to Amrita. He lacks manner and sophistication and the feeling of being nothing haunts him constantly. He thinks, he is in love with Amrita and when Krishna Sen Gupta, a Bengali youth who lives with Radha as a paying guest, talks to Hari about Amrita, he speaks of his position in a manner which takes away all the seriousness and appears to be very humorous. He says, "Every moment of the day I think of her, she is the nightingale of my heart, the star of my eyes, the juice of my liver, tell her that" (page 145).

Though Hari who has been portrayed as a weak character declares his love for Amrita, he is not able to face the opposition of his family. His family objects to his marrying Amrita, for a Bengali girl cannot fit into their family. It is at this juncture that Jhabvala comments on the issue of caste and community. Punjabis and Bengalis are considered to be poles apart. Their dress, food, language and social customs, everything is different, and hence they find a nice girl, Sushila Anand, a girl from their own caste and community. Prema makes Hari to realise the fact that Sushila is prettier than Amrita, that she has a melodious voice and of our own community. Hari protests mildly that she is in love with Amrita, and even goes to the extent of saying that, it is not proper for him to marry Sushila. But the whole matter is settled when Suri, Prema's husband intervenes and tells Hari in clear terms that he is to marry Sushila. It is here that Mrs. Jhabvala appears to be killing two birds with one stone. On one hand, she brings out ironically the conception of love in India, and on the other, she very aptly proves the victory of tradition over modernity. She proves that India is still a conservative society, no matter how its younger generation tries to break the shackles of old traditions and customs.

Hari's mother is very happy and is proud of her son. Amrita, on the other hand, proves stronger as compared to Hari. Though ultimately she gives in to the wishes of her mother and agrees to marry Krishna, their paying guest, yet she fights for her lover bravely. She not only faces the opposition of her mother Radha, who all along disapproves Hari, but also her grandfather, Pt. Ram Bahadur Saxena. He is not quite against her marrying outside the community and objects to the match on grounds, which are basically social and cultural. He feels that Hari would be total misfit in every aspect. Hari appears to him representing everything that is unacceptable to them. However, Amrita still thinks of the ways in which she can realise her love. As against Hari's weak protesti,.h is suggestive of Amrita's character and establishes the fact how ahead she is of Hari. Amrita is ready to give up her family, money and status for the sake of her love. She even goes to the extent of demanding help from Tarla's husband, Vazir Dayal. She plans to marry Hari in England where there would be no one to raise any objection. She is so enthusiastic about their plans for going to England that she sends Krishna to Hari to tell him of her plans. But Hari's response is discouraging and disappointing. Hari tells Krishna about his inability to leave Delhi, Krishna finds Hari incompetent to face the situation boldly. Mrs. Jhabvala proves that the lower middle-class is still weak and likes to stick to the traditions, whereas the modern Indian section at least has the courage to announce the disapproval of these old customs and traditions.

Another point which Jhabvala brings out in this novel is that, though the young generation (like Amrita) in the upper middle-class educated society are courageous and liberated, the older generation to a great extent continues to be conservative in its approach and attitude towards other. Amrita's mother Radha does not approve the match only on this ground. The ultimate conclusion is that Hari marries, Sushila and Amrita settle down for Krishna, a Bengali young boy of her own caste and community. It is a clear victory of tradition over modernity. Though we find Jhabvala deeply interested in the controversy between the two, her initial charm for Indian marriages and other social and religious customs can be seen throughout this novel. Hari's marriage provides, her with an opportunity to describe an Indian arranged marriage in detail. Her description of the marriage ceremony appears to be more business like than a social function. What is admirable is Jhabvala's keen sense of observation. It is this penetrative observation that calls for our attention. It is with minute observation that Jhabvala presents the activities of Indian women. What appeals to us most is her use of Indian words with which we are familiar, such as, ghee, Masala, Dal etc. This she does in order to give realistic touches. Jhabvala does not want to leave out anything, the climax comes when along with the marriage Jhabvala describes a funeral procession, a common site in India. The reason for presenting these two contrasts is that she likes to write about two different things simultaneously. The description of both is minute and true to life. India is a land were such social activities are common and one comes across these things so often that one does not reach to them as eagerly and violently as they should. Life is to be lived as it is and whatever comes is to be accepted in the same manner. What is remarkable about this novel is that the entire presentation is realistic and brings out Jhabvala' s enthusiasm for this wonderful land.

The Nature of Passion can be described as a social comedy which is Jhabvala's forte. The novel appears to be a continuation of her first novel, ***To Whom She Will,*** as she has again taken up a few aspects, of the day - to - day life of the rich class of Punjabis in Delhi. The novel is basically familial. It presents a story of two Punjabi families residing in Delhi, but it also focuses on many other related areas of a society which is involved in its state of change from the orthodox to the modern mode of living. ***The Nature of Passion*** projects several conflicts and cross-current of their changing society. The clash between the old and the young generations once again constitutes an important theme of the novel. Jhabvala still appears to be enchanted and obsessed by the Indian people, their dress, food, social customs and ways of life. In this novel she shifts her attention to child birth in Indian society.

After going through her first two novels one gets the impression that the Indian youth have failed to impress Jhabvala. As in the first novel, Jhabvala has portrayed Hari similarly here she portrayed Viddi as a weak character. It appears that in Jhabvala's world of fiction, Indian youth, especially unemployed appear to live in a world of imagination and enchantment. After completing their studies, they find it difficult to keep themselves busy. Jobs are hard to obtain and they are normally short of money and so they spend most of their time sitting in restaurants and coffee-houses planning for a bright future, when they will be able to translate their dreams and ambitions into realities. Jhabvala also throws light on the Indian Government offices and officials, their way of working and their corruption, which is an essential feature of the entire system.

The title of the novel seems to have been derived from "Swami Paramananda's translation of Bhagvad Gita", Jhabvala also quotes a passage from Radhakrishna's comments on this aspects of the ***Gita.***

> "The three modes are present in all human beings though in different degree. No one is free from them

> and in each soul one or the other predominates. Men are said to be 'satvika', 'rajasa' or 'tamsa' according to the mode which prevails——— while the actives of a satvika temperament are free, calm and selfless, the rajasa nature wishes to be always active and cannot sit still and its activities are tainted by selfish desires."[4]

The main emphasis in the novel is in portraying the process of "rajas" the worldly passion is marked by thirst for pleasure and which culminate in attachment, the "satvik" (Saintly) or the "tamsa" are merely hinted at in the novel in the behaviour of a few minor characters such as Phuphiji, Om Prakash and Viddi. It is the worldliness of Verma's or Lalaji's desire for money, his keenness to get rupees twenty-five lakh contract for the new building of the Happy Hindustan Trading Company, which is indicative of the fact that rajas" rules the world of Lalaji. The Novel presents two Punjabi families-the family of Lala Naryan Das Verma consisting of his wife, three sons (Om Prakash, Chandra Prakash and Ved Prakash) , three daughters (Rani, Usha and Nimmi) and his widow sister, Phuphiji and the other family is of Deve Raj another rich Punjabi businessman but he remains throughout in the background. Lala Narayan Das Verma, who is better known as Lalaji is the chief character of the novel. Starting his life as a Punjabi refugee and later on as a humble contractor he rose to become one of the most prosperous businessmen of the town. It is through his character that Jhabvala projects many aspects of Indian society and life of the rich class in Delhi. It is Jhavala's minute observation which grips our attention. It is evident in the portrayal of the life of Lalaji and other Punjabi families also acquired wealth and social status by dint of their hardwork but basically they remained the same as they were before they had money. They believed in simple living if not in high thinking. Their wealth and social status could not change their way of life. They had all the comfort and luxuries, yet their attitude to life remained what it had been before. Lalaji had seven marble bathrooms in his house but he preferred to use his garden-tap for cleaning his teeth. He slept outdoor in summer, even though he could afford an air conditioner and, in spite of having a well furnished bedroom, he disliked to share it with his wife. In this connection Jhabvala writes:

> "He did not like his bedroom nor did his wife with whom he shares it. It seemed wrong that just the two of them sleep there no children, no babies. No relatives come to stay, only pieces of strange and unnecessary furniture still one had to keep up with one's money. A bed room suite was a social necessity, so he had bought it."[5]

These lines clearly indicate that though refugees made money but basically they remained the same, unsophisticated and simple. In these lines Jhabvala calls a bedroom a 'Social necessity' Lalaji could not see as to why he should have a separate bedroom or a living room, for him a room is a room, where everyone can sleep sit and chat. In this novel Lalaji also represents the joint family system of Indian society a very important aspect, though going out of fashion with the passage of time. Jhabvala in this novel displays awareness of their special feature of Indian society- the joint family system which is almost unthought in the western world. Writing on this aspect of Jhabvala's fiction, V.A. Shahane comments:

> "Although joint family system is breaking down under various economic, industrial and social pressures, Indian society even in urban area still remains in-group, this in group feeling, mental out look and the get - togetherness of family ties Jhabvala shows her deep awareness of this aspect of Indian society."[6]

Lalaji is not only a traditional but also narrow minded typical businessman. Jhabvala ironically and humorously brings out the fact that whatever Lalaji does is in some or the other is connected either with his business or his family. He is regular in reading newspapers but only those columns which will be useful to him. He is not concerned with what is happening in world or even in India and Jhabvala takes keen delight in describing this aspect of Lalaji's character. She writes.

> "He read the newspaper, He read only the local report on pag three......He turned to the advertisements to contract tenders...........Out of habit also he looked the marriage." (pp. 111-21)

Nodoubt, this is full of humour and also has a satirical twist. Jhabvala is definitely laughing at the narrow mindedness of this class of Indian society. Though Lalaji has been portrayed as a traditional, simple and strict oldman, yet his reaction to Nimmi's getting her hair cut short is not what the readers would expect. Lalaji's reaction is confused and unexpected, and at this moment he appears, to be symbolising a synthesis between tradition and modernity. It is through various characters in various novels that different aspects of Indian society are presented by Mrs. Jhabvala. In this novel Lalaji's six children, three daughters and three sons aptly portray the different types of girls and boys found in the Punjabi families. Lalaji's three daughters Rani, Usha and Nimmi look apart from each other. Rani is married to a rich man and is well settled. His second daughter Usha is on her way to get married. In fact she represents a normal Punjabi girl, hailing from a rich family. Girls like Usha are supposed to get married and produce children. Describing this aspect of Usha, Meena Shirwadkar writes; "Usha is the symbol of womanly fulfilment, loving placid looking forward to marriage and children."[7] Though Usha appears to be happy with her life, Lalaji's wife is worried about her. She knows that after marriage she won't be able to continuo with this type of life. But Lalaji remains unaffected as he realises the power of money and the important role that money plays in Indian marriages. Hence Jhabvala tries to touch upon that aspect of Indian marriages which she has not done previously. Here she makes it clear that, in India marriages are more of business deals than anything else. Lalaji's third daughter Nimmi is a contrast not only to Usha but to her entire family. The following lines clearly bring out this contrast:

> "Juxtapose with her Usha is Nimmi, her siste,r enjoying college life friends, havin modern ideas, toying with English poetry, influenced with Parsi because he is member of a westernized club. She is ashamed of her parents whom she thinks unfashionable and orthodox."[8]

These lines aptly describe Nimmi, a young girl, trying to be modern and bent upon breaking all the shackles of old Hindu traditions. She goes to the college, has a fast friend Rajan, who comes from a sophisticated, modern rich family. She goes to the club with him and keeps it a secret from her family. She plays tennis in the club and puts on a dress which her family never approved of. What is significant is that Nimmi is well aware of what she is doing and also realises that the kind of life that she is living is not in line with the norms of the society she belongs to. In this connection, Jhabvala tries to show how the young generation is at war with old traditions and customs. Another fact that comes out is that, though the young people are revolting against their families, yet their stance is not pronounced and challenging. Nimmi does many things to which her family is apposed and yet she continues to do all such things in the presence of her family members. Her revolt reaches its climax when she develops intimacy with a Parsi boy Pheroz Batliwala. She does not mind accepting his invitation and going out to dinner with him, and after the dinner Pheroz offers a drive to Kutub Minar. Nimmi knows that it is not proper for her to do all this and yet she accepts the invitation and goes to Kutub Minar where Pheroz tries to kiss Nimmi. The entire episode is replėte with humour. The description brings out the fact that people inspite of being rich and prosperous and imitating the western world and becoming modern in their outlook, they remain the same backward and crude. Further-more, this craze for modernity makes them abnormal, for they remain neither Indians nor Europeans.

Lalaji's three sons, Om Prakash, Chandra Prakash and Viddi are like his daughters, different from one another and through them Jhabvala has successfully brought out three different aspects of Indian society. Om Prakash, the eldest son is a traditional young man following his father in every respect. He is not highly educated, married a girl from his own community and settled down in his father's business. He is blessed with two children and the third one is on its way. Like any typical businessman in India, Om is fond of good food and clothes and hence he has put on a lot of extra weight. It is through Om's personality that Mrs. Jhabvala has projected the joint-family system of Indian society. Om Prakash lives with his father in his house and works with him in his business, and as a result he is totally dependent on him for all his requirements and has hardly anything to worry about. Om asks his father to instal an air-conditioner in the office, but Lalaji does not give much importance to his demand and keeps putting it off on one pretext or the other. Om knows that his father is simply putting off the time and is fully aware of own initiative. This clearly brings out the fact that when a son works with his father, he is totally dominated by his father. But Om did not appear to mind this and the main reason for this submission is his lack of education. Hence he could not move in the modern westernized society. He was only mixing up with people of his own class and community. His idea about women and their place in society is also very narrow and old fashioned. It is through him that Mrs. Jhabvala brings out the fact that in old traditional Indian society, a woman's place is strictly in her house. Education plays no role in her life. She should live in her house, learn how to prepare food, get married, and look after her husband and family. Elaborating the idea of Om's traditionalism, Mrs. Jhabvala says:

> "Do you know what I will do with that One?.... When she is seven, I will find a good husband and bethroth her. Then she can back to the house and learn from her mother and her aunts to make chappaties and mango pickle. When she has learnt that well she can go to her husband's house and be a credit to us there. (p. 17)

The description, though apparently light, assumes significance. It clearly brings out the narrow view of an uneducated person regarding women in India. One can easily come to the conclusion that it is not Om only but the entire business community in India which thinks that education for women is a waste of time and money. The girls can only prove to be an asset to their family if they are experts in household chores.

Chandra Prakash is the second son of Lalaji and is a contrast to Om. Unlike Om, he is highly educated. He had been to England for higher studies, and on his return, instead of helping his father in his business, opts for government service. Not only this, he marries a girl of his own choice, outside his caste and community. He lives separately with his family. It is through Chandra Prakash that Jhabvala describes the Indian service class and the working of the Indian Government offices. Her stay in Delhi gave Jhabvala an opportunity to observe Indian Government officials very closely. According to her officers command a respect in society and try to maintain a decent living standard; yet they are always short of money (as their salaries are meagre) and it is this factor which makes them indulge in bribery and corruption. In Jhabvala's view corruption and bribery are an important feature of modern Indian economy. Since Chandra Prakash married a girl of his own choice his wife Kanta does not enjoy the confidence and love of her husband's family members. Chandra's salary is not sufficient even to provide them with a yearly holiday in the hills and for that also they depend on Lalaji's generosity. Mrs. Jhabvala writes about it quite humorously. Kanta tells Viddi.

> "We do not like to ask your father for favours. It hurt her that they so often had to doso, for Chandra's salary was sufficient only for their daily needs. Household and entertaining expenses were heavy. Anything extra like the cocktail party and the yearly holiday in the hill had to come out of Lalaji's Pocket'. (p. 196)

This is suggestive of the economic condition of Indian Government servants. It bears out the fact as to how ill-paid they are and how they need extra income to maintain a certain living standard. Chandra was lucky in having a rich father to supplement his income, but what happens when there is no one to add to their income; naturally bribery and corruption come in so much so that they had become a part of life and are not considered to be illegal or bad.

Lalaji's youngest son Ved Prakash or Viddi, had nothing in common with his two elder brothers. It is through him the Jhabvala juxtaposes the old traditional and the young generation of India. Like Nimmi, he runs after western culture. He and Nimmi are agents who make people aware of the western influence on the modern generation. Throwing light on this aspect, R.S. Singh in his article on Jhabvala observes.

> "Here the juxtaposition of the traditional made of life against the modern accentuates not only the changes that had become perceptible in cultural complex of the country but also the superficiality of the so-called modern life".[9]

Viddi is a graduate and now his ambition is to go abroad for higher studies. His intention is to be either an art critic or a journalist, but knows well that he cannot realise his desire, as Lalalji wants to him to be part of his business Viddi does not seem to have any clear cut idea of life. Like all young Indians, he also wants to go abroad just to be called a foreign-returned man. Mrs. Jhabvala examines this question and comes to the conclusion that it is not so much the studies they think about, it is the free life that they would be able to lead there eat, drink and enjoy life and the study part comes only after all this. Viddi also dreams of England and all those pleasures that his stay in England will bring. His repeated requests to Lalaji and Om to let him to go England fall on deaf ears. He does not like his father because of his craze for money and when Viddi's friends praise Lalaji's for his hard work and intelligence, he loses his temper and tells them as how crude, selfish and hungry for money and power he is.

Viddi's frequent condemnation of his father, brother and the entire family at times make readers wonder whether it was Mrs. Jhabvala's own impression about this new rich class of refugees. Mrs. Jhabvala seems to have used Viddi as her mouthpiece to criticise such people. It is quite obvious that whenever she wants to criticise India or Indian, she always does it through one of her Indian characters. Viddi's condemnation of Lalaji and Om Prakash is so acute that at times it appears a bit unnatural, considering the fact that in the Indian society no son would go to the extent of describing his father as an animal, and we often wonder it is the novelist's personal view regarding these refugees. Mrs. Jhavala uses Viddi not only to expose Lalaji's personality but also to expose their entire life-style. Viddi has no hesitation in telling his friend that the radiogram in their house is merely a showpiece. Books are another thing which have no place in his household. The only book they have is the ***Gita*** or some commercial registers and whenever he feels like to read something, he has to borrow it from others, because his father is against spending money on such things. The following lines are indicative of it.

> "We have a radiogram -— it is very big———---- it costs a lot of money. Nobody ever listen to the radio. Several times I have tried to listen to a concert of classical western music, but each time they have told. me that such noises, they cannot hear, turn it off" (p. 52).

The above lines once again bring out the fact that though these Punjabi refugees have acquired wealth yet basically they remain uneducated and crude with no taste either for music or for art. In this novel Jhabvala has tried to established the fact that art and artists have no future and value in Indian society. The artists get no employment and have no money and they waste their time and talent by sitting in cheap restaurants drinking coffee and thinking of ways to earn some money for their living.

Zahir-ud-din is an artist who has nothing to do. He is jobless. He decides to use Viddi as a means to get money from his rich father Lalaji. Tiwari a journalist having government job but is allergic to going to his office. Bhawa is dramatist writing plays on social problems and sometimes even stages them, but is unable to get success. It is through such characters that Mrs. Jhabvala has brought out the burning problem of unemployment in India. At the same time, she has succeeded in convincing her readers that talent has no value in India.

In this novel Mrs. Jhabvala has also described a few social customs with great enthusiasm. She has taken up the problem of arranged marriage In India. She brings out the fact that sometimes the marriages are arranged along with business deals. In other words, to get a certain business deal through the condition at times is that the interested party should agree to give away his daughter or son in marriage. For example, Lalaji is very keen on getting a big contract of the new building being put up by the 'Happy Hindustan Trading Company', at the cost of rupees twenty-five lakhs. He finds that one of the Directors of the company's happens to be the uncle of Devraj (Sunta's father) and feels certain that his work would be done through his connections. But when he talks to Devraj about it he comes up with a new proposal that he would get him the contract, provided he gives his consent to marry his youngest daughter Nimmi to the son of the director of the Happy Hindustan Trading Company. Initially Lalaji is opposes to the idea, but soon agrees to it as it is a question of getting or losing twenty-five lakh rupees. Besides the custom of arranged marriages in India Mrs. Jhabvala feels intrigued to see how the birth of a child takes place in Indian society. It becomes more or less a social affair, with this, Mrs. Jhabvala has also thrown light on the conditions prevailing in Indian nursing homes. The nursing homes have been presented a place of social intercourse. Ladies discuss all their problems there, and the men, along with their commitments discuss business.

In conclusion, we can say that ***The Nature of Passion*** is a novel written in a light mood. Mrs. Jhabvala has written about the Indian society and its problems as she saw them. The main theme of this novel is to project the rich class of Punjabi refugee in Delhi, their awareness of the power of money, and the clash between the old and the new generations. Its should be borne in mind that Mrs. Jhabvala wrote the novel under the influence of excitement and awe of the totally unknown society. There are many areas of similarities between ***To Whom She Will*** and ***The Nature of Passion.*** The character of Nimmi, Lalaji's youngest daughter reminds us of the character of Amrita the heroine of ***To Whom She Will.*** Like Amrita Nimmi falls in love with a Parsi boy who also hails from a totally different community and family background. Like Amrita Nimmi has to give up the idea of marrying Pheroz and she succumbs to the wishes, of her family members. She marries Kaku, a boy from her own case and social status. Mrs.Jhabvala appears to have tendency in exaggerating her characters and juxtaposing the situations to that extend that the characters appear to be caricatures. Lalaji's passion for money and love for Nimmi—the two focal points in the novel have been highly exaggerated. Lalaji's awareness of the value of money is also more than normal. Viddi's aversion to money and his entire family in the initial stage of the novel appears to have crossed limits of decency. Nimmi's quest for modernity and her sentimental love for Pheroz also has in it germs of exaggerations. It is through such characters that the evils that we find in our society get exposed and make the readers laugh. We normally find that her characters are found to be larger than life and this is perhaps Mrs. Jhabvala's way of projecting her characters. In her interview with Ram Lal this question had been very aptly asked and answered by Mrs. Jhabvala.

> "I think novelists can be classified in two schools—those characters are as large as life and those whose characters are larger than life. I am the follower of second school. That just happened to be the kind of novelist I am".[10]

This is the answer to the question why a majority of her character are larger than life. ***Esmond in India*** is a family story and covers the lives of three families in its narrative structure. The story revolves round the families of Har Dayal and Ram Nath, two friends who had studied together at Cambridge but who later on parted away to lead their own lives. While Har Dayal imbibed the English culture and injected it into his wife Madhuri, Ram Nath stuck to the Indian tradition even after his return and became a part of the freedom struggle. Har Dayal still relishes his stay in England and even tries to make a show of it whenever he gets a chance to do so. Ram Nath, however, though not very critical of the western culture, is more appreciative of the Indian ways of life and it seems that he has even forgotten that he had ever been to England for study. The only similarity between the two is that both had their share in the Freedom Movement. However, Har Dayal is an opportunist and Ram Nath is an idealist, and hence Har Dayal becomes a materialist while Ram Nath, the bookworm becomes an idealist.

Besides these two characters we have their wives, Madhuri and Lakshmi living in the worlds created by their husbands. Madhuri enjoys all the material comforts and luxuries that life can offer her, while Lakshmi, after losing everything in the freedom struggle lives more in her poverty-stricken present. Madhuri is blessed with two sons, Amrit and Raj and one daughter Shakuntala. Madhuri thinks most of the time about her daughter who has just finished her college education and is about to make a new beginning. Amrit is in service and is married to a nice girl Indu. Raja who is also studying at Cambridge makes his intention of marrying a European girl known to his mother. Lakshmi on the other hand, has only one son Narayan, a doctor who is an idealist and who is proud of being in the shadow of his father. He gives up all the opportunities of earning name and fame in Delhi and goes to the villages for service to the really suffering people of Indian society.

Between the story of these two families we have the story of Uma and her daughter Gulab. Uma, along with her husband, was also an active fighter for India's freedom, but unfortunately lost her husband just before independence. She now lives in her own narrow world comprising her daughter Gulab and grand son Ravi. Gulab, the most important character of the novel is married to Esmond Still wood an European residing in India. It is for the first time that we find Mrs. Jhabvala introducing a foreign character in her novel and it is through this character that the contrast between East-West is projected. She makes it clear that her initial enchantment and excitement about this mystic world the East is wearing off. Now she shows a deeper insight into this unknown society and is able to project it through these two characters. Both the characters are highly exaggerated and it is the Gulab-Esmond's relationship which is at the root of the novel. It is Esmond's real inability to love which explains his other feelings. When Esmond feels oppressed by Gulab, he runs to his mistress Betty, another European character in the novel."

Mrs. Jhabvala after writing about the rich class of Punjabi refugee in Delhi in her earlier novel is now attracted by the different type of freedom fighters India has during its long fight for freedom. Mrs. Jhabvala presents three types of freedom fighters. The first type comprises those who may be described as opportunists. They did all those things which freedom-fighters were supposed to do. They stopped putting on imported clothes and appeared only in Khadi. They did not have to sacrifice much to get the freedom, and after freedom was acquired, they enjoyed all the comforts in free India. Har Dayal can be taken to represent this type of freedom fighters. He is in possession of a big Bungalow and car and has many committee meetings at his residence. The way in which Har Dayal conduct himself during such meetings has been humorously described in the following lines.

> "As they all come, one by one driving up in their big car, Daddyji would come rushing out to greet tem full

> of affection and enthusiasm. He would receive them wit honour and modest smile."[11]

Although the entire description seems to have been written in a light tone, yet the ironic mode is quite obvious. Mrs. Jhabvala is in fact making fun of the way he received his guests, the fact that he did not hesitate in touching the feet of the Ministers just to serve his own ends. Not only Har Dayal's behaviour but even his appearance kept changing after he became a freedom fighter. He stopped wearing foreign clothes and instead put on 'Khadi' just to make a favourable impression on others. Not only Har Dayal even Prof. Bhatnagar, who had been a professor at Allahabad University and whose voice carried much weight in the ministry of education, wore only Indian dress. Jhabvala openly laughs at them and makes fun of their high ideas. Her sense of humour becomes obvious when she goes to the extent of saying that this change made them look so different that even their own family members found it difficult to recognise them. It is through Shakuntala that Jhabvala castigates them;

> "It was a change which had taken quite sometime to get used to. Before 1947 all her father's had looked just like English gentlemen but now they all looked like Indian Congressman." (p. 150)

The description is replete with satire as it brings out the hollowness and futility of the lives of these people. To highlight their way of life Jhabvala uses Amrit, and Shakuntala, a great admirer of her father praises him and his achievements, Amrita cuts short and remarks.

> "All this art and culture are very nice to keep old gentleman busy, but why we pretend they serve any useful purpose." (p. 55).

According to Amrit these committees are nothing but farce something which these rich people have created just to pass their time, and its seems that this is what Mrs. Jhabvala herself thought of these freedom fighters and their committees. It is with ironical and satirical remarks that Jhabvala ridicules the whole things and her intention in doing so is to bring out the hollow-ness and emptiness of their lives. We find Har Dayal's own son Amrit mak-ing fun of his father's activities and committees and this is done in such a natural way that we concur with what he says and enjoy every word he utters. This is how Mrs.Jhabvala presents the picture of India in her ugly shapes.

In contrast to Har Dayal we have his friend Ram Nath who dedicated his whole life to his motherland after his return from England. He plunged into the freedom movement and became a part of it. He has been presented in the novel as an idealist, a person who sacrifices everything to reach the target on which he has set his heart. He struggled before and after independence, first to liberate his country from clutches of the Britishers and later to survive in free India. Once again we find Mrs. Jhabvala using Shakuntala, Har Dayal's daughter to project Ram Nath's personality and character. After 1947, India got freedom and people like Har Dayal attained positions of importance whereas Ram Nath remained the same. He neither became rich nor important, and when once he was offered a high position, he refused for reasons best known to him. Ram Nath who refused a good offer seemed to be out of the ordinary life has no decent place to live, no servants and no glamour whereas those freedom fighters who acted as ordinary men without any ideals accepted what was offered to them, are important today. It is they who attend committee meeting and enjoy all the comforts and luxuries of life. Here what Shakuntala says is worth noticing.

> "Ram Nath uncle did not come to committee meetings. He was, she supposed not important enough"[12]

Such statements are so significant, ironic and full of meaning that they reveal the true face of Indian society. It also becomes clear that Mrs. Jhabvala chooses this young energetic graduate girl (Shakentalal to be her mouth-piece in this novel— a very proper choice indeed for who else can be better qualified to compare the two freedom fighters than one's own daughter and a good acquaintance of the other.

The portrayal of these two characters Har Dayal and Ram Nath is not only interesting but also very revealing. Both were at Cambridge and both returned to India and devoted themselves to the cause of India's freedom.

Har Dayal from the very beginning has been presented as a person who makes the best of what he gets in life, and in contrast to him Ram Nath is what he has been. While in Cambridge, it was Ram Nath who was important. It was he who helped Har Dayal to establish himself in that foreign land. Har Dayal in spite of being worldly and an opportunist never forgets what Ram Nath did for him and what he was in those days. Mrs. Jhabvala has made it clear that it is India, Indian society and its environment which can change a strong man like Ram Nath and leave him as nothing but a dried-up skeleton, still breathing to see the worse which is yet to happen to him, or till he himself realises that he has been a complete failure in his life. He would do nothing for himself or his wife. His only son Narayan who is a doctor and is working in the villages writes to his father asking him to find a bride for him. Ram Nath after many years gets an inspiration to move. He visits his friend Har Dayal after a long time and wants to arrange a marriage between Narayan and Shakunata but his offer is politely turned down by Har Dayal, and it is at this point that Ram Nath gives up and starts feeling that he is a total failure in life. The two types of freedom fighter have been convincingly analysed by Mrs. Jhabvala-one an opportunist who is in touch with the world and the other an idealist who is out of true with the world and is a complete failure.

Besides these two types of freedom fighters there is yet another category, of those who sacrificed their lives, who did not live to see what free India had to offer them. In the novel it is Uma's husband, Gulab's father who was an active freedom fighter and died of hunger strike in jail just before India got freedom. Mrs. Jhabvala does not even mention his name in the novel, but simply touches upon the "Gandhian policy of ahimsa" and hunger strikes. Uma's husband has been described as "giant" by Har Dayal dying of hunger strike in prison. Uma also remembers him as being extremely fond of good food and having a very magnetic personality and after reading the novel we are left to wonder to admire the Indian freedom fighters or to have pity for them. Har Dayal, Ram Nath and Uma's husband, are characters in the novel who have been used by Mrs. Jhabvala very successfully to portray the three sections of Indian society. The rich class, having all the comforts and privileges in modern India is represented by Har Dayal and the other extreme of the lower-middle class represented by Uma. Her husband was rich and at one time she had all the luxuries and comforts. Even now she has a large house and enough money to live on, but everything appeares to be a part of her glorious past.

Mrs. Jhabvala also writes about their families just to give a better and closer picture of Indian society in post-Independence India. In this novel women have a definite role to play. Har Dayal's wife Madhuri is a typical example of a rich Indian lady in modern India. Her daughter Shakuntala has been presented as educated and westernised fighting for her rights. A young girl with college education eager to break old traditions, and in between these two we have an ideal daughter-in-law Indu. Madhuri represents the rich women of Indian society. If Mrs. Jhabvala has observed those rich ladies she did not fail to describe the other set of Indian ladies who can be classified as middle-class Indian ladies. The sharp contrast between Madhuri and Uma is more or less a good example of a comparison between the two classes high and middle- class Indian society. Madhuri is westernised and is proud that both her sons had studied at Cambridge. She firmly believes that youngman must go abroad to learn fine manners. What Mrs. Jhabvala is trying to project is that the so-called rich Indian people feel proud of being noticed as weternised and foreign returned. It is this aspect of their life which is mocked at by Mrs. Jhabvala.

In the novel, Mrs. Jhabvala not only criticizes Indian woman but finds Indian environment and surrounding dull and drab. The only thing that she finds in plenty is "poverty". It is for this reason that even the country side in India appears to her to be life less and dull. This is presented when Esmond is taking the tour to Agra and on the way Betty, another European in the novel remarks,

> "The trouble with the Indian country side is that it is so frightfully dull" (p. 144)

Everything appears to be dull and colourless , and one has a feeling that the novelist is pointing at the poverty and all round depression in the country. The thing which takes the reader by surprise is that Mrs. Jhabvala's initial enchantment and excitement about this country did not last very long. It is this sordid picture of India which has been captured and presented in ***Esmond in India.***

The Householder is the fourth novel written by Mrs. Jhabvala in 1960. The novel comes as a pleasant surprise as we see Mrs. Jhabvala out of the despondent mood i.e. discernible in ***Esmond in India.*** She forgets the Punjabi refugees and the freedom fighters, and from the upper-middle class of Indian society, she shifts her attention to the lower middle-class society of India. She takes up the problem of young man, who is just entering the family life. The predicaments and the struggles of this young man have been presented in humorous manner but with a touch of irony here and there. The novel bares witness to the fact that the cycle was renewed in the case of Mrs. Jhabvala, because in this novel, whatever she has written is not bitter, it is a simple story written in a light vein, and it would not be out of place to mention that it is certainly refreshing heartening to see Mrs. Jhabvala writing about this country as a keen observer, rather than a bitter critic.

The Householder is a story of young man Prem, standing at the threshold of "Grihasthashram" *i.e.,* just entering the family life, leaving behind the care free life of student and also the protection of his parents. Prem's father was the Principal in one of the Colleges in Ankhpur and was held in high esteem by everyone in that small town. Prem passed his B.A. with second class mark and took the job of teaching Hindi in one of the private colleges in Delhi. So once again the background of the novel remains in Delhi.

The reader is introduced to Prem, the hero of the novel, as a married man teaching Hindi on a meagre salary of rupees one seventy-five per month. He has to support himself and his wife Indu who is in the family way and of course run the entire household. He has rented an apartment in one of the not-so-famous colonies and is supposed to pay rupees forty-five per month towards the rent of the apartment. He is naturally left with meagre amount to run his family and this, by no standard is sufficient. Hence from the very beginning we find Prem struggling hard to keep the house running in a proper way. The novel deals with this problem of Prem. Besides Prem, there are other characters in the novel, who have been successfully used by Mrs. Jhabvala to throw light on other aspects of Indian society. Raj, Prem's childhood friend, who works in a Government office in Delhi has been used for presenting the condition and the working of the Indian Government offices at a lower level. Mr. & Mrs. Khanna are the owners of the Khanna Private College, they have been used for depicting the state of private colleges in India, and how education has become a business rather than an academic venture. Mrs. Chaddha and Mrs. Sohan Lal two other teachers of the same college, embody the different types of teacher in India and their working conditions in such colleges. There are very few women characters in the novel. We have Indu, Prem's wife, who represents the life of young couple in lower-middle class Indian society and her relation with Prem's mother shows the mother-in-law and daughter-in-law relationship in India.

Besides these characters, the most important character in the novel in Hans, a German who happens to be in India in search of Indian spiritualism and is determined to find it everywhere. He has been portrayed by Mrs. Jhabvala in the first stage of excitement and enthusiasm. He has been used as an agent to unveil the knowledge of Indians (especially the lower-middle class Indian) who are unable to think beyond immediate needs and day-to-day problems as far as Indian spiritualism and religion is concerned. Another very important character in the novel is the "Swamiji". Mrs. Jhabvala for the first time comments on Indian Gurus and Swamis, what type of life they lead, how many people go to them when they are depressed, while others become their blind followers and live with them day and night. Through the Swamiji in the novel we are also able to see Mrs.Jhabvala's own knowledge about Hindu religion and spiritualism. All these characters seem to be mere puppets in the hands of Mrs. Jhabvala and she does not mind using them whenever and whereever she thinks fit to construct the plot of the main story, which revolves round the young man, Prem and his problem of low salary and high rent.

The very first line of the novel projects Prem as a very shy youngman who has recently been married and does not know his wife well enough to be able to buy a bag of nuts and raisins for her, as he has no idea of how she will react to this gift and ultimately he buys only for himself and eats it hurriedly before he reaches his apartment. Indu's pregnancy come to Prem as a great embarrassment and with a feeling of guilty he thinks

> "Now everybody would know.....what he did with her at night in the dark" (p. 8)

Not only the guilt but the prospective child instead of giving him any sense of pleasure is considered to be an added burden and a constant source of worry. He is worried about this new expense and this makes him con-stantly think about his low salary and high rent.

The main idea behind this entire description is perhaps not to ridicule the Indian youth but to bring out his utter helplessness. Mrs. Jhabvala makes it clear to the readers that in low-class Indian society marriage and child are considered to be a burden rather than as a pleasure. A householder, instead of enjoying the companionship of his wife finds her an added expense and Mrs. Jhabvala even advances reasons for this. The first and the foremost soon as he got his degree and before being able to earn enough to support himself and his wife. It was only four months ago that Prem got the job at Khanna Private College and his wife was already pregnant Mrs. Jhabvala uses Sohan Lal another teacher in the same college, to point out the evils of an early marriage Sohan Lal comments.

> Here in our India.......... It is so that while we are still children and know nothing of what we want they take us as tie us with a wife and children" (p. 97)

The early marriage system has thus been condemned by Jhabvala and once again this criticism comes from an Indian character. The other reason that Jhabvala hints for the prevailing discontent in married life in Indian society is the arranged marriage system. The marriage is arranged by the parents of the girl and the boy and at the most that the parents do is to allow them to see each other, and naturally the young couple takes time to like and to develop some kind of feelings for each other. Jhabvala has been intrigued by this custom of India from the very beginning. In ***The Householder*** Prem marries a girl, chosen by his parents and it is for this reason that at the start of the novel Prem finds it difficult to appreciate his wife and remembers his mother and the delicious meals she served him as compared to Indu's tasteless meals.

Prem fails not only as husband but also as a teacher in his college. He finds himself unable to maintain discipline in class. His inefficiency has been effectively highlighted by comparing him to the pompous Mr. Chadda, another teacher in the same college, who unfortunately shared the same classroom. Prem also finds it difficult to get over his diffidence that fails him to raise his voice against the injustice met out to him. Some how he gathers courage to go to the principal to ask for a rise in his own salary, but as soon as he enters his drawing room, he feels so nervous that instead of asking for a rise in his salary, starts pleading for his colleague Sohan Lal. This makes the situation more intriguing as Mrs. Khanna, who at that time was having an English breakfast, goes on giving comments on the importance of having a wholesome breakfast, Prem in his turn continues to plead for Mr. Sohan Lal's case and says, "It is very difficult for him to manage on his present salary. How can he support so many pecple on rupees seventy-five per month?" (p. 10)

While pleading for Mr.Sohan Lal's case he becomes so passionate and senti-mental that he even goes to the extent of quoting lines from the ***Panchantantra*** and for the first time a glimpse of courage is noticed in Prem. "Poverty" and "want" appear to have haunted Mrs. Jhabvala's own thoughts throughout her stay in India. She just could never reconcile with enormous giants of poverty and here Prem seems to be a mere mouthpiece of what Mrs. Jhabvala wanted to tell the world. Hence it is not only Prem's problem, but of the entire lower-middle class Indian society and particular to the youth.They constantly struggle to conquer this enormous curse of want which mars their lives. Marriage, baby and everything else comes to them as an extra burden. Prem is no exception to this. His basic problem is also poverty and want, and it is this curse which reduces him to the state of cowardice, and it is this which makes him an utter failure as husband, teacher and father.

Get Ready for Battle is the fifth novel written by Mrs. Jhabvala. It was published in the year 1962, i.e. almost after eight years of her stay in India. Mrs. Jhabvala after analysing the problem of lower-middle class householder, now leaves this problem and turns her attention to two other sections of Indian society, the rich and the poor. The conflict between these two sections has been brought out by her in a remarkable way. Not only the conflict but ultimate reconciliation has also been projected quite realistically. Mrs. Jhabvala also talks about the Indian social workers who act as a link between these two sections.

She has indirectly satirised them because ultimately they prove to be total failure as the rich businessman are able to buy social workers as well as they suffer themselves. Get *Ready for Battle* is more like her first two novels- ***To Whom She Will*** and ***The Nature of Passion,*** these two novels were written about the Punjabi refugee in and around Delhi, with no foreign character and no East-West counter and without any irony or bitterness. Her fifth novel ***Get Ready for Battle*** once again takes us by sur-prise when we see Mrs. Jhabvala in a light but gloomy mood. In this connec-tion Anna Ruther Ford observes:

> "Her first novels are peopled completely by Indians and are written from an Indian point of view. This euphoria lasted for a decades, then the poverty, hunger and the appalling conditions of which she had at first been obvious suddenly became visible. It was perhaps with this awareness that she wrote ***Get Ready for Battle***, her one novel that deals with India's social problems."[13]

For the first and the last time she writes about the poor sections of Indian society. She describes their colonies and the treatment they receive from the rich class. The novel ***Get Ready for Battle*** is an exception not only because (in this) it is new but she has written directly about the poor in many other ways also. The entire novel is a story of one family the family of a rich business man Gulzari Lal, whose obsession is to earn money, expand his business and give as much material comforts, as possible to his family. There are no foreign characters and no clashes between the old and the new generations. It shows Mrs. Jhabvala's awareness of the materialisation civilization in and around Delhi, as once again the novel has Delhi as its background.

Besides this major problem Mrs. Jhabvala has also for the first time taken up a few social problems in this novel. After describing the arranged marriage custom of Indian society in great detail in her first two novels, she takes up the problem of divorce remarrying and mistress in Indian society. Along with these problems, she also describes ironically the clash between the rich businessman and the social workers in India. As usual she uses characters to project the various problems of this unknown society. Gulzari Lal's wife Sarla Devi doesn't live with him as their spiritual values are dissimilar. He lives with his son Vishnu, his wife Mala and their daughter Preeti. Gulzari Lal has a mistress Kusum or Mrs. Mehara, widow of a retired army officer. Besides these characters, there are a few others, Brij Mohan, Sarla Devi's brother with whom she lives, Gautum a young ambitious lower-middle class person full of plans, his cousin Sankar and Sumi, Mrs. Sankar's youngest sister.

Get Ready for Battle is a quotation taken from the second chapter of the ***Bhagwad Gita.*** Lord Krishna, while explaining the yoga of knowledge calls upon Arjun to give up all fears and "treating alike pleasure and pain gain and loss, victory and defeat, get ready for battle." "Here lord Krishna tells Arjun that Kshtriya's duty is to fight against all evils; in Jhabvala's novel it is Sarla Devi, who sets herself against every form of evil, social injustice and oppression of the poor. However, the way Mrs. Jhabvala has inducted this quotation into the novel is not very effective. The story has been built around a poor locality, Bundi Basti, situated near Delhi. Gulzari Lal the big businessman wants to buy it and make money out of it. His wife Sarala Devi, who lives away from him is a social worker having entirely different views. She wants to help the poor who lives there. Throughout the novel we find her fighting for the rights of these people. Vishnu Gulzari Lal's son appears to be quite indifferent initially but being a businessman's son ultimately sides his father.

Although Mrs. Jhabvala focuses her attention mainly on the clash between the rich and poor, she had also taken up a few social problems of the middle and the rich classes of Indian society–the problem of divorce and the position of a mistress in modern Indian society. Kusum tries her best to persuade Mr. Gulzari Lal to get a legal divorce from his wife so that her position would not be that of a mistress and to achieve her goal. She adopts many tactics. She stops going to Gulzari Lal's house knowing fully well that in these eight years she has become indispensable for that household.Gulzari Lal not able to carry on without her, is forced to face the society and revises his views, the change in Gulzari Lal's attitude perhaps suggests the changing attitude of modern Indian society. The question that is left unanswered specially for a person who is not familiar with Indian society, is whether this change is accepted and practised only among the rich section of Indian society, those who can suppress the critics by the help of their money or by all section of Indian society. These new ideas, laws are only confined to a particular section, of Indian society. Mrs. Jhabvala is aware of the, fact and makes it clear through Sarla Devi who tells her husband Gulzari Lal'

> "I know what you mean when you speak of society — you mean the people like yourself, who have house and cars and go to club, for you, only these peoples or society, only they are human." (p. 50)

Kusum, an opportunist, tries to make the best of every situation, so that she can achieve her ultimate goal of becoming Mrs. Gulzari LaL. She encourages Brij Mohan and goes out of her way to be nice with him, as she knows that he is against the divorce, which is quite natural, he did not want his sister to lose all her rights in Gulzarilal's property and break the link with that family forever. But Kusum who succeeded in changing Gulzari Lal, does not find it difficult to change Brij Mohan's views. She uses all her tactics and goes to the extent of telling him that she is married, it will be once again like good old days. Ultimately Brij Mohan gives in and Kusum is now happy and ready to marry Gulzari Lal. Sarala Devi is so busy with the Bundi Basti problems that when Gulzarilal informs her that he is going in for a legal divorce, she replies. "I am ready to write anything you want" (p. 52)

It is indeed praiseworthy that Mrs. Jhabvala has tackled the problem of divorce in modern Indian society. She has been able to project the old traditional views as well as the changing attitude of those Indians who are literate, rich and want to be modern. We also have in this novel Vishnu, Gulzarilal's son and his wife Mala. Vishnu in this novel is a typical portrait of a rich man's son in India, who is economically dependent on his father. He lives with him in a same house, work in the same office and has been provided with all the comforts he can long for. Although his father tried to establish him and wanted him to be fully involved in his business, Vishnu was basically a timid man and depended entirely on his father, unable to do anything on his own, we find him dejected and helpless. Through the portrayal of this character Mrs. Jhabvala seems to confirmed that Indian youth are worthless, no matter what they do. However, at the same time, Mr. Jhabvala sucessfully uses Vishnu and Mala to project the familiar complexities of Indian society. Their fights reconciliations and love-making lend, touches of romance and realism to Jhabvala's novel. Vishnu and Mala have been portrayed as cowards throughout the novel. Besides Vishnu, Mala, Gulzari Lal and their problems Mrs. Jhabvala has also introduced the story of lower-middle class family– Shankar and his wife.

Shankar has been portrayed as a lower level, clerk. Mrs. Jhabvala has thrown enough light on the Indian Government servants and this appears to be another favourite subject with her. Right from her second novel to this one she has described them in different ways. Once again it is the damp rooms and poverty that find expression in her novel and a foreigner after reading her novels would always take Indian Government servants to be corrupt and untrust worthy. In this novel it is the lower-middle class and their daughters. Gautam in this novel seems to be Mrs. Jhabvala's mouth-piece, as towards the end of the novel the news suddenly comes that Sumi's parents have been able to find a boy for her and that soon she would be married. The fate of the lower-middle - class girl in India is that she must be married. As and when she reaches marriageable age, she must be married of to a suitable boy or else she is considered to be a burden and a disgrace. By dealing with such questions, Mrs. Jhabvala once again comes out as a social reformer. She wants to make the people of India aware of this evil, the arranged marriage custom of India. Along with these problems of Indian soci-ety, Mrs. Jhabvala has very successfully mocked at the modern westernised young generation of India. She has tried to show how they pretend to be all knowledgeable and intelligent, but are in fact bereft of these qualities. This group of young, smart and sophisticated youngsters is introduced through Vishnu.

Before marriage he, too belong to this set of people of Delhi. Besides discussing this problems, Mrs. Jhabvala for the first time describes Indian street hawkers in minute details and this associated the novel with a touch of realism. She even goes to the extent of writing the song they sing, to tell their cheap stuff and to make a fool of the innocent people. While describing their ways of life Mrs. Jhabvala uses Irony and satire and makes the entire situation.

Before concluding the study of this novel it will be pertinent to take up the main theme of the novel humorous the clash between the capitalist and the poor people in Indian society and those helpless social workers who sincerely work for the betterment of the downtrodden. Sarala Devi is seen working endlessly in search of her mission on this earth in hope that when her work is done, she will find a place in heaven. This has been beautifully commented upon by Yasmin Gooneratne:

> "The only one among the eight she has published, to centre almost exclusively upon India's extreme poverty and upon the exploitation of the poor and helpless by the corrupt, the wealthy and the hypocritical."[14]

Once again Mrs. Jhabvala is found to be bitter critical and ironical. She seems to have come to the conclusion that nothing in India is within its reach of being curved and changes for better.

A Backward Place occupies an important place among the novel written by Mrs. Jhabvala. The very title of the novel is suggestive of her impression of this country after settling down here for almost eleven years. These eleven years in the country have convinced her that India is one country which can never endear itself to her heart. Another important thing about this novel is that for the first time she is more concerned with the foreigner who happened to be in India. She concentrates on their reactions and different attitudes towards this country and as a result for the first time, she has more foreign characters in this novel. Earlier also Mrs. Jhabvala has portrayed foreign characters but in this novel they appear to dominate the entire story. The Indian characters are few and they remained mostly in back-ground. Another interesting feature which attracts our attention is that all these characters are women characters, and Mrs. Jhabvala has tried to view Indian society differently through each of these characters. Jhabvala found it difficult to adjust herself to this place either mentally or physically. Mentally she could never get over the poverty in this country. It haunted her constantly and made her restless and bitter. Physically, the Indian sun was up there only to ruin the good complexion and natural glow these foreigners had before they came to this country. Perhaps it is because of her weak nerves and oversensitive temperament that she found it very difficult to adjust in this backward land. This is her personal experience, but at the same time she suggests certain ways in which a foreigner can best adjust in this country. She suggests several ways and "The first and the best is to be a strong person who plunges in" (Page 9)

Another approach to India is to "accept it" with no expectation, no hope and no change. The best way would be to follow Gandhiji's principle *i.e.* to keep one's eyes, ears and mouth closed. The question is how many foreigners can do it. How many of them can kill their conscience and not think in the way they have been brought up. And it is the category where Judy, the protagonist of the novel, fits in. She is English, and has come to India after marrying an Indian youth Bal. She was only nineteen when she came to this country, and did not have the problem of adjustment.

She wore a sari, grew her hair long and lived with Bal's relatives without having any problems. Describing Judy, R.S. Sing observes.

> "Judy is far sighted soft-natured and understanding woman. She is mentally ready to compromise with life and help her husband to regain confidence and use his talent."[15]

Besides Judy, there are two more women characters in the novel Etta and Clarissa. Etta, like Judy, married an Indian youth and came to India at a very young age but even after being in this country for over twenty-five years, and marrying three Indian boys one after the other she never could like India, and on many occasions Etta seems to be her mouthpiece. Clarissa, another foreign girl, who came to India on her own, is altogether different. She is strong and one of those types who accept things as they are. She tries to make the best of all the opportunities that come her way, she knows she is not going back and hence she is happy in whatever condition, she finds herself in.

Besides these three main characters Mrs. Jhabvala has put in yet another category of foreigners in this novel. These foreigners who come here for a short time on some specific mission. They have a home to go back to and a job to look forward to. We have the Hochstadts, an old German couple, also living in Delhi. Dr. Hochstadt is a well - known economist and has come to India as a Visiting Professor for a period of two years. The Hochstadts react to this country in an altogether different way. They are mature and realize that to be happy in this country, one must try to be as much Indian as one can be. At the same time, they accept the incompatibility of the East and the West. They maintain their western views, yet they seem to voice surface appreciation of Indian art and philosophy.

The story of the novel seems to have been woven by Mrs. Jhabvala very deftly around these foreign characters. Besides these characters, there are a few Indian characters also, but they appear to be quite insignificant when contrasted with these characters. Bal, Judy's husband has been portrayed by Mrs. Jhabvala as a typical Indian youth. He is a graduate without a job, but full of plans and a dream of becoming a famous actor one day Sudhir another Bengali youth is also a graduate a brilliant student but he has failed miserably in the struggle of life. He failed to get a proper job and unlike Bal, presents a pessimistic picture of life. Sudhir's best friend Jayakar, an old retired man, has once again been used by Mrs. Jhabvala to criticise India. It is through him that the evils of Indian society and Government are brought out. Bal, Sudhir and Jayakar, all belong to the lower-middle - class of Indian society. It is they who are concerned about the poor people of this backward place. Besides these character there is another important character, Gupta, a rich man and owner of a big hotel. He represents the typical business class of Delhi, very rigid and traditional at home, but feels free to do everything once outside the walls of his house. He goes out with Etta and has fun. Through him Mrs. Jhabvala makes fun of the rich men who have money but not taste.

The only important Indian woman character in the novel is Mrs. Kaul, a modern sophisticated, educated, middle - aged lady.She is full of energy and ambition. She seems to be a caricature of western women or she stands for those modern Indian ladies who in their search to become western of modern, imitate western culture, but, ends up becoming neither Indian nor a Westerner. In this connection Connie Hay Ball observes.

> "Out of all her characters, Mrs.Kaul, Seceratry of the 'Cultural Dais' she is snobbish and affected.[16]

All these characters have been used by Mrs. Jhabvala to view this society from different angles. Delhi once again remains the battle-field and at times we wonder if Jhabvala's India is nothing but Delhi. Whatever she has seen and has written, whether it is social, political, religious or cultural, it is all in Delhi.

The story of the novel is simple and revolves round the

lives and familial entanglement of the foreign characters of this novel. The story starts with Bal and Judy. Bal is out of job and goes to the radio station, where he man-ages to get a small programme every now and then, and the rest of the time he spends in coffee houses or with his friends who are also jobless. Bal and Judy live in a crowded section of Delhi, with Bal's elder brother Mukund, his sister Shanti and an old widow, Bhauji. They have two children, Prithvi and Gita. Since Bal does not have a regular source of income, Judy goes out to look for a job.She is working for Mrs. Kaul in her "Cultural Dias", and is some how able to manage on her low salary. The entire situation appears to be quite ironical and the way it has been presented is such that one feels like denouncing Bal. He appears to be an idealist, living in a world of fancy, on the other hand Judy is practical, diligent and struggles as much as she can to maintain her family. Jhabvala is critical of all this and it is through Etta that she gives expression to her feelings. Etta asks Judy why she goes out and works, and what made her come to India to lead this kind of life? Etta's reactions are not normal. It is true that any foreign girl who marries an Indian, leaving her family and country forever, can at least hope to lead a comfortable life here. Etta not only criticises Judy for working but also for totally becoming one with the society-for putting on sarees and growing her hair long. She hates to see Judy living in this way and tells her.

> "You must leave him and get out. You're just rotting here. Look at you in that thing—and your hair too and – your awful. You have let yourself go" (p. 6)

In these words Etta not only denounces Judy but also Indian dress and hair style. It appears Jhabvala herself never developed any liking for sarees.She has criticised it many times indirectly, but here her dislike becomes appar-ent. Putting on sarees, according to Mrs. Jhabvala is the last limit of submission. She feels that to give up one's dress is to lose your identity for ever. Jhabvala has also criticised the way salaries are fixed in this country. After losing her first job, Judy runs from one place to another to find a job, and finally gets it in the Cultural Dias, at a very low salary and it is here that Jhabvala gets an opportunity to describe how salaries are fixed in India. The employer and the employee haggle, both trying to get the best out of the whole deal. Although Mrs. Jhabvala does not seem to be bitter apparently and it is not difficult to read her reactions and her total denouncement of Indian society. The meeting between Mrs. Kaul has thus been described by her. Mrs. Kaul interviewed Judy and "offered her a very small salary which Judy amazed at her own audacity but quite determined not to get less than she and the children and Bhauji could live on, had tried to make a raise. They had bargained — — both of them with the sharp looks on their faces." (p. 16)

After reading this it is very easy to see how bitter and critical Mrs. Jhabvala is of this society. In the Indian society one has to bargain everywhere, whether it is a bazaar or an employment office. An illiterate shop-keeper is no worse than an educated employer. Besides Bal, there is another youngman Sudhir and he is from Calcutta, He also struggled much to get a good job, but was unable to get one and here also Jhabvala points out as to how it is not the qualifications but the recommendations and relations that matter in India. Along with Sudhir we are also introduced to a retired old man and Sudhir's best friend, Jaykar, a revolutionary during the freedom movement. Jhabvala has successfully used him to point out so many blemishes of Indian society. Jayakar is extremely bitter and endlessly criticises the Government that Government for which he had struggled and suffered, Mrs. Jhabvala once again uses an Indian character to criticise the Indian Government. She uses Jaykar not only to criticise the Indian Government, but also to suggest as to what India needs most urgently in the present days. It is true what we have today is only promises but no plans, works but no deeds, and millions of Indians go without bread everyday. Indian poverty is a constant source of oppression to her and she goes on referring to it in novel after novel.

She wants to suggest as to how a starving society can

ever think of any kind of cultural activity, They have first to think of bread and shelter and nothing else ever enters their minds,After reading this one gets the impression that India is nothing but a land of corruption and want. Apart from all these problems Jhabvala makes references to a few other problems of modern India like servants, beggars an'd the other problems of lower- middle — class, society in India, Through this novel she brings out the real picture of India and this seems to be one problem which has found expression in her other novels too.

Jhabvala's ***A New Dominion*** marks a new phase in her career. In it, we confront India with a new perspective. It is no more a back-ward place, but rather a land of promise. The novel does not present the East-West encounter but rather East-West harmony or reconciliation Prof. V.A. Shahane oberves very rightly and says.

> "Jhabvala's A new Dominion endeavours to grapple with a vast and varied, harmonious and discordant noble and profane reality that is India."[17]

Jhabvala has poured all her experiences into the texture of this novel.

She has tried to record the experiences of various types of foreigners, mainly young girls (Lee, Margaret and Evie) who come to this land in'order to seek spiritual comfort and eventually takes shelter in an Ashram. Their experiences in India, which are evocative, inspiring, fulfilling and frustrating are shocking as an eye-opener to an average Indian or a foreigner. Besides these three girls, Jhabvala has also thrown light on the good work done by the missionaries with regard to the upliftment of India. Miss Charlotte, an old missionary and her dedicated work in this country is something to be admired. Besides these characters, there is Raymond, a typical Englishman a tourist. He is on a short visit to India. He came as a tourist and remained so throughout his stay in this country.

We also have a few Indian characters in this novel. Gopi, a young hand-some youth is presented as a typical

Indian. Jhabvala introduces him as a useless, out of job youth who is keen on meeting foreigners and ends up becoming a great friend of Raymond and Lee. It is through the Portrayal of this character that Jhabvala has been able to establish a relation between the East and the West, Rao Shib and his wife Sunita hail from Royal families and represent the sophisticated section of modern Indian society. Rao Shaib's widowed sister Asha is another important character in the novel and is a good example of westernised Indian women in India.Swamiji in the Ashram also emerges as an important character in the novel as he represents the fake Gurus in Indian society. He appears to be repulsive and awkward, and is in no way superior to an animal with all animal instincts. Banubai on the other hand is a pious old lady, whose small world is restricted to the world of God. She lives in Banaras and has a large following of admirers. Bul Bul and Shyam have been introduced as the domestic servants of Asha and Raymond and have been portrayed with a touch of satire and humour.

Mrs. Jhabvala has tried to project her views through the characters of her novel. In this novel, her characters appeared to be more individualistic, though some of them do try to get into this society. The novel can be divided into three parts- part one Delhi, part two in Banaras and part three in the Rajesthani town of Maupur. The main characters move from one place to another, and in doing so display many aspects of their experience, personality and destiny. The entire novel appears to be a collection of various episodes, each episode apparently renders the novel fragmentary, and the reader gets lost in the whirlpool of these episodes, but by the time a reader gets through the novel, he succeeds in getting a graphic view of Jhabvala's New Dominion *i.e.* India. Its social, cultural, spiritual and political aspects have been dealt with by Jhabvala through her various characters, Indian as well as European. These characters not only try to fit in with reality of this vast land but also relate to each other, thereby creating new relationships, which is one of the important ingredients of the novel.

The novel basically portrays the experiences and views of those West-erners like the three girls who come to India in search of spiritual comforts and to seek solution to their personal problems, but what they see and expe-rience do not tally with what they had expected on their way to India. Jhabvala chooses to be a social satirist in this novel and though she is not credited with having words of appreciation for India or the Indians in any of her nov-els, in this work, she seems to have reached the heights of bitterness against India. Writing about ***A New Dominion,*** Haydom Williams remarks:

> "Throughout the novel there is much psychological analysis, often extremely probing and painful, displayed against a backdrop and death betrayals, Hindu's holiness, ritual, custom, passion above all sexual passion, obsession and the frantic search for happiness which more often than not leads to the destruction of weaker persoanlity."[18]

Jhabvala not only denounces Indian characters, but the entire environment and landscape depress her and it also appears to be dull drab and colourless. The first episode of the novel, presents a depressing view of this vast land, and also projects, Jhabvala's own impression about the land. The novel brings out the bitter tone in which it has been written. Everything appears to be dull and drab to her, without any life, anywhere. Jhabvala always found Indian landscape dull and especially the Indian "Sun" depressed her. Even the characters presented in the novel appeared to be different from the other characters belonging to the western world.

Lee, Margaret and Evie, the three foreign girls cannot be compared to anyone of Jhabvala's foreign women characters portrayed in her other novels. Lee comes to India, as Jhabvala writes, " To lose herself in order to find herself" (p. 2) Not only Lee but Margraret and Evie also come to this country as they had become sick of the western way of life, its mechanical society, its materialistic and its commercial dealings. They try to find peace in Indian spiritualism and Swamis. Lee who seems to be most important in the novel comes here, with definite aim. She travels from one place to an-other accepts hospitality from various people, and goes through a variety of experiences. In Delhi she meets Gopi and Raymond, two important characters in the novel. Mrs. Jhabvala has very skilfully brought out the difference between the two, the difference between the East and the West. Raymond is happy to have a Lee as a friend and enjoys talking to her, whereas Gopi is not satisfied with that, he wants more. He knows that it would not be diffi-cult task to force Lee and get some physical pleasure. He takes her to a hotel room and indirectly makes his intentions known to her. Initially Lee refuses, but on second thoughts and in attempt to clear up all misunderstandings and also in her quest to merge herself completely in the society she agrees. Jhabvala's bitterness and irony is evident when she observes that Gopi does not waste any time and lies on top of her. Lee suffers rather than enjoys this experience.

> "But she was glad to be doing this for him, and at the final moment thought to herself that perhaps this was part of the merging she has so ardently desired, while looking out of the window." (p. 42)

The entire episode comes out rather badly. Jhabvala perhaps has tried to bring a union between, physical pleasure and spiritual quest. Lee in her desire to merge herself completely in this unknown society submits to Gopi's desire but to a normal reader, the situation is repulsive and degrading. We find Lee doing this not once but repeatedly to lose herself. Lee meets Margaret in the mission of Miss. Chartolles, another girl in quest of spirituality and peace of mind. She comes to know of a Guru who lives in Benaras, speaks English, and does a lot for his foreign disciples. Lee decides to go their along with Margaret, with the sole desire to find peace and that spiritual glory she has been looking for. In the Ashram they meet another European girl Evie, who has already won the blessing of the Guru and now is a sort of a personal secretary to the Swami.

Swamiji has a magnetic personality and has a remarkable capacity for impressing people and creating the illusion of hope through his eyes and words. He has the power to attract the foreigners and lives among them as God. He is the master of that Ashram. Everyone has to do what he wants them to do. But to the readers he is no more than a spurious godman as he is worldly sensual and sexual. He wants all his disciples not only spiritually but physically, he wants to possess them with their bodies and souls. Lee and Margaret are greatly impressed by Swamiji. Lee writes to Asha Rao Sahib's widowed sister, how Swamiji has influenced Margaret's view of life and the world. She writes that her eyes have been opened and how she has got adjusted in that Ashram. As regards herself, she wants "I can become the new person he wants to make me and I want much to be" (pp. 62-63)

The most astonishing thing is that we find all the three girls ready to submit to all his desires, whether physically or spiritually. In fact, there is a kind of mutual jealously among the girls about their proximity with Swamiji. They try their best to be closed to him and Lee in her desire to become a new person and to be with him walks alone into Swamiji's hut at midnight to get over the feeling that Swamiji has been ignoring her for a long time. Swamiji was waiting for her and without losing any time, takes her to bed stroking her like a cat. One feels aghast to see Swamiji's behaving worse than an animal. Lee's experience with the Swamiji, is worse than what she had with Gopi. Swamiji appears to be a moral humbug having no regard for moral or religious considerations. He readily claims the bodies of all the women he can get hold of.

Lee's total merger does not come in a pleasant way, but Margaret suffers even worse. She came to India with a definite purpose in her mind. She revolted against the convention ridden English society and was tired of its commercialism and hollowness. In desperation she turns to India and its spiritualism. She comes to this New Dominion to quench her thirst for self-fulfilment. Margaret also hopes to get this through Swamiji and does everything, she is asked to do. On one occasion, when the cook of the Ashram runs away, Swamiji discusses this problem with the three girls and ultimately tells Margaret "that by special decree she was appointed cook for the day" (page 100). Margaret, who is not mentally prepared for such a task tells him that she won't be able to do this job, but all protests made by her go in vain and ultimately, she touches Swamiji's feet for the first time and goes away. Perhaps this is her way of total submission. Margaret goes to the kitchen and becomes sick. She feels weak but she does not care for her sickness and all she desires is to be close to him. She feels that under the pretext of illness she is deliberately being kept away from the Guru. Thc doctor is called to her and on examination she is found suffering from infec-tive Hepatitis, but still Margaret and Evie feel that she can be cured in the Ashram and there is no need for her to be taken to hospital. Even Margaret does not appear to be inclined to go to the hospital and is happy to be with Swamiji. She tells Raymond "please don't be worried about me and further adds.

> "Doctor don't know a thing. These diseases that people get in India, they are not physically, they are pure psychic. We only get them because we try to resist India, because we shut ourselves in our little western ego and don't want to give ourselves. But once we learn to yield then they just fall away." (page 146)

In these lines Jhabvala is ironical, bitter and critical of India and of those Europeans who in their quest for spiritualism and a total merger in this world lose their good sense. Margaret goes back to the Ashram only to come after a few months in the last stages of her life, only to die in pathetic condition in the store room of a small hospital in Maupur. The entire situation appears of operation and one cannot help thinking whether this was her way of merging herself completely in this world the new dominion, never to come back again. Evie has her own way merging here. When we get introduced to her, she is already with

Swamiji and almost indispensable for him. She does everything Swamiji wants her to do without any hesitation. Her fascination for Swamiji appears to be beyond understanding and difficult to make out.

Besides these three girls we have another western woman character in the novel, Miss Charlotte 'a missionary' having dedicated more than thirty years of life doing charitable work in India. It is through her that we get to know the other side of Indian society. The condition of old Europeans who continue to live in India even after its independence and also the pathetic condition of poor Indian people. Miss Charlotte's work is selfless and full of dedication. She is neither a seeker nor a lover. She is in India with a definite aim to serve the sick and the needy. That is why when she learns that she will have to do away with her establishment in India and go to England for good, she does not resent it, in fact, she is happy at the prospect of going home. It is not only Charlotte who is anxious to go back, but right from ***Esmond in India,*** we see Jhabvala's western characters longing to go back to their native places. Raymond the only male European character in the novel comes to India as a tourist and remains so throughout his stay in India. He meets Gopi an Indian youth and becomes friendly with him. The only attraction he finds in India is Gopi who is still a student. Raymond remains an outsider and never tries to develop any kind of feeling for India and Indians. In fact, he has no respect for the Swamiji and people like him.

Coming to Indian characters in the novel, Gopi, Rao Sahib his wife Sunita, his widowed sister Asha Banubai and a young energetic Engineer Bob, are instruments in the hands of Jhabvala, who skilfully uses them to present the various sides of this vast Dominion. The most striking thing is that they have all been presented rather badly and appear insignificant and small when compared to the western, characters. They are all crude and full of animals instincts, they are sex-hungry and hypocritical. Towards, the end of the novel, we find Jhabvala summing up the East-West relations in the modern world. The west, hungry for spiritual values is turning to the East. And what the east offer is hypocrisy and crudity in the name of spiritualism. In this novel Jhabvala has tried to sum up her multifarious experiences and views as regards this mystic land.

Heat and Dust, published in 1975 is one of the most talked about novels written by Jhabvala. It is this novel which brought Jhabvala the famous Booker Prize. The most important thing about this novel is that for the first time Jhabvala changes the canvas of her novel. The setting of this novel is not in Delhi, but in a remote town of Satipur. This deviation makes one think that Jhabvala is perhaps fed up with Delhi. She writes about pre-independence India and goes back to 1923, when India was under the British rule. Explaining why Jhabvala felt inclined to recreate the India of 1923, Shahane observes:

> "Jhabvala's attempt to recreate India of the twenties and thirties are marked more by a flair for exotic, the strange the odd elements of life, rather than by the palpable rigid, realities of the situations."[19]

Jhabvala takes delight in presenting the life of a Nawab and British officer living in India in that period. Of course the contemporary India is still in her mind and makes it a point to describe it in its most repulsive aspects. Her hatred and disgust for this country appears at its worst, when she describes Indian beggars disease, food, smell, primitive customs like"Sattee", epidemics, communal riots. and of course poverty. This is well brought out by Meenakshi Mukherjee in the following lines

> "Poverty added an extra dimension of time to her fiction- going back of the past for the confirmation of a pattern that she had traced so far only in terms of contemporary India."[20]

The narrative element of the novel is as significant as it is in ***A New Dominion***. In ***Heat and Dust,*** we find the writer hoping between the India of 1923 and the contemporary

India of 1975, trys to established a link between 1923 and 1975. Jhabvala skillfully presents a situation in which the experience of two generations of Englishmen and women and their Indian counter-parts are brought in a very close association with a view to presenting the differences between them. It becomes more interesting to see the charac-ters moving around the same spot, the same centre and realise that experience. It is also important to note how differently these characters respond to the same situation. The most important character we get introduced to is a young European girl, Olivia, married to an Englishman Douglas the Assistant Collector of Satipur. Besides these there are a couple of old British officers and their families.

Mr. & Mrs. Beth Crawford, Mr. & Mrs. Minnies, Mr. and Mrs. Saunders and Harry an Englishman who lives with the Nawab as his official guest. A longwith European characters we have a few Indian characters representing the lives of Indians of those days. There is the young handsome Nawab of Khatm (a town near Satipur), his mother the Begum and other courtiers. The Nawab in fact, is the only Indian character who has been portrayed in detail. His presence is overwhelming and it would not be out of place if we say that he almost dominates – all the European characters. The story of 1923 in the novel is the story of Olivia and the Nawab.

In 1975, we have more Indian characters— Inder Lal a young clerk, his wife Ritu, his mother and a holy woman introduced as Maji. The European characters consist of the narrator of the story, a young man Chidananda and a young foreigner who came to India in quest of peace and spiritualism. The young narrator assumes importance as it is through her that the entire story is presented. It is she who is a link between the two periods. Mrs. Jhabvala nowhere mentions the name of the narrator but only presents her as the grand-daughter of Douglas and Tessie. Beth Crawford was her aunty, and Tessie. Beth's sister was her grand - mother. After divorcing Olivia Douglas married Tessie. The narrator is somehow in possession of half of the letters which Olivia wrote to one of her friends Marcia. In these letters she has written about herself and the Nawab and her life in India. The narrator becomes interested in Olivia and decides to visit India to unfold the mysteries of Olivia's existence, and the Juicy dismal oddities of her life. She comes to India to discover Olivia's India, her way of life, her friends, her partner, her going on and finally her elopement with the young Nawab. In this attempt the narrator makes a judicious use of Olivia's letters and is able to present India in proper perspective in the thirties.

The title of the novel is both important and suggestive. ***Heat and Dust*** are two things that haunt Jhabvala constantly in this novel. The entire story has been set in the summer months, when the heat is immense, dusty -storm are everyday occurrence and all these cause a mental depression. The readers are tempted to imagine that the heat and the dust - storms, are symbolic of Jhabvala's own state of mind. Jhabvala found it difficult to adjust in India and many times wished to stay away from this suffocating atmosphere, but was unable to do, as her strongest human ties, her Indian husband and children were in India. She was passing through a stormy period disliking everything India – Indian smell, food, landscape, language and people. That is why she wrote this novel in a bitter mood mentioning heat and dust-storms again and again.

The novel opens with the social and familial setting of Olivia's life and these lines are quite suggestive of the title of the novel, Olivia lives in Satipur as the wife of the Assistant Collector, Douglas wakes up early only to return at dusk. She has a bungalow all to herself which is large but dull. She feels bored and lonely in that large house. Describing her condition Jhabvala says,

> "The rest of the time Olivia was alone in her big house with all the doors and windows shut to keep out heat and dust." (p. 5)

Olivia in this novel represents the lives of those English girls who come to India with great expectations, but ultimately find it dull and drab. Olivia, who was young and pretty, loved Douglas immensely, so much so that when the summer is at its height and all the European ladies, Mrs. Crawford and Mrs. Minnies think of going to Simla and want Olivia to be with them. But she refuses to do so and tells Douglas, "She be bored, she would be irrita-ble, she would be hot, she would quarrel with him – all right. But please not to send her away from him." (p. 14)

Though Olivia loved Douglas, she was bored with her life in Satipur. She felt thrilled to receive an invitation for dinner from the Nawab of Khatm. She attended the party and thoroughly enjoyed it, for it came as a pleasant change in her monotonous life, also because the Nawab proved to be an excellent host. She for the first time found a person in the Nawab who admired her the way she was used to. Throughout the party, the Nawab acted as an excellent host, paying equal attention to all his guests, but;

> "His eyes often rested on her and she let him study her, while pretending not to notice. She liked it- as she had liked the way he had looked at her when she had first come in." (p. 21)

This party gave Olivia something to look forward to. She was aware of the fact that the Nawab liked her and would pay a call upon her very soon. The Nawab did come after four days and spent the day with Olivia. This was the beginning of friendship. The Nawab later on sent several invitations to Olivia and Douglas, but Douglas always declined them. Olivia, who was always very anxious to go to the palace and see the Nawab, gets an opportunity of going there with Mr. Crawford, who was a regular visitor to the palace. Yet Jhabvala gets an opportunity to describe the life-style of the ladies in 1925, in the palaces of the Muslim Nawabs, she writes, "These were also elegant, through more is Indian were also elegant, though more is Indian style, with floor level divans, covered in rich textures, and little mirrors in enamelled frames. (page 62)." This was just the beginning, and gradually Olivia's visit to the Palace became more and more frequent.

Harry, Nawab's guest and friend falls sick, and his sickness gives Olivia an excuse to go to the palace almost everyday. She does not even care to inform Douglas about her frequent visits to the palace. While talking about the Nawab and Olivia, Mrs. Jhabvala does not miss the opportunity to focus her attention on the society in the thirties, its evils and many age old conventions. She describes at length the *Sattee- Pratha-burning* of the woman alive with her dead husband. The discussion starts at the party which the Crawford gave after coming back from Simla. While they were away a grain merchant had died and his widow had been forced by his relative to burn herself with him on his funeral pyre. Douglas, who was looking after the affairs rushed to the spot but he was too late to save the woman. He, of course arrested the instigators and tackle the situation with exemplary com-petence, yet he did not look happy when everyone praised him for tackling the situation nicely at the party. During the discussion there is a difference of opinion on this issue. Everyone condemn the incident and describe the custom as most barbaric. But Olivia looks at the situation from a different point of view and points out Douglas that it is a part of Hindu religion and perhaps the best thing for them is not to interfere. Of course, no one sees eye to eye with her on this point, except for Major Minnies, who goes to the extent of relating a few other similar incidence of the past. The most impor-tant thing to bear in mind is that Jhabvala deliberately writes about this incident perhaps to tell that this society is what it used to be many years ago Prof. Shahane has the following to observe;

> "It seems rather strange to me that an incident of sattee could take place as late as 1923, though this is not impossible as an isolated case."[21]

Shahane found a solution to the problem by describing it as an isolated case, but the same type of incident was reported to have occurred on September 4, 1987 in Deorala a remote village in Sikar district at Rajasthan, where a young woman of eighteen Roop Kawnar burnt herself on her husband's funeral pyre. The episode was hailed by the Rajput community as one of the greatest events of the time. This is enough to prove that Indian society, to some extent, till continues to be barbaric and primitive. What Jhabvala wrote in 1975 was bitter and hurt her Indian readers but the allegations she has made are difficult to deny. Not only the *Sattee pratha* but even the communal riots between the Hindus and Muslims have been described by her. The problem which was faced by the Britishers then is being faced by the Indian Government now. Jhabvala has taken up an incident in 1923. It happened on the Husband's Wedding day when the shrine of Baba Firadaus was visited by more Hindus than Muslims. The Nawab was a Muslim, and so were almost half of his subjects. Most of them did not like Hindus visiting the shrine and so they created disturbances which lasted for a long time. This happened in 1923 but even today, after a gap of many years, we are faced with the same communal situations. Through these incidents Jhabvala perhaps wants to show that India is still a backward place and a new dominion is distant dream. Though Jhabvala makes a special effort to touch on these incidents, the main story of 1923 is of course, the one pertaining to Olivia and the Nawab. One day the Nawab invites Olivia for a picnic and drives her to the shrine of Baba Firdaus, where he tells her as to how his family came to have the title of Nawab. In this connection he tells her that it was one of his brave ancestors, Amanullah Khan who was a violent fighter but finally settled for a small state and title because by then he was completely tired. Although Olivia and the young Prince did not believe in the miracles of that shrine, both tie strings to get their wishes fulfilled. Then Nawab narrates many stories associated with the shrine. But what is funny is that while narrating the stories of his ancestors the Nawab shamelessly makes love to Olivia. He leads her away from the Shrine and both lie under a tree. Jhabvala writes-:

> "Not 'here' he said. He led her away from the shrine and they lay together under a tree. Afterwards he

> made joke 'It is secret of Husband's Wedding Day' he said. (p. 141)

His joke took on a reality when after a few days Olivia found that she was pregnant. It is quite ironical to note that Olivia became pregnant near the shrine and years later the narrator who visited the shrine with Inder Lal also became pregnant on the same spot. Inder Lal also told the narrator about the significance of the Husband's Wedding Day. He told her that the shrine was sacred to the childless woman for one day in a year only. Inder Lal went to the extent of relating the whole story. He said that years ago a childless woman was driven out by her husband so that he could marry again. On the day of his second wedding she came to this shrine to hide her shame and cried here. She had a vision that within one month she would bear a child and so it happened and hence the faith in the shrine.

Olivia's pregnancy sets into motion forces which bring about her decline. Douglas is extremely happy to discover her pregnancy and starts creating little castles in the air. While the Nawab, who is sure that it is his child, becomes more and more possessive about Olivia, who is in a dilemma because she knew that the child in her womb was not Douglas's but Nawab's.Olivia finds the situation extremely difficult and decides to go in for an abortion. She approaches the Begum who helps her and Olivia is taken to one of the quacks to bring to an end to her pregnancy. The entire episode smacks of barbarism and here once again the readers, especially foreign readers get a view of primitive India. Incidents like these make us think if it is the same India which boasts of its glorious traditions and culture. The quack was successful in her operation and Olivia get rid of the unwanted child. Olivia never returned to Douglas but went to the Nawab and he in turn sent her to the hills near town and there Olivia spent the remaining portion of her life. This is the story of Olivia and of 1923.

The story concerning the narrator gives us a glimpse of India that she sees in 1975 and it is through her that we get a picture of post-independent India. It is this India, to which Jhabvala seems to be allergic and describes with a tone of bitterness. She sees it in its worse form, and we find her in the last phase of the cycle through which every foreigner passes after coming to India. Jhabvala has reached the point where everything Indian is hateful. She looks upon India as a land of poverty, hunger, disease and dreadful smells, and this is what the narrator learns soon after her arrival in Bombay.She spends a night in the society of Missionaries where another foreigner lady who had been in India for a long time, warned her:

> "You have to be very careful with your food in the beginning boiled water only and whatever you do , no food from the street stalls." (p. 7)

The lady goes on to describe India in its, most ugly form. She tells the narrator about the famines and the smallpox epidemic. This is quite suggestive of Jhabvala's contempt for India at its worst. One gets an idea as to whether any land can be worse than this? What is striking about all this is that this is not the end but just the beginning of such detailed descriptions, like those of a beggar women, of hospitals, of poverty and diseases which Jhabvala has discussed in this novel. The descriptions are enough to give us an idea that India is no way better than the kind of hell we think of. Since the main aim of the narrator is to know as much as she can about Olivia, she reaches Satipur, where Olivia lived in 1923 with her husband Douglas. The narrator lives in a simple way in one of the crowded localities of the town. The way in which she lives amuses and also disappoints, her landlord Inder Lal, a clerk in one of the government offices. The narrator soon gets, adjusted to the new surroundings and decides to visit the Khatm where the Nawab lived. The town was a big disappointment as it was found to be full of dust and noise. Jhabvala once again gets an opportunity to describe the dull landscape and the horrible condition of Indian houses. It is through the narrator and the other character in Satipur that Jhabvala reveals the actual India in 1975.

Besides the narrator, we have a few more foreign characters who come to India in search of spiritualism and peace. Their experiences have also been described with a touch of ironical humour. The narrator meets an English girl alongwith two young men and asks them as to why they have come to India. The girl tells her that she has come to India in search of spiritual comforts. They felt tempted to visit India after listening to a lecture by a Hindu Swami in London. Jhabvala has written in detail about the lecture based on universal love. Mrs. Jhabvala has described in detail how they are cheated, robbed and even the girl molested by a party of Sikh youths. It is a horrifying description of their experiences and the treatment they received in this country. Jhabvala seems to suggest that every foreigner who happens to be here soon gets disillusioned within no time because of the treatment he receives from India. Though the entire description appears to be exaggerated, yet what she has written is basically true. The third foreigner, an ascetic (Chidanand) also came to India with a spiritual purpose. He was attracted by holy scriptures and decided to visit India. He was not disap-pointed initially, as he was able to find a lot of intrest in the temples of South India and spent quite some time there. He become fully one with India and its spiritualism, so much so that when he did develop dysentery and worms, he did not bother about them. Jhabvala describes this with a touch of irony and humour:

> "He too developed dysentary and ringworms but was not bothered by them; because of living on such a higher plane. Similarly he was not bothered by the disappearance of his few possessions from the temple compound where he lives. He found a Guru to give him initiation ......, He was given a new name Chidanand." (Page 27)

It was on the instructions of his Guru that he had set out on a pilgrimage on foot with a begging bowl in his hand, and this is how he happened to be in Satipur. But he could not continue his journey beyond Satipur as he was getting ill after a few days. He lay there with all his belongings. The narrator who had met him outside the travellers' home, felt pity for him and brought him to her room. Chid recovered within a few days, but didn't show any signs of leaving her chamber. The narrator not only provided him shelter and food but she also had to satisfy his hunger for sex; and this finds expression in the following lines:

> "He is always hungry, and not only for food. He also need sex very badly and seems to take it for granted that I will give it for him the same way I give him my food. I have never had such a feeling of being used." (Page 67)

We cannot understand why the narrator allows Chid to use her in this way. By way of explanation, she says she is physically much stronger as compared to Child and can easily put him off, but she does not do it, because she finds that it is due to some emanation, which comes not from within him, but some powers outside himself. Jhabvala seems to present altogether a new aspect of this land of heat and dust. The narrator is unable to explain her sexual experience with Chid, but later on she has physical contact with Inder Lal the clerk, who is also her landlord. They both visit the shrine of Baba Firdaus, and while she takes out sandwiches, Inder Lal takes out two strings to be tied in the shrine to get their wishes fulfilled and this reminds us of Olivia and the Nawab.After tying their string they are there alone and together. Their desire for communication become stronger and more inti-mate. The entire episode is a recurrence of the Nawab's attitude and actions. In fact, Inder Lal makes the same Joke the Nawab had made earlier, about what had happend there on the original Husband's Wedding Day to make barren wife pregnant and the thought that strikes our mind is: Why did Jhabvala repeat this incident? Is it to show to the world that India is the same and the people also remain the same?

Chid lives with the narrator and spends a lot of time with her, but ulti-mately he accompanies a lot of time with her, but ultimately he accompay Inder Lal's mother and his wife Ritu on a Pilgramage. Chid writes a number of letters to the narrator and it is here that the Jhabvala takes an opportunity of bringing forth the differences between the east and the west. Sometimes, we feel tempted to identify the narrator with Jhabvala herself. Chid is found to be utterly different from what he had been before and after his return from his pilgrimage and become bedridden the narrator takes him to the hospitals and informs his relatives in London and asked them to arrange for a ticket and he leaves the land of heat and dust forever. Besides Chid and the narrator, there is Harry who in 1923 was the Nawab's guest and spent many years with him in his palace. Though many years have passed since he came to India from England, many times he expressed his desire to go back to his native land. Ultimately, the Nawab had to send him back to his mother. Even after spending many years in India, Harry appears to have a very bad and sickening impression about India. Both Inder Lal's mother and wife Ritu have been portrayed as simple, traditional Indian women. As the entire novel has been written in the summer months, the months of heat and dust in India, Mrs. Jhabvala goes on to describe how Indians sleep out - doors during these months. The reader often wonders at the keen observation and knowl-edge of Jhabvala that she could acquire about Indian society. She describes everything in minute details and with exactness. Jhabvala seems to have been greatly oppressed by the time, she has written this novel and this makes, her to portray Indian poverty in its worst form. Mrs. Jhabvala is not satisfied with mere references to these poor people and long list of sufferings and misfortunes. The entire description of beggar though true is horrible and repulsive. The narrator in utter helplessness writes "Now a new thought new word presented itself to me, and it was this that old woman was dispen-sable" (page 117). Once again these lines reminds us of Jhabvala's own changed attitude to this country, from the beggar woman's story we are taken to the Indian hospital which are equally in bad shape. The narrator seems to revive the life of Olivia, just like Olivia she also became pregnant at the shrine. The stories of both Olivia and the narrator revolve around Baba Firadaus, shrine, pregnancy and motherhood. Olivia and the narrator both react differently. While Olivia gets rid of her pregnancy in morbid manner, the narrator faces it boldly. This certainly is a beautiful analysis of the past and the present as projected in the novel.

Heat and Dust is the last novel written by Jhabvala in India. It can be taken to be a sort of a declaration of her dislike and bitterness. She seems to have underlined the fact that India with all its good and bad points, is no place for Europeans. Nodoubt it is a beautiful novel but not as effective as ***A New Dominion.*** The novel marks an end to one phase of Mrs. Jhabvala's life as after this she left India for good and settled in U.S.A. She has publish one novel ***In Search of Love and Beauty*** after going there. It is our hope that after the oppressing heat and dust Jhabvala must have found an experience of love and beauty in the west. The novel can be taken to be a window through which the reader can see the changing image of Indian society as seen by Jhabvala. It is through her novel that Jhabvala presents the clash between tradition and modernisation. In presenting this, ***Heat and Dust*** seems to be no exception to the rule.

REFERENCES

1. Ruth Prawer Jhabvala's *To Whom She Will* p. 12.
2. H.M. Williams, *English Writing in free India,* p. 9.
3. Glasgow Herold review
4. *The Nature of Passion* Epigraph
5. Ruth Prawer Jhabvala, *The Nature of Passion* (London: George Allen and Unwin Ltd. 1956), p. 9.
6. V.A.Shahane, "An Artist's Experience of India" Jhabvala. Fiction in R.K. Dhawan, *Common Wealth Fiction* (New Delhi: Classical Publishing Company, 1971) p. 234.
7. Meena Shirwadkar, *Image of Women in Indo-Anglian Novels* (New Delhi: Sterling Printers, 1979), p. 42.

8. *Ibid'*.
9. R.S.Singh "Ironic vision of a Social Realsit " in *Indian Novels in English* (New Delhi: Gulab.

   Vazirani for Arnold Heinman Publisher India Pvt. Ltd. 1971), p. 154.
10. Ramlal Agrawal "An Interview with Ruth Prawer Jhabvala" *Quest* Vol. 91 Sept-Oct. 1974.
11. Ruth Parwer Jhabvala, Esmond in India (London: Geroge Allen and Unwin Ltd. 1958) p. 49.
12. *Ibid.*, p. 51.
13. Anna Rutherford "Ruth Prawer Jhabvala's Window In India" ACLALS bulletin 1975 —.LMysore Kurvilla) p. 27.
14. Yashmane Goonaratue "silence, Exile and canning". The Fiction of Ruth Prawer Jhabvala (London: Sangam Book Ltd., 1983.) p. 6.
15. R.S.Singh "Ironic Vision of Social Realist" *Indian Novels in English* (Arnold Heinmann Pvt. Ltd. 1971), p. 152.
16. Connic Hayball "Ruth Prawer Jhabvala India" *The Journal of India Writing in English* Vol. 9 July 1981, p. 44.
17. Prof. V.A. Shahane, *Ruth Prawer Jhabvala* (New Delhi: Arnold Heinmann India Pvt.Ltd, 1976), p. 113.
18. HYdn M.Wiliiams "Mad Seekers Doomed Lovers and Cemetries in India: Common Wealth *tl* Fiction" (New Delhi, Classical Publishing Company 1988) p. 256.
19. V.A. Shahane, "Jhabvala's *Heat And Dust"* A Cross Cultural Encounter" in Aspect of Indian writing, Macmillan Company of India Ltd. 1979), p. 225.
20. Meenakshi Mukherjee, "Journey's End for Jhabvala" in R.K. Dhawan's *Exploration in Modern Indo English Fiction* (New Dclhi) Bahri Publication Pvt. Ltd. 1982, p. 208.
21. V.A. Shahane, *Ruth PrawerJhabvala* (Arnold Heinmann Publishers Pvt.Ltd.), p. 133.

5

Irony, Satire and Humour

The structural pattern which Jhabvala employs resembles the form of 'New Comedy' which, in the words of Northrop Frye, tries to bring about a reconciliation between the individual and social themes. Discussing the various aspects of this new comedy Frye writes:

> "In all good new comedy there is social as well as individual theme which must be sought in the general atmosphere of reconciliation that makes the final marriage possible."[1]

Jhabvala's merit as a creative writer lies in her being intensely aware of her limitations. She writes about the only social segment of urban India that she knows at first hand. The general belief that she writes about only the sophisticated upper-class is rather an unfair exaggeration because her writings portray the lower middle class with sympathy and understanding. Her urban Indian is not urbane, in fact, it may even be described as a backward place. It is of course, involved in change, and therefore, her basic literary endeavour is to portray the human side of this society caught in the conflict of a change from tradition to modernity. Her art of fiction pursues the path of the comic and evolves the form of a social comedy, depicts men and women in society, that the setting of comedy is primarily urban, and that the comic writer presents a social and cultural outlook, with a view to determine man's behaviour against the established norms. Man's conduct is to be judged against a norm, rather than an ideal, and this norm often corresponds to a sense of proportion on a value. All writers of comedy present a point of view in which this norm is implied and for measuring eccentricity, abnormality, we must have a moral vision in view.

Jhabvala excels in presenting incongruities of human character and situations. These incongruities have social, familial and cultural implications and consequently they become the source of the comic. Jhabvala dramatizes the clashes between two families or two individuals in the context of the present day changes in urbanised India. The tension in Indian societies today such as those between the young and the old, the upholders of orthodox tradition and the rebels against that tradition characterize the social world of Jhabvala's fiction. These situations are individual in the deepest sense as well as representative of social change and almost archetypal in the universality of their consciousness. The experience of such individuals caught up in the whirlpool of social change is essentially Indian as much as it is universal in a large sense. Jhabvala is much preoccupied with portraying the predicament of individuals in their relationship to the family, to the social group, in a way which demonstrates her Indianness. Jhabvala reveals the pains and predicaments of her characters in a very effective manner, but while doing so she doesn't fail to make light of the situation by injecting into her fictional world doses of humour and irony. It is this way of writing which makes a direct appeal to the reader and the reader is left with no choice but to get involved in the world of Jhabvala and enjoy every moment of the life presented by Jhabvala. Her attitude to India and the world of her fiction grow more and more critical with the passage of time. As a result of this, she grows ironic, even bitter. Empathy is replaced by antipathy. Jhabvala is sincere in resisting false labels, and desire to avoid the mere appearances such as a Sari which will make her look like an Indian. She is also tempted to be 'Defiant and European', but in the end she visualizes the Sibilities of herself merging with the Indian earth. This transparent sincerity of Jhabvala in revealing her responses to the phenomenon that is India indirectly slows the process of her creativity. She may perhaps be considered a European writer on India, yet her creative work provides ample evidence of her closeness to India. In this connection, E.M. Forster observes "The oceans to be crossed, the distant brought near, the lands to be welded together."[2]

At first sight India might appeared to be an unlikely locale for comedy. The terrors of nature, over population, starvation, communal strife, death from chronic diseases all haunt fact and fiction in Indian history. The older traditional literature is heroic, mythological, poetic, philosophical, mystical, theological: the Vedas, the Upanishads, the Puranas and the Epics. Of these only the epics and the Puranas allow scope for wit and humour, the two components of comedy. Yet comedy in the highest meaning of the word, tolerant and balanced. Though comedy is critical but it is sympathetic representation of human being in their struggle to understand and accept the society of their fellows. Comedy is to be found abundantly in the prose fiction of Indian writers using English as their medium, in the last half century. Indeed, much of the finest achievement of this Indo-Anglian group of writers have been in the comic rather than the tragic mode.

Comedy is very difficult to define and only in the history of drama has it been allowed to take any specific shape. It can be divided into comedy of humour, manners and ideas. A critic has seen comedy as "A literary mode of thought."[3] It can be found in a variety of form and is as such, at home in the novel, the short story and the essay as in the drama. Later in the some place, this writer develops, the Coleridgean distinction between the desire to find ourselves, tragedy and desire to lose ourselves (comedy) man's natural pride finds its expression in tragedy where the hero is tested to the utmost. Man's modesty finds its expression in comedy, where the hero is thought painfully and with difficulty to submerge his difference and becomes a member of a social group and the family and the community.

The comic vision can be seen in general and on the whole acceptable but farce cannot be acceptable. Farce concentrates on exhibiting and correcting abnormalities on which are largely accidental. Hence the pre-occupation of farce with mistakes, domestic mishaps or idiotic accidents involve denudation. Whereas comedy in contrast is concerned with those abnormalities of characters and ideas which isolate the hero until he is forced or shed them and enjoy, as it were.

We can see how India lends itself to comedy as well as to both farce and satire. The comic writer finds his material as a well established rules of behaviour and also eccentrics and rebels inclined to pit themselves against the tradition and these are found in plenty in modern India. There is the further benefit to both comic writer and satirist alike of rapid modernization of a once highly coherent culture in modern India. These conditions are ideally found in India, Pakistan, Ceylon and Burma, rather than in Europe or America. On this point it is interesting to see that some of the best European comedies of the last seventy years have drawn material from relatively old-fashioned so-called backward society while in America the "ghetto" culture of immigrant Jews has produced some of the best comic writing of Leo Rosten and Bernard Malamud.

This kind of comedy is to be found in the novel of Ruth Prawer Jhabvala. She sets out to show India as it is and in many of her novels presents a picture which is instantly recognizable to both new and seasoned residence of the sub-continent— the Delhi scene is particularly well drawn. Yet her characters and plots when analysed suggest a view of India that is far from flattering. In some ways her comedy seems sterner and moves closer to satire. Sarla Devi, the ugly old heroine of ***Get Ready for Battle,*** is shown battling for the doomed refugees against her own husband's greed. She is so intent on helping strangers that she neglects her own son who is becoming a pocket version of his money grabbing father.

Jhabvala's comic touch is at its best in one of her best novels ***The Householder.*** The hero Prem, a young college lecturer, newly married is too immature to succeed as a husband or as a teacher. He longs for his care free bachelor days and is still emotionally attached to his mother. He is too timid to ask his employer for a raise in his salary and his landlord to lower his rent. Instead of trying to be a good "householder", the term has special significance for an orthodox Hindu as it is considered to be the second stage of life, in view of his wife's pregnancy and his lack of money he prefers to hang about with a German couple he has met who are in love with 'Spiritual' Indian. He feels flattered by their friendship and encouraged by their uncritical enthusiasm to turn for guidance to a popular new Swami. Jhabvala suggests ironically that Prem's liking for the spiritual life is only an attempt to compensate for his wordily failures.

It might be presumed that Jhabvala regards Indian religious experience with some scepticism if not with downright mockery. Jhabvala is fond of exposing the pretensions of the 'do-gooder' and those who expound political and religious rhetoric amids poverty, squalor and corruption. But it is only her simple and often religious character who achieve any degree of happiness as her Sarla Devi in ***Get Ready for Battle*** does in spite of cruel set back. Jhabvala is a prolific writer and has come to dominate the fiction written in English in India and about India in the last forty years. Kushawant Singh writes of Jhabvala having "Much in common with other writers dealing with irony and satire in India."[4] Jhabvala writes about one part of India which she knows by first hand experience-Delhi. She tends to write about. day-to-day problems of living, avoiding more obvious sensational, melodramatic or heroic subject in a comic spirit but avoids political controversy. She writes with a conventional novel structure. The background and history is sufficiently distinctive to invite comment at the outset there is considerable evidence in her novel, of the 'outsider' approach to India. But by comparison she seems to be limited in scope and vision. She writes about professional people expatriates like herself or about the elite businessmen who would regard themselves as superior to others. Her first novel ***To Whom She Will*** shows a girl in love with, but whose parents arrange a marriage to more suitable to their class and way of life. Jhabvala's main feature is her exclusion of her fantasy poetry and exaggerated comedy. She seems cool, detached and often sardonic.

Jhabvala presents foolishness of young generation of this country. Amrita and Hari in ***To Whom She Will*** fall in love and then out of love with equal ease .The system of arranged marriage doesn't seem to be so tyrannous. Romantic love is ephemeral and comic. Arranged marriage works out just as well or just as badly as one that depends on falling in love. It amuses Jhabvala to manipulate her plots to suggest this. She seems to say that romance doesn't and cannot bring lasting happiness. Her interest in the nature of the Indian joint family reflects perhaps her European origin. In Europe the family is nowadays often a small unit and it is not common for three generations to be housed together as they often were forty years ago. Jhabvala with her own personal history and exile and expatriation comes with great curiosity. Such an immensely secure and complex institution and yet within which such tension and rebellions can occur.

Jhabvala's first novel ***To Whom She Will*** reflects the spirit of comedy. While its individual theme is stated primary to the personal conflicts of Amrita and Hari, the social theme is explored through the complications which parents, as the responsible members or social institutions, induct into the marriage. The 'reconciliation that makes the final marrying possible' is quite ironically brought out when Amrita who, in the beginning loves Hari gets reconciled to the notion of marrying Krishna Sen Gupta. What makes Jhabvala's art particularly significant in this context is her conscious and deliberate use of the comic. There is an element of ambivalence in it, for it brings out the comic and sad nature of human experience since the comic mode basically affirms the disparity between the ideal and actual norms.

Jhabvala's comic point of view therefore deliberately presents this complexity, coming out of the contradiction in both character and situation. For instance, Hari is married to Sushila and on the eve of their marriage they are placed side by side to blink foolishly into the flashlight.

This reconciliation of Amrita with Krishna and of Hari with Sushila is rather ironically presented in the spirit of comedy. This integration on individual and social levels has a moral connotation. The moral norm has a positive as well as a negative aspects. It presupposes a moral code taking us back to the tradition of the joint Hindu family, to sense of authority of parents, to the wisdom of the elders guiding the inexperience young. At the same time the moral norms also indicate freedom from unfair moral restraints and purely conventional constraints.

Amrita under the influence of her mother and grandfather Pt. Ram Bahadur relents from her attachment to Hari Sahni, whom she first met at the Radio Station. Amrita is a Bengali girl working as an announcer in All India Radio where Hari too is an assistant. Their love like a radio play has too many sound effects. In the early stage Amrita tells Hari of her grandfather's opposition to their intention of getting married. Jhabvala sets the comic mode of the scene which for its exposure of adolescent sentimentality is remarkably effective. Hari says to her, "I am unworthy-you are goddess and I am unworthy of you:", Amrita pleads that she, like Pope's Belinda is no Goddess but Hari is assertive., "A Goddess" he insisted. You are Goddess I worship you." (Page 30)

Jhabvala is good at exploring comic element in sentimental love scenes and also in exposing the hollowness of pseudo-romantic epithets. Hari idealizes Amrita, calls her a Goddess and the irony in this exchange is a double-edged blade. It is as much directed against Amrita as against Hari. Moreover, a whole Indian pseudo-romantic poetical tradition is parodied in this light hearted encounter.

The cavalier mode of Hari's love-making is further

accelerated by his visit along with Vaidya to 'The Cavalier'. Amrita at first refuses but later consents to joining the two at *The Cavalier*. Vaidya's comments on Amrita. "She is what is known as a lady in our society..... That is to say she has been brought up to a sheltered and idle existence and taught never to think for herself" (page 56) are a half comic, a half ironic commentary on her personality. This implies that spiritually Amrita "Is still in pardah" an ironic reflection which is not merely directed against the Bengali teenager but against Vaidya himself. Vaidya becomes an object of Jhabvala's ridicule. Both Hari and Vaidya stare at the fashionable girls taste iced coffee through straws and comment on the appearances of women—the usual stances of the happy-go-lucky young men in India. The experience revolving round *The Cavalier* is symbolic of the Hari triangle in the narrative as well as the emotional instances and social values which emerge from it. The free easy and gay manner of adolescent love making is symbolised by the lovers' association with *The Cavalier*, which is again socially a symbol of an open society.

The social comedy of Jhabvala's fiction is quite often shown as emerging from human attitude of this free and open society. The freer the society the greater the variety of the individuality of the character, the men and women who constitute that society. Amrita and Hari both represents the female and male agents of this free society. Krishna Sen Gupta the paying guest in Amrita's house is a freak product of this free society. Jhabvala's men and women are involved in a search of self-identity in this open society. In this search they sometimes half find themselves and discover to a degree their associates and relations.

The principle of open society is implicit in Jhabvala's comic vision. The young men and women in ***To Whom She Will*** are caught up in crucial phase of social change from a convention-ridden and tradition-bound society to an open free society, free from the shackles of social customs and traditions. This is what is usually called a change from tradition to modernity. However, modernity is not always very 'mod' and is often restricted by forces of conventions thereby giving scope to the development of comedy. The adolescent love-making is in the style of most pseudo-romantic lovers who only care for one ruling passion, however momentary it may be. Amrita asserts her love for Hari in the studio, which has a dramatic quality. Her grand father is very keen to send her to England but she is against going there and prefers to stay with Hari. Hari says to her

However, this love-making scene ends in a note of frustration which is partly comic and partly pathetic. Hari and Amrita are alone in the big studio and she wishes to talk with him about their future plans. However, Vaidya comes in like a bolt from the blue and proposes a visit to a movie. Amrita refuses to go with him and says to Vaidya that he should go away. She leaves the studio and Hari follows her. She speaks to Hari in a similar tone asking him to go away. The disappointment and irony become evident in her tone and have a direct effect on him.

Hari is so uncertain of himself, and although he is conscious of Amrita's feelings for him, his response to her has never crossed the boundaries of superficial adolescent enthusiasm. His failure is essentially is one of individualising his experience, his passions, his feelings in a single, stable chord. His responses are utterly sensuous, sometimes ever sensual. The conversation between Krishna and Hari at the Bombay Coffee House, the resort of disillusioned men, about Amrita and Hari's real intentions expose the Cavalier quality of the young man's responses. Krishna comes to the restaurant as Amrita's messenger and representative, and wants to know Hari's real intentions. It is he who announces that Amrita is likely to go abroad. At this juncture Hari feels uncomfortable and begins to talk in a round about manner. The comic note and the ironic tone in Jhabvala's portrayal of scenes is unmistakable articulated in situations of this kind.

> "Love is not a game, Hari protested some what feebly. At the moment he could not help wishing that it were." (page 117)

This view of love as a game is implicit in the Hari-Amrita relationship. Its development in scenes and situations, characters and caricatures is both comic and ironic. Hari cannot help wishing that it were a game and this wishful thinking is marked by a double-edged irony. It is of course and irony directed against the human world, the society, the family which impels young men to play the game. Amrita's character and personality is viewed by other characters in the novel from various angles. Amrita again and again declares her passionate love for Hari who, quite in a funny way, admires her as Goddess in human form. She seems to him a modern Belinda who perspires and gives sufficient proof of being human, a real woman. Pt. Ram Bahadur Amrita's grand father, though not quite opposed to the idea of her marrying outside the immediate community, is against the match with Hari on grounds which are essentially social and cultural. He honestly feels that Hari, as a match for Amrita is a misfit in mind and soul. He is also found to be intellectually unsound and academically poor. However, Pt. Ram Bahadur's observations based on worldly wisdom and earthly experience are curiously undermined by the shrewd cynicism of Vazir Dayal. His words and the 'word of God' are quite ironic and expose the emptiness of the authoritarian approach to the problem of marriages of the young. Vazir Dayal is not always cynical since it is he who decides to offer money to both Amrita and Hari to go to England and be united in marriage. However, the money offered never arrives. Vazir plays a game of chess, an exact counterpart of the game of life itself. He offers to support the apparent non-conformism of Hari and Amrita, but the young do not prove to be genuine non-conformist at all. This incongruity in these motives of the young, seen in their attempt at rebellion against tradition and their readiness to surrender to the dictates of that tradition constitutes Jhabvala's comic and ironic mode.

However, tradition as a value of orthodoxy of the incompatibility of the old world with the new, is exemplified in situations which are serious as well as morally uncompromising. For example, the idea of arranging a family meet to enable the prospective bridegroom to see the prospective bride is a fairly new social development in Indian families. This in fact is an important step in the process of arranged marriages. Hari goes to the house of the Anand and is almost carried away by the charm of Sushila Anand. Her grandmother, a thin, harsh, uncompromising old woman does not approve of the trend of showing the girl to the boy with a view to settling marriages.

> "Sin, the old woman, audibly muttered to expose the girl to the eyes of the man she is to marry, that is a sin." (page 148)

This is a highly conservative and conventional approach to the problem of marriages as a social institution in India. In the past bridegrooms were able to see their counterparts only after the wedding ceremonies there by preserving the myth of purity and chastity of womanhood. This outdated attitude is represented by the Anand's grandmother, which many modern girls are sure to express their contempt for the old tradition. Jhabvala not only shows her awareness of the changing value, of a shifting Hindu society but underscores the comic incongruity in the behaviour both of Hari and Amrita in respect of their ultimate choices.

From conformity to non-conformity appears to be a clear individual and social transition, but the reverse of this movement from non-confromism to the desire to conform is quite curious and full of comic as well as pathetic possibilities. Jhabvala as a genuine comic artist fully explores the comic potentialities of this individual and social development. The resolution of the marital triangle is thus thought of in comic terms. The ironic tone of this resolution is quite pronounced as the seekers of love and social revolt have reverted to the position of the seekers of familial love, social security, claims of the community and convention. The rebels of individual fulfilment and social challenge have been claimed by conventions and the incongruity between these opposing poles provides Jhabvala great opportunity for bringing out the comic in her fiction.

Hari finally falls into the arms of Sushila Anand and Amrita into the seductive embraces of Krishna Sen Gupta. Krishna is her paying-guest, and quite comically the messenger of her love for Hari. He sincerely tries to bridge the gap between Hari and Amrita but finally fills in the gap himself. Amrita after her experience of calf-love and puppy- love reverts to a position which is found to be more sober and more pragmatic. Her life in the studios starts as a song of innocence and ends as in a song of experience.

Jhabvala portrays these situations with genuine sense of comic and a spirit of gaiety. The scene of booking the boy- a kind of betrothal— is not without its comic flourishes and ceremonial playfulness underscoring the comic mode which dominates its spirit.

> "Mr. Anand announces with an air of extra importance well, Suri Sahib, your boy is ours, we book him, here is our money, Suri holds the twenty-one rupees and responds heartily,' He is booked', This booking event gives rise to the usual sentimentalism of elderly women, their sobs of self-pity, a Curious combination of joy and grief. Hari's mother let out a loud sob while Hari desperately pretended not to notice what was going on" (page 150)

Hari thus marches on the road to matrimony but quite interestingly just three days before the date of wedding he talks to Amrita about their proposed action, the unusual world in which we live is in tune with basic comiciality of Hari's pretensions and Amrita's situations. While Amrita is seriously thinking in term of revolt and action including a visit to England with a view to getting married to Hari and settling down in that country, he quietly but surely gives into the pressures of his family.

To Whom She Will ends on a note of reconciliation realized through marriage. The wedding of Hari and Shushila is celebrated with gaiety while the union of Amrita and Krishna is presented in low profile. This, however, does not lower the intensity of the social comedy. The title, based on the ***Panchatantra*** story, is symbolic of the situations in the novel and the conflicts in the original are brought in close association with the central triangle of marriages. The wisdom of the ancient sages of India, implicit in this injunction is dramatized in the predicaments of Hari and Amrita, Sushila and Krishna and the complex tangle of their human relationships. Amrita, the attractive, self willed girl makes a bold, through abortive attempt to marrying her lover. She tries 'to give herself to whom she will', but does not achieve success. Sushila Anand and Hari both are married at a tender age to preclude the possibilities of their marrying for love and fighting for it. Hari marries Sushila not for love, but for social ad individual recognition and for preserving the Group values of the community and family life. Marriage, thus, appears to be a compromise in the social sense, an adjustment that two individuals have to make to follow a social norm. The two marital relations ***To Whom She Will*** only bring out this comic mode of a social compromise.

Jhabvala's social comedy in this novel offers a world-view in which we realize that the social world she projects, is the best of possible world and that we need the aid of the comedian to use the expression of James Feibleman to meet the in superable defects of actuality". We are inclined to laugh at the imperfections of the world of Hari's and Amrita's, Krishna's and Sushila's and Jhabvala's comic sense liberates us from the limitation of things as they are. We partly realise these limitations and dream of going beyond them. This dual view of the reality and the world brings charm to Jahbavala's art. The novel fits who into this comic paradox arising out of Amrita's attempt at marrying 'whom she will' and then getting reconciled to someone else. A major flaw in the novel springs from' the weak will' of Hari, Amrita, Krishna and the others who get involved in this family affair.

Jhabvala seems to show woman as a more powerful agent of revolt than man. Hari is presented to be passive and stupid, but quite ironically persons like him generally become the objects of love of girls like Amrita. However these defects do not in any way detract from the merits of the novel as an entertaining exercise in new social comedy. Reconciliation with contemporary reality is its main point and the process of reconciliation with that reality is also the process of getting reconcile to its defects. These defects are treated comically by the novelist to project a world view which is positive and affirmative.

Jhabvala's comic art brings out this gaiety and also a sense of acceptance of life. It thus becomes a case of affirmation of truth which is not lowered by the sense of failure. Amrita and Hari belong to this world of affirmation since they, in spite of their frustrations, continue to respond to life. The most positive and affirmative moments in comic art arise when men are released from the bonds of a pressing contemporary reality, and yet retain the confidence that their ideals are as intact as ever. The affirmation is not a mere moral statement, but a felt experience which is embedded in the souls of girls like Amrita who have passed through the crucible of adolescent love.

The Nature of Passion is both a novel of manners as well as morals. The title appears to indicate a work similar to a psychological novel. In fact its familial social cultural and moral aspects are more dominant and pervasive than its psychological trend and therefore it adequately fits into the general pattern of a social comedy which is Jhabvala's strong point especially in the early stage of her career as a novelist. The novel is basically a sympathetic portryal of two Punjabi families settled down in Delhi. The family of Lala Narayan Das Verma (Lalaji) including his wife, sister, three sons, three daughters and two daughters-in-law dominate the scene, while the other family of Dev Raj related to Lalaji, plays a secondary role. Jhabvala's canvas is primarily familial, though it includes many other related areas especially of a society which is involved in a state of change from a conventional to a modern mode of living. Lalaji the protagonist in this novel is very much involved in this change, though he embodies the old order genuinely attempting to reconcile itself to a new surrounding.

The Nature of Passion projects several conflicts and cross-currents of this changing familial and social surroundings and the persons who are involved in it. This is a novel which presents in concrete terms Lalaji's strong passions especially the feeling for his dear daughter, Nimmi. Lalaji's most delicate and inward responses to Nimmi are beautifully portrayed by Jhabvala. Nimmi too, seems to be a part of this whirl wind of passion. Even Lalaji who is generally concerned with life's petty or big monetary problems such as the ten lakh income tax arrears, the new Deputy Minister, the bribery and corruption case, the lawyer's report etc. cannot escape from being passion's willing slave. It is the private personal life of familial relations that overtakes his calculating and cool intellect. He surrenders himself to his heart's desires, his inmost affection for Nimmi his total involvement with her. This surrender to a genuine passion redeems his character and saves him from being a mere commercial success.

The novel derives its title from Swami Parmananda's translation of the Bhagvad Gita.

> "Know thou Rajas to be of the nature of passion, giving rise to thirst (for pleasure) and attachment. It binds the embodied by attachment to action."[5]

The main emphasis in the novel is on presenting the process of Rajas, the worldly passion which is accompanied by the thirst for pleasure and results in attachment. The Sattvika (the saintly) or the Tamasa (the angry) aspects, of passion are simply hinted at in the behaviour of a few characters such as Phuphiji or Om Prakash or Viddi. Lalaji is worried over the problem of getting the contract for the new building-Twenty-five lakhs of the Happy Hindustan Trading Company. He expects Dev Raj to help him in this deal. However this business deal is also linked up with the prospects of Nimmi's marriage. Thus the proprietary interests are brought in close association with the inmost feelings of personal relations. Rajas rule the universe of Lalaji and his community. Only Viddi revolts against the constant talk of money whereas the other children fall in line with him. Later on, even Viddi falls a victim to the lure of money. It is the money-civilization of a rising commercial middle class that is Jhabvala's primary subject-matter in the novel. It has, of course its own scales of values which are caught up between the conflict of tradition and modernity. Lalaji is deeply conscious of the value of money and what it can do to man's positions in life. In the closing scene of part one of the novel Lalaji is faced with the problem of marrying Nimmi and the dialogue between himself, his wife and Phuphiji is very suggestive. Even the women question his implicit faith in what money can achieve in life. When he suggests that the people who will receive as bride will be pleased with the huge dowry that they will get. His wife raises her tone of protest. Then Lalaji provokes his wife and sister:

> "You would have had my daughter brought up like a poor man's", asked Lalaji smiling. Poor man, rich man, his wife replied" a daughter is a daughter and there is only one me way." (page 87)

These elderly orthodox women are of course pleading their case against modernity, against permitting young women to join college, become independent and equal to men. While they argue in this way, and appeared to be opposed to Lalaji, they are as materialistic and commercial minded as he is. This is Jhabvala's way of presenting things which is at once realistic and comic. It is almost Dickensian in spirit. Where as in Dickens the characters are solitaries, in Jhabvala they are part of a socially well linked family group. Lalaji's idea of a room is not a room 'one's own' but rather a common room is for family get-together in which the individual merges into the group. Lallji, however, soon becomes adjusted to his newly acquired wealth, because he is aware of the bond between man and the objects he gains. It is this capacity and power to enlarge the area of one's possessions that characterise Lalaji's personalities. He has an outward as well as an inward looking personality. He thinks of his wife as his life's companion looking after his comforts, even in such trivial matters as knotting the cord of his Pyjamas. He is proud of his dearest daughter Nimmi, whom he looks upon as his finest achievement. This love for Nimmi, his first passion, shows his capacity to realise the most abstract element in human relationship. His affection for Nimmi is the most delicate aspect of his rather puzzling personality. When Nimmi in her quest for modernity has hair cut, Lalaji doesn't show any sense of anger on disapproval. Nimmi's new get-up shocks her mother and Phuphiji and even her elder sister Usha. But Lalaji's reaction to Nimmi's hair cut is marked by his generous attitude towards her:

> "Lalaji appeared at the bottom of the satires. He held a paper bag into which he peered with a very puzzled expression on his face. Nimmi could not help laughing. She leant over the banisters and called down Pitaji it is my hair" (Page 213: 214)

Lalaji in this moment symbolises the synthesis between tradition and modernity. He is of course alive to the power and value of money, but his inward self goes above the narrow confines of his materialistic bent of mind. Even his quest for money is a kind of fulfilment of self. Lalaji's nature of passion is to get rich and earn a place in society. His earthiness and worldliness, therefore, are the concretions of his abstract passions, love of children and the family as well as a desire to realise his true self. He has lost touch with his birth place, his native village, in the Punjab which after partition had become a part of Pakistan. Therefore in the soil of Delhi he begins to look for new roots. Lalaji's character reminds us of the nation of the father in 18th and 19th centuries English literature an index of familial involvement and social trust. Thackeray's Vanity fair, writes- Dorothy Van Ghent "With its panorama of western European international society as back drop to the heroine's activities is full of fathers, sick fathers, guilty fathers."

The old Mr.Osborne, Mr. Sedley an old Sir Pitt are the 19th century variations or the 18th century fictional fathers like Mr.Bennet or Squire Allworthy. These fathers present a stable social system of values and coherent world-view that the father as head of family represents a moral ideal in a society which is ethically and morally ordained. Becky Sharp in ***Vanity Fair*** represents worldliness and love for money, but this is distinctly different from that of Lalaji. Since the old man is deeply involved in his family and the happiness of his relations. Lalaji's craze for money is modified by his love for his daughter and thus the materialistic side in him is mellowed by the filial affection.

Although ***The Nature of Passion*** as a work of art is chiefly concerned with Rajas aspect of human behaviour, resulting in action and attachment, the other aspects of passion are pushed to the background. Nimmi's passion for Pheroze Batliwala is a kind of adolescent, sentimental love as she is carried away by his handsome looks, his visit to England and the way he talks. Nimmi gets her hair cut partly to please Pheroze. Nimmi is drawn towards Pheroze in a sensuous way and her passion is in tune with what she makes of her notion of John Keats' poetry. Nimmi represent's the quest for culture of the newly rich class in Delhi. Pheroze's attack on the business people in Delhi seems to be the voice of the pseudo-cultured against the invasion of their culture by the newly rich. Howeve,r it brings out a double-edged irony-an irony which is directed against the rich as much as Pheroze himself. In the contemporary American metaphysics, says Lionel

Triilling "Reality is always material reality." In Jhabvala's fiction too there is a genuine attempt to expose this material reality, the emptiness and hollowness of a money-civilization, the emotional poverty of a rich society. Jhabvala's approach to life and society is to accept both material as well as spiritual aspects of life but she is also keen on exposing their sharpness and shallowness where possible. She is also keen on exposing the crudity, the coarseness, the lack of sensitivity, the lack of an inherited tradition of the Punjabis who settled in Delhi after the partition of India. Jahbavala however, doesn't ignore the new fashions and attitudes developed by the so called rich people settled in Delhi. These newly rich classes have grown cut of a sense of enterprise, initiative and courage qualities which are capable of being noticed. Jhabvala's attitude to culture, or more specifically to European or westernised Indian culture in urban India, is not without the positive elements of that culture. She sometimes makes fun of these people, exposes them and subjects them to ridicule, brings out their hollowness and poverty of mind and yet she is alive to the fact that it is they who surround her world and give it solidity, strength and vitality. The novel is beautiful example of a fictional recreation of the commercial attitude of the new Indian society combined with familial sentiment. It is also a link between what it is and what it was, a synthesis between the modernity and tradition and a bridge between yesterday and today.

Esmond in India presents one of the basic modes of Jhabvala's art of fiction: the ironic mode. This ironic mode, placed midway between satire and comic spirit, is basic to Jhabval's world. The ironic mode in her world of fiction is not limited merely to verbal irony or the irony of the situation but rather to the total output of experience. Her irony sometimes springs out of a discrepancy between the appearance of a situation and the reality that underlies it. She follows the technique of concealment of real meaning or exposing the discrepancy between two levels of reality in portraying characters and situations in her novels. Jhabavala often expresses a meaning contradictory to the statement and this technique brings out her basic comic and ironic mode.

Before illustrating and examining this comic and ironic mode in ***Esmond in India,*** it will be pertinent to view this novel as presenting a basic pattern of Jhabvala's creativity. This novel India perhaps unconsciously presents Jhabvala's experience of living in India and brings out one of her deeper dilemmas. Jhabvala in her essay on ***Living in India*** has highlighted some of the complex problems of a European-more particularly a European writer who lives in India and who tries to give artistic expression to her experience. This dilemma of Jhabvala as a writer and a woman is not simply a personal issue. It has its origin in the process of her becoming an artist and Esmond in India is one of the fictional forms externalizing and expressing this problem of the inner life in its relation to the outer life.

Esmond in India is expressive of this inward dilemma of the artist to come to terms, with experience-the world that is India In this way the problem of Jhabvala the writer as artist is in tune with the problem of Esmond in relation to his experience of the human world that is . India. Esmond as a person is the very opposite of what a sensitive, intelligent, cultured European novelist, and his portrayal by Jhabvala is proof of her comic and ironic mode. However the character and personality of Esmond are at variance with the situation or the predicament that India projects. This is so because Esmond is an incomplete man and is one of several of Jhabvala's immature characters and his immaturity is manifold. It is emotional, intellectual and spiritual. His man preoccupation in India is a sort of a mixed bag: he acts as a tutor to European women on subjects of diverse interests. He teaches these Westerners especially the wives of ambassadors, Hindi or gives Sunday courses in Indian art and culture. He prides himself on his knowledge of Hindi and treats his servants in an imperious manner. He is not, however a sophisticated Englishman. He still retains his out-dated colonial attitude. Jhabvala's ironic attitude is quite evident in the following scene.

> "The servant wondered what the sahit. was saying, he could not even identify the language he was speaking." (page 14)

Esmond is both over-bearing and egotistic, though these characteristics are concealed below his handsome face, his attractive appearance and his ability to tackle women in a confident way. Jhabvala as a Westerner finds it easy to probe Esmond's weakness and also the shortcomings of Gulab, his Indian wife. We get introduced to Esmond and Gulab in the fifth chapter when they are already separated from each other. In fact, the scene of the dining table and the lunch underscores not only the difference in their attitude to food, but more importantly the wide gulf in their outlook of life, that divides them. Esmond is opposed to the idea of taking spicy things. Things to which the Westerner is usually opposed. On the other hand Gulab is very fond of spicy Indian food even to the extent of being indifferent to the environmental cleanliness. He become indecent in conversation and his sarcasm, his contempt is all lost on Gulab since, with her charming looks, she is very quiet and balanced. He tries to evoke some response some protest in her, but she remains very passive. He thinks he is trapped in her stupidity, in her dull heavy alien mind. At times he is very offensive and rude towards her.

> "you have got what I can only call a wonderful propensity to squalor. Tel me now, if pressed on the point, would you call yourself a slut?" (page 47)

A slut generally means either a dirty, clumsy woman careless of her appearance-as Gulab is or a woman of questionable character, but this irony has no impact on Gulab. This, however, brings out the hostile nature of Esmond who is indeed a culture snob and in this unkind domestic scene a heartless, dictatorial husband.

The Gulab-Esmond relationship is at the heart of the novel and constitutes the main core of personal and familial tangles in the novel. It is Esmond's real inability to love anyone which explains his other shortcomings. When Esmond feels oppressed by Gulab, he pays a visit to Betty his mistress. It is the company of Betty that Esmond feels at home and easy. The superficial and rather pompous Esmond does not represent European culture in India. He is simply a raw middle-brow and persons like him are not allowed to cross even the thresholds of the citadels of culture in Europe. However, he has certain qualities which present him in some favourable light. When Shakuntala, Har Dayal's daughter, comes to Esmond's apartment after a party, Esmond asks Gulab to welcome and meet her. He is all praise for

Gulab in Shakuntala's presence, even going to extend of remarking that all the interior decoration in the house is result of her creative brain. He behaves almost decently and we see an altogether different side of his character. He tells Shakuntala about Gulab: I yes, my wife is quite an interior decorator colour-schemes are her speciality.' Esmond's life his adherence to a superficial civilized code is quite visible in this scene.

Finally Gulab leaves Esmond and the apartment because her servant makes an unsuccessful attempt to seduce her. Gulab like all Hindu girls, respects her husband, but the moment she feels that her husband has failed to give her security, she is under no social or spiritual obligation to him. Gulab makes up her mind to desert Esmond for good. She takes her son, Ravi with her and this brings to a close for uneasy unstable and meaningless relationship with Esmond.

In ***Esmond in India*** the fortunes of two families are grouped together in its narrative structure. It is a novel of family relations, social import and the corporate life in which personal relations are mixed up with social and familial perplexities. Therefore, ***Esmond in India*** is neither about Esmond alone, nor about India only, but about the social context that functions as a setting for Esmond's experience. It is woven round the two families of Har Dayal and Ram Nath two friends who had studied together at Cambridge but got separated later on. Har Dayal the modernised liberal whose personality is sustained by the trapping of western education and culture and Ram Nath, the great idealist who had scarified everything during India's freedom movement, are studies in contrast. Har Dayal, the careerist the materialist and Ram Nath the book worm appear to sum up the two dominant aspects of society in modern Indian. Har Dayal recites his rather pompous and ornamental poems, encourages his daughter to cultivate her individuality and is not opposed to Shakuntala having a drink or a smoke at a party. A study in contrast is Ram Nath's brilliant son Naryan who is a very competent doctor and works in a village. He is keen to marry a sensible girl who will share his life and ideals. Ram Nath leads a life of austerity, want, neglect and social isolation where as Har Dayal is the embodiment of all social and cultural activities. They are indeed conceived as contrasted personalities.

Jhabvala shows a very rare insight into the world of sensuousness in which some of her characters get caught. For example Shakuntala, Har Dayal's daughter is carried away by the impressive appearance of Esmond. He has been assigned to give private tuition to her. Shakuntala is very immature teenager and like Nimmi in the ***Nature of Passion.*** She becomes an easy victim of the temptation of the flesh and the prompting of the senses. The scene in the Taj Mahal garden on a moonlit night is replete with sensuousness— the embodiment of the monument of love the evocation of Shelly's poetic charms and the agony of longing in a young heart give Shakuntala an intensity of feeling and withinno time she loses her heart to Esmond.

> "I do love you. From the very first moment i saw you I loved you. I can not hide it any longer. If I do it will break me, my heart will burst. Esmond I know your are married and also you have a child, but it tell you this means nothing to me. Only I know you have come into my life and now it is m duty to give everything I have to you, to adore you and to serve you and to be your slave." (page 183-184)

This portrayal of love scene is part of the nevelist's ironic mode. Jhabvala is completely detached in presenting how an adolesent, inexperienced girl, fed on romantic notions of love and feeling of sensuousness, becomes a victim of the temptations of the flesh. Esmond has affairs with Shakuntala but to him she is one more girl in a series of casual conquests. No love is involved and therefore, the scene brings out Jhabvala's comic vision in which the two levels of reality are constrasted. Although in the last scene Esmond is again in the company of Shakuntala, the tone of the novelist continues to be sceptical partly because it is the feeling of the moment not a moment of deep love and affirmation of life. Shakuntala's sensuus fascination for Esond is an act of recklessness and hence has no depth in it.

The relationship between Esmond and Gulab leads to disaster and separation. It springs from Jhabvala's ironic mode in which the possibilities of a positive relationship between a western man and eastern woman are shown as a futile and frustrating experience. On top of this negative note of marital discord, Esmond allows himself to be involved inanother equally frivolous relationship with Shakuntala. Jhabvala unduly highlights Gulab's weaknesses for Indian foods. Itis difficult to reconcile Gulab's utter passivity to Esmond's assaults upon her individuality and self-respect to the strength of her will. This determination made her to defy her family and marry him. And finally Jhabvala leaves Esmond utterly unconvincing. Laxmi, Madhuri and Uma project their points of view quite convincingly. However, there are humanness instances in ***Esmond in India*** which indicate the effectiveness of Jhabvala's basic comic and ironic mode. The hostess who gives a party attended by Har Dayal and Shankuntala stares at the girl with great naked blue eyes like hard boiled eggs.

The Billimoria sisters, very ultramodern, smoking cigarettes clap the loudest when the hostess announces that Har Dayal will give a recital of Sanskrit poems in translation. Jhabvala exposes the emptiness and hollowness of the so called cultured and sophisticated classes in India who under the superficial impact of the west either glorify or downgrade their heritage.

In Jhabvala's comic mode the pompous and the pretentious Esmond is cut to size and even reduced to a non-entity. The reference to Taj Mahal as a setting to his monumental tragedy is a masterly stroke of irony which is the positive aspect of Esmond in India. The fundamental passions which are evoked by situations in Esmond in India appears to end up in a negative response. Gulabs marries, for love but she does not find it at all, Shakuntala, too gives in to her passion without evoking any positive fulfilment. Esmond is frustrated in his marriage to Gulab and he allows his sexuality to get the better of him in his relationship with Shakuntala and his flirtation with Betty without realising and discovering the internal centre which will give him fulfilment of self. Esmond is of course, not deadwood. His problem is however, similar to that of Jhabvala herself. It is basically a problem of identity. Esmond is in reality a very ordinary figure and therefore unequal to the task of coming up to our expectations.

Get Ready for Battle is one of Jhabvala' s important novels, which projects the novelist's artistic and social pre-occupation with a money-civilization in and around Delhi, and also a protest against the values of that civilization. Jahbavala is successful in presenting the personal dilemmas and individual and familial predicaments of this society in post-Independence urban India. ***Get Ready for Battle*** is apparently a quotation taken from the second chapter of the Bhagvad Gita. Lord Krishna while dwelling on the Yoga of knowledge urges Arujana to shed all his fears, and "Treating alike pleasure and pain, profit and loss, victory and defeat, get ready for the battle ——-." (The Bhagavad Gita Verse 38)

In this novel it is Sarla Devi's duty to fight against every form of social injustice and oppression of the poor. However, Jhabvala's attempt to induce this quotation into a scene of the meeting between Sarla Devi and her son Vishnu is rather ambiguous and unconvincing. Vishnu has called on his mother who lives away in a solitary house, and whose relations with her husband are far from being good. Her husband Gulzari Lal's favourite notion about himself is that he should become a successful man of the family. However, his materialistic attitude and value-systems are diametrically opposed to the values of the spirit that his wife, Sarla Devi, represents. It is for this reason that they live apart from each other. Consequently, Gulzari Lal develops an intimate relationship with Mrs. Kusum Mehra a middle-aged, though attractive widow of an army officer. Kusum looks after all his comfort, shares his bed as well as his small domestic problems. She naturally wants this relationship to be given respectability by marriage and Gulzari Lal, too, is keen on marrying her. But the main problem is the divorce, at first he is unwilling to ask Sarla Devi to give her consent and even Brij Mohan her brother asked her for divorce. The divorce alone can clear they way for Kusum who is intent on marrying Gulzari Lal.

Sarla Devi has indeed reached a stage which is far beyond the bounds of worldliness and the barriers of self-interest. She is almost a saint who treats the pleasures and pains of this world alike, and who is non-attached to the temporary gains and losses of this earthly paradise of the poor and the suppressed, and is determined to fight for their causes. These poor people all to be removed from their tiny hutments under the skin of 'slum clearance' or providing them a better environment far away from their place of work. Their land is being acquired by industrialists, and profiteers and these people are being coaxed and threatened to vacate the area. Ironically, Gulzari Lal himself is the prospective buyer of this piece of land. Sarla Devi, who has gone beyond the self-urges her son Vishnu to lend his hand in lessening the miseries and agonies of the residents of Bundi Busti. Vishnu is indeed the little merchant's son and is carried away by the values of a money-ridden society. He has inherited this hunger for money from, his father Gulzari Lal. Conflict between what is and what should be is the central irony of the theme of ***Get Ready for Battle.*** However the theme of the novel is not confined to Sarla Devi or her championship of Bundi Busti. It is, in reality an aesthetic mode for creating a world of art surrounded by human and familial relationship. Jhabvala's art blossoms out of her deep awareness of the personal predicaments of her characters their ways of feeling, thinking and their actions.

Vishnu and his wife, Mala too, have their moments of serious disagreement and quarrel, though they love each other immensely at other moments. As Mala is keen on visiting her parents in Bombay, Vishnu refuses and is quite firm in rejecting her pleas. Mala respond to Kusum's view of modernity in marital relations and the need to permit divorce, if necessary. Mala and Vishnu quarrel again; she throws her Sari on the bed, he kicks at the piles of her saries. However this is only a storm in a tea-cup. The comic and ironic contexts of ***Get Ready for Battle*** are very skilfully displayed by Jhabvala in the complex web of human relationship in this novel. Kusum and Mala; Gulzari Lal and Kusum; Brij Mohan and Sarla Devi, Brij Mohan and Tara -all these have their moments of joys and sorrows. There actions, comic, as well as serious, operate as variations of the basic concept of ***Get Ready for Battle.*** However, it is not confined to battle, fights, quarrels and conflicts, it is very-neatly designed novel of domestic life and familial relations which are sometimes marked by intensity of emotion and other time jealousies and prejudices. Kusum, or Mrs Mehra, is a-well-drawn portrait compounding the varied qualities of a woman. She is Gulzari Lals mistress and yet her behaviour her behaviour and conduct is not odious at all. In fact she is friendly and affectionate and is genuinely concerned with Mala's and Vishnu's happiness; she is equally affectionate towards Brij Mohan, so much so that his responses to her turn from hostility to friendliness. She is always eager to make friends with Sarla Devi and praises the work done by her in social fields. Her relationship with Gulzari Lal is another story and is very keen legalise their unbecoming relationship by marrying him after he secures legal separation from Sarla Devi. She does all she can to achieve a stabilizing centre in relationship with Gulzari Lal and almost achieves success in it. Jhabvala succeeds in projecting Kusum as a complex character.

The relationship between Vishnu and Mala, the young couple is basically affectionate though they often adopt postures of getting ready for battle. The moments of their physical happiness are intense and Jhabvala presents them very convincingly. The sense of domestic intimacy between husband and wife is both sensuous and true romantic and realistic. At the same time, Vishnu passes his hand over her womb and remarks

> "Perhaps you will have another child, and she readily responds saying, yes, if you want" (page 221)

Mala is delighted to hear about the prospect of a new industrial enterprise at Chadnipet and the possibility of her living there with Vishnu and Priti. The break-up of large families into small units under impact of industrialization is indirectly brought out in Vishnu's quest for monetary and professional self-reliance. It is a measure of Jhabvala's compassion, reflected in the personality of Sarla Devi that prompts her to portray the last scene of the novel in which Sarla Devi walks her weary way in search of Tara to give solace to her wounded soul. Sarla Devi's heart is filled up with the vastness of space and the saint in her seeks the apparently on unattainable horizons. Her vision enlarges and tries to envelop the orange of the evening sky:

> "Sarla Devi looked up and above the street-remote but seemingly unattainable—she saw a sky huge and soft with evening. There was a last lingering, fading orange streak on the horizon." (page 223)

Sarla Devi' s quest for spiritual freedom is also hinted at in another context by Gautam the man of imagination. His main aim is to persuade people to keep their spirit free and not allow it to be overtaken by rigid conventions. He is very anti-materialistic and out rightly condemns Gulzari Lal's craze for money. He however, finds it necessary to seek his help in stabilising an ideal school for children. Jhabvala like G.B. Shaw and E.M. Forster, is deeply conscious of the value of money in modern life and the fact that all idealistic schemes of restructuring civilization will need money for their implementation in practical life. Sarla Devi and Gautam represent the visionary gleam in a world otherwise darkened and disturbed by Gulzari Lal's commercial attitude. Jhabavala has thus portrayed the two contrary aspects of modern India— the worldliness of the Gulzari Lal and Vishnu, and the other worldliness of the Gautams and Sarla Devis.

Get Ready for Battle is a domestic social comedy marked by satirical remarks. Jhabvala targets the spiritually blind people who have neither the brains nor the desire to understand the basic truths of life. Gulzari Lal and Vishnu represent this class and they cannot have equation with Sarla Devi and Gautam. However, the reference to the Bhagavad Gita citing the verse 38th from its second chapter implying an equivalence between Sarla Devi's outlook on life and the value-pattern of a Karma Yogi does not quite fit into the comicality of the domestic novel. The title appears to have been influenced by the comic spirit. Jhabvala's fictional perspective is in line with her comic and ironic Vision. The ambivalence in her value-patterns or the lack of commitment to any particular approach is a clear indication of her fictional perspective. As a European writer, she appears to be detached and it is this spirit of detachment which enables her to present situations, and characters getting ready for battle, and yet remain a smiling spectator of the whole thing.

The Householder reflects Henry James' conception of a novel as "a direct impression of life." Since it is faithfully highlights the personal predicaments, the familial and social problems of Prem, a Hindi teacher, with a second class B.A., in Mr. Khanna's private college. The world of ***The Householder*** is confined to the exploration of the consciousness of this central character. This consciousness however, projects Prem's responses to Indu, his wife, Raj, his friends, Chaddha and Sohanlal, his colleagues, Khanna his principal, Seigals his landlords, Hans Loewe and Kitty, his European friends, his old mother and the Swami. This completes the circle of ***The Householder*** who happens to be a middle class person. This consciousness springs from Prem's lower-middle class complex. At the start, he appears to be a little afraid of his students, incapable of maintaining discipline in class, and unable to assert himself anywhere except in his house. His visit to Khanna's house for a raise in his salary is replete with humorous connotation. Prem finds it difficult to support himself and his family with meagre salary he gets. What the ***Panchtantra*** says appears to be true of Prem in this context. In the ***Panchtantra*** it is written that "it is better to be dead than poor". "Poverty and wants are terrible things" -this statement unfolds the heart of ***The Householder.*** It explains not only the major problems of Prem as a husband, as a father, as a teacher, as a citizen but it is also central to the social structure so realistically and faithfully presented in the novel. In the first chapter Prem's main problem seems to be his low salary, Rs. 175 per month:

> "How to manage on that? His rent alone came to Rs. 451Per month" (page 9)

This problem of rent almost haunts him and this makes him represent his case to houseowner Mr. Seigal by bringing to his notice his growing expenses and even by imploring him to treat him as his son but all this falls on deaf ears. Prem is so nervous that he cannot ask directly, and therefore wants his wife lndu, to do the job for him. When he musters courage and asks Mr. Seigal, he gets a very cold response. Quite ironically the novel ends on a pessimistic note. Prem wants the rent of the house to be reduced and this is nothing but expressive of a tangible economic reality which is found to be haunting the self-conscious of lower middle class individuals in India perpetually.

The Householder is known for more fun than philosophy, more satirical and comic spirit than social documentation of the problems of lower middle-class individuals. Mr. Khanna does not mind using the staff room of the college as a guest room bringing in a bed and a towel with. "Work is worship, embroidered in it" (page 13)

The habit that some Indian's develop of being ponderous and knowledge — parading is satirised in Mr. Khanna's behaviour with Prem. While Prem tries to impress upon

Mr. Khanna the need to help Sohan Lal (indirectly Prem himself) by presenting a pitiable picture of the poor teacher's condition, Mr. Khanna delivers a short lecture covering the advantages of sumptuous breakfast.

> "You see, 'explained Mr. Kahnna', the gastric juices must be allowed to flow from early morning, otherwise they will become clogged and nasty indigestions follow." (page 14)

The Irony here arises from two opposites Sohan Lal's compulsion to leave home at six without any food and Mr. Khanna's pompous comment on the need to take plenty of salt 'with your food'. In the process of satirizing the characters, Jhabavala perhaps unconsciously makes them figures of fun, and ridicule , degenerating into caricatures. Mrs. Khanna, a short plump woman, too conscious of her husband's status, and almost contemptuous of his subordinate colleagues wears many gold ornaments and bright embroidered saries:

> "She looked as opulent and upholstered as her sitting-room, and consequently inspired Prem with the same feeling of shyness." (page 16)

Mr. Chaddha the professor of history appears to be a funny figure who has a remarkable capacity for flattering the principal and making a show of his knowledge. He is in the habit of using words and sentences pompously. He pays compliments to 'the gentle sex' for making it possible for men to enjoy an hour's leisure and ease in their charming company. He also cites examples from history of ancient heroes:

> "For respite from their battle to have their wounds dressed and their brows soothed by the hands of their consorts." (page 98)

He also lays emphasis on the need for good fellowship and companionship flowing from the High-tea. The tendency towards moralising and philosophising a peculiar characterisation of Indian character, is also to be seen in Prem's, remarks on ***The Householder.*** Prem is determined to request the Seigal to press his need for reducing his rent and wants to be treated 'as another son'. Instead Mr.Seigal while appreciating Prem's feeling, makes him appear as a 'mentor' to Romesh. Prem then assumes the role of an elderly adviser and guide while in fact he wanted to look young and foolish. In that assumed role prem observes:

> "In our ancient writings it is written .... that there are four stages to a man's life. When he is young he is a student, learning from his father and his teacher. After that come the life of the house holders .... In this stage a man must raise a family and see to their needs." (page 53)

These comments are self-explanatory and have a bearing on the theme of the novel. Prem is 'the householder' and in Sanskrit, it is called the Grihasthaashrami who is continually haunted by a sense of failure. However, he too indulges in the habit of citing ancient Indian scriptures for a common place things. He continues "The third stage when a man retires from his duties as a householder and spends his time in contemplation. While the samosa were served with tea, he quietly skipped the fourth stage (the Renunciation) of which he was not sure." (page 53)

This reference to the four stages in the Hindu view of life implies a link between the life of Prem, ***The Householder*** and the ancient scriptural tradition. However, Jhabavala does not, rightly play up the Hindu tradition. She concentrates on exploring the householder's economic, educational, familial and social predicaments in middle class urban social setting in Delhi, and creates in the process an excellent entertaining social comedy. Jhabvala's portrayals of the meeting of the eastern householder and the western tourist- cum-spiritual seeker is in part comic. Hans Loewe, a European youth, is a seeker after Indian's, mystery and philosophy and in this connection he asks Prem." Do you think a Westerner like me can reach to the spiritual greatness of the Indian yogis?" (page 61)

However, Hans is attracted to India in various ways.

He is up against Maya, the illusion and the concretes this-worldly realities of India simultaneously — in this country 'where everything is beautiful, the sunset and the fruit and the women, here you call it all illusion! How do you say -Maya?' (Page 39) Jhabvala has truly perfected the art of the ironic stroke. While Hans is greatly influenced by India's spiritual richness and declares enthusiastically that he loves Indian immensely, Prem feels impelled to make some timely comment and declares that since Independence Indian has made great progress.

This is equally true of the exchanges between Kitty, Hans' landlady, and Prem, which are indeed delightful strokes of irony. Hans and Kitty both desire to recruit Prem to join the group of the seekers after the spirit and invite him to live with them. Hans confesses that he is strong-willed and that he realizes God consciousness. Prem is astonished by the behaviour of these Westerners and their interest in Indian philosophy and yoga since he subscribes to the general belief that the west is highly materialistic. At Peggy's party Prem feels totally isolated and almost unable to communicate. Prem and Hans, the East and the West fail to communicate wit each other almost everywhere.

A significant aspect of Jhabvala's ironic mode is that, contrary to popular belief, the west is shown as seeking the spiritual value of life and the east is presented as deeply involved in materialistic pursuits. There are, of course inversions within this basic ironic inversion. There is also a Swami in ***The Householder*** who preaches Vedanta. Jhabvala's ironic thrust in other novels is directed not merely against fake Indian Swamis but also at the European seekers of the spirit. Hans and Kitty too are satirised effectively to expose their superficial enthusiasm for eastern philosophy and their high-sounding worldliness. One of the reasons why Prem and Hans cannot really communicate with each other is that they are carried away by words and words alone. Whereas Hans indulges in philosophical high sounding terms, Prem follows suit in using economic or political jargon. Since the two streams of Jargon do not meet at any single point, they cannot establish any link of genuine communication.

The Householder's marital relations with Indu are delicately and sensitively presented by Jhabvala. At one stage Prem feels that he is married to a woman who" was not only quite different from what he had wished and hoped for, but who also opposed him in his wishes." (page 68) This apparent marital dissonance later dissolves into experiences of real affection and love. He brings sweets for her and the scenes of this love making during day are marked by genuine involvement. After Indu 's departure for her home, Prem really feels drawn to her physically and emotionally. His mother comes, creates a little scene and then leaves for Bangalore. There are many scenes in ***The Householder*** which are moving. The first scene is the experience of love making of Prem and Indu on the roof on a glorious starlit night. Prem and Indu both feel great and supreme. They struggle, they love, they feel sated again and again and yet are united in each other's arms. They sense the solitude and the space—and experience a sense of unity with the earth, with nature and their other's self.

The second scene in which Prem gently touches Indu's growing belly is brief, but genuinely emotional since he instinctively tries to feel the baby in her womb, an extension of his own being. The sight of Indu's pregnancy, makes him feel a sense of shame because he feels, it will reveal to other people what he was doing to her at night. The third touching situation is the farewell scene between Hans and Premo Hans and Prem talk of their deep friendship and their pale eyes are loving and sad. Hans is almost overwhelmed but is checked by Kitty who talks of the infinite and Non-attachment, Hans then is divided between Prem's and Kitty's voices. "I forget the source of my being and so I become attached to friends and other things which are only Maya." (page 187) Her asserts that they must be non-attached and yet smiles as he shakes Prem's hand: "Hans tried to smile, but looking up Prem was surprised to notice that his eyes were swmming with tears. Prem was touched." (Page 188).

This scene demonstrates the triumph of the human spirit, of love and affection over philosophical catch words and metaphysical labels. ***The Householder*** is a sensitively portrayed social comedy of a lower middle class Hindi teacher reflecting not merely his economic and domestic problems but, also his complexes, his sense of failure and frustration and his minor fulfilment. ***The Householder*** calls for comparison with R.K. Narayan's ***The English*** *Teacher,* another comedy conceived in a similar ironic mould, and Bachelor of Arts. The story of married life, of Krishna and Sushila in ***Bachelor of Arts*** is very different in tone and spirit, from that of Indu and Prem in ***The Householder.*** Where R.K.Narayan's young English teacher indulges in creative, writing, adolescents exercises in verse - making on the pattern of Wordsworth; Nature poetry, Jhabvala's Prem is too prosaic and too pragmatic to involve himself in poetical experiences. And this is what makes the novel different from other novels dealing with social domestic situations of life.

Jhabvala's next novel ***A Backward Place*** presents several aspects of her art, her emotional and intellectual responses both as a person and as a creative writer. In its design, its human world and its controlling metaphor it has achieved on maturity which is found wanting in her early fiction. In the novel Jhabvala's central problems as a creative writer and as a foreigner living in India are most intricately combined in creating the tensions of emotions and attitudes of her experience of ***Living in Indian*** Jhabvala remarks:

> "The most salient fact about India is that it is very poor and backward. There are so many other things to be said about it but this must remain the basis of all of them. We may praise Indian democracy go into raptures over Indian music admire, Indian intellectuals- but whatever we say, not for one moment should we lose sight of the fact that a very great number of Indians never get enough to eat."[8]

While leading her own comfortable and easy life within

the four walls of an air-conditioned room, Jhabvala as an artist does not get away from what she believes to be an overwhelming aspect of the stark reality of India. The problem that India, as a stark reality or as a spiritual reality, evokes different responses. The reactions may assume the forms of affirmation or negation or ambivalence. All these areas of emotive and intellectual responses to this country are endowed with fictional art in ***A Backward Place.*** Jhabvala observes that.

> "Another approach to India's basic conditions is to accept them. This seems to be the approach favoured by most Indians".[9]

Jhabvala is also critical of the validity of the westernised Indians' attitude to the problems of their country. While Jhabvala appears to be dissatisfied with this unreality in the sophisticated westernised Indians' attitude to India, she feels more at home with the semi- educated but, deeply involved Indian joint families which share a genuine get-togetherness. Members of such families have their joys and sorrows, love and hatred, cunning and compassion -but what is more important is that they feel they form a family a social unit in which individuals, either conform or revolt. About this joint family life in Indian Jhabvala remarks:

> "There is actually something very restful about this mode of social intercourse and it certainly holds more pleasure than the synthetic social life led by westerned Indians. It is also more adapted to the Indian climate which invites one to be absolutely released in mind and body, to do nothing to think nothing just to feel to be. I have in fact enjoyed sitting around like that for hours on end."[10]

All these approaches of Jhabvala, the person, expressed prosaically in living in India are very subtly given artistic expression in ***A Backward Place.*** The most significant aspect of the novel which strikes us as a major element of Jhabvala's taught process is the dominate voice of affirmation which rings true and clear in the various chambers of its structure. Judy-appears to be the vital character in this novel who says "Aye" to all the challenges that her life and experience present to her more than Etta and more than Clarissa. Judy represents these authentic voice the dominate note of this international vision in ***A Backward Place***.

The controlling metaphor of the novel contains within himself the view points of the central intelligence, the characters who form its nucleus. One cannot says whether India or more specifically Delhi, appear to the Europeans a backward place? In the very first scene of the first chapter this attitude is projected by. Etta who is a Hungarian beauty married and divorced three times, and having to her credit numerous conquests of young Indians. She has a very superior attitude to the world and asks Judy to break off her relationship with Bal:

> "Marriage, my dear, are made to be broken, that is, one of the rules of modern civilization just because we happen to have landed ourselves in this primitive society, that is no reason why we should submit to their primitive morality." (page 5)

While Etta talks of Delhi or India as a primitive society of a backward nation, Prof. Hochstadts and his sensible wife appears to reinforce the same view as they acknowledge the incompatibility of East and West, through they seem to indicate surface appreciation of Indian art and physiology. At the end of the novel they are preparing to go back home and look forward to their little "Europe" as an escape from the backwards of civilization. The Hochstadts had, of course, passed through a phase of great admiration for Indian and great enthusiasm for the synthesis of East and West. Dr. Hochstadts says to Etta that Indians have something to teach them for the Indian spirit has in many respects surpassed the European. Dr. Hoachstadts confesses that experience in India take on a different tune from that of the life in Europe However, the Hochstadts leave India before this sweetness could really turn sour. The controlling metaphor, of India and Delhi being a backward place, illumises the human world in the novel with great complexity. A ***Backward Place*** presents Europe and India in proper prospective through the tone in which it is done is different. The induction or incursion of Europeans with their rational, scientific, materialistic heritage into the urban segment of India-Delhi presents aspect which shows the qualities of western civilization in a rather poor light. In fact, the Europeans inject into Indian society their own forms of coarseness, insensitivity and the meaninglessness of contemporary civilization.

Etta's contempt bordering on pity for Judy comes from this snobbish European attitude of injecting their value - judgement into the Indians' ethos. Jhabvala's irony is not merely directed against the European transitory visitors, it is equally forcefully directed against the westernised Indians like Mrs. Kaul or Sudhir who organised the Cultural Dais. Etta's attitude to the rural poor in India is matter-of fact and almost contemptuous. She remarks to the Hochstadts:

> "You sound like Clarissa, She is always on about the wretched people in their wretched villages or wherever they hide out. Clarissa likes her comforts Not, that I blame her. I am very keen on them myself, but what I cannot stand is all that hypocrisy about the simple life and the true values, that just makes me sick." (page 34)

This exposure of hypocrisy is not confined to a small portion of Europeans but can also be extended to include the westernised, educated Indians. Dr. Hochstadts beams with the new comer's enthusiasm of India when he talks of "correlation" as the most important aspect of this great country's civilization. He speaks not only of physical facts but also intellectual and spiritual aspect - the correlation of the old and the new of what has been and what is - This phrase seems to fit into the rhetoric of the patriotic, educated Indian of our post-Independence Establishment. The encounter between the Hochstadts and Etta presents not merely the gap between one European attitude and another but rather the division between the ideal romantic, positive perspective and a sheer negative and cynical attitude. What the Hochstadts seems to believe in is what is required to be developed in India. According to them Europe and India should be mutually contributory. It is this attitude of life and the people that needs to be cultivated so as to bring the two different civilizations closer to each other.

Jhabvala's chief concern, however, is the world of human relationships and not just intellectual rhetoric. Judy and Bal occupy an important place in ***A Backward Place.*** Judy meets Bal in London where he comes as an Indian delegate to a Conference of International Youth. She falls in love with his nice-looking face and his genial manner. Her home in England is cheerless and she is immediately taken in by Bal's youthful spirit. She marries him settles with him in a low-middle class joint-family house in Delhi. She is already a mother of two children when the novel opens and she is very deeply involved with them. Bal calls himself an artist and is associated with radio, stage and movies. Prithivi, Judy's little son has fever and he wants his father to stay with him, while Bal is keen on attending on Kishan Kumar, of Bombay film star on a visit to Delhi. While Judy is seriously concerned with Prithivi's rising temperature, Bal goes on talking on films, sings film songs while Prithvi asks for ice. Judy wants Bal to fetch ice but Bal is as different and careless as before. She asks him to do his duty as his father. Ultimately he submits but she is not happy with the kind of response she receives from him. Judy is a realist and dreamer in one- a realist she realizes Bal's weak points but as a dreamer she is thrilled by his fantasies. Judy loves him passionately, and in this she is not governed by any rational and logical pattern of life. More over she has a remarkable gift for giving and receiving affection. Although English by birth and alien by upbringing, she adjusts herself admirably into Bal's joint family. She has cultivated the English man's gift for adjustment, and she adapts for western modes to the requirements and claims of Indian culture. Her relations with Shanti, her sister-in-law and with Bhuaji, the pious old woman are very affectionate. Judy has inherited her father's mistrust of religious piety, since he associated it with the salvation Army. It appears to her external to human personality and something imposed from without, whereas to Bhuaji it was an in dwelling spirit and an article of a living faith. This good old woman tries to relate herself to religion and God in her daily life and finds spiritual joy in it. Judy, though she preserves her rationality, is inclined to believe that Bhuaji might after all be right. Judy thus moves closer to Bhuaji in spirit.

Judy seems to be truly an Indian wife and therefore appears closest to the point of affirmation. She loves Bal's fantasies partly because they sound cheerful to her in her cheerless middle class world. Bal and Sudhir are almost studies in contrast and Judy realises this difference in her relationship with them. While Bal is the embodiment of solid optimism, Sudhir shows a kind of be pessimism and even cynicism. Sudhir a sensible and knowledgable Bengali youth, is in charge of the Cultural Dais and Judy works with him. Mrs. Kaul, a showy, snobbish lady is the honorary secretary of the Dais. She is always a very well-kept and carefully groomed lady who quite often acts very coquettish and feminine especially to Sudhir.

While Sudhir wants to become a teacher just to open his mind, heart and soul to his pupils, Bal is enveloped in a world of the stage and the screen. He has always been anticipating his big chance, the moment of glory which will open up his talent and bring glamour to his personality. Bal's undying enthusiasm, however child like it appears, symbolising an element of hope in ***A Backward Place.*** He and Judy both demonstrate the sense of hope and adjustment in human character faced with flux of life, the sense that every dark cloud has a silver lining and that man must continue to dream and weave a web of fantasy in the hope that this dream may one day be translated into reality. Thus Bal's spirited enthusiasm is brought against the image of India as ***A Backward Place,*** an area of darkness filled with rays of hope for future.

The controlling metaphor of the backward place is also related to the concept of the masses who make-up India. Jayakar, the old revolutionary, who had been in jail for fifteen years, expounds his ideas of the masses and culture in relation to Sudhir's idea of the professional theatre. Jayakar raises the question of the quality of people who would respond to the professional theatre and asks Judy:

> "Were you thinking of the masses? To bring joy and jollity or perhaps culture and civilization into their drab lives? " (page 17)

Jayakar then advises Judy not to be worried over these masses. Jayakar and Sudhir both represent what we call a 'minority culture', the sophisticated as well as informal mode of behaviour of educated Indians. These Indians may be genuine and informal as Sudhir, or sophisticated and pompous as Mrs. Kaul. In the novel Jhabvala seems to reinforce the Arnoldian assault on the Philistine. Arnold's main attack on the Philistines in "Culture and Anarchy" is directed against their fake values, false tastes and the machinery of culture. The idea that etiquette is related to culture is the target of his attack on the Philistines who have a remarkable capacity in evolving efficient instruments and machinery of culture for the common people. A similar attack can be found against the upholders of the Cultural Dias in the novel. However, Judy an indirectly Jhabvala' s own concern for the poverty-stricken people of India in this quest for social improvement is not without a cause. E.M. Forster, in ***Howard End*** is basically concerned with portraying the Schlegels and the Wilcoxes the upholders of traditional culture and the followers of money civilization and at the beginning of chapter VI he writes.

> "We are not concerned with the very poor. They are unthinkable and only to be approached by the statistician or the poet. This story deals with gentlefolk, or with those who are obliged to pretend that they are gentlefolk".[11]

Even Jhabvala is not concerned with the very poor and her novels too, attempt to portray the people who pretend to be gentlefolk. However, the poor are presented by implication in ***Howards End.*** Similarly they appear to find a weak advocate in Judy. Forster's cultural point of view, the England of 1910 may appear to be as backward as India of 1965 primarily because both these cultures appear to be 'minority cultures' and more significantly Judy's important point of attack is not sustained by other characters in the novel. Jhabvala's irony In ***A Backward Place*** is thus two folds and the European as well as the Indian are brought within its framework. It is primarily through the flux of their relationships that the central metaphor of human relations operates and binds various characters and situations in one single unit.

A New Dominion throws light on the ethos of India but instead of being an area of darkness or a backward place, it is taken to be a promised land. India is no longer approached in negative terms, but rather in positive terms—as an ancient country with a rich heritage of philosophical thought and spiritual insight, challenging, provoking, inviting and inspiring three western girls Lee, Evie and Margaret. The novel presents an India which is at once harmonious and discordant, noble and profane. Thematically, the novel presents a three part division: part one is placed in Delhi; part two in holy city Benaras and part three in the Rajasthani town of Maupur. The characters both Indian and western pass from one place to another in doing so demonstrate various aspects of their personality and destiny. Jhabvala's main purpose is to depict the various aspects of ***A New Dominion*** the reality that is contemporary India in its social, cultural, religious, political and spiritual contexts. Since the scope of this reality is vast, she attempts, to grasp it in fragments through the characters that figure in the novel. These characters not only react to the large panoramic reality of the new dominion, but they also react to each other, creating a complex of human relationships which are central to the novel.

In this complex of relationships the west is represented by three girls-Lee, Evie and Margaret who are on a spiritual quest in the new dominion, and Raymond, a visitor represented as a tourist. Miss Charlotte a Christian missionary who has spent about thirty years in India in social work may be associated with Raymond since reason and common sense are their human norms. Raymonds finds it difficult to terms to the spirit of India and to him she is only a great panorama and a historical curiosity. For Miss Charlotte India is a challenging country whose immediate needs are social upliftment, education reform and a good life based on sound economic security. Whereas Raymond Miss Charlotte represent the rational, scientific and moral aspects of the culture of the west, Lee, Evie and Margaret embody a sort of dissatisfaction with it. These three girls are sick of the western way of life, its mechanical way of looking at things, its materialistic tendency and its commercial behaviour. Their reaction is not purely negative bordering on dissatisfaction and protest, but it is also positive in the sense that they carve the experiences of spiritually rich India, her God-men, her Swamis who, they are certain, will bring solace to their tortured soul, transform them into new beings and provide a life governed by the unity of mind body and soul.

The novel begins with a small episode-'Lee travels' and this is expressive of ***A New Dominion.*** Lee is the central figure in the trio and her main purpose in her journey is to lose herself in order to find herself. However, she is very sensitive to the smells of the poor in India because she is a very 'intense' girl. Lee meets Margaret in Miss Charlotte's Christian mission and finds in her a noble spirit engaged in a spiritual quest. Lee says about Margaret:

> "She is a very definite kind of a girl. Even her coming here was a definite decision. She didn't just drift into it the way I did. Margaret cane here because she had to. It was an active step of revolt against her life at home and her family." (page 37)

Margaret revolted against the convention-ridden household, the commercialism and falsity of English middle class society and refused to act her part as a bridesmaid in her sister's wedding. She revolted against the emptiness and nothingness of her English society. She turns to India and the Swamiji just to satisfy her spiritual thirst and her hunger for self- fulfilment. While Lee and Margaret do all they can to merge their selves with that of the Swamiji, as a symbol of India's heritage of mysticism and spiritual glory, Evie is even more intensely identify with what she believes to be the soul of India as represented by the Swamiji. She has unqualified faith in Swamiji's spiritual power and purity of mind and action. A reading in the ashram of a big book creates different responses in Lee, Evie and Raymond. Lee is anxious about the ailing Margaret whereas Raymond wants to take her to hospital for treatment. But the Swamiji is indifferent to Raymond's desperate plea for Margaret recovery and asks Evie to continue to read the bulky manuscript. He also asks Raymond to hold the manuscript and Englishman's reaction is hostile. The difference between the attitudes of east and west is prominently brought out in respect of an injured dog which cries terribly in pain near the ashram. Lee wants to have the dog put out of its misery, but the Swamiji bluntly rejects this, saying that 'everything must be experienced to the end' The dog, of course, dies the next morning after experiencing the full share of its pain. While Raymond shows almost a contempt for the reading of the holy book Evie is greatly pleased with it. Raymond's contempt for reading the manuscript earns Lee's displeasure and she shouts at him angrily in defence of the Swamiji:

> "How can you behave like that? Don't you realized what an honour he was doing you? I felt so ashamed of you." (page 134).

The Swamiji has of course a magnetic personality and he can create illusions of hope and bliss through a skilful use of words. The Swamiji is a type as well as an individual. He represents a new phenomenon in modern India which may be taken as the emergence of spurious God-men, but he is a person in his own right. He is worldly sensual, materialistic and he is in favour of claiming the bodies and souls of all his disciples. In fact the three English girls feel a sense of mutual jealousy among them as to their proximity with the Swamiji. Margaret fears that she under the pretext of illness, is being deliberately kept away from the Guru's presence. Lee in her attempt to become' New Person' is psychically disturbed and in that state walks into Swamiji's hut at midnight. She has a feeling that he is ignoring her. Lee's experience of sexual intercourse with the Swamiji is frightful and by contrast makes her recall the pleasant sexual adventure with Gopi she had in a hotel apartment near the Mosque. The Swamiji is indeed a spiritual and moral humbug and a religious hypocrite. He promptly claims the bodies of women, has no qualms either moral or religious and in fact becomes the cause of Margaret's ruin and death .He prevents her from being taken to hospital or even to a doctor for consultation. Margaret dies in pathetic circumstances in a dark store-room of a hospital. After her death the question arise~of her burial or cremation. Evie says that 'She was a Hindu':

> "Becoming a Hindu is not like becoming a Christian. You don't have to take formal baptism or anything but freely assent to the truth with in you." (page 207)

Evie declares that the relationship of the disciple will the Guru is the most powerful and neglects all other blood relationship..Thus the three English girls bestow all their affections their hearts and souls on the Swamiji and in return, the Swamiji seduces them, holds them by his charm and treats them as his personal properties, physical as well as spiritual. Talking to Raymond about them the Swamiji says,

> "They would sit all day and discuss about themselves for them their own personality is the most important subject in the world. But-poor girls—what personality do they have worth talking about? They are like little

> mice, quite undeveloped. And when I try to develop the, they run away from me. (page 178).

This pompous and ridiculous claim and the desire to develop their personality bring about the repulsive elements in the Swamiji's character. As a clever manipulator of men and women he says that in his relationship with Lee he is the injured party and that there is a contract between him and her which she has violated by running away from him. This contract certainly has many unwritten terms including midnight sex sessions, and yet he expects her to return. This seems to be the limit of human depravity and moral poverty. However quite surprisingly Lee in her psychic depth feels still attracted to him and probably wants to go back to him, Lee's relationship with the Swamiji is something beyond normal human comprehension.

Her relationship with Gopi has the same physical connotation. With Gopi, she suffers, rather than enjoyed her experience with him. What is worst is that Lee again rushes into similar areas of experience and even at the end of the novel, her predicament, implicit in her incapacity to distinguish between simple bodily pleasure and the joy of spiritual merger, remains as puzzling as ever. Evie's responses to the Swamiji are no less inscrutable. While the fake Swamiji was busy destroying and recreating Lee, he took possession of Evie's and Margaret's souls, Evie's fascination for the Swamiji is difficult to describe exactly, but surely it approximates to the grotesque when she speaks to Lee

> We'll go soon now. As soon as Margarets dead. She adds in a joyful voice: How happy he'll be to have us back!'" (page 198)

Whereas Lee Evie and Margaret try to become 'insiders' to the Ashram a prominent part of the 'New Dominion', Raymond, the rational Westerner, remains an 'outsider'. Raymond considers himself a tourist in India, whereas Lee tries unsuccessful to break the barriers of his stoicism. He makes polite conversation to her as Lee tells him that his favourite friend, Gopi, is with Asha. His face becomes flushed as he tries to control his feelings. Though Raymond is a tourist, an outsider, he is quite involved in his relationship with Gopi. Their relationship too, is inscrutable and the silences or ambivalences appear quite ominous. Gopi is a young energetic Indian with a pretty face and seems a curious Jhabvala version of the 'Divine savage' a significant phenomenon in the modern European novel.

Gopi is utterly sensuous and sensual and he provokes excites and entices Lee and Asha. Lee ad Gopi swim together in the hotel's swimming pool and finally Lee succumbs to his desire to sleep with her. Then Asha tries and succeeds in wooing him and he allows her to dote on him. Even Banubai, the ascetic prophetess, is very fond of Gopi as she thinks him to be childlike affectionate and even innocent. However, Lee seems to suspect some odd relationship between Gopi and Raymond. Asha the widowed sister of Rao Sahib formerly a prince of a small Indian state, is essentially a sensual woman. The fact that she is a non-conformists and definitely challenges all the norms of good behaviour is only one aspect of her sensuality. In a meeting of snobbish society women chaired by Sanita, Rao Sahib's wife, Asha smokes drinks openly and when she is bored she drums her feet on the floor and creates a great scene. In a midnight scene in her drawing room. Asha speaks to Lee of Love, its charms and agonies, and of her fear of being old. Asha finds in Gopi an amorous, youthful figure who could satisfy her thirst for physical enjoyment, and their stay in Maupur in the little desert pleasure-house can only be described as a sexual extravaganza. Gopi is by then engaged and preparations for his wedding are in full swing, but Asha, doting on him tries to keep him away from this event. Gopi too gives in her coquettry and dominating sensuality and at this ambivalent stage curtain is drawn on their relationship.

Rao Sahib embodies a new phase of modern India, its new political look, the transformation of prince into populist politician. But the basic factor in this change in man's craze for power which will assume various forms to assert itself. He talks eloquently on the political problem the new dominion and is appreciative of the values of the rising rich businessmen and shopkeepers in India. He is more aware of public causes than personal predicaments. He talks of India as a secular state, and of the policy of self -reliance, democracy and socialism using high-sounding words which he openly parades before Raymond. Jhabvala' s comment on this attitude is a fine example of civilized irony:

> "Raymond was sad; Rao Sahib's words were so big and Miss Charlotte's efforts so small." (page73)

Jhabvala's concern with the other side of this rising new dominion, too, is a frankly fearlessly expressed. She is always worried over that phantom like animal in Indian- the extreme poverty of the poor and the gap that divides the extreme poor from the excessively rich. Jhabvala's irony is two fold— it is directed against the indifferent new rich in India as well as the luxury loving foreigners in the new dominion. Against this background Rao Sahib's assertion of progress appears to be pompous. However, Deepak's assertion that India shall be self-sufficient within four years is almost ridiculous in this context. The fact that milk meant for children was sold in the black market brings out the corruption in public services. Explaining the significance of the title of ***A New Dominion,*** Jhabvala's observed "A New Dominion is an attempt to bring out the reality of India".[12]

The novel breaks new ground in technique also. Though Jhabvala carries forward her method of omniscient narrator in this novel too is a much greater emphasis here on what Percy Lubbock define as 'point of view' and therefore the novel is divided into small episodes highlighting the perspective of a particular character. The novel's unconventional mode is designed "to represent the random workings of the mind without the forced consecutiveness of a book."[13]

The novel projects the British and American view of contemporary India. The basic irony that runs throughout the novel is that while the British girls are running after a spiritual India to enable them to find their self-and-solve their personal predicaments, the India that they experience is the very opposite of their original idea. India in this novel comes off rather badly, and the Indians even worse, the total effect of it is very disappointing and negative. Granting that Jhabvala' s main position is that of a social satirist, and that she has the total freedom of the creative artist to choose her human material, her view of the new dominion has to be pronounced as very depressing and one-sided.

It was ***Heat and Dust*** that won for Jhabvala the prestigious Booker Prize in 1975 and made her an international figure. 'Heat' and 'Dust' appear to have become Jhabvala's major obsession, also the source and substance of her creative imagination. The first reference to the title occurs in Oliva's way of life, in fact, the first phase of it when, as the wife of Douglas, the Assistant Collector at Satipur, she lives in a large dull house. She feels bored and alienated in that large house:

> "The rest of the time Olivia was alone in her big house with all the doors and windows shut to keep out the heat and dust." (page 14)

The heat and dust thus embody an aspect of India, the one which the Olivias and Jhabvalas alike seem to react to India. The terms 'Heat' and 'Dust' project two unpleasant things to which most Europeans are allergic. Olivia's India as reflected in her diary and letters, is the India of the early thirties. Olivia, the wife of Douglas, eloped with the young Nawab of Khatma in September 1923 is one of the central characters of the novel. ***Heat and Dust*** is in fact, a novel of two women, Olivia and the young narrator whose name has not been mentioned anywhere. They stand for a generation gap in the attitude of European women towards India. The narrator is introduced to us as a young person and she was just three years old when Douglas breathed his last. Beths Crawford was her aunty and Tessie Beth's sister, her grandmother. Tessie married Douglas after he got a divorce from Olivia. The young narrator happens to be Tessie's, granddaughter and she is on a visit to India just to unfold the mysteries of Olivia's stay in India and the pleasent or unpleasant episodes of her life, her friends, her parties and many other activities with which she was connected. Thus Olivia's India was gathering dust which has been cleared by the narrators attempt of reconstructing her life in India. The narrator makes a judicious use of Olivia's letters in this attempt and the young inheritor too writes a diary of her first few day in India. Olivia's as well as the young narrator's (having been identify with Jhabvala's) imagination slowly but surely gathers heat, gains momentum and becomes evocative in removing the dust that has come to be settled on the India of early thirties. The young woman's responses are clearly different in tone, rhythm and spirit from those of Olivia and the creative interchange of dust and heat thus stands for the process of the creative imagination itself.

The narrative element In ***Heat and Dust*** is as significant as it is In ***A New Dominion.*** In both these novels Jhabvala presents a grasp of narrative mode and maturity of technique which underline her later fiction. ***Heat and Dust*** is essentially a story of Olivia alternating with the story of the narrator, the past is thus brought in close association with the present and this subsequent change in outlook is skilfully projected.

As the novel opens, the social and the familial setting of Olivia's life is slowly unfolded and the oddities of Anglo-Indian families in individual and social responses are brought to the force. Mrs. Crawford and Miss Minnies ironically call themselves 'tough old hens', and Olivia's predicaments are highlighted in presenting the differences among European women in India. While Jhabvala is unsparing in her irony, especially against Mr. Saunders, she also sounds a negative note in making her feelings to India as an artist. Olivia's attitude to life is not, however, always constant and she surrenders to the Nawab and to the call of the body without giving any serious thought what she is going to do.

Olivia is invited by the Nawab to a picnic and a visit to the shrine of Saba Fridaus. They sit by a little spring of bubbling water between two rocks amidst a green grove in a desert, and he talks of miracles. They playa game of musical chairs and Olivia gets drawn towards the young Nawab. Even Harry too is attracted to the Nawab as is indicated by his willingness to live in the palatial suits. The relationship between Harry and the Nawab is puzzling though there are moments when they are genuinely involved in affection. At first Olivia appears to be deeply in love with Douglas, though she is opposed to the Anglo-Indian official stereotypes. She is against going to Simila along with Mrs. Crawford as an escape from the 'heat' and 'dust' of the unbearable Indian summer because she wants to be with Douglas and also be part of the Nawab's parties. She also actively takes part in a discussion of the Indian customs of 'suttee' caused by a grain merchants's death and the consequent force used on his wife to burn herself along with her husband's body. She was forced to burnt herself by her relatives and since this was an instrumental in instigating them. He tackled the situation in a becoming way and was praised by the Nawab for his immediate action.

Mrs. Jhabvala tries to recreate the India of the twenties and thirties and this is marked by a flair for the exotic, the strange the odd elements of life rather than by the rigid realities of the situation. Jhabvala also focuses her attention on incident concerning the dacoits, the gay parties, the hijras so as to break out that aspect of India which has always turned the Europeans against Indian. She also throws light on modern Indian which is projected to be one-sided, unbalanced and incomplete. The narrator come across a young Englishman and his girl quarrelling for a place with the watchman of a travellers' rest-house. This young man, it seems, was attracted to Hindu religion after listening to a visiting Swami in London on Universal Love. The Swami described love as an ocean of sweetness that surrounds all men and women. He spoke about love in a very convincing and effective manner and those who heard him could not resist the temptation of visiting India to see the various mysteries surrounding her. The young man and his girl decided to visit India to experience at first hand this universal love and India's great spiritual heritage. He came to India lived among the Sadhus and finally found a Guru who gave him initiation a new existence and a new name. He got converted to Hinduism and changes his name to Chidananda and his friends simply called him Chid. After a few days the narrator, while walking with Inder Lala in the Royal Tombs, hears a groan and enters one of the ruined building She recongnizes the deserted man as Chid whom she had met at the travellers' rest-house. He is sick and therefore given a shelter in the narrator's small room. Soon he recovers from his fever but doesn't want to move out of the room. He wants the young woman to give him food and he is also hungry for sex. Sexual appetite is most intricately compounded with religious or spiritual pursuit in ***Heat and Dust.*** The narrator has the following to comment on Chid.

> "He is always hungry, and not only for food. He also needs sex very badly badly and seems to take it for granted that I shall give it him the same way I gave him my food." (page 65)

But the appetite is not so simple as that and the narrator has a feeling of being used by Child to reach a higher plane of consciousness through the powers of sex. She has no idea about all this and yet she permits him to go ahead and satisfy his hunger for sex. She is physically stronger than him, and can easily defeat in the game, but she doesn't do so simply because she feels it is due to some emanation which comes not from within him, but from some powers outside himself. Normally he seems so utterly sexless to her—his chicks having been smooth without much growth of hair and is terribly skinny like one recovering from a prolonged illness.

Jhabvala skilfully brings out an intricate design in which the experiences of two generations of English men and women and their Indian counter parts are brought in a very close association with a view to projecting the differences between them. The characters appear to move round the same spot, the same centre, and relive that experience. And how differently they respond to the situation and the spot. This only highlights the young narrator's knowledgeable comment: "India always changes people" the perspective on sex finds a variety of expression in ***Heat and Dust.*** For instance, Mrs. Saunders develops an abnormal fear of the Indian's sexuality. She is too ill to know the truth and yet very susceptible to the fear of an imaginary sexual onslaught. Olivia visits her to enquire about her health and finds her sitting on a sopha rather than lie in bed. Olivia, is surprised, but Mrs. Saunders whispers, "It is not good let see you in bed, the servants your don't know what goes on in their heads" (Page **119).** And then she tells her of a lady from Somerset who lives in Muzzafarbad. This adds one more variation to the rather superficial and sensual treatment of sex theme in ***Heat and Dust.*** To cut the matter short, sex in ***Heat and Dust*** has hardly any heat or real life-giving fire. It stays too much on the surface, or becomes an instrument of disaster.

The Nawab and Olivia visit the Baba Firdaus Shrine and although the young prince apparently disbelieves in miracles, he and Olivia both tie strings to get their wishes fulfilled. The Nawab tells Olivia of his ancestor; Amanullah Khan who got his title in 1817. He was a violent fighter and finally settled for a small state and title because he was tired. The present Nawab goes on to tell Oilvia of Amanullah Khan's valour and fighting spirit. Once a Marwar prince displeased him by not offering opium in the appropriate silver pot-but Amanullah Khan did not take it as an insult though it was only a very small thing a clear sign of lack of manners. He invited the prince and his colleagues for a party, a ceremonial tent was put up and there were the usual civilities of reception and embracing. The guest sat up in the tent a secret sign was made, the ropes of the tent were cut and the prince and his men were entangled in the canvas and trapped. Then Amanullah and his inhuman companions stabbed each one of them with draggers and no one was left alive. The young Nawab speaks with pride about this shameless act of homicide, the treacherous killing of invited guests and says to Olivia:

> "We still have that tent and the blood so fresh and new; Olivia its is as it has happened yesterday." (Page 137)

This passage fills us with bitter disgust not merely for Amanullah Khan, but his equally incredulous and treacherous descendant, the young Nawab. Going through this episode it is not possible for us to call the Nawab a romantic hero. He is not even a picaresque hero. He is however very erratic and sometimes childishly funny which probably attracts Olivia to him.

The basic reason, however, is that Olivia is too bored with Douglas and the dull, morality-conscious English setting and Indo-Anglian social background. It is strange that after narrating the story of the treacherous blood both in the tent, the Nawab takes Olivia to bed. He leads her away from shrine and they lie together under a tree. The Nawab jokes about the secret of the Husband's Wedding Day and indeed it makes Olivia pregnant.

Olivia's pregnancy sets into motion forces which bring about her decline. Douglas, when he comes to know of his wife's "'pregnancy, create-little castles in the air of his son's future. The Nawab, however is sure that the child is his, and he dismisses Douglas from his thoughts. Olivia visits the palace frequently, the Nawab strokes her growing belly, becoming more and more possessive of her. It is strange that Olivia is taken to a quack and the crude operation performed by him is supervised by the Nawab's first wife, the Begum. Olivia returns home, Douglas takes her to hospital and Dr. saunders soon realizes the true cause of her abortion. This becomes known to Douglas and his friends and Olivia leaves the hospital for the Nawab's palace. He finally keeps her in a house where she dies after a few years.

In this sordid tale of amorous adventure the Naawab as well as Olivia appear to us awfully puny and small creatures. They come off badly and to explain their relationship in terms of genuine love or fellow-feeling nothing is sort of a travesty of truth. Jhabvala's description of princely India is extremely unrealistic and pseudo-romantic. She, however makes a realistic attempt to show the Nawab's human quality, his lavish hospitality, his generosity and his capacity to get involved in other people's problems and affections. He is, of course, very erratic and lacks a stable emotional balance.

Sex and pregnancy appear to be parts of a recurring rhythm of the sequence of events in ***Heat and Dust.*** The young narrator, too, gets pregnant and does not want Inder Lal to know about it since he will start worrying over it. Unlike Olivia, this young narrator will have her baby and she hopes to go upto the mountains and join an ashram. She cherishes, as Olivia did two generations earlier, the view of the high, snow-covered mountains and clear, deep blue sky. Heat and Dust ends thus:

> "That is what I expec to see, perhaps it is also what Olivia saw: The view on vision-that filled her eyes all those years and suffused her soul." (Page 180)

It is difficult to relate Jhabvala' s constant sneering of the experience of India, as presented in the attitudes, manners and gestures of the characters in ***Heat and Dust,*** to anything like a Himalayan vision of snow-covered peaks and the vast arch of a heavenly blue sky. We just cannot say whether the puny Olivia and the erratic Chid whom she has, created will become on with the vast spaces of the Indian earth and the Indian sky and in this process they go beyond their smallness and their punny dimension. However, at the end of the novel the English appear to be packing their luggage and getting ready to go back home. Ironically, the Nawab, too, goes to London to lead a rather sedate life there. As if this is not enough he dies later in New York. ***Heat and Dust*** is a skilfully manipulated picture of princely India put against an equally deftly drawn picture of modern India, and both these parallels are presented from the European point of view. There is hardly a scene in the novel which is genuinely moving or touching.

The main cause of Jhabvala failure as an artist in Heat and Dust is that she does not make any use of the ample opportunities of exploring the inner like of her characters. Ritu is a psychological case and so is Chid. Jhabvala keeps these doors and windows of their psyche totally shut and we have to remain content with merely their outward appearance. ***Heat and Dust*** is a remarkable work of art as it artistically presents the processes of change, the processes of 'becoming' of two English women; and one of them the young narrator, acknowledge this meaningfully in words which appear to be the heart of matter.

> "India always changes people, and I have been no exception. But this is not my story, it is Olivia's as for as can follow it" (page 9)

However, the reader knows that *Heat and Dust* is as much Olivia's story as it is the young narrator's. This technique of double narration enables story as it is the young narrator's This technique of double narration enables Jhavbala to develop a sense of detachment. It also enables her to highlight her vision amidst a human an natural landscape enveloped in heat and covered by dust.

REFERENCES

1. Northrop Frye; "The Argument of Comedy." *Comedy Marvin Felhieim,* New York, 1962, p. 237.
2. "Passage to India" Walt Whitman Gay Wilson Allen and C.T. Davis, Walt Whitman's Poems, New York 1955, p. 235.
3. L.J. Potts *Comedy* (London 1949), p. 10.
4. Khuswant Singh, His remark about Jhabvala, R.K. Narayan and other India Writer Writing in English, *Illustrated Weekly* of India, 197
5. Myself in India' in *An Experience of India,* p. 8.

6. Doroothy Van Ghent-The English novels. From and function New York, 1953, p. 148.
7. Lionel Trilling. The liberal Imagination, London 1949, p. 30.
8. 'My self in India' in *An Experience of India*, p. 8.
9. *Ibid.*, p. 8.
10. *Ibid.*, p. 14.
11. E.M. Forster, Howards End, A Vintage Book, New York, 1921 p. 45.
12. Ram Lal Agarwal" An Interview with Ruth Prawer Jhabvala *Quest*. Bombay Sept. Oct. 1974" p. 35.
13. David Lodge, *The Novelist at the Crossroads*, London, 1971 Page 13

6

Stylistic Patterns

Ruth Prawer Jhabvala occupies a distinguished place among the novelists of Indo-English literary scene. She undoubtedly ranks foremost among the outstanding novelists of the post-Independence era and is considered second to none but the big three-Mulk Raj Andnd, Raja Rao and R.K. Narayan. Just like Kamala Markandaya, Nayan Tarashagal Anita Desai and other female writers she too enriched the literary horizon of post-Independence period with the varied hues of her fictional mosaic. In spite of her divergent culture and up bringing she has remained in tune with her contemporary literary milieu. She seems to the observation that "Women are natural story tellers even when they don't write or publish."[1] Margaret Atwood too subscribes to this remark when she comments that with their skills in communication women are extremely good at finding thing out and so providing themselves with material.[2]

> "Novelist use a combination in varying proportions of what they have experienced what they have discovered and what they have imagined"[3]

Jhabvala uses this creative faculties with rare insight and displays an amazing range of experience and imagination in perceiving the reality of her surroundings Jhabvala in her fiction presents a blatantly realistic picture of the post independence familial and social scene of urban India.

Though Jhabvala is not an Indian atleast by birth yet she IS endowed with keen power of observation. She observes the life around her in a detached and dispassionate manner.

She is often compared with Jane Austen for her realistic delineation of the familial and social scene in urban middle class life. Some of her novels are ironic illustratonof inter cultural dichotomy.

The fictions of Jhabvala clearly fall under two distinct groups. Her first four novels namely ***To Whom She Will, The Nature of Passion,*** The Householder and Get Ready For Battle are gentle comedies of manner having a totally Indian cast of character dealing with the world she was exposed to and knew best - that of the urban middle class. The second group of novels namely ***Esmond in India, A Backward Place, A New Dominion*** and ***Heat and Dust*** deals with a problem much closer to her own heart- that of being an alien in her adopted country

In almost all her stories and novels Jhabvala takes on the role of an in this method Jhabvala tells a story with several perspectives without, of course, personally getting involved in any of them. She is presented at the site of the character as she continuously watches them and comments on their actions and modes of feeling. She thus appears to be an outsider ·of -while- yet she plunges into the small circles, enters the consciousness of her characters and then describes what she has observed and assessed so meticulously. As a European writer, Jhabvala' s frequent emphasis upon painting or describing minute details of apparently unimportant scenes or events is a significant feature of her art. The western intelligence thrives on comprehensiveness and thoroughness in subject under review. As an artist. Jhabvala inherits this western intellectual discipline and highlights it in her fictional world. Jhabvala is also aware of the fact that she is writing for western audience who are not familiar with Indian cultures or modes and therefore her comprehensiveness receives additional impetus. Her area of observation is very wide and she renders all that she observes in a comprehensive coverage. Sometimes this tendency carried to a greater degree with the result that an Indian reader is almost bored. But the western reader, who is unfamiliar with the scene, gets thrilled

Jhabvala doesn't succeed in cultivating the art of organic description or narration. Modern novelists make description an organic art implying that it is an important part of plot, characterization or symbol. Jhabvala's art of fiction highlights this organic quality, the modes of narration and methods of characterization. Like Somerest Maugham Jhavbvala seems to give much attention to food and eating mode of the characters in fiction. Her outlook appears to be governed by one notion. Since food is one of the essentials of living, especially in India the food habits of Indian or their sense of intense enjoyment of spicy food preparation may be of primary interest to western readers. Excessive emphasis upon food however makes a clear departure from the modes of her organic art and the descriptions are neither related to the character portrayal nor to thc development of plot or theme. This seems to hang on to characters or situations without much significance. However the love of spicy food becomes an aspect of the sensuous pleasure-loving character of individuals. Gulab, the Indian wife of an Englishman, Esmond, is very fond of spicy dishes and this scene in Esmond in India brings out Jhabvala's mode of organic art, highlighting food habits.

> "Ravi was already taking the cover off the little earthen ware pots. "carrot halwal' Gulab looked pleased herlarge melancholy eyes flashed for aninstant with a wonderful food. In the other posts were gram, tomatoes andpotatoes swimming in red curry and chunks of meat soaked in curds. Everything would be highly spiced. Gulab smiled with pleasure." (page-19)

Bachani then tells Gulab that she will make hot parathas for her which pleases her and Gulab lies on the floor very comfortably and very Indian. Jhabvala succeeds in catching and convincing the 'Indianness' of Gulab's mode of life and the food and other habits and their long descriptions become part of this strategy of character portraying. Jhabvala is a skilled artist in employing environment as a means for revelation of character. For example at a simple level a person who has an over decorated drawing room over flowing with glossy heavy furniture, ornate curtains may be feather-brained creature. Jhabvala's art of environment as a means of portraying character crises or conflict in human relationships is an important feature of her art of fiction especially as a European writer she responses intensely to the tropical sun of Indian horizons. In ***Get Rea for Battle*** Sarla Devi and her daughter-in- law Mala, are shown involved in moments of crisis, of values and human relationships. While Sarla Devi speaks with sincere passion, Mala is too excite~ too angry, too hot to listen. Her face is flushed and her ripe bosom goes up and down. The room is warm; "It was intensely hot on the veranda; heat, seeped from the stone floor and the tall pillar and the garden, all that beautiful green, lay dead in the white sun" (page -89)

The hot, red hot tropical sun of the Indian sky is Jhabvala's constant obsession. It is the sun which seems an ordeal to the quiet European given to cool climates and organized life. The order of his life is violently disturbed by this unbearable heat and he loses his temper, he shouts, he quarrels; he gesticulates in anger and hatred so much so that the heat appears to disintegrate his personality. Under its influence, he makes love to all kinds of women or vice-versa in cheap restaurants or turns spiritual. The heat distorts his quest for India and spiritual disillusionment is the inevitable dark harvest of his frustrated efforts. Environment thus, plays a major role in Jhabvala's fictional world.

In this way her technique becomes part of her vision. It becomes a discovery. In fiction the reader's response to characters is governed by the way they talk. A voice in a drawing room or market place enables the reader to visualize the person, his qualities and his way of life. The dialogue is also expressive of that person's culture, manners and morals. It may some times suggest a class, high-brow, middle-brow or low-brow, or at other times a social fabric which goes beyond accepted social categories. In Jhabvala's fiction the dialogue between Indians and Englishmen sometimes appears to emerge from this social fabric partly because it arises out of the coming together of two different cultures. In the ***Householder,*** Prem calls on Hans, a European seeker of Indian mystical experience and is puzzled by the atmosphere of the place. Hans,.1 landlady invites Prem to come and live with them.

"What a marvellous idea! cried Hans who entered just then. Come and live with us Prem ! 'And be our love, said the landlady. Shechuckled:That's a quotation, you know, come andlive with me and live withus Prem ! 'And be our love, said the landlady. She However, the dialogue becomes highly artificial when the western man is confronted with a genuine Indian experience unfamiliar to him. The dialogue between people belonging to two different cultures highlights the artificial nature of the relationship between east and west. However, Jhabvala succeeds in dramatically projecting the Indian modes of behavior in an appropriate phrase which is authentic. In ***To Whom She Will*** Radha speaks to Tarla," You with all your committee shommitte, you must know you must know somebody (Page-l 60).

This sound-variation of committes is authentic Indian style, which goes very well with Radha's attitude too busibodies among women. r Just now they are coming' is a typical Indian use of English, almost a translation of an Indian vernacular expression in Hindi. The Indian fondness of the indiscriminate use of the present continuous has been well rendered into English and made fun of by Jhabvala. Jhabvala's use of Indian English is faithful and gives a realistic picture of the Indians' linguistic modes and oddities.

> "There is a dinnerpartytonight, Usha told Aruna' you will come? (Page 54)

The Indian distortion of the interrogation mood is characteristic of the cultivated people's manner of speech in India today. Jhabvala records not merely the peculiar Indian patterns of speech realistically, but she also captures the movement of typical Indian gestures. Language thus becomes gesture and a mirror of modes of behavior. The syntax is primarily logical and highlights the important aspects of character or situation. Jhabvala' s use of situational segments of English language may be termed, in linguistics, as a 'register'. A register is governed by the range of vocabulary and syntax proper to the occasion or the person who speaks. Each register indicates a quality of speech or the speaker. Jhabvala frequently uses a single register since she assumes the rolel the omniscient narrator. However, she uses varied registers to project the peculiarities of characters and situation to highlight the comic tone. For example; we can quote pompous use of language in Mr. Chadda's talk at the principal's tea party in ***The Householder:***

> "A sense of Comradeshipmoreover' I saidMr. Chadda, that will survive and trumph over any buffets of fortune that in might be our fate to encounter (Page 102)

Mr. Chadda's Indian English brings out victorial pompousness and of ponderous moral tone. This register is of course different from Jhabvala's own register as, third person narrator. She also uses other registers marked by philosophical ideas as reflected in some of the titles of her novels such as for Battle, The Householder and The Nature of Passion -Since Jhabvala is basically a writer of domestic comedy with ":.,on emphasis on irony or social satire, her language hardly acquires any poetic tone. Imagery in fiction is given high rating in modern criticism, but Jhabvala's novels have little evidence of the use of image. She makes use of imagery in a very usual and selective manner.

Jhabvala's use of irony must be distinguished from her use of sarcasm or satire. Irony is a kind of utterance which presents a double audience comprising one party that hears but does not understand, and another party which hears as well as realizes the deeper significance of the expression.

Jhabvala in her ironic tone succeeds in splitting her audience between those who perceive and those who do not. She expects the reader to perceive the hidden meaning that lies beneath the surface statement, the gulf that lies between the appearance of a situation and the reality that underlies it. Jhabvla makes use of different forms of irony such as verbalirony of rhetorical irony, but herfiction does not offer many examples of drmtic or tragic irony. She is also ironic in the generlsense of that word sometimes used by the New Critics to indicate that total context of a poem projecting several disaparate elements of experience. Her fiction is iron because it takes in account and presents the complexities and incongruities of her aesthetic experience.

Jhabvala's style is the 'subject' and not 'the man' and this 'subject' is India in relation to a western creative writer'ssensibility. This is both natural as well as human. Although technique is in a certain sense discovery or vision, often a point, technique and talent appear to go their own way sin different directions. Modern fiction in English is full alive to its techniques and tools. The modern novelist tries to explore and interpret the complex nature of the modern spirit and in this context almost all Indo-Anglian writers, with the exception of Raja Rao, seem to indicate an odd failure. In a realist like Ruth Prawer Jhabvala we find a very sensitive creative writer. However, she is often preoccupied with environment only, with India as its focal point. Elizabeth Bowen's comment on the fiction of the D.H. Lawrene can be cited as an example.

> "We want the naturalist surface, but with a kind of internal burning. In Lawrence every bush nurns."[4]

The vision of Lawrence finds an objectification in his technique projecting passionate private world of vales. But in Ruth Prawer Jhabvala the bushes are neat and green but they never seem to burn. There may be writers in whose work there is burning but no bush, where as in Jhabvala there is a bush without being burnt. As Jhabvala tries unconsciously to identify herself more and more with India- the objective correlative of her aesthetic emotions - it seems likely that her comprehensive world will picture more bushes with not merely flourish but also burn, and this combination of talent and technique will, in the days~e bring into the great artist in all her true glory. It goes without saying Ruth Prawer Jhabvala has come to be recognized as an international novelist and short stories writer. It is an established fact that she appears to be better known abroad than in India. Her achievement as a literary artist is distinctive and at the same time limited. It is distinctive because she has developed and demonstrated the qualities of a literary artist which are her own and which naturally emerge from a social and cultural fabric peculiar to her-self. She has sometimes been described as an 'inside-outsider' and other times as an 'outside-insider'. These apparently contrary expressions are more meaningful than more high-sounding literary terms since they are concerned with her literary and personal situation. She is basically a European writer who lived in India and who has given to her experience of life and society in India as an artistic expression. From the western point of view she may appear to be an 'Outsider - insider' while from the Indian artistic view point she can be taken to be an 'inside-outsider.' Both these positions indicate a basic change of perspective, though one of them is inherent in her literary situation. Whether Jhabvala is an 'inside-outsider' or 'outsider-insider' is not, however the most significant feature of her literary achievement. What is most significant is her awareness of man, society, human and moral aspects that she projects in her experience. This awareness also includes her knowledge of the human heart, both in its individual and universal context, as well as the inward understanding of the social and cultural patterns and values. This appears to be central point of all literary art and the final evaluation of creative writer depends upon the kind of performance and achievements with which they credit themselves.

John Read, while evaluating Jhabvala's artistic achievement, observes that "Jhabvala is better equipped than even E.M. Forster to deal with the mysteries of Indian psyche"[5] she is unlike E.M. Forster not really involved in the mysteries that India or Indians present to a creative western writer. Her worldliness and realistic approach to life indirectly helps her in avoiding the pitfalls of sentimentality or superficial involvement with varieties of Indian religious or mystical beliefs. Her merit as creative writer is guided by her awareness of her limitations. She writes about that urban India with which she is well acquainted. The general belief that she writes about only the sophisticated upper class is rather an unfair exaggeration because her writings, as we find in A backward place present the lower middle class with sympathy and understanding. She also portrays the rising commercial class which is by no means really sophisticated. In fact, this is the new rich class which has sprung from the brink of poverty and want, and which is mad after culture refinement and respectability. Thus in enlarging the area of her social and cultural setting in her fiction, Jhabvala shows her awareness of the variety and complexity of the post-independent Indian Society.

Jhabvala's art of fiction fatrows the path of the comic and develop the form of a social comedy of manners. According to George Meredith, comedy depicts men and women in society, that the setting of comedy is primarily urban, and that the comedy writer presents a social and cultural outlook with a view to determining man's behavidr against an accepted norm. Man's conduct has to be judged against a norm rather than an ideal, and this norm takes into account a sense of proportion. All writers of comedy present a point of view in which this norm is implicit, and for measuring eccentricity, abnormality, we must have a moral consideration in view. Jhabvala is good at in presenting incongruities of human character and behavior. These incongruities have social, familial and cultural dimensions and consequently they become the source of the comic. In The Nature of passion, Nimmi speaks of her college and the lecture on Keats poetry and Om makes fun of the whole business of girls going to college.

> "This college is only a waste of time and good money, and will perhaps even given her wrong ideas. At this Usha laughed. She had failed many times to pass Inter and reference to this always moved her to good humored laughter." (Page 17)

The idea of sending girls to college in Lalaji's family creates conflict between the old and the young, tradition and modernity. But this difference in values is presented comicall and in a sarcastic mode. The incongruities in human behavior are highlighted through the character and behavior of Lalaji sitting in his office and receiving persons who would call upon him for help. Jhabvala has remarkable capacity for observing Indian modes of behavior. The Indianness of India writers in English or European writers on India has often been raised in relevant critical forums. Sometimes this question itself has been taken to be insubstantial because creative literature deals with the universals in human passion and reason rather they any specific area and part. Sometimes the problems of Indian sensibility, Indian cultures and traditions and Indian way to living have been considered very significant in creative writing. It is of course true that the Indian creative writing especially fiction has to be judged primarily, as art and only secondarily, as an expression of social ethic or values. However, the ethic or values are closely linked up with the aesthetic form of the great art of literature, and should not be considered in isolation. The Indianness of India art of fiction in English is therefore very much a part of that art itself. The Indianness of Indian creative writing in English must be judged by the awareness of the author of certain specific and special characteristics of societies and cultural patterns in India. For example Indian society has always been more a compact society than its counterpart in the west. Although the concept of the joint family system is losing its relevance under various economic and social pressures, Indian society even in urban area still preserves this compactness and the get-togetherness of family ties, Jhabvala shows her deep awareness of this aspect of Indian society. In fact, many of her novels are primarily concerned with portraying either the fulfillment or frustration of individuals in the undivided Hindu joint family system. Lalaji in ***The Nature of Passion*** behaves almost like a benevolent person having in mind the welfare and happiness of his children and members of the family. ***The Nature of Passion*** is almost like a family chronicle and in this sense essentially Indian. It is also India in the way in which it highlights the conflicts between two families in the context of the present day changes in urban parts of India. The gap between the young and the old, tradition and modernity and the rebels against that tradition mark the social world of Jhabvala's fictions. These situations are both individual and general at one level or the other. The experience of such individuals caught up in the world of social change is basically Indian as much as it is universal in a wider sense.

Jhabvala takes much interest in portraying the predicament of individuals in their relationship to the family, to the social group, in a way which highlights her Indianness. Lalaji's second son, Chandra Prakash, a government official who is married to Kanta, is to some extent isolated from the family but in part allied with it. He looks forward to his career as the head of the department and his wife is deeply aware of their newly acquired western culture. He regards himself an intellectual and tries to prove at every step that he is different from his family members who know only the art of making money. He and his wife both however need the money and the financial help that the joint family, and especially Lalaji, provides. The dislike of the commercial class is thus combined with a peculiar sense of dependence on that class and this brings out the contradictions prevailing in the present day Indian society.

There is another aspect of this Indian familial setting which Jhabvala portrays with considerable power and deep sense of inward understanding. The experience of European women married to Indians or of Indian women married to Europeans who are brought face to face with this peculiar situation of the Hindu joint families is sharply projected in her fiction. Gulab's marriage to Esmond has brought about no change in her life style. She is still fond of the spicy food that her mother or the cook prepares for her and Egmond is left with no choice but to dislike the strong smells of spices. European women such as Peggy in ***The Aliens*** gets cultural shocks when her sister-in-law comes to her room and opens all the drawers without even seeking her permission. This is not merely a minor question of social manners or surface formalities, but one which presents difference between the individualistic European families and the socially close-knit Indian families. Jhabvala displays her acute awareness of this difference in the characters and the situations, they are faced with, in her fiction. In this sense she is both European and Indian thereby making her distinctive position among creative writers in English solid and tangible. In ***The Aliens*** Jhabvala highlights the sufferings and predicaments of Peggy, an English girl married to Dev and made to live in a joint family of Punjabi Hindu businessman. She feels rather isolated in the family because she does not approve of the coarseness of her mother-in-law

> "Some of the split water came trickling into Peggy's lap. She got up and murmured in order to make a point of keeping up her manners she went beck into the study where her writing paper still lay on the desk. She sat down and suddenly she was writing very fast. All of a sudden she stopped, not because there wasn't plenty more to say but because she wasn't sure whether the word she wanted was spelt 'course' or 'coarse'. She knew she would never send any such letter" (In Like Birds Like Fishers Page – 99)

Peggy with he English background s repugnant to this insensitivity and coarseness of men and women of a civilization which is immensely guided by monetary considerations. However she does not dispatch the letter to her parents in England because she has acquired there stoical attitude to life.

She feels cut off from the main stream of life, and yet she manages to 'live and let live' in her Indian husband's family. Peggy is repugnant to Indianness in manners and modes of behavior and this is well trough out by Jhabvala. The interaction between two cultures European and Indian has always been Jhabvala's pet theme. It is in this area that her personal experience in India gets developed into art. She knows that India reacts strongly on foreigners and they either love it or dislike it or do both. She has herself gone through this cycle of great enthusiasm for India where everything seemed marvellous to the other extreme.

Jhabvala's creative self appears to be the main occupant of her individually-designed room from where she could view the outside world. It helps her to keep up an attitude of ironic detachment since it is a room very distinctive, and also different from the world outside. Yet there is a change within the room itself, for instance, when the air conditioner is in operation it is cool and comfortable. It creates the proper atmosphere for Jhabvala's, sense of the comic. But sometimes the electric power becomes inoperative the room cooler stops functioning, and this results in the atmosphere becoming warm and suffocating. This outer atmosphere affects the inner sense of Jhabvala's mental attitude. Then her attitude to India and the world of her fiction hardens; she grows critical, ironic and even bitter. Empathy is replaced by antipathy because the room ceases to be her own. It loses itself In a larger India and the creator of fiction merges into her created world. She writes about the way India affects her.

> "India swallows me up and no it seems to me that I am no longer in my room but in the white-hot city streets centre a white – hot sky." (Page – 42)

The heat in India is murderous, yet, Jhahvala figures out many situations 2Y~J-' and characters in it which exercise a grlat enfluence on her imagination and a creative self. A smiling leper being driven in a cart by another leper and the image of Siva being worshipped by people catch her imagination and present that aspect of India which is both human and divine at the same time. She is well aware of the fact that religion and religious devotion have deep roots in India. Even old, semi - starved widows and the disadvantaged and the surpressed can be seen dancing in the country side. Jhabvala feels that the Indian sky which is hung expansive and clear dominates the destiny of man. Jhabvala greatly admires Indian devotional songs of Bhakti cult on the themes which draw parallels between man's love of God man's love for woman. Khuswant Singh finds that Jhabvala is very much Indian and has no hesitation in calling her the 'adopted daughter of India', she is sincere in opposing and highlighting false labels and is very anxious to expose them in public. This transparent sincerity of Jhabvala in exposing her response to the phenomenon that is India indirectly underlines the processes of her creativity. She may perhaps be treated as a European writer on India, yet her creative work gives ample proof of her Indianness, the aesthetic aspect of her art, shaped by her experience of life in India. It is the European's 'Passage to India'; but very different from that of Kipling or E.M. Forster. Jhabvala at the start has a different picture of India but as she came to know more and more about India, this idea underwent a great change. With the passage of time this developed into maturity and her vision of India became more soild and tangible.

This can be seen in many of her other novels. Thus, the growth of Ruth Prawer Jhabvala as an artist shows the working of a process of isolation-alienation in a mild form, and its transformation into creative art. Alienation is a much misused word and has several layers of meanings. It is therefore more pertinent to look at Jhabvala' s art from a different point of view. Looked at from a different angle, it would be clear that Jhabvala is both Indian and unIndian and this needs to be explained at length.

The growth of Ruth Prawer Jhabvala as an artist presents the working of a process of isolation. In Jhabvala,s world the context and connotation of alienation is purely social. Her novels portray the break-down of a traditional social order thereby projecting the alienation or isolation between one individual and another in marital relations and in family life. The Marxist critic may take it as a satirical portrayal of a capitalistic and commercial society.

The breakdown of tradition is the primary source of this alienation.

Its social context is one in which man is placed against the power of money. Alienation takes place when man is reduced to the position of a thing, as he is pushed away from the earth and his fellow men. Once reduced to the position of a thing, he falls a victim to the power and lure of money. Jhabvala's quest for material reality is thus in line with a meta physic that inevitably leads to a process of alienation. A sensitive reader rightly understands the alienation in such novels, but fails to give expression to it in categorical terms. The world of Jhabvala's fiction is coloured by this mild, soft sense of alienation. As a representation of western culture and tradition, she inherits a life view, which does not appear native to the sons of the soil. She knowingly or unknowingly brings out the Indian ethos in the context of the western rational and scientific attitudes which invariably become instrumental in judging Indians, their moral behaviour and their emotional or sensous responses to environment. She has a remarkable capacity for portraying conflicts of individual and domestic friction, which are social or familial reflections of individual and domestic friction, which are social or familial reflections of alienation.

Jhabvala's great merit as an artist lies in her success to give artistic expression to this sense of mild alienation in her awareness of man and society in India. Man and society in India today are engaged not merely in a change from tradition to modernity but in a process of cultural fragmentation. She brings out this change with a remarkable sense of awareness and sensitivity. She also tries to counter-balance her presentation of material reality with the presentation of aspects of India's spiritual reality. The search for the Sadhus and the pursuit of the spirit in her novels can be taken to be to her journey back to the Indian earth. Jhabvala's main problem as an artist crops up when we find her dealing with India's traditional and culture and knowledge of its heritage of civilization. She tries her level best to deal with the most important feature of Jhabvala. As a creative writer the major themes in Jhabvala's fiction are 'East-West Encounter' and 'marital disharmony' which are interlinked in their negative context. In the positive context these may be described as fruitful and happy relationship between East and West resulting in marital harmony and happiness. Jhabvala deals with both these aspects, but the elements of encounter and disharmony have an upper hand in her fiction. In her two novels ***Esmond in India*** and ***A Backward Place*** these two things are treated with great sensitivity and success. ***In Esmond in India*** Gulab marries a European, Esmond Stillwood and their marriage ends in failure. East and West and the difference they represent in their ways of living, cultural patterns and values is convincingly highlighted by Jhabvala climaxing in marital disharmony and break-up of human bonds. Gulab and Esmond get away from each other owing to temperamental differences as well as cultural gap. In ***A Backward place*** Judy married to Bal a handsome youth dreaming of career in films tries to make success of her marriage, but the kind of success they should credit themselves with is found missing. Ultimately, we find Gulab and Esmond moving away from each other and this is brought about through errors of misunderstanding and loss of trust.

The theme of domestic disharmony in Jhabvala's fiction has a much wider canvas than is evident in East-West confrontation or coexistence. Indian husbands and their Indian wives too appear to fall apart in a purely Indian familial and social situation. This conflict springs of a clash of interests, personalities, temperaments and also values. In ***Get Ready for Battle*** Gulzari Lal and his wife Sarla differ basically in their attitude to life. His view of life is so much governed by materialism that he finds it difficult to be of one mind with his wife Sarla. The clash of interests and personalities forms the basic theme in Jhabvala's ***Householder.*** This clash is between Prem and lndu, who are married only to find that their life styles are more contradictory than complementary. This conflict between a growing sense of individualism and the orthodox tradition of a man-ridden Indian society is genuinely representative of the post - second war period of Indian society. In ***To Whom She Will*** Prem and Suri also betray a lack of domestic harmony. Marriage, according to Jhabvala, could be merely an adjustmet, rather than a real involvement, in human relationships and love. Mrs. Kaul in A Backward Place becomes a society lady devoted to social work and cultural activities simply because her husband Mr. Kaul is too busy traversing the road to self-glory and the advancement of social status. She becomes a willing victim of self-deception. She joins the armies of the benighted who fall from the high position lit by the inner life to the earth below representing merely the outer glory of life. The satirist in Jhabvala artistically brings out Shaw's estimate of the British institution of Marriage as convenient solution of Britain's acute housing problem of allotting one room for two persons Jhabvala exposes these aspects of the Indian society today which is caught up in a major conflict between the old and the new. The New society woman in urban India is a phenomenon in itself. But what is significant in Jhabvala's portrayal is a deeper awareness of this society oman's personal predicament. In her search for the outer life there is a sense of defeat and frustration, a sense of failure of the inner life. Mrs. Kaul in A Backward Place or Sarla in Get Ready for Battle ample demonstrate the Indian society lady's personal perplexities. This rings out the fact that Indian society lady's personal perplexities. This brings out the fact that Indian man and woman struggle hard to come out of the narrow, traditional world in which they live. Even after coming out of this narrow world they find it difficult to adjust themselves to the new surrounding in which they find themselves. The gap between their outer life and their inner life is the theme of Jhabvala's fictions and this find expression in novel after novel.

Jhabvala as an artist highlights, three kinds of reality the social reality the cultural reality and th spiritual reality. She primarily a novelist of domestic life, its joys and sorrows, its harmony and friction, its, fulfillment and frustration. Since she IS concerned with the monetary aspect, of life in its domestic setting, she attempts to present the material reality, which assumes significance in her fictional art. However, the approach to her fictional world has also a spiritual aspect partly expressed in the charm that Europeans have for the Gurus, the inheritors of India's spiritual glory. In this way Jhabvala's quest for the material reality is combined with her search for a spiritual reality. This dual quest finally results in the basic unity of her art in which the real and the ideal, the mundane and the spiritual are combined into a unified vision of her art.

In the field of fiction, Jhabvala's place in Indian writing is not only unique but also permanent in the sense that she writes with her domestic sensibility, employing the confidential technique often reminding us of writers like Lamb and Hazlitt. However, in her fiction, although sustaining the same tone, she gives a comic ending and this is something which makes us to see the inner recesses of life. She explores themes of escape and estrangement, loneliness and detachment, obsession and search for identity, in the Indian context. Her novels deal with the ironic experiences of the Indians and at times touches upon the psychological problems with which her characters are confronted. Today fiction has become the main source of entertainment the world over. It appears that this part of Indian literature is amply serving the creative urge in keeping with the modern trends, Jhabvala has accumulated in her fiction all those things which have a direct bearing on our life. Jhabvala exposes the current human situation with understanding and sympathy and suggests the need for the reconstruction of humanity; every character is an experiment ir truth and phase in his soul-search. Her heroism lies in her struggle for a pure existence against the collective external evil of society. Jhabvala can be described as a comic humanist, hers is a comic humanism. She exposes and laughs at the stupidity in the meaningless struggle of the heroes. Her heroes are comic personage_picked up from the lower and middle class families of the society. Each character has the latent urge to be prominent in his society his struggle is slow in serio-comic colour. In other words, the hero leads in his dream world of achievement and is finally disillusioned. He attains spiritual transformation in the Upanashadic tradition.

> "From dreaming to reality,
> From ignorance to knowledge,
> From darkness into light Thus
> The hero is the comic a mode of
> Study in maturity."[6]

Her characters make us laugh at the selfishness of man, show us how civilization has tempered human folly and illustrate the importance of the Upanishadic way of illumination. In his mad quest for happiness man may snatch an occasional moment of happiness. But is it real? Where does the quest end? He often faces fiasco, a series of minor setbacks. In his mad pursuit, he will be caught in the trap of disastex: ultimately and the quest appears mock-heroic at the end.

Nevertheless Jhabvala's fictional aim IS quite obvious. Her novels are a plea for adjustment; she has designed her novels to create rhythm, employing a special technique, which is her own. Everyone of her protagonists takes some sort of journey, and the heroes symbolize the different stages in the spiritual journey of a pilgrim. She seeks the realization and pure action as the means of purifying the soul for salvation. Jhabvala taking a grown-up man as the hero symbolizing the spirit presents the various developing phases the hero's evil life, repentance, self awareness, regeneration and finally salvation. Her novels provide food for thought. The apparent comic simplicity is a mean of entertainment suggesting the spiritual. She tries to blend philosophy and human drama and thus presents life with all its limitations. Jhabvala achieves raising human drama to the heights of excellence in fiction. She has a remarkable capacity for presenting her characters in lovely humorous hues. And there is nothing strange if they have received warm tributes from scholarly critics of the West and East. Jhabvala, believes that repentance purifies the soul. And a single, whole-hearted, pious act coupled with deviation is enough to purge off all evils and regenerate the soul which at the end will be awakened from the dream of life into salvation. Jhabvala seems to preach and teach this single truth in effective term through her works in ***Heat and Dust*** in particular.

It was after ***Heat and Dust,*** When Jhabvala could no longer come to terms with India that she decided to leave. However, even twenty-five years after leaving India Jhabvala could not cool:d-A:e4: discard her Indian experience and she absorbed it into ***Three Continents*** (1987) which she wrote after she made New York her home. As a European writer in India Jhabvala had problems of communication and this she says was because:

"When one writes about India as a European and in English (as I do), inevitably one writes not for Indian but for western readers. How to translate the idiom of one language into another, how to present a scene to an audience unfamiliar with its most obvious ingredients (such as temples to Azores and motorcycle rickshaws); All these problems however very quickly disappear - not because however very quickly disappear not because they have been solved but because a much larger one swallows them up and that is how to explain within the limits of western terms and concepts what it is like to live in India."[7]

However, Jhabvala tries to overcome this problem through her western characters and through narrative techniques using not only evocative syntax but also regional colour. In her development as a writer she has learnt from her favourite novelists and also from her experiences as a screenplay writer and absorbed themes and techniques from these into her fiction. In studying the development, of the psychological trend in her fiction, Jhabvala appears to have derived some of the ingredients, of this psychological study of the human mind from Chekhov. We can see that Chekhov begins to use nature as a foil for human emotions. As Chekhov matures in his writing, his portrayal of the conflicts within the character corresponds to the elements outside. In his deeply emotional play Uncle Vanya the storm raging in Vanya's heart corresponds to the storm raging out outside side there home. His love for Helena over powers him, but he knows it is futile even to think of marrying her. As he weeps tears of grief and frustration, Nature weeps outside. As there is thunder and lightning, Vanya says despondently:

"Soon the rain will be over all living things will review and breathe more freely. Except me. Te storm won't revive me. Day and night m thoughts choke me, haunt me with the specter of a life hopelessly wasted. I have never lived. My past lift has been thrown away on stupid trivialities and the present is so futile, it appalls me."[8]

A similar technique of using nature in this way is developed by Jhabvala in her fiction. In A new Dominion the conflict between the physical and the spiritual emotions in Lee corresponds to the strange night out side the hut where a beautiful moonlit night is disturbed by dust storm. The moonlit night is comparable to the spiritual peace she feels and the violent dust storm to the physical passion she feels for the Swami:

"There was a full moon but it wasn't bright it was dimmed out and pale like the pale shreds of clouds floating across it. The sky way torn up by these clouds shifting and sailing rather fast as if they were being driven and making everything up there look very disturbed, and on the earth it was disturbed too with the little hat winds blowing through the air."[9]

The events that follow correspond to these natural phenomena. Lee's visit to the Swamiis hut and his subsequent attack on her creates in her the same emotion as the dust storm in its frenzy. Just as Chekhov doesn't need to explain the intensity of his character's feeling. Jhabvala, doesn't need to explain Lee's. However, in using this technique

Chekhov brings out the pathos in the situation while Jhabvala highlights the sensual aspect. As Jhabvala matured as a writer her style and techniques became more and more varied. From a satirist who highlighted the comic aspects of Indian life she became a more analiticl and philosophical writer. As her attitude to India changed and she saw the hypocrisy in society, her irony began to reflect the outrage she felt at the from a satirist who highlighted the comic aspects of Indian life she became a more analitical and philosophical writer. As her attitude to India changed and she saw the hypocrisy in society, her irony began to reflect the outrage she "New Delhi façade, people electing each other, talking of democracy, calling press conferences What does it mean? It has nothing to do with what I know of India"[10]

Her irony becomes tough and brutal like Chekhov's and like him she begins to expose the hypocrisy in society. In ***Get Ready for Battle*** she contrasts Sarla Devi's genuine battle for the Poor with the hypocritical promises of the women's organization. Mrs. Bhatnagar is the widow of a rich Industrialist who organizes social welfare meetings where the discussion is more about parties and the snacks served than about help for the poor. Jhabvala's ironic vision seems to echo Chekhov's in the portrayal of the attitude of the rich towards the poor. It highlights the total lack of communication between the two classesin society.

It is clear therefore that part ot significance of Chekiov work in relation to Jhabvala clearly lies in the similarities between the cultural situations of 19th century Russia and 20th century India *I* but it certainly goes beyond that. The above examples illustrate to a certain extent how Chekhov's writings influenced Jhabvala. Chekhov's concerns are close to Jhabvala's. Like him she is keen to make people aware of what is happening in their societies and in order to do so she learns from Chekhov's similar themes, techniques and style of writing. Jhabvala' s skill as an artist lies in the fact just as she did with Jane Austen, that she adapts these to suit her purpose. Her exposure of the foibles of

Indian society is similar to Chekhov's of Russian society who, like Tolstoy and other realist novelists of his time writes about conditions in Russia. Jhabvala being influenced by the Great Russian writers also writes realistically abut India. However she alters the themes she has taken from them to suit the customs and conditions in India particularly the relationships between the east and the West. She differs from contemporary Idia writers in doing so because as a westerner she is able to view India objectively. As a European married to an Indian she has the additional advantage of beign part of the society she writes about. She is, therefore better equipped than other European writers like E.M. Forster who has written about India. Jhabvalal viewed India in the same way as Chekhov viewed Russia, in all its various manifestations, whereas Forster only saw the mysteries which he conveyed to the western reader.

REFERENCES

1. K.R. Srinivasa Iyengar Indian Writing in English (New Delhi: Sterling Publisher Pvt. 1963) p. 436.
2. Flora Alexander, Contemporary Women Noelists (London: Edward Arnold 1989), p. 12.
3. Ibid.
4. Elizabeth Bowen 'Notes on writign an novel' in Collected Impressins. London, 1950)
5. Quoted Shyam M.Asnani in Jhabvala's Novels: A Thermatic stude- The Journal of Indian Writing in English Vol. 1 NO. 2, January 1974, p. 47.
6. C.D. Narasimhaiah India Writing in English p. 135.
7. Moonliht, Jasmine and Ricker, P. 36.
8. Chekhov Jncle Vanya in the Oxford Chekhov Vol. 3 (London Oxford Unviersity Press 1964) p. 34.
9. A New Dominaion P. 167.
10. Jhabvala' A Novelist of India reflect two world's in the New York times 17 July 1973' p. 7.

7

Open Spaces in Feminism

A Maternical Feminist V/s Englightened Feminist

For a correct comprehension of the emergence of feminism ‹s a self conscIous and concreted approach to life and literature during the past five decades or so, it is necessary to have the historical perspective of it. The out burst of feminism in the 60' s throughout the world, particularly in the advanced west was not a matter of chance, but the natural product of centuries of struggle for women's. In this context, Mary Wollstonecraft's *A Vindication of the Rights of* a *Women* is the first landmark which can be regarded as the manifesto of modern feminism Incidentally in the same period some women writers in England- Fanny Burney, Maria Edge worth, Jane Austen and others- came out of the obscure, suffocating feminine shell and presented life and art from the point of view of women. Margarate Fuller's *Woman* in 19th century and John Staurt Mill's *The Subjection of Women* are milestones of modern women's path for emancipation, for self definition and self assertion. In the twentieth century Virginia Woolf can be regarded as the first avowed champion of feminism A Room One's Own and her numerous essays, are an open attack on orthodox society, which, in her view, is the root cause of educational, economic and cultural backwardness and disabilities hampering women's creative culture and social growth and stature.

However it was the *Second Sex* by the French woman writer Simon De Beauvoir, that brought about a revolution and radical change in western society, and thus it can be rightly regarded as the true foundation of the present day feminism. This radical book is a powerful and comprehensive critique of the age old cultural belief in woman as simply the 'negative object' and man as 'the defining, central subject' representing the entire humanity. American modern feminism began with the publication of Mary Ellman's persuasive book, *Thinking about Women,* and it was followed by Millett's hard hitting influential work *Sexual Politics* which exposes Frued's male prejudices and some novelists'-degrading presentation of women as objects of sheer sexual gratification. Though in its modern sense feminism became conspicuous for the first time in the eighteenth century, its seeds are as old as human race. A close scrutiny of the term 'feminism' - woman's voice against injustice and inequality - tends to unfold the fact that feminism is the result of the culture or of the society shaped and governed by men to suit their needs and interests regardless of women's basic needs and happiness.

Literary feminism may be of two kinds - explicit and implicit. The first focuses on the writer's explicit intention to reveal some significant aspects of feminism and his concern with the problems and hardships faced by women who attempt to cross the barrier created by the man-dominated society. Than there are some other forms of feminism which point out the same problems facing women today. Psychology has interpreted feminism in its own terms. Differing from the views on feminism which are political, social and economic, psychoanalytical feminism though at times overlapping with socialist feminism, is primarily based on Freud's stress on 'the instability of sexual identities', and approaches the notion of gender as a problem. It is a fact that the true femaleness and maleness are not fully attainable permanently and this suggests a comparative openness which allows changes in them. Feminism is still in process of evolution to attain a definite entity. It has now acquired the position of an ideology and in the words, of Warhol.

'Feminism can be thought of as an ideology that has

operated in political and social theory and spiritual studies'.[1]

True, feminism aims at grabbing power that is to position to dictate and direct action and thinking of others- from men. In modern time economic strength is all considered to be powerful and can be achieved through intellect alone. In olden days physical strength was considered to be vital force to acquire good position in society. Since women can earn a lot and can be economically strong by virtue of intellect and education, they can rush into for power and can fight for gender equality or even better position. But economic power and independence, imparting woman freedom of every kind, cannot give her satisfaction and inner happiness. She needs a man's loving company, and thus feminism cannot be anti-male and cannot be contented with lesbianism. It is almost impossible for feminism to attain its goal of complete equality, for no man-woman relationship can exist on the principle of absolute equality. If feminism is based on the wrong attitude of hostility towards man, it will not work, for the two genders are nct only complement and supplementary to each other but also absolutely indispensable for each other for full growth and fulfilment. Since the feminist movement till today doesn't have a common, well accepted positive ideology, ultimate goal and right direction, it is doubtful if it will ever be able to make earth a blissful seat for women in particular, and for mankind in general. Ann Curthoy's, the well known Australian feminist thinker observes that:

"Many feminists are in the process of defining their dissatisfaction with women's movement as it is. There is dissatisfaction with many of the women's centre and service set up b the movement, dissatisfaction that as the women's movement grows in size it is diluting its perspectives, programmes and aims. These dissatisfactions, can e ruined up as a losses of direction which itself is losing right of our ends. our ultimate goals. We have not, that is to say, a clear notion of our feminist Utopia".[2]

The novels portrays the multifaceted problem of life

and presents the reactions of ordinary men and women. It is a mirror of society which is as good a gauge as any for arriving at a judgement. The novel has a special way of looking at things and people and bringing out the significant features of life. The form and content of the novel have their connection with specific cultural and social patterns. Similarly the position of woman may be regarded as an index to the quality of its culture and character of its civilisation. It unfolds the established philosophy of that society. There has always been a remarkable quantity of first rate works by Indian writers in English in the fields of autobiography, religion and philosophy. The growing demand for social reforms, the revival of past traditions, the search for a national identity, and the increase awareness of the role by the individual in society gave birth to the Indo -Anglian novel. This automatically gave rise to a new look at the status of woman in the Indian society. In fact, the whole burden of civilization is summed up in its feminine image.

The Indo-Anglian writer, like Indian society is torn between two extremes, on one hand he glorifies, and idealises Indian woman and on the other hand he is compelled to brood over pitiable condition. Since the writer primarily aims at projecting the total view of Indian life and culture, a large number of novelists have concentrated on the experience and exploration of cultural clashes when East and West meet. The theme of East-West cultural clash glorifies Indian woman to the point of saintliness as through her the writer speaks of Indian values. She is drawn in a sharp contrast with everything that is modern because in India modernity is generally bracketed with westernisation. Women figuring in most of the novels in general and Jhabvala's fictions in particular strive hard to project the best of their cultures, to manifest India's timeless traditional values. In the interculture theme we can divide characters into two opposite groups, the personal and the impersonal in the sense that they fulfil their duties beyond personal self.

Thematically speaking, novels written on or set against

Gandhian background, depict women of unprecedented courage and determination. The earliest novels on freedom movement show the same spirit as do the same time there are novels which deal with subjects particular to the Indian scenes such as hunger, famine, joint family system, industrialisation, and superstition where woman is the victim of natural or man made cruelty, injustice and exploitation. Only novelists like Ruth Prawer Jhabvala, Nayantara Shfi.gal and Anita Desi deal with woman as the central theme of their novels expressing her sensitive state of mind. In Indian life and so in Indian fiction, role of expectations are highly specific and institutionalised. Thus woman's role in the family has remained multifarious. Raja Rao has rightly said that "Life is made for woman, man is a stranger to this earth."[3] Despite quite radical change the status of woman, more than that of man, is bound up with the traditional wife and mother's role. 'Ideal' house wife is the favowite image, virtually moulded in the same fashion in all these novels. We find that service, sacrifice, submissiveness come to them naturally. Excessive endurance and the list of adjustments she makes is endless. Faithfulness and obedience perfect her. Ruth Prawer Jhabvala protest against monotony, drabness, injustice and humiliation. Her women refuse to be taken for granted and do complain against this condition. Largely the Indo-Anglian novel depicts the paradise of the husband while it gives us the pitiable and pathetic account of the wife. Independence has hardly made any change in the wives plight. The only cry "you do not understand me," fills her whole being with pain. The final and sublime role of the feminine image is in the words of Anand Coomar Swamy "For everything feminine is of the mother."[4] The wife and the mother are related in ***The Serpent and the Rope*** "Her womb is her life"[5] The strong material instinct essentially runs through the veins of every feminine heart in Indo-Anglian novels. They exemplify self -transcendence through self-effacement. The image of a woman as a mother is divine and unparalleled indignity and serenity. Thus, the observation shows that home is the main area of rooted that no Indo-Anglian writer touches other spheres of activity for woman.

The constitution of India has vested the Indian women with equality of status and opportunities with men. However, a study of the Indo-Anglian novel proves that the contrary is true. From the Vedic age, the birth of a son is a blessed favour, and we find this in some of the novels of Jhabvala.

Social taboos, superstition, and poverty make her condition still worse. The stark reality is described by Jhabvala and what Arun Joshi observes in ***The Foreigner*** hold true:

> "It is very bright outside, I stand turning to Sheila she was getting my shoes from under the divan and I was filled with a sense of sympathy for all Indian Women who always have the back arched stooping to someone's service."[6]

Jhabvala's women feel that they grow smaller every day trapped in a myth of the wife and the mother. True, the new woman in the work of women writers tries to protest but the psychological odds against which they fight are peculiar. But when all is said and done the question arises whether these women are simple straw feather idealised and created only to project the 'Indian image'. Are they treat merely as vehicles to carry the writer's deliberate interpretation of the East and not as human with real feelings *I* The answer is, sadly, yes. They are merely types with stock situations made to entertain foreign audience. The obsession to justify 'Indianness' forces them to be myth-conscious. It seems that a tradition with most of them is to go back in time in order to provide the desired mode. Hence the importance of mythology and legend. Even the very names Sita, Savitri, Gauri, Laxmi, Mera and Parvati are suggestive of their epic and myth parellels to their names. And this impact of myth is mainly responds for creating stereo typed characters. They are ideal rather than facts, shadows rather than actual living beings of flesh and blood, they do not question the terms and crime of their lives but painted as models of virtues. Society speaks in them but they are not supposed to speak for themselves. Their mythological pomp and superlative politeness make them more of Goddesses without power rather real woman on the earth.

One of the most deep-rooted obstacles in aschieving the goals of women'~ liberation, is the ideologies in the form of religion. Major, a religions allover the world preach the superiority of men over women. Weather it is "Koran dictating dominance of men over women,"[7] or The New Testament which goes on to say-. "It is shame for women to speak in the church."[8] In contrast Hindu religion in its fundamental form gives women a place of deep respect in society. In fact, power, the ultimate and final source of energy is embodied in the feminine form of Shakti. Great writers all over the world written with the assumption that behind every successful man is a woman. Shakespeare heroines are known to be the moving force of his plays. Ruskin goes on to say." Shakespeare has only heroines, no heroes." George Bernard Shaw believes and propagates the theory that women are the central driving force of this world.

Women are held in great esteem in India. They are treated as 'Devi I by men. In Hindu custom men pay obeisance to young girls hailing them as incarnation of deities. All this sounds very impressive and mind - boggling too. A feminist writer would certainly be shocked to read these lines because all is not so well as it appears to be. As long suppression and torture both mental, physical and emotional has forced her to stand up to fight the male-dominated society. Previously women were deprived of the privilege to education where as men were given all the facilities in this field. Women's role was to accompany men in their beds, provide them with emotional and egoistic satiation so that they were re-affirmed of their supremacy from time to time. In Indian society, the identity of a women is attributed to her husband. She is a decorative piece who is expected to accompany her husband everywhere and meet the people whom her husband approves. She can never expect to have her own association and defiantly not of the opposite sex or else she is relegated as infidel.

Indian women novelists can be said to be highly conscious of the women's liberation movement. By and large they have portrayed women and their stories with consciousness of the injustice being meted out to women by society. These novels have a feminist undercurrent. Usually these novels have a woman as the central character. If we look at these fictional female characters, a large number of them rebel against the existing social set-up. They discard the idea of being submissive, suffering and sacrificing. Rebellion is not easy process. It demands determination and a will to stand by the cause of rebellion at any cost. These heroines in the novels of Indian women's novelists have often come up to paying the prize of their rebellion rather than submitting and dying through suffocation.

Ruth Prawer Jhabvala as a major woman novelist is less concerned with the personality development of her women. She is attracted by the double standard of Indian women. In general she can be said to have dealt with distortion of modernity as women's liberation. Her female characters don't go against tradition without any firm conviction, they do so in order to pose modern. Jhabvala will be considered as a modern writer of contempo-rary India. She is neither brutally frank like Nirad C. Choudari, nor traditional in her themes like Mulk Raj Anand or R.K. Narayan. She has chosen for her a subject matter, the most vitally modern, the aspect of marriage in the con-temporary Indian life. She has been writing for the past fifty years and during this period she has written a number of novels focusing her attention on many problems facing men and women in India. Change is the law of life, and a state of changelessness is stagnation. The woman in India has long been worshipped using the choicest terms of address. But the woman of Independent India is not ready to enter another dark era of drawing hero-worship. With cumulative wisdom being passed down to her through the ages she has learnt to recognise her self. One notices two main tendencies in the Indian social frame work today- one may be called the centripetal while the other has come to be termed as centrifugal or running away centre or the family. Neither of the two trends can be said to be completely in vogue. Often, they overlap and the nature of a particular character is the sum total of all the actions and experiences in the course of the work of art.

The spirit of revolt arising out of mechanical life, mismatched marriages or wayward ways of husbands have forced the women to come out in the open to raise her voice. But the revolt doesn't take her out of her home. The home still remains for her the only refuge. There may be temporary withdrawals but on the whole, a centripetal spirit of compromise can be seen on the part of the women.

Jhabvala' s characters, chosen mostly from an Indian middle class or upper class family, are by no means, sophisticated. She peeps into the af-fairs of an Indian middle class family as if it is a comedy of the restricted human consciousness. Her vision maintains a limitation and avoids falling into sentimentality or superficial involvement. She wants to stress ironically in her novels that living in India doesn't mean sharing the Indian vision of life. The East-West encounters are in fact a legacy of colonial past. But Jhabvala's approach is a bit different as compared with other novelists like Anita Desai and Kamala Markandey.

Jhabvala is a novelist who is concerned and known for her behaviourism rather than psychoanalyst approach. Her characters follow a distinct code of conduct affecting the various fields. The conflicts delineated in her novels are primarily outer ones; yet she is humane enough to feel the ache at the heart of humanity. Her characters encounter variegated existential problems such as the adjustment between husband and wife, between man and soci-ety. The problems of her characters arise from their social and cultural inter- action. Thus her writings show her awareness of man and society in their human and moral dilemmas. Her awareness of a group of people, their cul-ture and the tradition, at times transcends the racial barriers and becomes one with the universal human beings. She is herself a

European married to an Indian and has lived in India for quite a long time. She displays a deep under-standing of her women characters especially the European ones living in India. This can be studied biographically also. In the beginning of her arrival in India she was very happy about everything she saw around. For that reason her earlier novels have the comic attitude and later ones are satirical She herself accepts this

> "I suppose it could be put down to my change of attitude towards India". I loved everything during my first year here - I really loved it and was wildly excited by it and never to go away from here. But later that change. I saw a lot that horrified me."[9]

In her first two novels ***To Whom She Will*** and ***The Nature of Passion,*** she has taken up the theme in a comic mode. In these novels she has depicted a clash between tradition and modernism at personal and familial level. In fact, the modernism of Amrita and Hari in ***To Whom She Will*** and of Nimmi and Pheroze Battlliwala in ***The Nature of Passion*** is pseudo-modernism which loses ground as soon as it faces real problems of life. In both the novels when the parents come to know about the love affairs of their daughters, they don't lose any time to arrange marriages for them. The irony of the situation is that the girls also accept the proposals, made by their parents. Both the novels pose the question whether the "arranged" or "love" marriage is conducive to happiness. Jhabvala excels in exploring the comic element in sentimentalized love scenes and also in exposing the hollowness of pseudo romantic epithets. The transition from conformity to non-conformity is obvious on individual and social planes but in these novels we find the reversal of the movement from non-conformist to conformist. In the beginning , both the female protagonists are non-conformists who are trying to come but a convention-ridden and tradition-bound society to an open, uninhabited society free from the shackles of social customs and conventional constraints and proper love marriages, but in the end both become conformists and agree to marry according to their parents' choice. These novels end on a note of reconciliation achieved through marriage. Hari marries Sushila, Amrita marries Krishna Sen Gupta and Nimmi marries Kuku not for love, but for social and individual graces and for preserving the group values of the community and family life.

Jhabvala's European characters are more impressive than the Indian ones. She has a deep understanding of European life where as she has only outer knowledge of Indian characters. Being a European, She cannot probe the Indian psyche as deeply as she can the European one. But this is enough for her purpose of writing social comedies. She is a European writer who primarily writes for western audiences. She has the knowledge of human heart, both in its individual and universal contexts along with the understanding of the social and cultural patterns and values. As a European, she views, the game of human affairs in an Indian Family from an objective and external point of view. Without being prejudiced, she presents a convincing account of the individual life, but at personal, social and familial levels. She talks her characters from the social and familial background. Her worldliness and down- to- earth approach to life indirectly help her in avoiding the pitfalls of sentimentality. She doesn't falsify or merely idealize life. She portrays the predicament of individuals in their relationship to family and social group. She shows the way for the harmonious life by bringing to light the cause of disharmony.

(The major theme in her novels is marital dissonance which arises from maladjustment. In ***Esmond in India,*** Gulab, cutting across colour and racial frontiers, marries a profligate Englishman he easy going Gulab, with her Oriental taste for carrot halwa, spices and hot-red curries, her typically Indian bashfulness and indifference towards modern furniture, is a glaring contrast to her husband, Esmond, with his inmate craze for orderliness, smart and sophisticated society, and upto date furnishings. The long descriptions which Jhabvala gives about Gulab's way of living and eating become a part of her strategy for character portrayal. Gulab likes the comfortable way of living without any formality, she enjoys lying on the floor and is not bothered at all about her appearance or dress. Food is one of the fundamental of her living and Gulab is greatly fond of spicy dishes which seem to become an aspect of the sensuous and pleasure seeking characteristic in her. Jhabvala eminently succeeds In catching and conveYing the "Indianness" of Gulab's mode of life.

> "Ravi was already taking the paper off the little erarthen ware pots. 'Carrot Halwa!' he cried Gulab looked pleased, her large melancholy eyes flashed for an instant with a wonderful fire. In the other pots there were grams, Tomatoes and potatoes swimming in red curry, and chunks of meat soaked in curds. Everything would be highly spiced, Gulab smiled with pleasure."[10]

Gulab is neither physically comfortable nor mentally satisfied in husband's house. She has been living with him due to her inbred instinct which tells her that her husband is her God. The true picture of Gulab can be seen in Ram Nath's description of Indian wife.

> "So like animals like cows, he said with sudden revulsion; 'Beat them starve thm, maltreat them how you like they will sit and look with animal eyes and never raise a hand to defend themselves, saying "do with me what you will, you are my husband my God, it is my duty to submit to my God." (page 97)

But the marriage fails because their basic attitudes towards life are different.

The root cause of their dissonance is not only racial and cultural gap but temperamental differences also. Esmond is selfish and mean, and Gulab is sluttish and unsophisticated. The sharp contrast between the two ways of living and thinking, causes awkward and unseemly situations In conjugal life. Though Jhabvala is a European yet she has not all admiration for the sophisticated western society. It is true that she is more for the accepted traditional view of life which has stood the test of time. She feels that most of the Indian women have been adversely affected, by the westernized education.

By bringing to surface the causes of dissonance, Jhabvala has tried to bring about the way which will result in marital assonance. Mostly her novels show a few years of married life in the beginning. This is a stage which need proper adjustment though it is not always easy, as two grown up people brought up in different circumstances and situations come together and want to establish their identity. Each wants to dominate. Unless there is proper understanding, the marital harmony cannot be achieved.

In ***The Householder*** Prem's; wife Indu is passive and submissive. She accepts the dictates of the society and tradition. She tries to keep her husband happy and works a lot to keep her house nice. Whenever Prem gets irritated and scolds her, she tires to keep quiet in his presence. ~

> "It made him uncomfortable to think of her crouching alone in there, crying quietly to herself. She always cried very quietly. He had by accident discovered her on two occasions....."[11]

Indu is child-like and frivolous. She is married for a few months only when the story begins, and one can see lndu and Prem to be little more than strangers. They are yet to discover their affinities and cement their bond by love and understanding Behind lndu's girlish giggles and sullen pouting there is the concern for her husband Even when she is angry she prepares his food carefully though she serves it silently. While Prem is observed in the thought of getting his salary raised, rent reduced and the expenditure, lndu tries hard to be a good housewife, attending to household duties meticulously and tolerates her mother-in-law silently. As H.M. Williams says, Jhabvala

> "Suggests very skillfully the duality of her school-girlish frivolity and her basic emotional superiority to Prem"[12]

When Indu goes away her mother-in-law takes charge of house-cooking his favourite dishes and serving him lovingly even while sighing over the unending duty of a loving mother. The mother's feelings are depicted with psychological insight. Indu's absence makes Prem to realize what she means to him By learning to adjust to each other's shortcoming and accommodate other's point of view, Indu and Prem strike a harmonious balance in marital relationship. This adjustment can be regarded to oneself, to family or society. For happy and harmonious life proper adjustment and mutual understanding are essential.

In Get Ready for Battle once agin Jhabvala delineates the problem of martial dissonance though with a variation. Gulzari Lal and Sarla Devi are husband and wife but one is totally materialistic and other is totally idealistic. There is little scope for assonance. As a result they fall apart .Sarla Devi leaves her husband and goes to live with her brother and Gulzarilal Keeps a mistress Mrs. Kusum Mehra who is a widow with grown up children.

The problem has been elaborately sketched by Jhabvala. Sarla Devi s idealistic who has left her millionaire husband whereas Kusum is materialistic who defies all the rules of society and traditions for the personal comforts. For Sarla Devi materialism is everything. Just as birds of the same feather flock together, so Gulzaui Lal and Kusum join hands. There develops a love between the two, but the way divorce case is handled is really intriguing. Kusum is a measured morality. Her advice to Mala shows her worldliness.

> "You see, child, sometimes it is necessary to be a little bit strict with men.lt is not good always to say yes to them/ it spoils them. Sweet heart, men are like children in this, one can spoil them with too much kindness"[13]

Kusum's love with Gulzarni Lal is a calculated one. She wants him to take divorce from his legal wife so that she can marry him and be his legal heir. The respect which she has for the conventional and traditional ways of life is only at the superficial level. She regards them as long as these serve her purpose or give her social security otherwise she cares a foot for anything. The way she talks about the divorce case with Sarla Devi and her brother shows her shrewdness.

There is yet another couple Vishnu and Mala, the son and daughter-in -law of Gulzari Lal who present a real contrast to Kusum. Both of them are generally interested in each other and are not materialistic. For Mala, the love for her husband is everything. Mala dislikes modernity. She cannot share her husband's interest in the club and the get -together parties. She is conventional and disapproves the easy talks, the dancing to the gramophone and the educated girls with their educated views. She dreams of going away to the village where Vishnu proposes to start business because she hopes that there would be nowhere for him to go and he would have to be with her Mala appears to be immature. She is yet to grow and learn to accept her place and responsibilities as a housewife and mother. She behaves hysterically when her mother-in-law visits her. In comparison to Mala, lndu in ***The Householder*** seems to have learnt quickly as evidenced by her controlled and dignified behaviour with her impetuous husband and nagging mother-in--law. Both Mala and Indu stand testimony to Jhabvala's comprehension of Indian domestic life and familial relationships.

Whatever Jhabvala's relationship with India and Europe may be , as far as her fiction is concerned, India seems to be her theme as well as obsession. Her awareness of various aspects of Indian life establishes the Indianness of her fiction. Her close personal experience of Indian life and her exclusive interest in it as a novelist as well as her ability to identify very closely with Indians, notably with Indian women, take her nearer to native writers like R.K. Narayan and Raja Rao[14] She gives us in her fiction the experience of European women married to Indians or of Indian women married to Europeans who are confronted with inevitable situation of Hindu Joint families.[15]

As a woman writer with her sensitive perception of the human relationship Jhabvala handles the situations from the perspective of relationship between man and woman-in and out of marriage-which naturally is most intimate and hence most complex. The problems of the expatriates, their psychological turmoil and cultural schizophrenia are dealt with insight and understanding. Jhabvala speaks of the emotional stages which every European living in India undergoes. She says "First stage, tremendous enthusiasm-everything Indian is marvellous; second stage everything Indian not so very marvellous; third stage, everything Indian abominable."[16]

But Judy of ***A Backward Place*** is an exception to this emotional upheaval She doesn't dislike India or Indian way of life .She marries an Indian for love and she sticks to him in spite of the testing times they have .Judy tries her level best and almost succeeds in adapting herself to Indian ways of life .Her positive attitude to life helps her to accept the challenges of life. Her readiness to identify herself either the lower middle class Indian family in which she lives gives her a sense of belonging and saves her from the theme of cultural alienation. One can see that "The marriage of Bal and Judy is difficult not because of the difference in race so much so because of the clash in their temperaments between the dreamer and the pragmatist':' 17 She retains her English pragmatism and Anglo- Saxon coolness, but these very qualities, instead of working as barriers in her coming closer to her people, help her put up with Bàl's childish irresponsibility and impractical optimism Judy is happy because she is neither like Etta, who hates and despises India nor Clarissa who is victim of self-deception. She retained her English qualities like imperturbability and cool composure while adapting Indian ways of life and dressing. There is no problem with character like Judy who accepts India and adjusts to it. But Etta and Clarrisa in the same novel find it difficult to cope with India. Etta, a middled-aged Hungarian woman, has come to India as a result of he marriage to an Indian student.

The marriage has proved to be a failure and Etta has had a number of love-affairs after that. She is conscious of waning beauty and is at pains to retain the love of her recent lover, Mr. Gupta. The rapid changes that age brings on her, coupled with her fear that she is losing hold on Gupta, make her feel desperate. She is unhappy because she tries to resist India instead of being absorbed by it .She despises the country, describes it as primitive society with primitive morality. She feels that "The Indian sun has been put specially into sky to ruin our complexions" (Page 7) Trapped and imprisoned in a country which she hates, Etta become depressed and even hysterically at the thought of isolation and loneliness awaiting her. It is true that" Jhabvala treats Etta with sympathy mixed characteristically some irony aimed at her pretentiousness"[18]

Clarissa unlike Etta has come to India inspired by the works of Vivekanand and Romain Rolland. She describes herself as a spiritual seeker and says that she is in India out of conviction and idealism. In spite of her professed quest for comfortable life. She professes love for India, wears sarees, praises Judy for attempting to be an Indian wife, appreciates her house because it has' character but hesitates to use their bathroom. She pretends to be too busy chasing the eternal values to care for worldly matters. Yet she lives comfortably on the hospitality of her rich friends. Though she claims to be as free as a bird, she is prisoner to her own delusions about Indian. Both Etta and Clarrisa are trapped in India and are condemned to live there.

In ***A New Dominion*** Jhabvala portrays the Westerner's attempt to grapple with the spiritual India. In this novel there are three girls; Lee, Margaret and Evie who have come to India to seek spiritual solace from the hollow, pretentious and materialistic life of the west. Unfortunately they come across a spurious Swami. Jhabvala's attitude to the spiritual guides in India is obvious in the presentation of the Swami. Her satire, however, is not combined to the worldly materialistic god men alone. The spiritual seekers from the west too are not spared. The west turns to the East, not because it believes, trusts and admires the spirituality of the East, but as an act of rejection of the western materialism and to fill the vacancy in their lives. One cannot find fault wit Jhabvala for the distorted picture of the Swami, for india has not dearth of such fake Swamis.

These girls are runnign away from the vacuous aimlessness of English society. They look at the Swami as a symbol of India's spirituality and seek complete identification with him. The tragedy is that they don't know what they want, nor they know wher they can find it. They get confused between physical union and spiritual communion. Thisis the reason why they submit to the lust of the Swami. Teh attracton they feel towards the Swami is not devoid of sexuality and that explains their jealousy for one another.

The irony is obvious that the trut seekers of th ewest end up by mistakign sex for spirituality. Raymond and miss Charlott embody the rational scientific and moral aspects of the culture of th ewest; Lee Margret an Eive represent a sort of disssatisfaction with it. They have come to India to be transformed into new beings who will be capable of unity of mind, body and soul. But for Miss Charlott India is a challenging coutnr whose crying need is social amelioration, educationalreform, and good life based on economic security. Then, there is Asha, the widowed sister of a Rao sahib, formerly a prince of a small Indian state. She is non conformist and challenges all the norms of good behaviour. She finds in Gopi an amorous, youthful figure who could quenc her thirst of physical enjoyment. Even Banubai, the ascetic prophetess, is very fond of Gopi as she considers him affectionate and childlike. The basic irony implicit throughout the novel is that while the English girsls are seeking spiritual India to enable them to find themselves, the India they experience is th every opposite of their original concept.

In Heat and Dust Jhabvala portrays the sad and touchign story oftwo English women of two differen tgenerations who came to India and become its victims. A young English woman comes to India to reconstruct the story of her grandfather's first wife Olivia who had an affair with the Nawab of Khatam. Olivia is pretty young woman, rather vain, pleasure seeking and a little petulant. When she came to India with her husband Douglas, She had much love for Douglas that he seemed to her noble and fair. But within a short time she got bored with life in Satipur and started looking for entertainment and admiration which she was used to. An invitation to Nawab of Khatm's place provided her with what she had sought .Instinctively she knew that he would calion her again .She was so excited about his visit that in his company she forgot her boredom and the oppressive heat outside. The way Olivia was attracted to the Nawab and submitted herself to him shows a that there is something frivolous about her.

While Olivia's choice was for the Nawab, the narrator allows Child, a wandering Westerner to use her to satiate his desire. She is also intimate with Inder a Government clerk. The Nawab was extremely charming and the attraction Olivia felt for him was more physical than anything else. In spite of her efforts to keep out the heat and dust by shutting all the doors and windows, Olivia becomes a victim of the heat, an inherent passion in her .As her sister Marcia put it, Olivia was passionate by nature and it was this passion which took her into the Nawab's arms unresisting and willing. Olivia's change of attitude is evident in her changed opinion of Douglas which made her think derisively of him, "What manliness? He can't even get me pregnant." (Page 120) No conscious effort was made on her part to resist the temptation. Her wish to have a baby so that "everything would be alright-she would be at peace and also at one with Douglas" (Page 111) was prompted more by her guilt complex rather than by her love for Douglas.

When she became pregnant, she told the Nawab first and only then Douglas. She got her pregnancy aborted for fear that the baby might look like an Indian and thus would betray her to Douglas. It was only when everything became public that she decided to leave Douglas and go to the Nawab. Olivia seems to be lacking in frankness and courage. The narrator is everything which Olivia was not. If Olivia tried to create a little Europe in her house, the narrator tries to Indianize herself as much as possible. Unlike the English community that lived in India as representatives of British empire and behaved like superior to natives and led an isolated life; Whereas narrator is not prejudiced against the natives and has in fact come to India to seek a simpler and more natural way of li~Olivia hides her pregnancy from Douglas out of fear and guilt complex, the narrator keeps it from Inder to spare him embarrassment. From the narrator the readers come to know that Olivia had led the same kind of lonely and isolated life on the hills in the house of the Nawab. Yasmine Gooneratne observes that the narrator "belongs to a new generation of liberal-minded educated travellers from the West who consciously strives to communicate with India" 19 and so her decision to stay on the hills would be a step further in her attempt to understand India. She wants to take permission of the Swami to go up the hill. The narrator's wish to go up the hills suggests her wish top know spiritual India too.

1(1 The novel shows that the passage of time has not changed human p ssion and emotions. Changed circumstances and customs might bring in different attitudes but the basic instinct and responses remain unchanged. Olivia and the narrator are set apart, separated by fifty years of time but get caught in similar situations. If their responses and reactions differ, it is In accordance with their attitudes. On the whole, the heart of the matter IS jhabvala's preoccupation with what India does to Europeans. It also shows how woman's stepping out into the wider world has widened her scope and perspective espically when one thinks of the limited world of Jane Austen with whom Jhabvala is often compared.

A Study of the non-Indian women characters in Jhabvala's novel reveals that women, irrespective of the difference in race religion, culture and graphical situation, are prone to be emotional, sensitive and sentimental. What they long for is emotional fulfilment and stability. Jhabvala presents western women in India as frustrated souls in search of peace and fulfilment. Dejected by materialistic values of the western society, they seek anchor and refuge in Indian spirituality. There are numerous impulses and tendencies in human beings. And these traits are described in Jhabvala's world. Jhabvala herself speaks about her of characterization

> "I use one character and split that character up. I have certain leading figures in my life and I seem to use them again and again presenting different facets of their personality so one person can play the role of fifty" [20]

These characteristics represent the human personality in the fictional world of Jhabvala. Her women characters, may broadly be placed in four major categories. First there are women, who are passive or submissive , who accept the unquestioning resignation the dictates of the society. They adjust to the texture of personal life, no matter what it may be . They are self sacrificing and modest like Judy in ***A Backward Place*** or like Indu in ***The Householder.*** Second, there are women who are aggressive and assertive. They are dissatisfied and rebellious. They yearn for fulfilment often identified with love, and when they encounter social conventions as impediment, they attempt to control and change them for example, Etta in ***A Backward Place*** Kusum in ***Get Ready for Battle*** and Olivia and the narrator in ***Heat and Dust*** A .Some women are both submissive as well as idealistic for example Indu in ***The Householder.*** She tries to follow the conventional way but she has the idea of individual freedom. When Prem wants to dominate her, she defies him for the sake of her ideal. And finally there is a category of women who are aggressive but at the same time idealistic. They can take any drastic step to realise their ideals, as Sarla Devi in ***Get Ready for Battle.*** These four types of impulses reveal the personality of any woman character. However, nobody can have only one type of impulse always. These vary according to the environments and human beings reaction to different circumstances in different ways.

> "A person's behavior depends not only on the situation in which he finds himself, but also upon the way in which he views himself, and what self attitude he has."[21]

What makes the study interesting is the revelation that women Western or Eastern are loveable and loving, sensitive and sentimental, individualistic and assertive and that pride, vanity, Jealousy and selfishness are weaknesses common to both.

Conclusions

In the last three decades of twentieth century Indian Englis. fiction has witnessed the introduction of new themes anc techniques with their new found confidence. Indian Englisk writers have boldly experimented with language and technique. The most noticeable change however, is to be found in the use of language by these writers. Most of these writers belong to that section of society where English is used as means of social communication. There is a vigour and flow in their language. The contemporary Indian English novelists have made a very evocative use of language by breaking, inverting and twisting the language. The new generation of Indian English novelists is not trying to write English or American English, they are writing a living.

Perhaps the most striking feature of the contemporary Indian English fiction has been the emergence of feminist literature-feminist in the sense of being written by women novelists as well as in the sense of giving voice to the sufferings, aspirations and assertions of women in a traditionally male-dominated world. Beginning with Anita Desai the list would go on including novelists like Ruth Jhabvala, Shashi Deshpande, Bharati Mukherji, Manju Kapoor and Sobha Dey.

These novelists writing in English attempt to project women as the central figure and seem to succeed in presenting the predicament of woman most effectively. The works of women writers have given a distinct dimension to the image of woman in the family and society. Among the women writers mentioned above, Ruth Prawer Jhabvala is variously described as insider outsider and outsider insider.

Ruth Prawer Jhabvala, Polish by birth, educated in England came to India as a bride and picked up the threads of Anglo-Indian fiction, with a new perspective. She has a unique place among the Anglo Indian novelists of post-Independence era. The question is why she is so different from other Anglo-Indian novelists? And the answer is obvious. She came to India when British Raj, was no more. India's struggle for freedom was over, but was over, but was faced with many other problems which came with freedom. Jhabvala naturally got involved with these problems and wrote them, humorously, ironically, critically and even bitterly. She never mentions Britisher or the problem of the ruler and the ruled. Her canvas is purely social.

Jhabvala is essentially an European writer who lived for sometime "' India and expressed through her work the experience of Indian life and society. Whether she wrote as an outsider or as an insider is not so important. The most important thing is her awareness of society, human and moral dilemma and aesthetic design that she projects in her novels. Jhabvala's contribution to Anglo-Indian fiction will always, remain incomparable and unique. The Indian image that she has projected in her novels, will always be remembered by her reader. Her deep understanding, her sense of observation, and deep insight into the unknown society make her novels worthy of careful study and analysis. Jhabvala is credited with having written eight novels and three collections of short stories in India. Her works are like a screen on which we see thirty years of post independent India projected in many of its hues and colours.

Mrs. Jhabvala's first novel ***To Whom She Will*** is about Amrita, a modern Bengali girl, the grand daughter of an Anglicised retired barrister. She falls in love with a Punjabi youth, Hari Sahani in the first flush of her youth. Both of them embody the aspirations of the modern dedicated work-a-day century in their romantic world and seriously find themselves mature enough to marry for love. But the over-protective nature of the young lover's parents frustrate their attempts as in their opinion, they have not matured emotionally. Hari unable to stand even the slightest hurdle in his way I finds himself in the world of phantasy when love would be only a glorious feeling 'Connected with flower and moon light and music in lotus bowels'. Being in love, for Hari, is of course wonderful, not only wonderful but also necessary. It is what he has always thought of all through adolescence. But he has not thought that the world in which he lives will be so complicated. Similarly, Amrita, too despite her education and modern westernised thinking is still emotionally immature and unable to handle the situation she is in. Krishna Sen Gupta a noble, attractive, amusing and always helpful young lecturer staying at her home as a paying guest is found to be a suitable and ideal match for Amrita. But ironically she never thinks of him in the beginning. The irony is poignant in the fact that she makes Krishna a means through which she continues her contact with Hari. And Hari once mad after Amrita now quietly allows himself to accept Sushila as his wife on the insistence of his parents. Amrita, though apparently more stable and determined in her love, submits herself to be married to any person of her parent's choice. She feels overjoyed to receive a letter from Krishna. Such discrepancies between loud pronouncement and actual actions are projected with comic reticence and playful irony. The title of the novel has its origin in the ***Panchatantra*** which describes a tender girl determined to marry a boy of her choice.

In ***The Nature of Passion*** Nimmi — once again a modern young girl-strongly believes in women's emancipation going to clubs playing tennis, keeping bob hair, dating, dressing stylishly and attending lecture on English romantic poet. But all these are not permissible in her community. Nimmi's brother Viddi shares her aspirations and joins in her quarrels with the elder brother Om. But the irony of it all lies in the fact that these youngsters longing for a better way of living should yield to something even more superficial and swallow than what they oppose in the traditional way of living. To them would-be-sophisticated, the surface glitter and glamour of high society makes up the essence of culture.

The implicit irony is clearly hinted at in the discrepancy between overt assertions and basic instincts in that scene when Viddi expresses his wish to become an art critic or writer of book in some western country. On the other hand, Lalaji, tired of these irrelevant past times, takes upon himself the task of teaching his son the value of money. At first, Viddi reacts violently to his suggestion but ultimately sees the light of reason and finds weight in the suggestion of his father. He accepts calmly the proposal of his father to launch him on business with an initial salary of Rs. 500 a month. Jhabvala appears to point out that most of the young man and woman live in a world of fantasy and when they return to the world of hard realities they find themselves unfit to cope with the situation they are in. Their responses, mental process and attitudes and sentiments are too much influenced by a social structure in family bonds are overpowering. The keen and observant eye of the novelist moves in a wide compass noting all kinds of oddities and mannerisms in people. Lala Narayan Das in ***The Nature of Passion***, has constructed a bed room suite. It is done merely for social necessity since he prefers to sleep in the open for most of the year. He never uses anyone of the seven marble bathrooms in the house and prefers to wash by the garden-tap and clear his teeth with a twig. The novelist has succeeded in portraying the old habits like yawning widely, rubbing the knees while talking scratching the thigh quite often, slapping each other while laughing burping loudly after big dinner with much accuracy and detail. Now all these may be true of a certain section of Indian society, but to present such oddities repeatedly gives an impression that the novelist's chief concern is to provide maximum fun to the western readers even at the cost of sounding childish.

No society, however sophisticated and advance is free from typical mannerism and racial characteristic. These are the things which one can notice in any community and sections of the globe. A comic writer is not supposed to load his or her theme with such, common place and odd detail for effect and appeal. A comic writer like Ruth Prawer Jhabvala is supposed to rise above such banalities and direct her attentions at those things which look odd to all at first sight. The way in which she portrays the characters in the novel is no doubt praiseworthy but her effort to create humour by exposing the oddities and banality with such character is objectionable. The effect of irony lies in the writer's ability to touch upon those aspects of life which lie hidden from the eyes of common people. It is only when it is done that the effect of irony is felt more acutely.

Jhabvala's third novel ***Esmond in India*** presents a new dimension in her creativity. In this novel the strands of comedy, irony and satire mingle and fuse to make a fabric of fiction that teases and fascinates at once. Mrs. Jhabvala after following the same stream of thought and ideas in her previous two novels suddenly changes her entire approach. She shifted from the Punjabi refugees, their culture and focuses her attention on the rich Indian families living in the post- independent India. Not only are the characters different but also her entire approach has changed in this novel, yet the basic canvas remains the same. She writes only about the families residing in or around Delhi. This is quite interesting and of great importance as she makes it a point to write about only those characters whom she knows very well and has observed minutely.

This novel ***Esmond in India*** is a family chronicle and moves around the lives of three families. The story is woven around the families of Har Dayal and Ram Nath two friend, who studied together at Cambridge, but later on they separated apart to lead their own lives. Har Dayal from the very beginning has been portrayed as a person who makes the best of what he gets in life and in contrast to the Ram Nath changes completely. While in Cambridge it was Ram Nath who was important, it was he who was helped Har Dayal to establish himself in that foreign land. Ram Nath however, though not being critical of western culture, was more appreciative of the Indian ways of life and it appears he had even forgotten that he had even been abroad for study.

The only similarity between the two is that both fought for India's freedom. However, Har Dayal was an opportunist and Ram Nath an idealist and hence Har Dayal becomes a careerist and materialist while Ram Nath remains a recluse, the book worm and an idealist.

Besides Har Dayal and Ram Nath we have their wives, Madhuri and Lakshmi living in the webs erected by their husbands. Madhuri enjoys luxury life while Lakshmi after losing everything in the freedom struggle lives in a poverty. Madhuri has her own family of two sons, Amrit and Raj and one daughter Shakuntala. Like every Indian mother Madhuri worries most of the time about her daughter who has just finished her college education. Lakshmi on the other hand, has only son Narayan, a doctor, who as an idealist follows in the footsteps of his father. He decides to go to the villages to serve the really suffering sections of Indian Society.

Between the story of these two families we have the story of Uma and her daughter Gulab. Uma along with her husband was also an active freedom fighter. She lost her husband just before independence and later her entire world comprised of her daughter Gulab and grand/son Ravi. Gulab, the most important character of the novel is married to Esmond an English, who just forgets to return home and stays on to guide tourists around the ruins of the ancient country. Esmond is very fastidious and wants his house to be kept clean and beautiful and also Gulab to take to western ways of life which she refuses to do

Though Gulab bears the bullying of her husband meekly, her mother Uma does not. She worries herself to death and constantly keeps asking Gulab to leave her husband for good, but Gulab, true Indian wife considers Esmond her lord who could treat her as he liked. Esmond and Gulab are unable to understand each other and so their marriage becomes a cold affair. Both the characters are highly exaggerated and it is the Gulab Esmond's relationship which is at the heart of the novel and forms the main core of personal and familial angles in the narrative.

Esmond gets involved with Shakuntala, a silly, upper-middle class college girl during his Agra tour. Shakuntala can be compared to Amrita of ***To Whom She Will*** and Nimmi of ***The Nature of Passion.*** In all three novels these young girls represent the modern youth in India. Mrs Jhabvala has portrayed Shakuntala as being totally under the western influence. She goes to parties with her father and is attracted towards Esmond. But Shakuntala's infatuation with Esmond, who is married to her cousin, is something that leaves a bad taste in the mouth.

Esmond is a pathetic figure in Independent India, earns his living by giving lectures on Indian culture which he hates. But he cannot show his hatred. He was attracted towards India the way he was attracted towards Gulab, but staying in India and with Gulab under the same roof soon makes him realize that underneath the beautiful facade, there is something which causes real repulsion. As Gulab proves to be slovenly woman, India, the land fo Taj Mahal, turns out to be a scene of unredeemed poverty.

In this novel Jhabvala is in a less tolerant and less forgiving mood than she was in her earlier novels. This perhaps because she is no longer totally detached from the scene she writes about. In the earlier novels she was an observer but in this novel she is confronted by her own experience of India. The thing which astonishes the reader most, may be the Indian reader more than other is the Mrs. Jhabvala's initial enchantment and excitement about this country did not last very long. In fact, she wrote her first novel in 1955 and this novel in 1958 a period of three years is not a very long time to be so critical of any country.

Jhabvala's next novel ***The Householder*** is once again a light novel dealing with problems of young man — Prem— a middle- class man who at the threshold of "Grahasthashram" is faced with so many problems. This novel comes as a pleasant surprise because once again she becomes an innocent observer of this unknown society writing with a tinge of sympathy about the predicament of young man in Indian society. She takes up the problem of young man, who is just entering the family life. The predicaments and the struggles of this young man have been dealt with in a humorous manner but with a touch of irony here and there.

The Householder is a story of Prem, the protagonist of the novel, a young teacher in Mr Khanna's private college. He is a B.A. who teaches Hindi and is married to Indu, a girl chosen by his parents. He is weak and diffident but by no means unintelligent. He is aware of his precarious financial position but knows he cannot get a better job because of his poor qualification. His position becomes even more precarcious when he realizes that his wife is with child. He threfore, wants to improve his condition by either getting a raise in his salary or a reduction in rent.

Besides Prem there are other characters in the novel, who have been successfully used by Mrs. Jhabvala to throw light on other aspect of Indian society, Raj, Prem's childhood friend, who is also working in one of government offices in Delhi has been used for showing the condition and working of Indian government offices at a lower level. There are also few women characters in the novel, Indu, Prem's, wife who represents the life of young couple in lower middle class Indian society and her relation with Prem's mother, shows the mother-in-law relationship in India. Beside these characters another very important character in this novel is the 'Swamiji'. Mrs. Jhabvala for the first time touches Indian Gurus and Swamis. Through the Swamiji in the novel we are also able to see Mrs. Jhabvala's own knowledge about Hindu religion and spiritualism.

From the beginning of the novel Prem has been portrayed as a very shy young man who has recently been married to a girl, chosen by his parents. He is unable to appreciate his wife and remembers his mother and the delicious meals she served him as compared to his wife Indu. He is not happy and his discontentment can be seen after a few days of his marriage. Through these Indian characters Jhabvala is ridiculing the Indian arranged marriage system. The marriage is arranged by the parents of girl and boy and naturally the young couple takes time to like and to develop some kind of feeling for each other.

'Poverty' and 'Want' seem to have haunted Mrs. Jhabvala's thoughts throughout her stay in India. She just could never reconcile with the enormous giant of poverty and here Prem appears to be a mere mouth-piece of what Mrs. Jhabvala wanted to tell this world, and hence it is not only Prem's problem, but of the entire lower-middle class Indian society and particularly the youth. Prem is no exception. His basic problem is also poverty and want which make him a coward and it makes him an all-round failure as a husband, teacher and probably father.

Just as in her other novels in this novel too Jhabvala juxtaposes the rich and the poor and shows how money makes the rich crude, insensitive and hypocritical and how the absence of money makes people shy and diffident. Though ***The Householder*** is a novel about lower middle-class people money plays an important part in it by its absence. It would not be inappropriate to say that though this novel is written with a simple theme and quite sympathetically, yet it is full of ironic humour and there are certain aspects of Indian society which Mrs. Jhabvala has analysed quite skilfully.

Jhabvala's fifth novel ***Get Ready for Battle*** once again has been written in a lighter mood and instead of being critical she appears to be sympathetic. This novel is an exception not only because in this novel Jhabvala wrote directly about the poor but in many other ways also. The entire novel is a story of one family, the family of a rich businessman, Gulzari Lal whose only aim is to earn money, expand his business and give as much material comforts as he can to his family. There are no foreign characters and no clashes between the old and the new generations. It shows Mrs. Jhabvala's awareness of materialistic civilization in and around Delhi, as once again the novel has Delhi its background the same old canvas but with new colour.

Gulazari Lal is a brash businessman, who throws big parties to dazzle petty government officials. His married life is completely disrupted and his wife has left him. He has a mistress called Kusum, or Mrs. Mehra widow of a retired army officer. Kusum spends most of her time with Gulzari Lal and rules his household. Vishnu, Gulzari Lal's son and Mala, his. wife get used to her presence in the house. Gulzari Lal does not see that there is something wrong in having a mistress in the house. He thinks that after he returns home from office he needs someone like Kusum, who knows how to please him and not a simple and religious woman like Sarla Devi, his estranged wife. Kusum wants Gulzari Lal, to divorce his wife but Gulzari Lal does not want to divorce his wife because such action would bring disrepute to him and spoil his business prospects.

Jhabvala after describing the arranged-marriage customs of Indian society in her first two novels and dealing with the dilemma of a young householder, she takes up the problem of divorce, remarriage and mistress in Indian society. Along with these problems she also described the clash between the rich businessmen and the social workers in India.

As against the type of degenerate bourgeoisie represented by Gulzari Lal's and Brij Mohan, Gulzari Lal's brother-in-law, there is Sarla Devi, who takes the side of the poor and wants to improve their lot by organising them and representing their case to the government. But she loses her battle with her unscrupulous husband. Sarla Devi also loses the battle on the home -front as Kusum finally succeeds in influencing Gulzari Lal to think in terms of divorcing Sarla Devi.

Sarla Devi, however, is not an idealised character. Her philosophy of treating pleasure and pain, gain and loss, victory and defeat alike makes her a little too unworldly. On the other hand Kusum, her counterpart, is a little too shrewrd and practical. She ensnares Gulzari Lal and plays tricks on him.

Beside, Gulzari Lal, Kusum and Sarla Devi, there is

Vishnu, Gulzari Lal's son and his wife Mala. Vishnu in this novel is a typical portrait of a rich man's son in India, who is economically dependent on his father. He lives with him in the same house, works in the same office and has been provided with all the material comforts he can wish for. Similarly, Mala has been portrayed throughout the novel as a submissive wife. She is not very happy in Delhi and wants to go to Bombay, but Vishnu never feels inclined to go there as he is totally dependent on his father and this makes Mala very unhappy.

Mrs. Jhabvala in this novel not only emerges as a social reformer but at the same time she has very successfully satirized the modern westernised young generation of India. She has tried to show how they pretend to be all knowledgeable and intelligent but have neither of these qualities. All they know is a little western culture, which they follow blindly and as a result are neither Indian nor Westerns.

After ***Get Ready for Battle*** Jhabvala wrote three more novels in India -***A Backward Place, A New Dominion*** and ***Heat and Dust***. As all these titles of her novels suggest her attitude towards this country. She is bitter, critical and ironical. Probably she has reached the last stage of her cycle, where everything Indian is abominable, and the cycle is never renewed again. ***A Backward Place*** is a novel in which Jhabvala for the first time is more concerned with foreigners, who happen to come to India. Jhabvala concentrates on their reaction and different attitudes toward this country, and as a result, for the first time, she has more foreign characters in the novels.

In this novel almost all the foreign characters are women and Mrs. Jhabvala has tired to view Indian society differently through each of these characters. Jhabvala herself found this place to be very strong for her nerves and was unable to adjust either mentally or physically. Perhaps it is because of her weak nerves and oversensitive temperament that she found it very difficult to adjust in this backward land. This is her personal experience, but at the same time she suggests certain ways in which foreigner can adjust in the country and one such best way, would be to follow Gandhiji's principle, that is to keep one's eyes, ear and lips closed. And under this category Judy the main character of the novel comes. She is English and has come to India after marrying an Indian youth Bal while he was in London on a short visit. Her parents were working-class people and she suffered in the English cold. She found Bal handsome and married him in hope that he would take her to a warmer place. But Bal himself came of a lower- middle class family and did not have a regular job.

Besides Judy, there are two more women characters in the novel, Etta and Clarissa. Etta, like Judy married an Indian youth and came to India at young age, but even after being in this country for more than twenty-five years and marrying three Indian boys, she never could like India. Mrs. Jhabvala uses Etta to criticise India, and on many occasions Etta appears to be her mouth-piece. Etta appears to be one of those wrong types who are never adjust here. Clarissa is her opposite. She is meek but she too uses a set of cliches which some Europeans use to show their love for India. Between them, they characterise two attitudes the one of intense hatred and the other of condescension. Jhabvala suggests that both the attitudes have become obsolete, because Europeans living in India are no longer conquerors but the conquered ones.

In contrast to Judy and Etta who came to India as a result of their chance marriage there is another foreign character in the novel — the old German couple the Hochstadts belong to altogether a different category of foreigners in India. Their reactions to this country are different from Judy's, Etta's or Clarissa's. They have neither merged in this society like Judy and Clarissa, nor do they hate it like Etta. They can see the shortcoming of Indian society and at the same time are appreciative of so many Indian things. They have time and a mental state where they are able to see some good points in India. The reason perhaps is that they have come to India with a definite purpose and definite length of time. They leave India before the enchantment and excitement about this mystic land starts to fade away.

Hochstadts and Judy represent the extreme situations in which westerners find themselves because the former are in India for a short time and the latter is better off here than in her own country.

A New Dominion marks as a new phase in Jhabvala's literary career and a deviation from the norm which marked her earlier works. ***A New Dominion,*** is of course, India again but with a new perspective. It is no more a backward place but rather a land of spiritual and peace. The theme of this novel does not present the East-West encounter but rather East-West harmony or ultimate compromise. Jhabvala has endeavoured to store all her experience in this one novel. She has tried to record the experiences of various types of foreigners.

A New Dominion projects the experience and views of the Westerners like the three girls —Lee, Evie and Margaret who come here in quest of spiritualism and to solve their personal problem, but what they see and experience come out rather badly. Jhabvala chooses to be a social satirist in this novel and though she never has appreciated India or the Indian characters in any of her novels, in this novel she appears to have reached the climax of bitterness against this land. She not only denounces Indian character, but the entire environment and landscape depresses her and it always appears to be dull and drab.

All three European girls Lee, Margaret and Evie reached the Ashram of Guru in Banaras with a hope to find peace and that spiritual glory for which they were looking for. Swamiji has a magnetic personality has the power to create the illusion of hope, through his eyes and words. He has the power to attract these foreigners and lives among them as God. He is the ruler of that Ashram. Everyone has to do what he wishes them to do. But to the reader he is no more than a spurious god man, as he is worldly sensual and sexual. He wants all his disciples not only spiritually but physically. He wants to possess them with their bodies and souls.

Besides these three European girls, we have Raymond, the only male European character in the novel comes to India as a tourist for a year and remains a tourist through out his stay in India. He has come on his own, and has no definite plans. He does not know when he may go back. He comes here as an outsider and remains one. He is never able to develop any kind of feeling for India, Indians and Swamis. In fact, he hates the Swami and wants to hit him, when he treats Margaret's illness with indifference.

Coming to the Indian characters in the novel, Gopi, Rao Sahib, his wife Sunita, his widowed sister Asha, Banubai the prophetess, and a young energetic Engineer Bob are instruments in the hands of Jhabvala, who skilfully uses them to project the various sides of this vast Dominion. The most important thing is that they have all been portrayed rather badly and appear insignificant and petty when compared to her western characters. They are crude and full of animals instinct. They are sex-hungry, pretentious, egotistic and hypocritical. The only exception we have is in the character of Banubai the prophetess.

In this novel Jhabvala is ironical, bitter and critical of India and also of those Europeans who in their everlasting quest for spiritualism and a total merger in this world lose their good sense. She has tried to sum up her multifarious experiences and views as regards, this mystic land. In this novel Jhabvala moves away from the centre of social activities to the centre of spiritual activities. The novel is dominated by sex and spiritual talk. The Indian characters in the novel too are different from the Indian characters in her earlier novels.

Heat and Dust, the prestigious Booker Prize winner for 1975, unfolds the sad and touching story of the English women of two different genetrations who came to India and became its victim. A young English woman comes to India to reconstruct the story of her grand father's first wife

Olivia, who has an affair with the Nawab of Khatm. While reconstructing the story of Olivia by actually visiting the places where she lived, the narrator (who remained unname up to the end) records her own life in her diary. **In** this manner it is the story of Olivia alternating with that of the narrator. The novel shifts back and forward from 1923 to the present with ease and felicity. The story moves on two levels the past and the present with diary and journal as narration techniques. The past narrates how Olivia and her husband Douglas came to India how she fell in the amorous spells of the Nawab and eloped with him. We also learn that the affair resulted in Olivia's pregnancy and abortion. Olivia had to run away from the hospital to the Nawab's palace. She was later on given a cottage in the hills and had to be satisfied with the status of a mistress of the Nawab.

The present records the narrator's liaison with Chid, an English man turned Hindu. She meets Chid and helps him in his sickness, but he will be satisfied with nothing less than sex with her which he gets. Once again the spirituality and sex are intermingled and the tragedy of the thirties seems, to be repeating itself. The narrator also becomes pregnant but unlike Olivia, she does not go in for abortion. In the hope of having a baby she joins an ashram and suffers, quietly. Both the women are destroyed by the heat and the monotonous parched and barren landscape.

Jhabvala's image of India as portrayed In ***Heat and Dust*** is extremely disturbing. It is again depicted as a backward place inhabited by poor, sensual and imbecile people. Its stronger climate is oppressive enough to devour European who are sensitive to it. Her feeling of India, its squalor, its misery, its excitement, the enticement of its, paradox is in fact, nothing more than skipping over the surface of Indian life with all too clever observation of its external characterisation. Not a single character impresses or amuses the reader. It is difficult to feel involved in the personality of any of the characters. All of them have turned out to be card-board-cut outs. This is Jhabvala's major weakness in this novel.

Strange things happen in this novel not only because India is strange but Jhabvala has made the country, stranger in her imagination over heated by hatred. ***Heat and Dust*** is the view of an outsider of a foreigner at best of an Anglo-Indian like Kipling or John Masters, she cannot be 'said' to have travelled even halfway through the inner life of the Indian people in comparison of E. M. Forster. Even the approaches of these two artists are dramatically opposed in grappling with the east -west theme.

On the whole Jhabvala deals with the traditional Indian Family life gently. Jhabvala does touch on some of wider aspects of society of which corruption is one of them. The whole plot of ***The Nature of Passion*** is based on Lalaji's fear that his involvement in a corruption may be revealed. It isn't because he manages to persuade his civil servant son Chandra to lose certain incriminating evidence. Chandra, with his English sense of in public life is shocked but he cannot maintain his smart way of life without Lalaji' s money. Nor is this the only example of alliance between the smart and educated, and an Indian capitalist, somewhat grubby money. Gulzari Lal in ***Get Ready for Battle*** too, employees unfair means to get the Bundi Basti evacuated for his material gains. Jhabvala beautifully points out the showing off syndrome of Indians/ Lalaji's spoilt daughter Nimmi reacts to her rich sophisticated young friends suggestion that she should become a teacher to escape an arranged marriage.

Though Jhabvala is not a feminist, yet some of her novels central focus in on women. The women in Jhabvala's fiction are shown as the victim of merciless social customs. They are shown as puppets in the hands of social tradition oppressive man dominate society. The presence of Westerner is a very vital aspect of Jhabvala's fiction. In the social context Indian and European meet fall in love, get married and face either mutual dissonance or familial friction. In the cultural context they face the problem of adjustment of divorce backgrounds Jhabvala shows concern with the problems of European men and women trying to get adjust to Indian Society. In the spiritual context she portrays European who are facicnated by Gurus, the torch bearers, the beacons of light of India ancient spiritual heritage. The spiritual element in these Gurus may be bizarre or genuine. Yet the charm they hold for the Westerners is unmistakeable. The presence of Guru in todays world has become a thing of the past especially since these Gurus have materialistic outlook. One hears of flesh trade, prostitution and a rape on the premises of the ashram. A pious place where man goes for peace from the worldly miseries is turned into hell. Most holy places have not been able to retained their sanctity.

In Jhabvala's fiction, a Westerner is drawn towards India spiritualism. The oriental mysticism and the meditative which gives peace to man is described. The Guru; disciple relationship plays an important role in her novels. At the same time spiritualism has been portrayed in a negative light. The holiness of God man, who teaches the philosophy of the holy text and shows the path of good and bad, have been portrayed as fake god-men in the name of spiritualism all immoral activities take place. The Swamiji in ***A New Dominion*** exploits the English woman sexually and goes to the extent of rape of Lee who doesn't accept him. The logic behind this sexual assault is that in order to attain certain super consciousness one has to overcome the desire of passion. The Swamiji has the capacity to reduce his victim and then finish them off. He believes in transformation of the old into the new by sexual exploitation where the person would totally become his. All his actions are immoral and revolting. He is a man who runs after material and physical pleasure.

Jhabvala suggests that the sexual exploration in the name of God is immoral as all religions have a method of super consciousness. The 'God-men' according to her, concentrate more in promoting evil than good. They are spiritual imposters who don't have the high calibre of moral values due to which frustration comes in and disintegration takes place. In the name of God individual builts false empire of spiritualism which exploits man. Almost all her Westerner characters undergo pangs of disillusionment in the novel like A New Dominion and Three Continents.

Jhabvala writes In a deliberatelly down-to-earth language, emphasising realisation details of incident and object while under playing the complex working of the human mind. She never allows us to know the characters from inside. One wonder if her aim as a novelist makes her to choose this method? The transparent sincerity of Jhabvala in revealing her suspense to the phenomena that is India indirectly shows the process of her creativity. She may perhaps consider a European writer on India, yet her creative work provides ample evidence of her Indianness, the aestheic design of her work moulded by her experience of life in India. It is the European's "Passage to India" but very different from that of Kipling and E.M. Forster. Jhabvala in the early years of her experience of this country appears to try to transplant a little Europe of her own in India, but with the passage of time the plant has grown into a tree with a native growth, which is waterned and nourished by Indian soil. Her Polish and German heritage seems to suggest Goethe's idea that a man doesn't learn to understand anything unless he loves it. In this sense Jhabvala's love for India becomes a gracious, beautiful and erotic art.

Having spent many years in India she presents in her fiction the minuts details of the People and place and their problems. The problems of martial discord is partraied in almost all her novels and to her characters pass through crisis after crisis and almost all of them are in quest of better partner searching their heart within. The institution of marriage based on social system to satiate the inborn urge of sex is of immense importance. The concept of marriage is age old and has been popular and prevalent in human society since time immemorial. Thus marriage is practically a universal social tie. Though it is regarded as an obstacle in all adventure of life. The principle of marriage and its practice based on free choice of boys and girls are only popular in the western world. In India, it is used for strengthening relationship or for creating new alliance but in no case the decision to marry a particular person rests with a boy or a girl. In this way marriage in India is a sacred bond to the truly, two souls together. It remains an infinite bond of two souls from life to life and birth to birth. Thus, it is amply demonstrated in the fiction of Jhabvala that marital discord is the central theme of many of her novels.

In conclusion, we can say that Jhabvala's contribution to Indo-English fiction is remarkable. Her approach to the theme and situation of Indian set up is realistic and photographic. She doesn't dispense with the minimum requirement of art to entertain and engage the readers. She works in the style of a painter who is given visual and imagination description of life rather than to phychological analysis on exploration of the inner world of the characters and the Indian society to which they belong.

Human feelings, ideas passions, experiences, joys, sorrows, aspirations frustrations and the struggle in life form the core of Jhabvala's literary art. Among the women novelists the sensibility of Jhabvala is characterised by the native Indian scenario and sometime focusing on the plight and vision of Westerners. A close observation of her fiction reveals both negative and positive aspects of life. Religious sensibility is stirred when the focus of vision lies on man and society in relation with cosmic forces. Jhabvala's attitude to life and man is thus coloured by the greater perspective in which life is taken up for better examination and analysis.

8

Index

***